SPIDERS IN THE BATH

BY
PAUL BREEN

A statement from Merseyside Police

The Force Solicitor claims, *"some of what you say is simply scurrilous abuse, some of what you say will undoubtedly be libellous and the individuals concerned will of course take such steps as they feel necessary to protect their reputation. . . you must of course make contact direct with any trial judge or barrister you suggest may be affected by your publication. I have copied your letters to the Police Federation in respect of individual officers. It will need time to consider the position."*

Consequently the foreword of this book has been withdrawn on legal advice.

The author would like to thank
Mr. Lynch
brilliant English teacher
Cardinal Godfrey High School 1971-1976

First published 1993 by Paul Breen, 7 Faversham Road, Norris Green, Liverpool, L11 7BG
This edition published 2005.

Copyright © 1993 & 2005 Paul Breen

The right of Paul Breen to be identified as the author of this work has been asserted by him in accordance with the Copyright, Design and Patents Act 1988.

The characters and situations in this book are entirely imaginary and bear no relation to any real person or actual happening.

Printed by Birkenhead Press Ltd, 14 Appin Road, Birkenhead CH41 9HH.

British Library Cataloguing in Publication Data.
A catalogue record for this book is available from the British Library.

Please note: From 1st January 2007 ISBNs will contain 13 numbers. These numbers will be the same as the present number printed below the barcode (ie. starting 978). Please continue to use the 10 figure number until 31st December 2006.

ISBN 0 9522875 1 X   ISBN 978 0 9522875 1 3

Chapter One:

The Power Struggle.

Liverpool, during the early 1980's. An era of recession, redundancy and hard times. The children from the baby boom of the sixties had grown into embittered adults, with no hope and no future. Overworked over stressed, and underpaid, the police were used as a pawn in the struggle to keep the lid on a powder keg of bitterness and unrest.

Bad housing, police harrassment, and lack of opportunity, was an insult to a generation that had been taught to expect more. Seeing their parents used, abused, and discarded as they approached middle age, instilled a determination into the youngsters that nobody was going to do it to them. Forced into a choice of kow-towing, grovelling, and a lifetime of hand-outs, they took the only way out open to them - and turned to crime. Young men with guts refused to accept the hand life had dealt them, and kicked the table over. The hard pressed police became the front line troops of a government that was tightening its belt in a war against the cream of a generation that regarded the Prime Minister as a pimp. Young lions became engaged in a guerilla war against anyone and everyone who tried to suppress them - and the legend of the "Spiders in the Bath" was born.

It was a little after tea time on a Friday evening. Four twelve-year old schoolboys were playing football against a neighbour's fence, using it as a goal. They hadn't been playing long, when the door flew open, and a middle-aged woman came running down the path. "Go on, sod off down your own end of the street" she cried. It was the third time that night they had been moved on. "Piss off, you old bag" shouted little Maca, as they slunk away. " You wait until I see your mother" called the irritated woman. "Kiss me arse" muttered little Maca as they reached the corner. "Where are we gonna play now" asked Sykesy. "Dunno" shrugged little Maca. A man in a mac walked slowly up to the bus-stop in a quiet village. Two women were already standing there. He sighed and looked at his watch. It had been a long day at work, and the bus was overdue. Just across the road, he noticed four lads sitting in a powerful car. The driver sat with his elbow out of the window calmly chewing a match. The man wondered what they were waiting for.

The four schoolboys sat huddled together on the steps of the local pub, cold and bored with nowhere to go. Sykesy produced a packet of chewing gum from his back pocket and passed it around just as a police car stopped nearby.

"Here we go," said one lad as the two policemen approached .

A car pulled up outside the bank at the top of the village. It was the local supermarket manager banking the day's takings in the nightsafe. The man at the bus stop stamped his feet and rubbed his hands. It was getting cold. The supermarket manager opened the glove compartment and pulled out the bank wallet. He tucked it discreetly into the front of his jacket.

"Empty your pockets," the first policemen ordered the schoolkids.

Little Maca produced a front door key, an old snotrag and three pence in change. "What's your name?" asked the policeman.

"Philip McFaye," replied the youngster uncomfortably.

"Where d'you live?" continued the policeman.

"Over there," said little Maca pointing across the street.

"Where d'you live'" snapped the policeman angrily, hitting him in the stomach.

"Twenty Tenwall Road, Norris Green," coughed little Maca.

"That's better. Where d'you live?" he asked Sykesy.

"101 Eastham Road," replied Sykesy nervously.

A petrol bomb smashed against a policeman's riot shield and exploded in a ball of flame. The plastic began to melt. The policeman was forced to drop the shield and retreat.

The supermarket manager stepped out of the car and walked calmly towards the nightsafe. The people at the bus stop watched in surprise as the powerful car screeched away up the street. The four young men's heads lurched backwards as the car surged forwards. The supermarket manager turned to see what was going on. The car skidded to a halt at the bank. The startled supermarket manager froze in shock. He was caught in the no-man's land between his car and the bank. The car doors flew open and two raiders flew towards him. He recovered quickly but it was too late - they were on him. He turned away as the first man grabbed the bank wallet and tried to wrench it away from him. The second assailant grabbed him by the hair and volleyed him in the face as he fell. The supermarket manager released the money as his head bounced on the pavement. The man at the bus stop came racing up the street. The two men were back in the car in a flash and it scorched away round the corner. The man cursed them as he reached the bank. It was too late. There was nothing he could do. It was all over in the time it would have taken to snap his fingers. The supermarket manager was lying on his back trying to clear his head. His head and nose were cut. The man helped him to his feet.

It was 1980 in Northern Ireland. It was autumn and the dark nights were drawing in. Albie Kinsella, a corporal in the Paras, was on a foot patrol coming down a dimly lit street in riot torn Belfast.

A sniper with a high powered rifle positioned himself on a roof four streets away. From his vantage point he had a clear shot in between two houses halfway along the street. A street lamp adequately lit up his target area. He patiently set his sights on it and waited.

2

Albie was on the point as the patrol progressed uneasily down the street. Albie was an old campaigner, a veteran of four tours of duty in Northern Ireland. Perhaps he had developed a sixth sense, but although he couldn't put a finger on it - something was wrong, and he knew it. Maybe it was because the kids who played in the street were nowhere to be seen. Maybe it was because the street was empty and quieter than usual. He snapped his fingers and signalled his men to cover. They scrambled into doorways, hid around corners and threw themselves flat on the floor, desperate for any cover they could find.

One soldier stood behind the street lamp. The sniper eyed him carefully. He could hit him easily but he couldn't be sure of killing him - patiently he waited.

Albie pressed himself in a doorway. There was a tense forboding in the air. Albie could taste the dryness in his mouth and the sickly feeling of anticipation in his stomach. The pub door opened at the end of the street and broke the uneasy silence momentarily. Twelve army rifles zeroed in on the unaware drunk in an instant. The drunk stopped and pulled a whisky bottle out of his overcoat pocket. He began swigging it back. This man was no threat to them. Albie surveyed the positions of his men again and noticed the raw recruit taking cover behind the lamp.

"Hey dickhead what are you doing there? You can be seen for miles...Don't move a muscle until I tell you and then run like hell over here, got it?"

"Got it, Corp," the young man replied, visibly tightening up.

The soldiers began switching positions to give him cover. The sniper watched the frightened soldier coldly through his telescopic sight.

The drunk stopped slurping his whisky and burped. He tried to focus on the figures down the street.

"Go home, you English bastards," he called and hurled his empty whisky bottle down the street. The bottle smashed next to the frightened soldier who spun round instinctively with his gun at the ready. The sniper fired as his target stepped out of cover. The bullet went straight through his neck. He lay dead in the gutter. His head lay lopsided and his eyes stared accusingly at the drunk.

"Jesus," murmured the drunk and turned to run. He didn't get far. Albie ran across the street and kicked his legs away from him before diving into cover on the opposite side. The drunk fell heavily, banging his head on the floor. Albie dragged the dead body out of the lamplight. His squad was already after the sniper. Albie closed the dead man's eyes and lay him gently in the gutter as an army landrover came hurtling up and stopped by the drunk. Six soldiers poured out of the back.

"Baines, Watson," Albie called in fury heading towards the drunk. The two squaddies seized the prone drunk and tossed him roughly into the back of the landrover. Albie kicked him in the kidneys. The drunk grunted. Albie smashed him in the ribs with his gun butt. The drunk started to cough blood. Albie seized him by the collar and screwed his face up next to the stunned Irishman.

3

"What's his name?" growled Albie.

"Mother of God!" moaned the drunk.

Albie pulled the man towards him and butted him full in the face. There was a terrible crack.

"Where is he?" demanded Albie.

The drunk slumped away from him mercifully into semi-consciousness. Albie kicked him in the jaw, then again and again in the ribs and face trying to vent his anger. He jumped out of the landrover into the street where Baines and Watson were waiting.

"Get anything out of him, Corp?" asked Baines.

"No," growled Albie. "Beat the shit out of the bastard then dump him somewhere."

"Yes sir," replied the two paras.

They jumped into the back of the landrover and closed the door behind them.

An hour later the sniper walked into a pub near Belfast's docks. An older man greeted him. There was a pint of Guinness on the table waiting for him.

"Hello Michael-Edward. How are you? Long time no see."

"Fine, Dermot," replied the sniper. "Wish I could say the same for my little ones."

"Aye, this is no place to bring up your children. I hear this was your last job for the cause?" said Dermot, taking a drink of his pint.

"For now," replied Michael-Edward. "I've got myself a job over the water, a sexton with Liverpool City Council. I'm tired of living in squalor, killing soldiers, scrimping for a living. I feel like a Red Indian bumping off the white men. The more you do it the more they come."

"And how will you manage over there, have you got any money?" asked Dermot.

The gravedigger shrugged. "I'll get by. I always do."

Dermot smiled and pulled a piece of paper from his pocket. He handed it to Michael-Edward. The gravedigger opened it. It was a telephone number. Michael-Edward looked puzzled.

"What is it?" he asked.

"It's a legacy from me stay in prison over the water. The man's an old cell mate of mine. He'll have plenty of work for you, a man with your talents, Michael. You could earn yourself a lot of money."

Michael-Edward stared coldly at his friend waiting for more information.

"There's trouble brewing in Liverpool," continued Dermot. "This man is an up and coming gangster. He's left his old boss and set up on his own. His boss doesn't like it one bit."

Dermot took another drink from his pint. Michael-Edward watched him and said nothing.

"There's going to be one terrible clash of heads me boy, you take my word for that. And the people on the winning side are gonna be in the pink for life."

Michael-Edward smiled, and tucked the phone number into his top pocket. "That'll do me," he said. "Cheers."

The two men joined their glasses and laughed. They swigged their ale down and Michael-Edward ordered two more.

An hour later in Liverpool, two policemen stopped at a set of traffic lights waiting for the lights to change. A stolen Jag nosed up next to the police car. It was being driven by Albie's younger brother, Jerry. In it with him were his three friends, Marty, Smigger and Dougie.

The two officers looked across at the car. Jerry scowled at them and looked away. Marty was sitting in the front passenger seat.

"I think they're looking for a mug shot," he said, undoing his trousers.

"So do I," said Smigger sitting in the back. The lads dropped their trousers and waited for the lights to change, ignoring the dirty looks the police were giving them.

"Hey there's no need for that," said Dougie in a huff.

"Behave. It's a shed," said Marty nodding towards the police car. "They'll never catch us."

The lights changed to amber. Jerry banged his hand down hard on the car horn. The startled policemen turned quickly to see what the trouble was. They couldn't believe their eyes when they saw the two bare bottoms spread across the car window. Jerry put his foot down and scorched away.

"Cheeky bastards," growled the driver as he banged the car into gear and gave chase.

The Jag was pulling right away from them as Jerry clogged it down the dual carriage way.

The policeman was on the radio. "This is Charlie Delta Foxtrot One in pursuit of a stolen red Jag down the East Lancs Road towards Kirkby. I'm losing him. Request a Tango Charlie pursuit vehicle to intercept."

"Can you see him Doug?" asked Jerry spotting Dougie looking out of the back window.

"No, we're away," laughed Dougie.

"Better turn off though," warned Marty. "Soft shite will have been on the radio."

Jerry swung the car right at the lights and then turned left into a suburban street.

An old man walked out of his house and climbed into his mini. He started the car just as Jerry turned into the street. The old man didn't even look to see if there was anything coming. He backed straight out into Jerry's path. Jerry slammed on the brakes and swerved to avoid him.

"Shit" cursed Marty in desperation.

The Jag smashed into a tree plummeting Marty head first through the windscreen. Jerry instinctively pushed the car door open. He knew his arms were broken and his rib cage was smashed. He staggered out of the car trying to catch his breath. He could hear the police car in the distance getting nearer. He knew he couldn't get far. He half-staggered, half-sneaked into the nearest front garden and hid behind the privets. Smigger couldn't get his door open. He wound the window down and climbed out. Dougie was still dazed. Smigger gaped in shock at Marty's mangled face as he lay slumped across the bonnet.

"Stupid old bastard. Shouldn't even be on the fucking road," he screamed at the old man, just as a police car turned the corner. Smigger turned and sprinted down the street. He ran twenty yards and then up a garden path into the back gardens as a police car slammed on next to him.

Dougie was collared as he was climbing out of the car window.

"All right, you've got me'" he shouted as he was roughly manhandled into a transit van that had just arrived on the scene.

Jerry listened as Dougie was carted off. In great pain he tried to catch his breath. He watched a policeman walk up to Marty and pick his head up by the hair. Pieces of windscreen were still embedded in. Marty's grotesquely gashed face. The policeman winced and dropped Marty's head back onto the bonnet.

Dougie was dumped on the floor of the transit van.

"Who's the driver?" one policeman asked.

"What time is it?" asked Dougie, trying to act soft.

The policeman kicked him sharply in the groin. Dougie groaned and curled up on the floor, his face contorted in pain.

"Who's the driver?" the policeman asked him again.

An old woman peeped nervously out of her flat window. The flashing lights and the noise outside aroused her curiosity. Her mouth dropped open in awe at the drama she saw before her. A slight movement in the garden, attracted her attention. There was a man hiding in her front garden. She tapped angrily on the window. Jerry cursed and tried to turn. It was too late. They were on him. Two burly policemen bundled him unceremoniously into the back of the transit van. The policeman was still trying to get the driver's name from Dougie.

"What's his name?" said the officer angrily, kicking Dougie in the stomach. Dougie groaned in pain. Jerry was trying to catch his breath on the floor.

'Hey twat' I'm the driver," growled Jerry in anger.

The officer stopped for a moment, surprised by the open hostility of the youth.

"Hardcase, eh? What's the name of your mate who got away through the back gardens. The one with the mouth," snarled the policeman.

There was a silence.

"D'you mean the one with the arse?" quipped Dougie. Another officer punched him in the jaw. Dougie's head bounced against the side of the van.

"I'm talking to you, hardcase. What's your mate's name?" continued the first officer.

6

There was a silence. Jerry stared defiantly at the officer. The policeman snapped and kicked him violently in the ribs. Jerry wheezed in agony like an old man.

"What's his name?" demanded the policeman, kicking Jerry in the body again. There was a moment's silence as Jerry caught his breath.

"D'you know the next time I'm in a robbed car and you're on the beat - you're dead," growled Jerry. The policeman stopped him in mid-sentence with angry blows with his hands and feet.

"Get off him, you bastard," yelled Dougie being forcibly restrained by two other officers.

Jerry could see the man striking him in a blur. He could feel no more pain. He slipped into unconsciousness.

Shanley Pybus was Liverpool's top gangster. He sat quietly at his desk in his pent-house suite, patiently twisting a pen in and out of its lid. His two top lieutenants, Patsy Lucas and Jimmy Nesbitt, two powerful sombre looking men, sat in silence, waiting for their boss to speak. There was an air of expectancy in the room. Nesbitt got up from his seat, sighed and walked to the window. Pybus watched him for a moment and then returned his gaze to his pen. Nobody spoke.

Outside, the lift reached the fifteenth floor. A small balding, bespectacled man clutching a dossier under his arm stepped out from the lift. He looked nervously at the two bodyguards guarding the door to the suite. The peroxide blonde, Mr Pybus's personal secretary, stopped cleaning her nails and looked disdainfully at him. She flicked on the intercom.

"Mr Crawford your accountant's here to see you, Mr Pybus," she piped.

"Send him straight in," came the reply.

Crawford headed for the suite. A bodyguard stepped in front of him and frisked him. The man nodded to his friend. The second bodyguard opened the door. Mr Crawford entered.

Nesbitt turned and watched him coldly. Patsy Lucas remained impassive. Pybus pointed to the chair in front of him. Crawford sat down and nervously opened his file.

"Well," said Pybus.

"In the last six months the turnover in the gaming clubs and the brothels that Mr Russell used to run are up by thirty percent," began Crawford. He waited for a reply. Pybus eyed him impassively.

"The insurance business is flourishing with an intake of twenty per cent more than it was, and the narcotics industry is booming", continued Crawford, placing two sheets of paper in front of Pybus.

The gangster looked at them for a moment. "Give it to me in plain English," he said.

"Well to be blunt, Mr Pybus," started Crawford, "Mr Russell has fiddled you out of close to a quarter of a million pounds in the last year alone."

He held his breath and waited for the coming storm. None came. Mr Pybus nodded to himself for a moment and then pointed to the door with his pen.

Crawford got up and furtively left. Lucas and Nesbitt watched him go. Mr Pybus reached across and got himself a cigar out of his cigar box. His men watched him silently as he almost chewed the cigar alight in the corner of his mouth.

"I want him dead," he said in a puff of smoke. "See to it," he ordered.

Lucas and Nesbitt got up and left without saying a word.

It was Friday afternoon. Russell was drinking wine with a friend, in the downstairs bar of a pub he owned. The pub was fairly empty except for a courting couple, some young girls who'd been shopping, and a couple of young men at the bar. A married man paid for a pint and a glass of lager, a bottle of lemonade and a packet of cheese and onion crisps for his six year old daughter who was sitting happily drinking another bottle of lemonade through a straw, next to his wife.

Russell sat on a stool next to the bar. "Who are Liverpool playing tomorrow, Vin?" he asked his friend.

"Dunno," replied Vinny the bar manager, sipping at his drink. "Birmingham, I think."

"Don't know whether to go to the match or to Haydock," replied Russell.

One of the young girls noticed the first of four gunmen coming down the stairs and screamed.

"What the fu..."said Vinny, cut short as he saw what the trouble was.

Russell was over the bar in a flash. A shotgun blast tore away part of the bar where he'd been sitting. There was pandemonium in the bar as screaming, frightened women dived for cover underneath the tables. Nesbitt caught Vinny full in the stomach with the second shotgun blast. His white shirt was splattered with a large blob of incandescent red. Russell scurried into the cellar as mirrors and glasses were ripped to pieces by shotgun blasts. Lucas leapt over the bar after Russell. Vinny stood clutching his stomach in disbelief. He tottered over to the floor, dead. The married woman screamed in shock as she saw his gaping mouth and staring eyes. Russell swung a keg of lager against the cellar door as Lucas tried to get in.

"Bastard!" cursed Lucas and tried to kick the door in. Lucas and Nesbitt shouldered the door open but it was too late. Russell had escaped through the delivery shaft. The angry gunmen made off back up the stairs and out of the pub into a waiting car.

The shocked customers slowly recovered their wits in disbelief. Everyone seemed scared to move. No-one wanted to go near the body in case it was catching. The bar was like a pocket in time, silent except for the frightened whimpering of women and the choking smell of gunsmoke. The married man got up from his wife and daughter and covered Vinny's head with his jacket. He returned to his family and cuddled them closely.

The police were on the scene in minutes, led by three plainclothes men. They stopped and surveyed the scene. One officer checked on the dead body, another went into the cellar, the third approached the shocked people.

"What happened?" he asked.

No-one seemed in a hurry to reply.

"Four fellas came in with shotguns," said the girl's boyfriend in a quiet voice. "The fella they were after got away over the bar."

The policeman nodded in understanding. "Was he a big man in his forties with a big broken nose and going baldy?"

"That's him," butted in the girlfriend.

The policeman made a note in his book. "Did anyone see the gunmen clearly?" he asked slowly.

"I did," ventured one of the teenage girls, gingerly.

"Did you get a good look at them?" he continued.

"Yes," she nodded slowly.

"Would you know them again?" he asked.

"Yes...Yes, I think so," she replied, not too sure of herself.

"What's your name?" the policeman asked, preparing to write it into his notebook.

"Hey love, what are you thinking of?" growled the married man.

The policeman looked at him in surprise as he was joined by his colleague who had been examining the dead body. Everyone turned to look at the married man. "Stop for one minute and have a word with yourself," blurted the man angrily. "We are talking about gangsters now. Even if you identify him d'you think you'll live to testify against them? Those people think nothing of killing, you've just seen that. If you're lucky enough to testify d'you think you'll last a year afterwards?... No chance!"

"Behave yourself," interrupted the second officer.

"Never mind behave yourself" growled the man. "Just as though you'd give two shits about the girl once she'd testified. You'd just take your promotion and slot your extra fifty quid a week in your arse pocket!".

"We could give her police protection, a new identity, a new start in life," said the first policeman.

"She still wouldn't last twelve months. You know it and I know it."

The teenage girl watched the heated argument intensely. The enormity of her position slowly dawned on her.

"Excuse me," she said quietly, interrupting the argument. There was a moment's silence. "I can't remember what the men looked like now."

The two policemen looked at each other in dismay.

"Does anyone remember what these men looked like?" asked the first policeman.

The witnesses looked away and made no reply.

"D'you know we could do you for perverting the course of justice?" growled the second policeman at the married man.

"You could do a lot of things to me - but it wouldn't kill me."

Whitey was a sly looking young man in his late teens. He walked slowly along the industrial estate checking if there was anything worth robbing in the long line of parked cars. He noticed a baby buggy in the back of a Capri. That should be worth twenty notes to him at least. He looked furtively around. There was no-one about except for a mechanic working in the forecourt of the garage across the street. Whitey approached the car furtively and tried the door handle - it wouldn't budge. He selected a key from his bunch of keys and jiggled it carefully into the lock. He cursed and jiggled the key harder when the door wouldn't open. Accepting failure ungratefully he moved on to the next car.

He noticed a Sharp radio recorder in the dash board. Carelessly he tried the door without looking around. The mechanic stopped work and watched him with interest. He had already seen Whitey tamper with the door of the Capri. Whitey had no luck with the second car and moved on to a third car as the mechanic was joined in the garage forecourt by a work-mate. Whitey jiggled a key into the lock.

"Hey!" shouted the mechanic.

Whitey panicked and the car alarm went off in a deafening blare. Whitey saw the mechanic running across the road towards him and sprinted off up the street.

It was three o'clock in the afternoon. The seven till three shift in the Giro was emptying out. Two young men streamed out of the office into the car park with the rest of the workers. One young man was dressed in a suit, his companion wore a leather jacket and carried a motor bike helmet.

"Where are you off tonight, John, seeing it's pay day?" asked the lad with the helmet.

"Town on the sniff," came the reply. "Where are you off?"

"Southport on the arm. It's me tart's birthday. I've booked a room in the old bed and breakfast for the night. She doesn't know it yet though," laughed the youth.

His mate grinned. "I'll see you on Monday."

"Yeah, tara John, see you Monday," replied his friend, climbing astride a big powerful motorbike. He put his helmet on and kicked the bike into life, revving the engine loudly. He backed slowly out of his parking space and moved powerfully towards the main gate, waving to his friend as he went past. He swung out onto the main road and slowed down as he approached the traffic lights. The lights changed and the bike shot away. He felt the persistent rush of wind in his face and the power between his haunches as the bike ate up the road before him. He swung the bike left, his eyes streaming tears, and eased back the throttle as the road opened up before him. He threw the bike down a couple of gears as he raced towards a narrow hump-backed railway bridge. He almost left his stomach behind as he flew over it towards the village. He eased the bike left through the crowded shopping village and shot up the outside of the congested traffic as all the lights seemed to turn to green. He breasted the rise and scorched into the dip. The packed shopping village was just a blur behind him. He eased back on the accelerator and banged the bike down a couple of gears as he approached a box junction. He banked the bike heavily to the right and flew up the road through the industrial estate. The bike roared as he accelerated down hill and the large hill of a railway bridge loomed up before him. Head down he accelerated up the hill, oblivious to the fact that he couldn't see the road on the other side. The bike almost took off and the gears screamed as he screwed back the throttle, up the narrowing road into the estate.

An irate young man was waiting for a break in the traffic on a bend on the road through the industrial estate. He edged the car forward when there seemed to be a gap in the flow of traffic. He braked sharply and cursed, banging the steering wheel with his hand as the gap closed again. The youth on the motor bike came tearing up the road towards the bend, gaining hand over fist on a heavy goods vehicle. He braked sharply and looked over his shoulder, there was nothing behind him. Without a moment's hesitation, he decided to overtake. He swung the bike into the middle of the road and opened up the throttle. The bike flew forward past the slow lorry. In the same instant the car driver spotted a gap in the oncoming traffic and shot out in front of the slow, approaching lorry. The biker just had time to see the white car before his bike crumpled into it with a terrific bang. His bike stopped dead in a tangled mess under the car wheel. His right leg severed from the knee down, flew across the road under the wheels of the oncoming traffic. The biker flew through the air and saw the ground racing towards him in a spectacular blur. His broken body landed on the floor in a heap and was tossed away viciously onto the grass verge like a broken doll. His body lay crumpled in a twisted gory mess of blood and bones.

"Fuckin hell," gaped Whitey in surprise, who was passing by on the way home. He ran over to the lad and looked down at him. The lad wheezed and gasped heavily, obviously dying.

"Shit," he groaned.

Whitey looked down at him in shock. He noticed the thick wage packet in the lad's pocket. The corners of a wad of thickly packed five pound notes in a brown pay packet brought him back to his senses. Whitey looked up at the people who had stopped. They were wincing and in shock. One woman held her head in her hands and cried. The man who was driving the other vehicle involved was being violently sick at the back of his car. Whitey noticed the playing field behind him and turned to look at the inviting wage packet.

In a flash Whitey had made up his mind, whipped the money and was sprinting into the playing field. The biker lay dead.

"You dirty bastard!" shouted one driver.

"You twat!" called another.

Whitey ran like hell across the field towards the cemetery with the wind pounding in his ears.

A police patrol car arrived on the scene and the angry motorist pointed out Whitey and what he'd done. He hadn't yet reached the cemetery wall. The policeman picked up his radio.

"Delta One to Tango Two - come in Tango Two."

A police car was parked in a quiet lane that ran by the other side of the cemetery, inside was a policeman and a policewoman petting heavily. She ran her fingers through his hair and kissed him passionately. He lurched hungrily towards her, feverishly groping inside her tunic at her exposed left breast. They ignored the radio message at first.

"Delta One to Tango Two. Come in Tango Two." The policeman, the same one who had worked Jerry over, reluctantly picked up the radio, but the policewoman wouldn't be denied. She clung firmly to him and nibbled hungrily at his ear, playing with his crotch.

"This is Tango Two, Come in Delta One," said the policeman.

"Hello John...Bill here...Got a right bundle of fun coming towards you. He's just picked a dead man's wage packet from a traffic accident and got off through the cemetery towards you."

The policewoman was busily fixing her tunic.

"He's about five foot eight, dark hair, wearing a green bomber jacket, jeans and training shoes."

"OK, Bill, Tango Two out," replied the officer.

The police car sped down the lane to the cemetery gates. They skidded into the cemetery and roared up the path. Whitey spotted them and changed direction towards the old golf course.

"There he is," said Police Constable Ash. Whitey ran across the field, leaping over grave stones, trying to get over the fence into the old golf-course before the police car reached him. The police car tore down the narrow pathways throwing up gravel as it went in a desperate effort to cut him off. Whitey reached the fence first and ran through the small gap into the long grass of the dilapidated old golf course. The police car skidded to a halt twenty yards behind him. Police Constable Ash was out in a flash and after him, followed by WPC Thatcher who was restricted in running by her skirt and the fact that she insisted on hanging on to her hat.

Whitey strode manfully through the long grass and bumpy terrain with PC Ash bounding along behind him, making headway all the time. Whitey was knackered. Realising he was going to be caught, he threw the wage packet away into the long grass just as Ash brought him down with a, rugby tackle. The pair disappeared heavily into the long grass. Ash pinioned the out of breath Whitey to the floor with his knee and had him handcuffed by the time WPC Thatcher arrived.

"See if you can find the money," growled Ash, dragging Whitey to his feet. Thatcher nodded and waded into the long grass whilst Ash roughly bundled Whitey away. Tired and out of breath, plus the impediment of his hands handcuffed behind his back, Whitey stumbled and fell on the rough terrain, under Ash's feet.

"Get up you stupid bastard," growled Ash, and kicked him in the kidneys. Whitey gasped and staggered to his feet.

WPC Thatcher noticed the money in the long grass at her feet. She watched stoically as Ash hauled Whitey away through the fence and out of sight. She looked slowly around, checking nobody was about. It was lonely and quiet except for the constant trill of the birds. She hurriedly picked up the money and stacked it inside her breast pocket. Then she pretended to search through the long grass.

Ash dumped Whitey into the back of the car and then climbed in the front. Whitey looked disdainfully out of the window. He could see a middle aged woman putting flowers on a grave in the distance.

"What's your name?" asked the policeman hurriedly dragging his notebook from his pocket.

"Joey White," conceded Whitey.

"Where d'you live?" continued Ash. "108 Gerald Road Croxteth," replied Whitey, realising he had a chance if the policewoman didn't find the money.

"And why did you rob the money?" asked Ash.

"What money? I don't know what you're talking about," persevered Whitey.

Ash whacked him with a rabbit punch across the top of his head. Whitey yelped and held his head in his hands as WPC Thatcher climbed into the car. A large swelling appeared above one eye.

"Any luck?" asked Ash.

"No," replied Thatcher. "It's like trying to find a needle in a haystack."

Ash glanced at Whitey and caught him smiling so he whacked him again across the face. The swelling burst and began to bleed.

"I was only walking through the cemetery," whimpered Whitey, "that's all. I panicked and ran when you came teararsing towards me."

"Yeah and I was pissing out of me earhole," growled Ash unbelievingly as he started the car.

"I haven't done nothing," moaned Whitey.

"The way I remember it, you were already running when we came into the cemetery," Thatcher butted in.

"That's right," growled Ash and lunged another wild swing towards Whitey's head. Whitey yelped and deflected the blow. He cowered with his head down expecting another blow in another moment.

Jerry sat disconsolately on the hard wooden bench in the cell. His eyes were black and his sides were stiff from the beating he'd taken the night before. He sat in silence and stared at the graffiti that had been scratched and written on the cell walls and wondered what the people were like who wrote the gloomy messages.

"No ale, no bail, loads of jail," wrote one poet.

"Tommy loves Karen and his little baby girl," was scraped forlornly by a large heart and cupid's arrow.

"Lakey is a grass," condemned one angry message.

13

The rest of the graffiti were mainly names and dates of people sent down, only one message of hope was scrawled thinly on the wall.

"Sheila Morton is bang at it," followed by a phone number.

Jerry's attention was diverted by Dougie trying to slip a newspaper under the door.

"Go on, throw it," he called across to the cell opposite. An arm appeared out of the small square hole in the other door, clutching a cigarette. It threw the cigarette awkwardly towards the newspaper.

"Did you get it?" blurted a face appearing at the hole.

"Yes," called Dougie eagerly in a low voice. He slowly drew the newspaper back into the cell and appeared triumphantly with the cigarette in the hole in the cell door.

"Now when you get to Risley don't tell no-one your business," shouted the voice.

Dougie looked across at the three lads trying to cram their heads together in the small hole. They were three lads from Croxteth, Ged, Collo and Cagsy.

"I remember the first time I went to Risley," called Collo, pushing his way to the front and trying to get his head through the hole to see if the screw was coming. When he was satisfied he continued, "This fella got eleven years for a shotgun job, and the only evidence they had against him was from this woollyback who heard him talking in Risley. The woolly was expecting seven years. Him and his mates screwed some Paki's supermarket and got interrupted by the old Paki and his daughter. His mates raped the daughter and he bummed the arse off the old Paki."

Dougie guffawed laughing. "What happened then?"

"The Woollyback was only expecting three years after he grassed on the other fella," answered Collo.

"Didn't the woolleyback get done in?" asked Dougie.

"No," replied Collo. "They shipped him out to the hospital wing."

Collo heard the key in the lock and the jailer approaching. The jailer marched Whitey in, clutching a wet flannel over his cut eye. He locked Whitey in the next cell to Dougie.

"Got a light please boss?" Dougie asked as the jailer passed. The officer produced a lighter, lit the cigarette and walked away. "Thanks boss," said Dougie gratefully. "Alright Whitey lad," chirped the lads from Croxteth. "What are you in for?"

"Alright boys," said Whitey gleefully, recognising his mates. "Burglary," he answered.

"Cagsy," called Dougie.

Cagsy pushed his arm through the hole realising Dougie was trying to throw him a blanket. Cagsy caught it.

"Are you one of those pricks who rob houses?" Dougie asked Whitey.

"No, it was a factory," lied Whitey.

14

"What happened to your face?" asked Ged.

"A copper worked out on me," replied Whitey.

"That's all they're good for, that and swearing your life away on the Bible," said Ged. "You should wait for them to come home bevied and smack them across the head with a spade."

"What are you in for?" asked Whitey.

"A car," said Ged, "but they're trying to tie us in with a snatch on a video shop, so they gave us a three day lie down."

"Oh," said Whitey.

"Have you got any old newspapers in there?" asked Ged.

"Yes," said Whitey looking around.

"Well give them to Dougie to pass into us when the Risley bus comes. We'll have to make up two beds."

"What are you in for?" Whitey asked Dougie.

"A car," said Dougie. "We got remanded for seven days. We were going to plead guilty anyway. We got caught red handed but we've got a mate in intensive care, so they're waiting to see if he turns his toes up before they decide what they're going to do with us."

Marty's Mum and Dad sat quietly on a bench in a lonely corridor outside the intensive care unit. They sat holding hands worriedly in silence, each alone with their thoughts and memories of their only son. Marty lay in an oxygen tent not twenty yards away from them up the corridor to their right. There was a drip attached to his arm, along with another machine monitoring his heart beat. His head was half shaven and full of stitches. His face was dragged together by a mass of stitches and one eye seemed to be slightly lower than the other. His parents sat solemnly outside in disbelief. They couldn't believe that if he lived he would be a vegetable for the rest of his life.

The Risley bus arrived in the car park behind the police station, its last stop on the way to the remand centre. The jailer let the officers into the cell area.

"How many have you got for us today?" asked one

"Six," replied the jailer.

The prisoners were let out of the cells. The officers began handcuffing the first two together, left arm to left arm so they couldn't run.

Dougie passed a handful of newspapers in to Cagsy.

"See if there's any blankets or old books-left in the empty cells," said Cagsy.

Dougie ran round the cells and re-appeared with two blankets and half a dozen dilapidated old cowboy books.

Ged and Collo were kneeling on the floor each spreading out a blanket and packing one side of the blanket with newspaper, then they folded the other half of the blanket back over the newspaper.

"What's that for?" asked Dougie, puzzled.

15

"Insulation," replied Collo as he worked. "The floor is damp with sweat and condensation. Pick a number one to three," he continued.

"Three," replied Dougie, puzzled.

"It's me," laughed Cagsy cheerfully. "The bench is mine."

The cell was one of two reserved for drunks in the police station. The bench was less than six inches off the floor and there was a toilet in the corner.

"Rather you than me," said Dougie, catching a whiff of the pungent unkempt toilet. "Banged up twenty four hours a day in this yard - no exercise, no visits."

The officers were about to handcuff Jerry. His left arm was in plaster so they had to handcuff his right hand. Dougie walked over to be handcuffed to him.

"Hey, you look after yourself," called Cagsy. "At least the scoff is sound in here. It's out of the police canteen. Our dog wouldn't eat the slop they give you in Risley."

"You get a bit of entertainment often when the drunks come in and start punching the walls and shouting they've got six hundred witnesses," laughed Collo.

Dougie smiled as he was handcuffed to Jerry.

The prisoners were led into the yard and onto the bus two by two, where they were unchained and placed into narrow cages rather like pigeon coops. Jerry swapped places with a girl who was let out of her cage and into the passage way as there weren't enough pigeon coops to go round. She sat down outside Jerry's pigeon cage and the officer locked the door.

She was a rough looking girl in her early twenties. She wore a short brown checked coat and a pair of pink cut offs. Jerry sat in silence and looked at her bare legs. They were shapely but unshaven. Jerry noticed the golden hairs sprouting roughly out of her legs.

The bus pulled out of the yard. The prisoners began shouting rude remarks.

"Pamela" shouted a shrill voice at the back, "show us your tits."

There was a roar of laughter around the bus. The girl ignored it as the bus sped along the motorway. She sat quietly staring out of the window. The wolf whistles, cat calls and dirty remarks died down as the bus got into open country and its occupants began to reflect on how they'd got themselves there and what lay ahead of them.

The men stood in the lobby of the main building waiting to be processed into inmates. Jerry's name was called out, followed shortly by Dougie's.

Jerry walked up to the officer at the first table. He verified Jerry's name and address and read the charge. Jerry moved on to the next table where he was frisked. He was sent into another hall to wait, followed by Dougie.

One of the inmates weighed him after he had been questioned. Jerry stood in silence. He was told he was being moved to the hospital wing. Dougie was asked the same questions.

"Name and address?"

"Have you been here before? If so when?"

16

" Do you take drugs?"

" Have you any history of serious illness? "

"Are you a homosexual?"

The officers either ticked or put an 'X' after each question and then referred Dougie back to the queue.

Dougie's name was called out in turn. He walked into the small room from where the call came. He stood on a pallet board and was ordered to strip. A bored prison officer watched him. An inmate placed his clothes in a box and issued him with a small towel that barely stretched around his waist. He was told to go up to the stores and get kitted out. He was issued one striped blue shirt, a pair of brown canvas trousers, a pair of brown plastic slippers, one pair of grey woollen socks, a pair of white 'Y' fronts and a white vest. He was then ordered to get a bath. Clutching the towel around his waist and his kit, he walked into the bathing rooms. He enjoyed ten minutes in the hot bath although the bottom was grimy and needed cleaning. He re-appeared at the hole where his kit had been given to him, went back to the next room and was given a stodgy meal of thin bangers, mashed beans, a small dollop of butter and a handful of bread on a plastic plate. He was also given a plastic fork to eat it with and a plastic cup of tea that was more like a bucket than a cup. He was then ushered into the cage to eat his meal with the rest of the men who had been processed. Jerry was sitting there waiting for him.

Mrs Mullen was sitting in the living room watching television when the phone rang in the hall. It rang several times with no sign of any one answering it. Reluctantly she got up from her favourite TV programme and answered it.

"Hello, double six four one," she said poshly.

"Hello" replied the caller. "Is Angie there?"

"Angela - it's for you," the woman called upstairs. "She won't be a minute," she said, putting the phone down and going back to the living room.

Angela was Pybus's secretary. She had not long got out of the bath and was sitting at her dressing table wrapped in a short towel, drying her hair. She bounced down the stairs, expecting one of her boyfriends to be on the phone.

"Hello, Angie? It's Mr Russell," said the caller.

"Oh, hello Mr Russell," replied Angela, "What can I do for you?"

"I'm told Mr Pybus was at an important meeting this afternoon. I was trying to get in touch with him," lied Russell.

"Oh no," replied Angela. "I'm sure he wasn't."

"Well, was there anyone who was with him this afternoon for any length of time?" continued Russell, still fishing.

"Well, now you come to mention it, there was Patsy Lucas, Jimmy Nesbitt, Tucker Fielding and Arnie Davidson. Mr Pybus was very upset with them. I could hear him shouting at them from the lobby I've never seen him so annoyed," she disclosed, like one gossip to another.

"Thanks very much, Angie," replied Russell, "You make sure you don't tell anyone I phoned, after all we don't want to embarrass the lads, do we?"

"Oh no," replied Angela, shaking her head.

"That's a good girl. There'll be something nice for you in the post in the morning" continued Russell. "Bye."

"Oh thanks Mr Russell, goodbye," said Angela and hung up.

Russell put the phone down.

"Embarrass them? I'll friggin' embarrass them," he said, turning to the four heavies sitting silently in the smoke-filled apartment. "Sydney. See our friend Angela gets something special in the post in the morning," he said, taking a cigar out of his mouth and pointing to the smallest of the four men. The man nodded.

Dougie walked slowly along the corridor on the second landing in C Wing of the remand centre. He was one of the tail enders of a group of eight men walking along with their bed rolls under their arms, waiting to be banged up. He was ushered into the last cell on the landing with a lad from Huyton. Dougie stood looking round the small green painted cell. The other lad started making his bed. Dougie noticed him and followed suit.

"What's your name?" asked the lad.

"Dougie," came the reply. "What's yours?"

"Yozza," answered the lad. "Is this the first time you've been here?"

"Yes," replied Dougie.

"Well try not to piss in the bucket too much and make sure the lid's on properly when you do, otherwise it stinks the cell out. It's a good idea not to think of what your mates are doing on the outside, especially at weekends when they're on the ale."

Dougie looked at him puzzled. "Why?" he asked.

"It makes the time go quicker and it stops getting you down," replied Yozza.

"What's the scoff like in here?" asked Dougie.

"Don't worry. You'll shit some fine turds in the morning," laughed Yozza. "The screws reckon the food is spot on when it comes in here. If it is somebody's making a good fiddle because it's bladdered by the time it gets to us."

Dougie smiled and climbed on to his bed. "Nobody forces you to eat it," he commented

"Don't worry, you'll eat it, just wait till you're hungry. You'll have to eat it," said Yozza.

A prison officer's eye appeared in the peep-hole. Both lads went quiet and looked at it before it disappeared

"Who was that?" asked Dougie.

"The butler," replied Yozza. "How d'you want your eggs? Fried or boiled?"

Russell sat quietly next to his brief, Cyril Bletchley, a bald fat man who was also a local, councillor looking disdainfully across the table at the detective sergeant interviewing him.

18

The sergeant stubbed his cigarette in the ash-tray.

"You ask me to believe that?" said the D.S.

"I don't care if you believe in Father Christmas," said Russell dryly.

The detective glanced angrily at Bletchley and ignored the provocation. Russell was lucky his brief was there.

"Perhaps you'd like to go through it all again?" said the sergeant restraining himself and taking a deep breath.

"Certainly officer, seeing as you're either simple or hard of hearing. Watch me lips this time," said Russell, goading the man.

"I'm gonna have you, smartarse," growled the sergeant.

"Really Inspector?" chirped Bletchley addressing Detective Inspector Benson who was standing behind his sergeant. "You must control your men. Threatening people in front of witnesses - most unbecoming."

"When I want the monkey to speak I'll rattle its nuts," snarled the angry sergeant.

"As long as it's these nuts and it's with your mouth dear boy," chirped Bletchley gaily, referring to his genitals.

The sergeant jumped up in anger.

"Johnson," snapped the Inspector.

The detective sergeant froze in mid air. The inspector beckoned to him with his head, ordering to him to stand behind him.

The inspector placed himself in the sergeant's seat. Russell and Bletchley watched him warily, realising from past experience that Benson was a different kettle of fish than any hot-headed young sergeant.

"That reminds me, Bletchley. Are you still hanging around public toilets of a night?" said Benson, raising an eyebrow, waiting for an answer. None was forthcoming. Benson smiled and continued.

"Councillor Cyril Bletchley, prominent solicitor, champion of the poor, the oppressed, this stinking bastard," referring to Russell " - and champion arse bandit."

The two men remained silent, refusing to rise to the bait. The sergeant watched their obvious discomfort with glee.

"Now gentlemen, to business. Let me tell you the way it is," continued Benson. "There is a war starting between you Russell, and that other king shit of ill repute, Shanley Pybus. As far as I'm concerned, you can knock hell out of each other. I know one of you will end up floating down the river with the rest of the turds and the other one will end up doing life." The inspector paused, looking for a reaction. Russell shifted uncomfortably in his chair.

"Unfortunately, the Chief Constable doesn't see it the way I do. One innocent bystander is already dead. How many will die before this sorry affair is concluded?" shrugged the inspector, almost inviting a guess.

"If you know all this Inspector, perhaps you'll be good enough to sting us with a charge?" said Bletchley smugly.

19

The inspector got to his feet and moved towards the door.

"Be patient. Don't worry - I won't disappoint you," replied the inspector, leaving the room, followed by his sergeant.

Russell watched them go and looked at his solicitor for advice. Bletchley just shrugged and waited. The sergeant closed the door and looked worriedly at the inspector. Benson shook his head, rebuking the man and then turned and walked up the corridor, followed by his hapless companion.

"Experiences in life," chirped Benson, mounting the stairs. "You're dealing with the big boys now. Not some spotty-faced kid or hard faced drunk."

Benson turned left in to a large consulting room full of plain clothes policemen. The chatter and lighthearted banter stopped as he entered the room. Benson sat himself down in front of a large screen. Sergeant Johnson headed for the projector.

"Has everyone been briefed?" asked Benson.

"Yes sir," replied Johnson. "The situation is simple, gentlemen. Our friend Russell has been stung - now it's his turn to sting back. Something which he won't be doing while we're holding him habeas corpus. However, his hatchet men aren't nice people - so Johnson is going to tell us all about them. O.K, Johnson," said the Inspector.

The detective sergeant nodded towards the back of the room and the lights went out.

It was about that time that Russell's four heavies left his club and walked the short distance to the car. Animal slipped the pick-axe handle, hidden in the front of his jacket, into the back of the car and then climbed in after it. Mad-dog hauled his powerful frame into the front passenger seat. Bombhead passed him a small hatchet and checked his sawn off shotgun was loaded. Sydney, the driver, sat waiting until they were ready.

Bombhead nodded to Mad-dog indicating he was ready and Mad-dog gave the order to go. Sydney eased the powerful red Jaguar onto the deserted road.

Mad-dog's prison picture flashed onto the screen in the police consulting room

"Joshua Macready - nickname Mad-dog," started Sergeant Johnson. "Age thirty six. Implicated in several malicious wounding charges in recent years. None of them proved. Has beat two charges of perverting the course of justice by intimidating the witnesses. Believed to be Russell's new right hand man since the split with Pybus. He used to work for Pybus as a doorman until he bit off a customer's nose in a fight. Pybus dropped him like a hot stone, consequently he was sentenced to three years in prison during which time Russell looked after his wife and four kids financially. Not to be approached alone."

Mad-dog loosened his sleeve by his elbow and tested the weight of the hatchet in his hand. He licked his finger and ran it along the weapon's cutting edge - well satisfied, he sat back in his comfortable seat.

20

Animal sat silently in the back, his beard encroached bearishly across his face. He picked up his pick axe handle and stood it between his legs, resting his powerful hands on its thick head.

The picture changed on the screen as Animal's prison photograph appeared. "Anthony Reid," continued Sergeant Johnson. "Nickname Animal. Age forty six, a woollyback, the only one from out of town. Ex-professional wrestler, broke a man's neck in a bar room brawl. Served twelve years for manslaughter. Believed to have been recruited in jail by Macready. Not to be approached alone," warned the sergeant.

Animal glanced across at Bombhead and caught him picking his nose. Bombhead examined the large curd on his finger tip and then furtively wiped it under the seat. Animal scowled in disgust.

Bombhead's picture appeared on the screen. It was an unpleasant picture taken after his last fight.. His face was swollen and there was a cut bleeding profusely below his left eye.
"Matthew Mark McCoy", began Sergeant Johnson, "Nickname Bombhead. Age forty. No prison record. Ex-professional boxer. One time holder of the central area middleweight title. Unfortunately he fought with his face and was forced to retire punch drunk. Very childish in some of his ways, but regarded in some quarters as the top street fighter in the city. Reported to have the fastest head in Liverpool. Again not to be approached alone."

Sydney drove along the road straightfaced and silent.

His picture appeared on the screen. "Sydney John Dalrymple," started Sergeant Johnson, "Nicknames? None. Age fifty-two. A homosexual. The best jockey in the business. Has served two terms in prison for his part in armed robberies. Always carries a stiletto. The thing to note, gentlemen, it's a stabbing weapon not a slashing weapon," concluded Sergeant Johnson.

Sydney drew up outside the first house. It was three thirty in the morning. Arnie Davidson was sound asleep in the front bedroom with his wife Julie. There was a loud crack as Animal burst in through the front door, followed by Mad-dog and Bombhead. Arnie sat up in bed and heard the heavy footsteps on the stairs. He realised what was happening too late. He was hardly out of bed before Mad-dog and Animal were on him. He tried to cover his head with his arms as the blows rained down on him. Mad-dog chopped away at his body with the hatchet. Animal tried to break his legs with the pickaxe handle. Julie Davidson screamed in terror. Bombhead placed the shotgun against her head, raising a finger to his lips he said, "Shhhhhhh."

Mrs Davidson was almost paralysed with fear. There was a still moment when the only sound was Mad-dog's hatchet ripping into Arnie's body and the sickening sound of wood on bone. Bombhead was distracted by a glimpse of Mrs Davidson's large bosom in her low-cut negligee. He seized the top of it and ripped it off. It was left hanging on by one strap. Mrs Davidson clutched her naked breasts in her hands. Bombhead chuckled like a naughty schoolboy and unzipped his fly.

"Not now," said Mad-dog, out of breath. He was finished with Davidson.

"The only reason Arnie's not dead is because he's an old friend," panted Mad-dog.

Arnie was curled up on the floor, a mass of broken bones.

"But he's finished, and that's good enough," said Animal.

The three men left the room. Julie Davidson sat in shock for a moment on the bed, clutching her nakedness. The groaning of her husband brought her back to reality. She jumped out of bed and tried vainly to tend his wounds.

"Oh my God," she kept murmuring. She got up and ran for the phone in the downstairs hall. She bounced down the stairs, oblivious to her nudity "Come on, come on," she implored wanting the dial to turn faster. She dialled nine, nine, nine.

"Ambulance, Fire Brigade or Police," answered the voice.

"Ambulance," Julie blurted.

"What address?" asked the voice.

"9 Rakesdown Road and hurry," urged Julie.

She hung up and began dialling another number.

The phone rang in another part of town.

"Come on, answer," urged Julie in distress. The phone kept ringing. Tucker Fielding climbed out of bed and put his dressing gown on.

"Who the bloody hell's this at this time of the morning?" he moaned to his wife.

He walked grudgingly downstairs and picked up the phone.

"Hello Tucker? It's Julie. They've just done Arnie and they're on their way over there."

"Who is?" asked Tucker impatiently, still half asleep.

"Russell's men," shouted Julie in hysterics.

Tucker heard the gate open and the footsteps on the garden path.

"Shit," he cursed as he realised.

The door burst open. Animal flew in.

"Tony, John," screamed Tucker, trying to escape up the stairs. It was too late. Animal whacked him on the back of the neck with the pickaxe handle, bringing him down on the stairs. Mad-dog grabbed his flailing left leg and started chopping at his ankle with the hatchet, trying to chop his foot off. Tucker screamed in agony and tried to cover his head with his arms. His two teenage sons appeared on the landing, followed by his hysterical wife. The eldest lad, John, charged straight into the melee, armed with a hammer. Animal whacked him with the pick axe handle across the head and left him spreadeagled on the floor. Tony, the youngest, had frozen in terror at the frenzied attack. A line of blood spurted up the white artexed wall from Tucker's almost severed foot. Tony turned and ran. Bombhead waded through the carnage after him. Tucker's wife screeched hysterically at the top of the stairs. Bombhead butted her full in the face knocking her on to her backside. He rushed into the bedroom. Bombhead surveyed the room. All was quiet. His suspicious gaze returned to the wardrobe. He approached it slowly with a wicked grin on his face and gently opened the door. Tony was in tears, cowering in the corner, trying to protect his head with his hands.

"Oh God," he whimpered as he saw Bombhead. Bombhead smiled and whacked him on the side of the jaw with his gun butt. Two teeth immediately flew out, his jaw bone smashed, Tony slumped slowly to the bottom of the wardrobe into unconsciousness. Bombhead smiled and closed the wardrobe door.

Julie Davidson hung her head low in defeat, the telephone pressed close to her ear. The heartrending screams died down. The only sound was that of wood and metal on flesh and bone and then silence. She sat curled up on the stairs and began to sob. Two ambulance men came rushing into the house. Julie looked up at the two startled men. "Patsy's not on the phone and I don't know Jimmy's phone number," she blubbered uncontrollably.

Patsy was awake, making love to his girlfriend.

"Oh Patsy," she moaned, clawing at his naked back, the two bodies gyrating to a climax. "Don't stop," groaned the girl even louder as they convulsed in ectasy.

There was a strange calmness in the room, rather like the stillness before a storm. Patsy blew his fringe out of his eyes and rolled off her as the red Jag drew up outside. Patsy lay serenely on his back staring at the ceiling in satisfaction.

The front door blew in. The three gangsters raced up the stairs. Patsy realised what was happening straight away. He jumped out of bed and opened the window. Animal burst into the room and threw his pick axe handle at Patsy just before he jumped out of the window. The pick axe handle struck him across the back. Patsy landed naked in the front garden and rolled forward. Mad-dog threw his hatchet at him and just missed. Patsy sprinted off down the street, clearing the garden fence in one leap. Bombhead pushed the other two out of the way, trying to get a clear shot. The blast ripped away the road under Patsy's feet. but Patsy ran on for his life, unharmed. Sydney swung the car round and accelerated after him down the street. The naked man jumped onto the pavement in desperation and ran as fast as he legs could carry him down the empty street, his powerful genitals swinging comically in the air as he went. Sydney smiled the twisted smile of a sadist and banged his foot down hard. The gap between the man and the car closed rapidly second by second. The Jag bounced onto the pavement only three or four yards behind its quarry as Patsy threw himself through the air towards the haven of the entry at the end of the street. The car flashed past and Patsy landed in a heap against the foot of the entry wall.

"Bastard"' cursed Sydney and slammed on the brakes.

Winded and coughing Patsy picked himself up and ran off down the entry. Sydney reversed up to the entry. It was to no avail. The entry was empty. Patsy Lucas was away. He'd live to fight another day.

Jimmy Nesbitt's wife sat up in bed, woken by a loud crashing sound. It was the front door caving in. Her husband was out. She pulled the blankets up to her chin as she heard the rush of heavy feet on the stairs. She gasped in surprise as the three powerful men gathered around her bed. Bombhead dragged the bed-clothes out of her grasp. She whimpered. Bombhead laughed lewdly and looked lecherously at the attractive woman dressed only in a skimpy nightdress. The woman stared at Bombhead in surprise.

"Where's your husband?" asked Mad-dog.

"What?" answered the woman, still shocked.

Bombhead ripped off her negligee revealing her ample bosom. She covered her chest with her arms.

"Where's your husband?" repeated Mad-dog.

"Out fishing," she replied in fright.

There was a moment's silence The woman looked anxiously at them. Bombhead unzipped his fly. "Now?" he said.

"Yes," replied Mad-dog, "but I'm first."

It was eight o'clock that morning. Mad-dog, Animal and Bombhead stood handcuffed in front of the charge desk, surrounded by a posse of policemen. The desk sergeant starrted his speech.

"Joshua Joseph Macready, Anthony Reid and Matthew Mark McCoy, You are jointly charged with the rape of one Mary Nesbitt on the 4th March 1980. Further charges will also be preferred regarding various incidents on the same night. You are not obliged to say anything unless you wish to do so but anything you do say may be given in evidence."

There was a moment's silence. The three men stared defiantly at the sergeant.

"Have you anything to say?" continued the sergeant. Again there was silence. Animal made a deep, gutteral noise as though he was dragging something up from his boots. He cleared his throat and lobbed a large green blob of green catarrh towards the charge desk. It tumbled gracefully through the air and landed with an unceremonious 'splat' on the charge sheet. The sergeant stared at him in disgust. He picked up the charge sheet by the corner and shook it violently over a waste paper basket until the larger part of the spittle dislodged itself. He ripped off the carbon copy and stuffed it into Animal's top pocket.

"I'll see you later," threatened the sergeant. Animal laughed. "You better bring a fucking army with you".

The sergeant nodded to his men and the three gangsters were led away to the cells.

Detective Inspector Benson watched from a distance. "What happened to Dalrymple?" he asked.

"No sign of him yet sir. Probably at one of his boyfriend's," replied Sergeant Johnson.

It was a pleasant late winter morning. The taste of spring was in the air and the chill of winter had gone. People were sporadically making their way to work up the quiet street.

The postman cycled up to number eleven and got off his bike. It was Sydney. He rested the bike against the gatepost and walked up the path to the door, carrying a parcel.

Mrs Mullen answered the door.

"Recorded delivery for Miss Angela Mullen," said Sydney, handing Mrs Mullen the pencil from behind his ear. Angela was still in bed.

"Tch," said Mrs Mullen and signed for the parcel in a hurry. The sausages frying in the kitchen needed turning over.

"Angela, there's a parcel for you" she called up the stairs before rushing in to the kitchen.

Angela was hopeless at getting up but the thought of the present perked her up no end and she flounced gracefully down the stairs in her nightgown. Her mother was pouring boiling water into the teapot.

"Where is it?" asked Angela, wondering what the gift was.

"On the washing machine." said her mother checking the toast wasn't burning.

Angela happily carried the parcel into the living room. She shook it and held it to her ear. There was no reaction. She held the parcel to her chest and dragged roughly at the wrapping paper. There was a loud bang and a ball of flame. The front windows blew out into the street, the flying glass scything down two housewives on their way to work.

"Angela! Angela!" screamed Mrs Mullen, trying to fight her way into the front room, but was beaten back by the flames.

Sydney sat calmly in the red Jag and watched the two women lying lifelessly in the street "I bet you're sorry you didn't have that extra piece of toast now," he said quietly, starting the car. The car drove leisurely away.

It was almost eight o'clock in the morning. The prisoners at Risley Remand Centre had been released to slop out and clean up for breakfast. Dougie sat disconsolately on the toilet at the far end of the block. For security reasons the only privacy offered was that of a three foot by eighteen inch door placed six inches off the ground, which left little or nothing to the imagination. Scores of prisoners flashed past going about their daily business, some of them letting on to Dougie. Dougie was cursing the harsh toilet roll when he was joined by Collo and Cagsy.

25

"Alright Dougie?" they chirped, "how's it going?"

"Just finished," quipped Dougie, wiping his backside.

The lads laughed.

"How did you get on?" enquired Dougie.

"Sound. They couldn't link us with the videos," replied Cagsy.

"What about the other fella?" continued Dougie.

"Who - Whitey?" replied Collo.

"Yes," said Dougie. "There's something about him I don't like."

"He got off," said Collo. "They didn't have enough evidence against him."

Dougie flushed the toilet. "Never mind, maybe next time," he said.

That afternoon both Jerry and Dougie got visits. Dougie's mother and his girlfriend came to see him bringing him some food and drink. Jerry was visited by his sister Karen and his girlfriend, Teresa. Jerry sat quietly across the table from them in the claustrophobic room full of anxious and worried families visiting their loved ones. Some of them were old hands at the game. Jerry broke the silence. "I don't like you seeing me like this, Teresa. Don't come to see me any more."

"O.K." said Teresa meekly.

"There's no need to be like that. She's lost a day's pay to come and see you," said his sister Karen.

Jerry gave her a hard stare and she shut up. "How's me mum taking it?" asked Jerry.

"Not very well," replied Karen. "Blaming everyone but you, as usual."

Jerry smiled. "How's Marty?"

"Well, he's not going to die but I don't know if it's a good thing," said Karen.

Jerry nodded despairingly. Out of the corner of his eye he noticed one inmate necking his girlfriend and fondling inside her blouse. The girls caught Jerry's gaze, saw what was going on and said nothing.

"Another reason why I don't want you coming here," said Jerry to Teresa. "There's a lot of nutters in this place and half the time you don't know who you're talking to. The other day after Karen's visit I was sorting out my swag," he said, referring to the food Karen had passed in, "with this other guy who had a terrible scar on his throat. Anyway we got talking and he seemed like a sound lad. Next thing you know I found out he was in for trying to cut his mother's throat then his own"

"Oh my God," said Teresa in shock.

Jerry just shrugged and laughed. "It's always a good thing never to tell any one your business in a place like this," continued Jerry. "Two guys were talking the other day, one was from Macclesfield. The other guy asked him if he knew such and such, a girl up there. It turned out he did, so the guy told the Macclesfield lad what a good grind she was and how he'd had her. Anyway the Macclesfield lad walked back into his cell, took the batteries out of his radio and put them into his sock. Then he came back and hit the other guy over the head with it until he was dragged off."

The girls waited wanting to know the reason for the unprovoked attack.

"Anyway, it turned out the girl was this guy's wife, unlucky," shrugged Jerry, matter of factly.

It was about two o'clock in the morning. The constant stream of insults and abuse from the young prisoners wing began to die down. The lighting in the hospital exercise yard cast a dismal shadow of the bars and cell grill on the wall in front of Dougie. Dougie stared anxiously at the wall deep in thought. Along the corridor came the pitiful sound of a grown man blubbering like a child.

"Let me out you bastards, let me out. I haven't done nothing," the man cried. His plea fell on unsympathetic ears. The screws ignored him. There was a banging sound on the wall and an Irish accent called out.

"Reeves, do your bird."

Again there was silence, Dougie turned to Yozza.

"Yozza, you didn't tell me what you're in for," said Dougie.

Yozza looked at him for a moment, reluctant to be drawn. "I'm in for mugging an old lady," he finally admitted. "But I didn't do it," he hastened to add. "Two young fellas I was with did it but they got away and I got the blame."

"How long are you on for if you do go down?" inquired Dougie sympathetically.

"Five," replied Yozza. "But that doesn't bother me....It's me ma. It's put about ten years on her. The mud sticks, neighbours and people she's known for years shunning her in the street and all that."

"Can't you get 'em to own up?" asked Dougie.

"No, not while I'm in here," replied Yozza. "Tomorrow's me last chance. I'm up for commital. I'll have to do a runner out of court, and see if I can get them to own up."

It was eleven o'clock the next day. Jerry, Dougie and Yozza waited downstairs in the damp tunnel from the cells to Huyton Magistrates Court. It was a pleasant sunny day and the adjacent shopping centre was packed with people.

The jailer came down and called out Jerry's and Dougie's names. Their case was ready to be heard.

"Good luck, Yozza, look after yourself," said Dougie, shaking hands.

"I will," replied Yozza.

"See you Yozz. Don't forget, hit the back gardens as soon as you can," warned Jerry and with that the two lads disappeared up the stairs.

Yozza despondently watched them go. It was now or never.

Smigger sat alongside the girls in the courtroom. Jerry smiled at his mum while the charge was being read out. It was good to see her again.

"How do you plead?" asked the clerk.

"Guilty," replied the lads simultaneously.

Suddenly the tunnel door flew open and Yozza came flying out past the startled jailer, over the dock into the courtroom. He shouldered the usher out of the way, ran across the court pews to dodge the second policeman and out through the courtroom doors into the packed waiting room. He paused for a moment to see which way to run. He made a dart for the open door to the car park. A policeman tried to dive on him but a man waiting for his case to be heard deliberately stood in his way. The two men tumbled heavily to the floor. Yozza was away out the door, running for his life with frenzied shouts of "Go on lad, run" ringing in his ears.

The policeman dragged the man to his feet.

"You're nicked sunbeam," he growled.

"Who me?" asked the man to a roar of laughter in the waiting room. Amid the melee sat a small dignified woman with a set of rosary beads in her hand, silently praying as fast as she could.

Yozza was out and running, across the road into the shopping precinct, with three policemen in pursuit. He dodged through the heavy crowds, screaming at them to move and headed for the car park towards the sanctuary of the back gardens. A policeman bundled heavily into a middle aged shopper knocking her onto her backside and ran on regardless. A policeman on duty In the car park saw Yozza running towards him and tried to cut him off. Yozza skirted around past the policeman and headed for the main road. Seeing his quarry escaping the policeman threw his truncheon at Yozza's feet. Yozza stumbled, ran on a couple of steps and then fell headlonginto the path of an oncoming bus. A woman screamed. There was a rasping sound and a sickening crack as Yozza's skull caved in under the back wheel. A woman fainted.

"Jesus Christ," exclaimed the startled policeman trying not to vomit.

"You murdering bastard," yelled one heavy woman shopper as she set about him with handbag and her shopping. She was restrained by other officers arriving on the scene. One placed his jacket over what was left of Yozza's head.

The policeman still in shock, gave way to the compulsive urge to be sick and vomited violently over the pavement.

"You will go to prison for six months," Jerry was told. Dougie had only got three. Their families stood in silence. Dougie shrugged. It could have been worse. The courtroom door opened and Yozza's mum was led away by a policewoman. She was crying uncontrollably. It suddenly dawned on Dougie what had happened.

"You dirty stinking bastards. He didn't even do it. He didn't even do it," he yelled as he was dragged downstairs by two policemen.

Jerry stood in silence and stared impassively at the judge. The judge returned his hostile gaze.

"Take him down. Next case please," said the judge.

Jerry was led away shaking his head. "He's only a jumped up shopkeeper probably a fuckin' florist or something," growled Jerry in disgust.

It was about the same time that Marty was wheeled out of the intensive care unit. His half shaved head and grotesquely scarred face lay lopsided on the pillow. A nurse sat him up in bed and placed a spoon in his hand. She began the long thankless job of trying to teach Marty how to use a knife and fork again.

Chapter Two:

Inspector Benson sat in his office studying a file. There was a knock on the door. It was Sergeant Johnson. Benson tossed the file on the desk in front of him and lolled back in his chair.

"O.K. Johnson. What have you got for me?"

"Pybus is locked up tighter than the crown jewels. No-one gets into the building or out of it. His men are out searching for Russell all over town."

"Any sign of Russell yet?" asked Benson.

"No sir. We haven't run him to ground yet. But all his usual haunts are staked out. By Pybus's men as well as our own."

"Well pull them in - loitering with intent, carrying an offensive weapon, anything," ordered Benson.

"Yes sir," replied Johnson.

"What about Dalrymple?" asked Benson.

"No sign of him, sir."

"Well find him. I want that bastard's arse. Anything else?"

"Yes sir, Jimmy Nesbitt. He's gone on holiday with his wife until she gets over the rape."

Benson waited. There was nothing unusual in that.

"Well?" he asked.

"I'm told he's personally going to cut the balls off Macready, Reid and McCoy."

"Good luck to him," replied the Inspector. "He'll need it. Keep me informed."

"Yes sir," replied Johnson and left the office. Inspector Benson returned his attention to the file on the desk.

Russell was holed up at Sydney's boyfriend's flat. The man's name was Shirley. He sat curled up on the couch, his hair tinted a brazen bronze colour, his face full of make up topped off by a large black earring in his left ear. He studied his book with avid interest, stirring only to turn a page.

Russell sat at the table near the fire bearing all the hallmarks of a hunted man. He sat there playing patience his shirt and tie undone. A cigarette puckered in the corner of his mouth, his eyes beginning to water as he studied the cards through the thick cigarette smoke. The ashtray was full of dog ends - some still lit. The only other object on the table besides the half-empty whisky bottle was a small plate containing two thick cheese sandwiches, one with a bite taken out.

For the umpteenth time Russell withdrew his handgun from the holster under his arm and checked that it was loaded. He stubbed out his cigarette and immediately lit up another one, tossing the used match into the fire.

Shirley watched his agitated guest pace up and down in front of the fire and wondered what was going through his mind. With his best men out of the way and the rest in hiding the odds were stacked heavily against him.

29

There was a knock on the door followed by three more knocks then a pause. Russell was behind the door with his gun at the ready after the second knock. Three more knocks came in steady succession then silence. The two men eyed each other anxiously. Russell motioned Shirley to check the peephole. It was Sydney.

"Did you get it?" asked Russell, closing the door behind him.

"Yes, boss" replied Sydney, walking to the cassette deck and inserting the tape from Russell's private answer phone.

Russell returned to his seat at the table pulling heavily at his cigarette. Sydney started the tape.

"Hello John," spoke a voice in a thick Irish brogue, "Dermot here." Russell smiled instantly recognising the voice of his old cell mate.

"A friend of mine will probably be in touch soon," continued the voice. "I've an idea you might have a bit of work for him," he said jovially.

The three men looked at each other with interest. Russell shrugged at Sydney's searching gaze.

"Do things his way, John. He's the best and maybe we'll have a little drink after all this is over." The phone was hung up. Sydney stopped the tape.

"Who is he?" he asked.

Russell smiled. "An old friend," he replied.

The tape continued. "Russell, you're dead meat," growled a voice; "and so's your wife and daughter after I've fucked them." The phone went dead.

"Nesbitt," said Sydney.

Russell nodded as he stubbed his cigarette out on the cheese sandwich, much to Shirley's disgust.

The phone rang again. A soft spoken Irishman came on the line.

"Russell? The phone in the pub where you had your first pint with Dermot! Be there twelve o'clock Friday." The man hung up.

The two gangsters looked at one another for a moment.

"What have I got to lose?" shrugged Russell.

It was twelve o'clock on Friday. Michael-Edward stood at the bar of a small dockland pub studying the racing page of the Daily Mirror with a small pencil behind his ear and a pint of half drank Guinness on the bar next to him. The pub was a rough working man's pub frequented mainly by old dockers and seamen plus the odd prostitute trying to make a fast tenner now and again. About a dozen men were in the bar, and an old prostitute waiting for the morning shift to finish and come for a pint on pay day. She sat alone in the corner with a bottle of light ale on the table in front of her. The haggard woman stared roughly up and down at Shirley as he walked in followed by Russell and finally Sydney.

Michael-Edward scrutinized them carefully in the bar mirror. Shirley stood in front of Russell as he surveyed the bar with his hand in his pocket. He and the man behind him were obviously armed. On Russell's approval Shirley went straight to the bar and ordered the drinks. Russell and Sydney went and sat in the corner next to the prostitute. Russell sat seemingly unconcerned with his head down and his hand on his gun watching every move in the bar. He nodded and Sydney got up to check out the toilets. Michael-Edward took a swig out of his pint. He folded his paper under his arm and walked along the bar to leave. He nonchalantly pulled a cut throat razor out of his jacket pocket, swept it cleanly across Shirley's buttocks and back into the same jacket pocket in one swift unseen movement whilst walking calmly round the end of the bar to the door.

Shirley's lower jaw dropped and his eyes stared in shock as the cold steel ripped deeply across his backside. His trousers ripped open and there was no reaction for a split second other than the man seemingly to stand on his toes for an instant. The barman placed a pint on the bar in front of Shirley and gaped in awe at the startled look on his face. Shirley cried out like a boiled crab. The blood gushed heavily out of his backside, his buttocks visibly flopped open. Shirley dropped to the floor landing first on his side and then face down clutching vainly at his bottom, squealing in agony. The men at the bar stood back in surprise. Russell looked on in horror as Sydney returned from the toilet, gun at the ready. He glanced at Russell then at his prostrate boyfriend and the surprised men around him. He noticed the door just closing at the end of the bar. His adversary was getting away. He ran down the bar and jumped over his squealing boyfriend's pain-wracked body as the dockers scattered away out of the armed man's path.

Michael-Edward pinned himself against the wall next to the pub door. Sydney came rushing angrily out of the door with his gun at the ready. The Irishman stepped in behind him with a cutting back-hand stroke of the cut throat razor across the man's buttocks, pushing him forward into the street. Sydney screamed in pain as he felt the cold steel and the rip of trousers and flesh. He dropped his gun in the street as he fell and clutched vainly at his bottom.

"You bastard! You bastard!" he wailed pathetically.

Michael-Edward stepped over his stricken adversary and walked round to the other pub doorway calmly wiping the blood off the razor on his jacket sleeve before folding it and tucking it carefully into his jacket pocket.

Russell looked in panic at Shirley's pathetic face as the man lay whimpering like a child on the floor holding his bottom. Russell realised he was alone in the pub and the look of agony on Shirley's face and the running mascara served only to put the fear of God into him. He felt a hand on his knee. It was the old prostitute leaning across to proposition him. Russell whipped his gun out and fired in a wild panic straight into the smiling old hag's make-up splattered face. The bullet entered through her forehead and left through the back of her head followed by an explosion of blood, bone and brain that splattered up the wall for nearly a yard. Russell fell away from her panicking blindly at the ugly smiling face that was wierdly transformed in a split second to that of a drunk who had been knocked out but hadn't hit the floor yet. The old hag flopped back onto the seat dead.

The men in the bar stood back in shock. The only noise was the unnerving wail of Shirley on the bar-room floor. Russell was in a highly agitated state. He pointed the gun at the men in the bar and made his way slowly and carefully to the pub door he'd come in. When he got there his nerve snapped. He turned and ran blindly out straight into a vicious head butt that caught him across the bridge of the nose. His gun dropped onto the floor. Michael-Edward dragged him by the lapels to the back of the stolen transit van and tossed the semi-conscious man into the back. Russell looked round in a blur at the navy blue rust eaten old van floor, but everything was too much of a rush for him and he passed out into unconsciousness. Michael-Edward slammed the back door shut and picked up the gun from the pub door way. By the time the first nervous dockers ventured out of the pub doorway the old van was driving away up the road.

Russell smelt a strong whiff of pungent ammonia and jerked his head away sharply. He still refused to escape the nightmare he was having. Michael-Edward sat on the wheel-arch of the van and watched the bleary-eyed man beginning to come round. He repeated the dose of smelling salts and sat back. The patches of purple paint began to stop chasing the patches of deep rust around. A pair of brown working boots seemed to smudge together across the floor. Russell came to his senses and rubbed his eyes in wonderment. A man dressed in old working clothes wearing a black mask sat holding a pistol with a silence attachment pointed at his head.

"Top of the morning to you Mr Russell," chirped the man in his deep Irish brogue. "I believe you have some work for me?"

Russell smiled in relief. He picked himself up and nodded to the empty wheel arch behind him. The gunman nodded his approval and Russell sat down.

I need three men dead as soon as possible," began Russell, his shrewd business head beginning to re-appear."These people aren't easy targets. Each one is highly dangerous in their own right and difficult to get at."

"Nothing worthwhile in life comes easy," said Michael-Edward. "Except death," he added menacingly. "Twenty thousand a head. Plus a nice little bonus every month once the business is running well again."

"Agreed," said Russell and shook hands with a smile.

"I need someone to find out the personal details of each hit, photographs, place of work, address, habits, all the usual gen," said the Irishman.

"No problem," replied the gangster. He reached into his pocket and handed Michael-Edward a business card. It read,

J.T.Mitchell

Photographer of the highest class

Cheap rates for weddings and parties

His address and phone number was on the back.

"Who is he?" asked Michael-Edward.

"John Thomas Mitchell," replied Russell. "Ex-sergeant with the vice squad. Retired due to ill-health".

"And the rest," said Michael-Edward.

Russell laughed. "He wasn't averse to turning a blind-eye or helping one of the young ladies out provided the money or whatever he wanted was right."

The two men laughed.

"Of course, nothing was ever proved," continued Russell.

The joke was over. Michael-Edward's voice hardened.

"The police will know that it's you behind these killings. I dont want any contact with you whatsoever. If you want me put an advert in the Echo. SPECIALIST WORK REQUIRED, no phone number, no address, nothing. That way you won't be bombed out with unemployed specialists and I'll know you want me."

"Specialists in what?" asked Russell puzzled.

"Exactly," replied Michael-Edward. "Is there anything else before I go?"

"Yes," replied Russell. "I want people to know that if they cross me this is the justice they'll get."

Michael-Edward looked hard at him almost asking for a reason without saying anything.

"It will keep the bad mouths in line when I take over the whole operation," answered Russell.

Michael-Edward nodded. "It will cost an extra five grand if I think of something."

Russell agreed. The two men shook hands. Michael-Edward pointed to the back of the van. Russell got out onto a large area of debris in the middle of nowhere. Michael-Edward started the van and drove away.

Detective Inspector Benson and Detective Sergeant Johnson stood solemnly in the lift watching the flashing green light indicating their rapid rise in altitude. The light stopped at number twelve. The doors opened automatically and Benson stepped into the hospital corridor, followed by Johnson. They turned left and left again, their footsteps echoing off the polished hospital floor and walked in silence through two hospital wards towards the tall police constable standing guard outside the room at the end of the corridor.

"Morning sir," greeted the constable.

Benson nodded stoically and was followed into the room by Johnson.

"Morning sir," said the police sergeant getting up from the seat next to the bed, discarding the book he was reading.

Benson nodded but said nothing.

Sydney lay face down on the hospital bed. A cage had been placed across his waist to keep the blankets off his backside.

The two detectives regarded him in silence. Benson eventually pulled up a chair and sat down next to the bed. He smiled at Sydney but there was no reaction other than the defiant look of contempt on his face.

"Well I must say, it couldn't have happened to a nicer fella," said the Inspector sarcastically. There was no reaction other than the scowl of a professional criminal who knew from experience that no matter how bad the situation was, his only chance was to say nothing.

"What's the form on this kind of thing?" continued the Inspector in an effort to goad the man by pretending he didn't know."

Still there was no reaction on Dalrymple's face other than that of hate.

"You should know," continued the Inspector. "You're usually on the other end of the blade."

There was a moment's pause as the Inspector showed his obvious delight at Sydney's predicament and Sydney stubbornly refused to be drawn.

"At least three months on his belly and at least another three months before he's walking again if he's lucky," stated Detective Sergeant Johnson matter-of-factly.

The Inspector smiled in delight at the information but Sydney just scowled, refusing to speak.

The Inspector realised his ploy was getting nowhere. He switched his strategy and let his obvious disgust for the man show.

"Been playing postman lately?" growled the Inspector.

There was no reply

"Sean Atkins, Theresa Atkins mean anything to you?" asked the Inspector. Again there was no reply.

"The four Delaney children, Mary, Sandra, Karen and Donna?"

There was still no reply, just a scowl of defiance.

"No," said Benson shaking his head. "Just six kids you saved the expense of a mother's day present when you delivered Angela Mullen her little gift. You may as well talk to me now as later," raged the Inspector, "we've got plenty of time and you're not going anywhere."

Sydney just ignored the man, knowing he was annoying him all the more.

The Inspector realised the fact and began to calm down.

"Well if you're not going to talk to me I may as well call the police guard off. I'm sure Mr Pybus would like to talk to you. Dead or locked up for life. Make your mind up now," said the Inspector.

"Now now Inspector there's no need to be like that. This man's possibly a witness to murder. You've got to protect him," said Councillor Cyril Bletchley, breezing into the room.

The Inspector stared at Dalrymple's lawyer, his eyes blazing in temper.

"The man's no use to me unless he talks," said the Inspector. "Therefore I've got no choice but to call off the police guard."

"Now now Inspector," chastised Bletchley again," that would be unwise. What with all these killings and no-one brought to book! Screams of police corruption, payoffs, and politicians calling for heads to roll! Definitely not very wise."

Don't give me that shit," growled the Inspector on his way to the door. "You're not talking to a novice. You'd never make it stick."

"Shit's not proud," beamed the Councillor. "It doesn't care where it sticks."

"The problems you queers have. Terrible, isn't it?" replied the Inspector on the way out the door.

The room was at the top floor of an apartment block. It was full of lights and other photographic equipment plus clothes and props scattered over the floor in disarray. It was silent except for the rapid squeaking of the bed in the corner and the panting of an out of breath man excitedly making love. Suddenly - it was all over. The fat man groaned and heaved himself off the pretty young schoolgirl beneath him, leaving her drenched in his sweat. She winced in pain as he flopped back half-dead. The girl jumped out of bed, skipped past her school uniform which adorned a chair next to the bed and into the shower. She tested the water with her hand and stepped into the cascade of water when she thought it was warm enough. She began to wash herself in a lather of soap.

"Do you really think you can get me into films?" she called with the soap in her eyes.

"I don't see why not," called Mitchell, "as long as you keep doing the right things," he replied.

The phone rang.

"Hello, J.T. Mitchell," beamed the fat man, answering the phone next to him in his best telephone voice.

"The man with the big nose said you could help me with the groundwork on three undesirables," said a voice with a soft Irish tone.

"Ah yes," said Mitchell, instantly recognising the childhood name of Russell - his life long friend - and curiously eyeing the naked schoolgirl putting her uniform back on. "£1,000 a head was the price he quoted."

"Agreed," said Michael-Edward.

"Who are we playing with?" asked Mitchell.

"Shanley Pybus, Patsy Lucas and Jimmy Nesbitt," came the reply.

"It'll take about three weeks," replied Mitchell, unimpressed.

"O.K." said Michael-Edward. "I tell you where and when to leave it, when it's ready."

The phone went dead.

Mitchell smiled at his young model. "Now then dear, where were we?" he asked.

The girl was packing her bag ready to leave. She threw him a disdainful look which said it all. You've had all you're getting today, you fat bastard she thought.

"I've got to go," she said cheerfully. "Mum's expecting me."

Three weeks later Michael-Edward had just fiinished a long shift at the cemetery. He strolled along the narrow path towards the gravediggers' hut with his shovel slung lazily over his shoulder. It was early evening. The sun was beginning to set. A strange peacefulness that only happened at that time of the day had settled over the cemetery. The only sound came from the birds calling to each other and the sporadic voices of children playing on a rope swing next to the cemetery wall in the distance.

Michael-Edward tossed his shovel into a wheel-barrow along with the other tools of his trade and sauntered the last couple of yards to the hut where he kicked his muddy boots against the wall before wiping his feet on the doormat. On entering the hut, the first thing he did was to put the kettle on. He swilled his face and hands in cold water and groaned as he dried himself. He plonked himself wearily into the chair at his desk and unlocked the top right hand drawer. He took out a large brown envelope and thumbed casually at the three files inside. He picked one out and yawned as he tossed it on the table in front of him, replacing the envelope in the drawer. Printed in capital letters across the file was the name - Shanley Pybus. Michael-Edward opened the file. Just then the kettle boiled.

Michael-Edward walked slowly into the church. It was empty. A huge statue of the Crucifixion hung over the altar and a tray of candles burned slowly in the corner for the repose of the souls of dead relatives of the local parishioners. Michael-Edward looked up in awe of the huge statue which dominated the church. There was a strange silence and a loud foreboding that was trying to tell Michael-Edward that what he was about to do was wrong.

The old priest was in the sacristy. His back ached. He tottered over to the cupboard and opened a drawer. His pain killers were hidden in the corner under the pentecost robes. He walked to the sink and poured himself a large glass of water. He felt light-headed and sat down on a chair. For sixty years he had been a loving and faithful servant to his master. He wondered how long he had left. Maybe it was age, maybe it was all the pills he took, but the attacks of giddiness were becoming more and more frequent now and he wondered whether God would grant him his wish to die in his sleep. He placed three pills in his mouth and swigged back a mouthful of water. Michael-Edward watched him coldly for a moment and then swiftly and silently coshed him as he finished drinking the water. The glass bounced on the floor. Michael-Edward caught the priest before he hit the ground.

"Forgive me Father," he whispered as he dragged the old priest to the closet at the back of the sacristy. He lay the old man down comfortably in the bottom of it and placed some clothes under his head as a pillow.

Shanley Pybus sat comfortably in the back of his bronze Rolls Royce. It was Thursday evening. Every Thursday Pybus went to confession in the church in the neighbourhood where he grew up. The phone rang. One of the two heavies passed it to the boss.

"Hello Boss," said Patsy Lucas.

"Hello Patsy. What's the do?" replied Pybus.

"Something maybe nothing. I don't know."

"What is it?" asked Pybus.

"Me you and Jimmy have got our names printed in the obituary column of the Echo," said Patsy.

Pybus laughed. "It will just be Russell playing games. Letting us know that he's still around.

"O.K. Mr Pybus, just thought you'd like to know," said Patsy. The phone went dead.

Michael-Edward bowed his head and piously walked up the aisle to the confessional solemnly clutching a Bible. A young boy sat with his mother waiting for the priest. Michael-Edward smiled at them as he entered the confessional. The woman acknowledged him.

"Evening Father," she said.

"That's not our priest," said the little boy, loudly.

"Shush," scolded his mother. "Father Murphy's probably having a little holiday."

"Oh," said the young boy, apparently appeased.

Michael-Edward closed the confessional door behind him and sat down. He took a pair of black gloves out of his pocket and put them on. He reminded himself that he'd have to wipe the outside door handle with a handkerchief when he left. The green light over the confessional door went on. The woman nodded to her son and pushed him towards the confessional. He opened the door and knelt down on the small pew before him.

"Bless me Father for I have sinned," he began. "It is three weeks since my last confession".

Michael-Edward placed a small plastic bag - usually used for banking five pounds worth of ten pences - full of freshly dug top soil on the small table at his side.

"I've swore and told lies," said the little boy reverently.

"Hm hm," grunted Michael-Edward, pulling a gun out of his cassock.

"I've been disobedient and won't do what me mum tells me," said the little lad nervously.

"Is there anything else?" asked the unholy priest, quickly fixing a silencer to his gun.

"I drew a rude picture of the teacher on the blackboard," admitted the lad piously.

"Did you get caught?" asked the priest.

"Nah," said the little lad, almost insulted.

"Good lad," replied the priest mischievously, as he checked his gun was loaded.

"Say two Hail Mary's and one Our Father," continued the priest. "Now then ... I confess ..." said the pirest, starting the child off in the Act of Contrition.

"... to Almighty God," joined in the boy. The priest began to mumble in Latin.

Pybus arrived outside the church. One of his bodyguards walked into the church and looked around. There was only one woman in the church. She was obviously waiting to go to confession. The man nodded to his boss. Pybus got out of the car flanked by two armed men. They walked the short distance to the church door and stopped. Pybus entered the church alone. He dipped his hand in the font and blessed himself. He walked slowly up the aisle and stopped at the pew where the woman was sitting. He genuflected to the altar and slid along the pew next to her. He nodded. She smiled in return. Pybus knelt down and prayed for forgiveness, little did he know it would be his last chance.

The little lad stepped smartly out of the confessional and smiled at his mother. He walked joyously down to the front of the church to do his penance, full of the warm feeling a good confession seems to give. The light changed to green. The mother got up out of her pew and went into the confessional. Pybus slid along to the edge of the bench. He was next.

"Bless me Father for I have sinned. It has been three weeks since my last confession," said the woman. "I don't know where to begin Father. I've got three teenage lads. They don't go to church any more. They say it's a waste of time. They're on the dole and say they're bored all week, why should they be bored for an extra hour on Sunday."

"Hmm," said the priest, careful not to say too much.

"They're always in trouble with the police," worried the mother. "That Mrs Hannah across the street, her kids are never in trouble with the police. Sometimes I wish they were, so the stuck-up cow can see what it's like. They think its funny - me having to go down the cop shop every two minutes."

"Now now," said the priest calmly.

"Sorry Father. But somehow I think it's my fault but I can't think where I've gone wrong."

Outside the church, the three bodyguards stood around the door laughing and joking. The chauffeur sat in the car calmly reading a book. Half of his job was sitting around waiting. It was always handy to keep a good book nearby.

The confession door opened and out came the woman. The burden visibly lifted from her, she walked to the front of the church to do her penance.

The light changed to green. In walked Pybus. He knelt down in the pew, his face right up against the grill.

"Bless me Father for I have sinned," he began. Michael-Edward eyed him coldly. This was definitely the man he had been waiting for.

"It's been a week since my last confession."

Michael-Edward squeezed the trigger at point blank range. Pybus didn't even see it coming. There was a dull thud followed by a "thwack" as the bullet entered the middle of Pybus's forehead. His eyes and mouth stayed open in shock. The power of the blast threw his body against the opposite wall. Michael-Edward shot him again in the heart and then in the stomach, his body slumped sideways to the ground. Blood trickled slowly from his mouth as Pybus stared aimlessly up at the ceiling. Michael-Edward reached through the grill and emptied the plastic money bag full of soil over his face and body. He calmly put the gun away and took off his gloves. It was time to go. He stepped out into the church and wiped the door handle clean of any fingerprints. He looked furtively around. The mother and son were making their way out of the church.

The three gangsters stood outside the church smoking. They stepped aside and let the two people pass. The young boy skipped along the path bursting into song.

"Sheena is - a punk rocker."

"You hurry up, hard face," called his mother. "We've got to get to the shop before it shuts to get some tea before your dad gets home from work."

She smiled at the men and made her way down the path. They watched her go in surprise and then grinned between themselves, obviously finding something comical in the pair.

"Evening gentlemen," said a voice from behind, catching them by surprise. It was Michael-Edward.

"Evening Father," replied the three men, nervous as though they had been caught out. Michael-Edward walked slowly down the path out of the church into the street. A few moments later one of the guards checked inside the church. The green light was still on but no-one was waiting. The man couldn't see the boss anywhere. That was unusual. He tapped his colleague on the shoulder.

"Enry," he said.

Henry looked round and quickly came to the same conclusion. Just then Father Murphy came staggering out of the sacristy holding his head.

"Shit," cursed Henry drawing his gun and running into the church followed by the others.

"Stay on the door, Tom," called Henry.

The old priest saw the two armed men come running past the confessional towards him.

"What the devil's going on?" he cried, blocking Henry's path.

Henry brushed him aside the way a young bull tosses a matador. He and his compatriot pressed themselves flat against the wall on either side of the sacristy doors, guns at the ready, ignoring the old man trying but unable to get up. The old man passed out again. The two armed men burst into the sacristy, expecting the worst.

"Nothing," said Henry.

There was a split second's silence then both men exclaimed in unison - "the confessional!"

They pressed themselves flat against the church wall. The heavy pulled open the confessional door. Henry stepped into the doorway gun at the ready. Pybus lay dead at his feet. Henry was unmoved. They checked out the priest's door in the same careful manner - nothing. They returned to the confessional and studied the corpse of their dead boss. Henry put his gun away and shrugged. There was nothing he could do now. The two men walked briskly out of the church into the Rolls Royce and away.

Inspector Benson and Sergeant Johnson stood in silence watching Pybus's body being placed in a plastic bag and then onto a stretcher. The fingerprint men were already hard at work in the priest's confessional.

"Sacrilege!" muttered Johnson.

Benson nodded in agreement.

"It makes you wonder what kind of mind is behind this," said Johnson. "Names in the obituary column, sitting patiently listening to confessions, attacking a priest, murder in church and then just ghosting away unseen - but it's the soil that makes you think."

39

"We're dealing with a very dangerous man," agreed Benson. "It's the names in the obituary column that eats at me".

"How do you mean?" asked Johnson.

"When you were a kid did you ever catch a daddy-long-legs?" asked Benson, walking towards the sacristy.

Johnson looked at him puzzled.

"You'd never be content with just squashing it," continued Benson. "You'd always pull its legs off before you crushed its head."

"I reckon it's just Russell's last throw," said Johnson. "If Lucas and Nesbitt go the same way as Pybus nobody's going to stand in his way taking over the Pybus operation."

"True," said Benson, arriving at the sacristy. "But you don't understand what I'm getting at. Letting the man know he's dead and then catching him unawares. Killing him with his pants down. It suits this killer's mind toying with his quarry, letting it know it's got no chance before he puts it out of its misery."

The old priest was sitting in a chair having a head wound attended to by an ambulance man.

"Are you sure you didn't see anything, Father?" the Detective Inspector asked him again.

"I just felt a presence behind me," said the priest. "I heard a noise, no pain and then I just felt myself being spirited away."

"O.K. thanks a lot, father," replied the Inspector on the way out of the church. "The noise was probably the crack on the head," he said to Johnson on the way out.

Outside, a police cordon held back the calvacade of newsmen and television cameras. They surged forward but were unable to break the police line as Pybus's body was brought out. The cameras flashed. The photographers pushing and shoving trying to get a good picture as the body was loaded into the ambulance. Benson and Johnson watched from the doorway of the church.

"You know," said Johnson, "I've never liked pressmen. Bloody parasites all of them. The vultures of modern day society feeding off other people's misery and misfortune".

"Sometimes I agree," said Benson. "but we've all got to put a loaf on the table."

The two men were mobbed by the press on the way to the car. They harassed them with questions from all sides.

"No comment," said the Inspector pushing his way through to the car.

Johnson's temper finally cracked as they reached the car.

"Can't you tell us anything at all, sergeant?" persisted one anxious reporter.

"Do I owe you a living lad?" growled the policeman.

"The public have a right to know," said the man taken aback by the policeman's animosity.

"All in good time," said the officer, getting into the car and slamming the door.

That night the hospital ward next to Dalrymple's private room was quiet and restful. A tall young policeman stood guard outside the door, tired and bored. Inside the more experienced police-sergeant was sitting in an armchair reading a book. Sydney was sleeping comfortably on his belly. In the ward the elderly patients were snoozing happily, oblivious of the various ailments of age that had put them there in the first place. One old woman woke, perhaps disturbed by some nightmare or discomfort.

"Nurse...Nurse..." she whined croakily.

The nurse was talking to two big powerful men in the ward's kitchen unit.

"Hold on a wee minute," said the Scottish nurse before she breezed into the hospital ward.

"Is that you again Nellie?" she scolded in good nature.

"Can I have a drink of water?" moaned the old woman.

"Of course you can," said the nurse taking the opportunity to fluff up the pillow and stuff a thermometer in the old lady's mouth.

She disappeared and returned a couple of minutes later with a glass of water. She removed the thermometer,checked it and replaced it in her tunic, giving the old lady her water in the same movement.

The old lady gulped greedily at the water and then lay back on the bed.

"D'you feel better now?" asked the nurse.

"Yes thanks," replied the old woman.

"Well you go back to sleep. We want you looking your best when the old man visits tomorrow," scolded the nurse as she settled the old woman down again for the night. "You wouldn't want him to think we weren't looking after you properly now would you?"

"No," replied the old woman.

"Good," said the nurse, walking back into the kitchen. She ignored the two men and put the kettle on. Patsy looked at Nesbitt.

"Will you do it?" he asked the nurse.

"Why should I?" replied the nurse, placing two cups on a tray.

Nesbitt placed a twenty pound note on the work top. the girl looked at him unmoved and carried on placing cups, saucers, milk and sugar on a tray. Another twenty pound note landed on the table as she placed the teabags in the pot.

"How do I know you won't hurt anyone?"

"I promise you," said Nesbitt. "I give you my word that we only want to talk to him. He's an old friend."

"What will I say to the police afterwards," she asked, still not convinced.

"Just say we threatened you," said Lucas.

The nurse looked at him for a moment, saying nothing.

"O.K." she finally relented, "But it will cost you another twenty."

The money landed on the table. The nurse picked it up and tucked it into her tunic. The men watched as she tipped a capsule full of laxative into the teapot. She poured the boiling water in and gave the teapot a good stir. She placed some biscuits on the tray and walked off up the corridor with it. The young policeman was made up when he saw the refreshment approaching.

"Thanks a lot nurse, great stuff," said the constable taking the tray off her and carrying it into the room. He set it down on the table next to the sergeant and poured it.

Ten minutes later the constable was standing outside the door again. He heard his stomach rumble and felt his bowels begin to shift.

"Sarge, I'll have to go," he called into the room

"O.K. son," said the sergeant, still deep in his book, his tea untouched.

The policeman walked briskly along the quiet corridor down the stairs and into the toilet. The nearer he got the more desperate he felt. He was undoing his belt as he opened the door. Patsy whacked him across the head as he walked in. The policeman sank like a stone unconscious. Patsy fumbled in his pocket for the handcuffs, just then the policeman farted. Patsy stopped and looked up at Nesbitt.

"Looks like he didn't make it," he laughed.

The two men dragged the fallen officer in one of the cubicles and handcuffed him to the toilet chain.

The police sergeant sat comfortable in his chair, too deep in his book to notice anything was amiss. Patsy peeped at him through the small glass window in the door. The sergeant jumped up as the door flew open. He was too late. Patsy stunned him, coshing him over the head and then knocked him out with a back hand stroke across the jaw.

Dalrymple woke up in alarm.

"Hello Sydney," said Nesbitt cheerfully.

Sydney took a second to realise what was going on. He scowled at Nesbitt and resigned himself to the fact that he was helpless. Patsy tipped the teapot out of the window, making sure there would be no comeback on the nurse.

"Got a few questions for you, Sydney," smiled Nesbitt.

"If you're going to kill me - kill me. Don't think I'll give you the satisfaction of telling you anything," growled Sydney, knowing he was about to die.

"Don't fuckin' tempt me, shitty arse," growled Patsy. "Been trying to run any nudes over lately?" he said, referring to the night Sydney had tried to run him down.

Sydney didn't reply. It was Nesbitt who spoke.

"Maybe we can make a little deal here. Your life for some information?"

Sydney laughed. "D'you expect me to believe that?" he said, disregarding the lifeline.

"I give you me word," said Nesbitt, "that I won't harm you tonight in any way. We'll pursue our little dispute when you get discharged from hospital - provided you tell me what you know about this hitman."

"I don't know much," said Sydney taking the lifeline seriously.

"Well," said Nesbitt, "as long as you don't hold nothing back, it's a deal."

The two men shook hands and Sydney began his story.

"When Russell was in hiding he sent me to pick up a tape from his answer phone. There was three calls on it. One from you," he said, referring to Nesbitt, "one from an old friend of Russell's to recommend the mechanic and one from the mechanic arranging the meet."

"Which old friend?" asked Nesbitt.

"I honestly don't know," said Sydney shaking his head. "but I'm pretty sure it was a paddy."

"What about the hitman, was he a paddy?" asked Nesbitt.

"Don't know for sure," said Sydney. "He spoke in a mick accent but any soft cunt can take off that accent."

"What else?" asked Nesbitt.

"That's it," said Sydney. "You know the rest what happened in the alehouse where we met him."

There was a moment's silence. The two men looked at each other.

. "The guys no mug," said Sydney. "I'm top class and he managed to cut out two of us and cart Russell off without anyone getting a look at him".

Nesbitt nodded, obviously in thought. He got up and moved to the door keeping his part of the bargain. Suddenly Patsy grabbed Sydney's foot and wrenched his leg half out of the bed, ripping open his old wound. Sydney squealed in agony. The nurse came running.

"I gave the man me word," said Nesbitt as Sydney sobbed hysterically in the background.

"I know you did," said Patsy. "That's why I didn't kill the bastard."

The nurse got to the room the same time as Nesbitt reached the door. Everyone stopped. The nurse could see Sydney wailing in the background.

"You bastard!" she said and socked Nesbitt on the chin.

Nesbitt was taken by surprise and rode the shot on his chin before replying with a straight right that smashed the good looking nurse's jaw and tossed her unconscious into the corridor. The two gangsters walked through the ward of panicking elderly patients and down the stairs.

"You bastard," said Patsy,"I was going to pull her."

"So what's the crack now?" asked Nesbitt, considering their next move.

"I'll take Henry with me and run things from here for a while. You take the other two lads who got a look at the priest, Andy and Joe, back to Wales with you until your missus gets over the rape. That way there is less chance of the bastard sneaking up on us," said Patsy.

"Just in case we get a tug over this, you've been in Wales all the time anyway."

The two men walked silently out of the hospital and into the car park.

"If we can get to Russell first we're in business," said Nesbitt inferring they had a chance.

"Maybe no money's changed hands yet."

Patsy looked at him inquisitively as they got into the car.

Nesbitt slammed the door and explained.

"If the guy can't get paid he won't want to play. Would you work for nothing?"

The car drove off.

That night the wind was blowing a gale. The cemetery was alive with ghouls and unsettled spirits chasing each other across the grave-yard. Ghosts ran manically round the cemetery shrieking in anguish and the trees ranted and raved at each other like demons in the dashing wind. Michael-Edward lay in his double bed next to his wife. He was in a deep tormented sleep. An empty whisky bottle lay on its side next to the bed. A glass of undrunk whisky stood at its side. Michael-Edward lay on his back facing the ceiling. Cold beads of sweat began to break on his brow. His nightmare was beginning to come to life.

The strange foreboding atmosphere in the church settled in the room. A choir of angelic voices began singing a strange incomprehensible hymn in a slow rhythm. The choir seemed to grow in numbers and the noise in volume as the dream went on. The newspaper photograph of Pybus's body being carried out of the church appeared in his mind's eye. The headline read:

"THE MAN GOD COULDN'T FORGIVE!"

"God sends his angel to slay the gangland racketeer," read the follow-up.

Pybus's face re-appeared at the confessional box window. Suddenly there was a gun blast and a hole appeared in his forehead. Michael-Edward dreamed the whole grisly murder over again. The wind outside raged louder as though there was pandemonium in the cemetery and the multitude of voices in the choir began building up to a crescendo. Another newspaper heading flashed through his mind. This time the priest was quoted as saying,

"IT WAS AS THOUGH I WAS SPIRITED AWAY."

Michael-Edward's mind went back and relived other murders he had committed, car bomb attacks and shootings. It instilled on his mind of how the apparent serenity of ordinary everyday life was shattered by violent death. He tossed and turned in his sleep but he still couldn't escape his ghastly dream. Faces of his victims came to his bedroom window. Some called to him, others laughed at his torment. He dreamt he was lying in the bottom of a grave. His tormentors tossed a coffin down on top of him. It landed with a thud. Shanley Pybus woke up in the coffin, the bullet still fresh in his forehead and began scratching and tapping to get out. The choirs of hordes reached fever pitch. The coffin lid flew open and Pybus flew out of his coffin to get the gravedigger. The spectre - its face contorted in anger - tapped angrily on the bedroom window. Michael-Edward sat up in bed, jolted awake by the frightening apparition. The music stopped. The faces disappeared from the window. Outside the television aerial tapped repeatedly against the window in the relentless wind. A cold sweat drenched the agitated man. It was only a dream. He turned to go asleep and noticed a weird face laughing at him from his wife's side of the bed. He looked again. It was only his wife's dentures in a glass on the cabinet next to the bed. He rested his head on the pillow and composed himself like any adult who has a bad dream. He smiled to himself and settled down again for the night. Slowly he began to doze off. The strange atmosphere from the church settled in the room and the voices started singing again. The nightmare was about to repeat itself. Slowly but surely Michael-Edward was going mad.

The next morning Michael-Edward walked the short distance from his house to his hut. The birds sang shrilly and the trees dripped with rain from the previous night's storm. Peace and tranquility had returned with the break of day. Michael-Edward pulled a file from his drawer. He tossed the file on the table in front of him. Printed in block capital letters across the file was the name - Patsy Lucas.

Henry was a bear of a man often described as the missing link. He was of mixed race about six foot two, twenty two stone, with no neck and a little head stuck on massive shoulders. He was bedecked in jewelry. The granny chain which hung around his neck was that thick you could have tied the New Brighton Ferry up with it. His fingers were covered in sovereigns. Since the death of Pybus, he had been assigned to minding Patsy Lucas.

It was Saturday morning. Patsy usually took his girlfriend shopping on a Saturday - today was no exception. Patsy was a face. He couldn't afford not to be seen around, especially in his present predicament. Men of his calibre were thought by mere mortals to know no fear. In his line of work he couldn't afford to show weakness.

The two men and the woman walked from the house to the car.

"You're next Boss," warned Henry, not wanting to take unnecessary risks."

"Yeah. But this time we know he's coming," replied Patsy, drawing a magnum from inside his jacket.

Henry smiled as the car drove along.

"It won't come to that Boss. If I get my hands on his neck I'm gonna squeeze so hard they're gonna be picking his brains off the ceiling for a week!"

Patsy and his girlfriend laughed. There was something reassuring about having Henry around.

The car stopped outside an enormous boutique. The chauffeur swung the car over onto the pavement, disregarding the double yellow lines. Patsy and his girlfriend got out of the car, followed by Henry.

Henry had a good look around as he followed his boss into the boutique. The chauffeur settled down with his nose in a book.

Michael-Edward watched the car from the opposite side of the street, inconspicuous among a crowd of shoppers at a bus stop. Presently a traffic warden strode confidently up to the car, spotting the Roller parked on the yellow line. He tapped angrily on the window of the car. The chauffeur ignored him, apparently deep in his book. The traffic warden tapped again even louder. The electric window came down.

"You can't park here," lectured the warden.

The chauffeur pulled the book away, revealing a loaded gun pointed at the man's face, only inches away from his mouth. The man's chin dropped. He went white. The chauffeur stared menacingly at him.

"You move and you're dead," warned the chauffeur, impervious to the passers-by. He stared intently at his man.

The warden nodded, still dumbstruck.

"Put hands on the door and your mouth on the gun,"ordered the chauffeur. The man placed his hands on the door and gingerly leant into the car. He had no choice. He carefully spread his lips around the muzzle of the gun. His tormentor watched him coldly. Just then Patsy's girlfriend came out of the shop laden with shopping. Patsy had been spoiling her again. She was followed by her man and Henry. She climbed into the car, noticing nothing unusual.

"Henry, is this anyone we know?" asked the chauffeur, figuring that perhaps this was the hit man.

"No," said Henry, frisking him. Patsy stood back in the shop doorway, his hand on his gun. The two men got into the car. The traffic warden was transfixed to the spot in terror. The chauffeur moved the gun from his mouth.

"Goodbye," he said and drove away up the street.

"You done well," said Patsy, "This is a sly bastard we're playing with. You can't afford to take any chances."

Michael-Edward watched them enter a department store across the street from him. He crossed the road and walked calmly into the shop. The chauffeur's head was stuck in the book again.

The shop was packed with customers. Michael-Edward could not see them anywhere. He cursed himself. They must be on a different floor, he thought.

He walked over to the lifts and stepped into the first available one with a crowd of shoppers. He turned round to see Henry towering over him, staring straight at him. For a minute Michael-Edward froze. He thought he was dead. Henry turned his back on him, not recognising his enemy. The lift doors closed. Michael-Edward breathed a sigh of relief. The doors opened again and they were on the third floor. Patsy and his girlfriend got out, followed by Henry and a handful of shoppers and, finally, Michael-Edward. He walked slowly to a trolley of clothes and began browsing through them, watching his quarry from a distance.

"Can I help you at all?" asked a pretty young sales assistant.

"Oh no thanks," said Michael-Edward, taken by surprise. "Just looking."

He watched Patsy thumbing through a row of trousers.

Surely if he bought a pair of trousers he would try them on first? Michael-Edward decided to take a chance. He picked up a pair of trousers to try on and walked into the changing room. He pulled the curtain to and waited.

"I don't want these trousers, mam," complained the little boy in the opposite cubicle.

His harassed mother had two other young children in the cubicle with her. Her son was standing on a chair. She was holding the trousers so that he could step into them.

46

"You'll get what you're given," she nagged.

The little boy wiped his nose on his sleeve, his little face puckering indignantly. He stepped into the trousers and his mother pulled them up around his backside.

Michael-Edward saw Henry take a brief look inside the changing room. It was alright. Surely Patsy was safe in a crowded shop full of people. Patsy came walking in with a pair of trousers to try on and entered the cubicle next to the young mother.

The young mother fastened her son's trousers and stood back to see if they fitted. Next door Patsy removed his trousers.

"Stop picking your nose," scolded the mother, smacking one young child on the arm. Suddenly she heard a man preaching from the Bible.

"Sinner repent ye your sins for the day of judgement is at hand."

Patsy was bent over trying to get his foot into his new pants when he realised what was happening. The first bullet caught him in the lower part of the back, jolting his body upright, his face contorted with pain. The second in the rib cage and the third smashed into the back of his head. The soil came sailing over into the cubicle. Patsy clutched at the curtain in his death throes.

"What's that mam?" asked the little lad, referring to the preaching voice.

"Someone's been on the tablets son," she said.

Just then the curtain came down and Patsy fell into the cubicle, dead, with his trousers round his ankles, knocking the little boy off the chair. The mother screamed in terror, clutching her little children.

Henry came running. He was sure he knew the man who'd left a moment earlier from somewhere. He stared down at the dead body of his friend and realised who it was.

"Shit," he cursed. "This bastard's getting me a bad name."

That night the Rolls Royce drove up a crispy gravel path to an isolated cottage in North Wales. A man with a pump action shotgun watched the car approach.

The car stopped and flashed its headlights three times. The guard recognised the signal and flashed his torch in reply. The car pulled up outside the cottage. Henry got out.

"Alright Andy," he said, acknowledging the guard.

"Alright Henry lad," said the guard. "Not having much luck lately, are you?"

"Fuck off," came the stern reply.

Henry entered the house, passing Joe, the other heavy, on his way. Jimmy Nesbitt was waiting up for him. He wore a white open-necked shirt and black trousers. His day's growth sprouted roughly out of his face in an almost navy blue seven o'clock shadow. Henry sat down on the couch, still upset. He and Patsy Lucas had been good friends. He hadn't come all this way just to face the music.

Jimmy poured him a large brandy and placed the bottle on the coffee table in front of him in silence.

Henry knocked back the brandy and poured another one.

47

"I saw the bastard in the lift," he recollected with himself in disgust. "I didn't recognise him until Patsy was dead and shitty arse was doing an 'off man'."

Henry shook his head in disgust staring at the drink in his hand before tipping it back in anguish.

"You'd know him again though, wouldn't you then?" asked Nesbitt, already knowing the answer.

"Too right," replied Henry.

"O.K. We'll let him come to us," said Nesbitt. "Everything is running sweet in town business wise. There's just one thing left to do."

"What's that?" asked Henry.

"I've got a package to pick up," replied Nesbitt.

"Dope?" said Henry.

Jimmy Nesbitt nodded.

"Can't you get someone else to pick it up?" asked Henry concerned.

"No," said Nesbitt, "It's got to be me."

"So," said Henry, "That's when the man will make his move."

"Either there or somewhere on the way back," shrugged Nesbitt, having already resigned himself to the fact.

"The only way we can beat the man is by making him show himself," he said, trying to convince Henry.

At the same time, not too many miles away in Liverpool, a file lay on the desk in a certain cemetery, in a certain gravedigger's hut. Jimmy Nesbitt was printed across it in block capital letters. The room was dark, lit only by a small gas lamp. Michael-Edward relaxed half in the shadows, in his rocking chair, rolling a cigarette.

"So, Mr Nesbitt," he said quietly, talking to himself. "You go to work on Monday. You sit in the canteen for two hours," he said, lighting his cigarette and discarding the match. "Then you disappear to the toilet for half and hour and when you come back? There's a nice little parcel waiting for you. And that's you. Finished for the day! It's a hard life," he said, taking a deep breath on his cigarette as he considered his options.

It was ten to six on a Monday morning. A light drizzle - the kind that soaks you - descended slowly in a haze on the six hundred men starting work on the early shift at the local motor factory. The men, some tired, some still drunk, and some with the bad taste of the ale from the night before on their mouths, trudged mundanely into work. Jimmy Nesbitt dressed in working clothes, walked unnoticed into the factory, flanked by Henry and Andy. Joe had been assigned the job of looking after his wife in Wales. The three men made their way upstairs to the works canteen and sat down at a table. Nobody spoke. Andy dipped into his pocket and pulled out a set of playing cards. He gave them a fast shuffle and started dealing them.

It was about that time that Michael-Edward walked quite freely into the factory. He was dressed in the firm's overalls, a cap, a donkey jacket and working boots. He walked unchallenged past the security guard with his lunch box tucked under his arm. He made his way through the massive car plant to the toilet at the press shop.

It was fairly big for a factory toilet. There were four cubicles against one wall. The urinals were in an 'L' shape opposite them and the wash basins were in the middle of the room.

Michael-Edward made straight for one of the cubicles - the one on the end. He turned and locked himself in, pulling the toilet lid down at the same time. He took his coat off and hung it on the hanger on the toilet door. He settled down on the toilet seat and began eating his sandwiches whilst reading a book at the same time. A strange foreboding settled in the room, the same aura as in the church and a choir of voices began to sing. Unmoved, Michael-Edward sat deeply entrenched in his book.

Upstairs in the canteen the time went slowly. Henry watched the time tick slowly by on the canteen clock. He was nervous and edgy, plus the fact he was losing at cards. He tossed his hand in in disgust and went for something to eat. Andy smiled, winning again. Nesbitt glanced at Andy and watched Henry's agitated swagger up to the canteen's service area. Henry wasn't usually the nervous type but with the last two killings and Jimmy unnecessarily putting his life at risk he was in a mean mood. There was a queue of men along the canteen service area waiting for breakfast. A young chef was serving them with set breakfasts already laid out on plates. Next to them were separate trays of bacon, eggs, sausages and toast. Henry walked straight to the front of the queue. Nobody argued. Henry just scowled, not taking notice of anyone in particular. The young chef watched in amazement. Henry picked up four plates of bacon, egg, sausage and tomato and tipped them onto one plate. He grabbed a handful of sausages and about a dozen rounds of toast.

"Haven't you got any crusts?" he asked.

"No mate. We always throw them out", answered the young lad.

Henry just scowled. He picked up his scoff and walked past the girl on the till making no attempt to pay. She looked at the young man without saying anything. The lad just shrugged. What could he do? The men waiting for breakfast watched in astonishment, whispering between themselves when Henry was well out of earshot. Henry sat down at the table with his food. Andy tried to pinch a piece of toast. Henry rapped him across the knuckles with his knife.

"If you want some go and get your own," he said with a mouthful of bacon.

Andy backed off with a scowl.

Michael-Edward checked his watch. It was nearly five minutes to eight. He attached the silencer to his gun and stuffed it inside his shirt. He stood on the toilet to check nobody was around. There wasn't. He climbed out of the cubicle leaving it locked and began washing his face. He yawned and noticed a gap on one side of his mouth. He pulled his lip to one side and probed it with his tongue.

"Looks like I need a filling," he said to himself.

A man came into the toilet with a newspaper in his hand. He walked straight into the middle of the three available cubicles. He flushed the toilet before use then dropped his trousers and sat down. Michael-Edward returned his thoughts to the problems of his teeth.

Nesbitt came strolling along the corridor on the way to the toilet flanked by his men.

"You stay outside in case you see the cunt," he said to Henry. "You stand inside and keep an eye out while I have a shit," he said to Andy.

The two men nodded in turn.

Henry stopped outside the gents with his back to the wall. His two colleagues went in. Nesbitt went straight to the end toilet. Michael-Edward had his back to them. He watched them in the mirror. He saw the heavy disregard him with a smirk and carried on shaking himself dry unmoved.

Nesbitt dropped his trousers and settled down to study the racing pages of a newspaper.

Michael-Edward began washing his hands and face in the sink.

Andy decided there was no danger and he wanted to go to the toilet himself.

"Henry," he called, "will you give us a blow? I could do with a shite myself."

Henry smirked and sidled into the room. Andy went straight into the toilet. Henry cast a lazy eye over the room and didn't pay much attention at first glance to the man drying his face.

"Shit!" he exclaimed, realising who it was and fumbling inside his jacket for his gun.

Michael-Edward took his time, his face red and his eyes cold. He squeezed off one bullet that caught Henry straight between the eyes. Henry looked at him for a moment before he crashed to the ground, dead, the bullet hole giving the illusion there was a tiny blob of bacon stuck to his face.

Andy heard the noise of Henry's body hitting the floor.

"Henry, is that you?" he called, drawing his gun and trying to pull his trousers up at the same time, but not quite managing it.

Michael-Edward stood casually pouring soil over Henry's body. Andy's cry seemed to distract him. He ripped two shots through the toilet door. Andy was standing on his feet with his trousers round his ankles. He took both bullets full in the chest. He fell back against the wall, and slumped to the floor dead. His hand protruding through into the worker's cubicle. The worker was full of drink from the night before and couldn't hear anything for the noise in the factory.

"'Ere y'are mate," he said, reaching down and passing the protruding hand a roll of toilet paper, his head still in the newspaper. Only when the man didn't take the toilet roll and he looked down and saw the blood trickling over the hand did he realise something was wrong. At the same time Nesbitt calmly drew his gun and sent six shots splintering through the toilet door, not even bothering to get up from his seat.

"Sinner repent ye your sins for the day of judgement is at hand," whined Michael-Edward. Nesbitt tried to fire again but to his surprise - his gun was empty.

He took that look of surprise on his face to his grave. Three bullets ripped through the door. One caught him in the stomach, another in the chest and the last one took away part of his head. He fell to the floor, dead.

A large pool of blood trickled into the workers cubicle. He, by this time was cowering on the toilet seat with his trousers down, frightened to step into the pool of blood in case it was catching.

"Oh my God! Oh my God!" he whimpered in panic as the soil came sailing over into the two adjacent cubicles.The man was close to tears, closed his eyes and prayed.

Michael-Edward kicked down the toilet door of the toilet he'd been using. He calmly picked up his things and left.

Five minutes later a foreman discovered Henry's body and heard the whimpering coming from the middle cubicle.

"Fucking hell!" he declared.

He summoned up the courage to kick the toilet door in. The worker was still clinging to the pipe leading to the cistern with his trousers round his ankles, praying for all he was worth. The foreman helped him down.

"Come on son," he said, trying to comfort him. "It's alright now."

The man broke down and cried like a baby.

"Why didn't you hurry up and get me out, you bastard," he whimpered like a young child.

Russell sat at the back of the court room. Inspector Benson sat a couple of benches in front of him, angry and alone in defeat, bearing the scowl of a bad loser. The prosecutor was at the bench in private consultation with the three magistrates - acutely embarrassed. The three prisoners had been remanded in custody for four months and the police still had no evidence to offer. Cyril Bletchley, acting for the defence, sat smugly in the front of the court like a beached whale. He scribbled absent-mindedly on the folder before him, enjoying the prosecutor's obvious discomfort.

It was the day of the committal for Animal, Mad-dog and Bombhead. The three men sat comfortably in the dock, happy at the thought that they were about to be acquitted. The Inspector sat in silence disgusted at the scene before him. Three guilty men cocking a snook at the judicial system. Animal removed his front teeth and flicked his tongue in and out as though he was licking at something small and intricate. He replaced his teeth, a smile beaming all over his gummy face, as the prosecutor finally announced that he had no evidence to offer. The three men were discharged.

The Inspector fixed his gaze in anger on the courtroom clock as the three hostile men walked past, growling and gloating at him.

"Lick it bitch," encouraged Mad-dog as he sauntered past.

The Inspector visibly cringed under the remark, using all his powers of concentration to hold himself in check.

"Stick to giving out parking tickets, sonny," patronised Animal on the way past.

"One of these days I'm gonna kill you, you fuckin' binman," growled Bombhead, happy at the thought of being released but remembering the dirty bastard who had locked him up for four months, (banged-up three in a cell, for twenty three hours a day living on slops).

The Inspector nodded, chewing his lip, watching the magistrate retire. The last bitter remark cheered him up. It showed that at least these bastards weren't getting it all their own way.

An hour later Inspector Benson was sitting in the Chief Superintendent's office.

"Well John, what have you got?" asked his boss.

"We know that the hitman works for Russell but we can't prove it. Russell has been staying in Spain waiting for this to blow over. Now he's set to take over where Pybus left off," answered the Inspector.

"What are you going to do about it?" asked the Chief Superintendent.

"I'm going to harass him at every possible chance, no matter how petty the reason," answered Benson.

The Chief Superintendent looked at him inquisitively.

"We've had enough bad publicity over this already," he warned.

"It's a question of having to," replied Benson.

The Chief looked at him, waiting for him to enlarge.

"If we don't keep pestering him, he'll realise something is wrong," continued Benson. "We've got a man on the inside."

"Regarding what line of enquiry?" asked the Chief.

"Drugs," came the terse reply.

"Good," replied the Chief. "Glad to hear we're getting somewhere at last."

Shanley Pybus's old Rolls Royce arrived outside a big apartment block - Pybus's old apartment block. Russell stepped out followed by his three goons. They walked past the guards into the lift. The lift stopped at the top floor. Russell marched into the office, followed by his three men. He relaxed comfortably in Pybus's old seat and laughed out loud. Now he was the man.

Chapter Three:

It was a sunny Sunday morning. Little Maca, Sykesy and two friends were busy making bikes in the front path of little Maca's house. Sykesy was showing one lad how to mend a puncture by dipping the inner-tube into a bowl of water. The other two kids were putting the front wheel on another bike.

Upstairs in the back bedroom, Vicky lay asleep crushed up against the wall in her small single bed.

Dougie lay on his chest, half hanging out of the bed, half uncovered by the blankets and tired from the previous night's exertions. Vicky's eyelids flashed open - the peace and tranquility disturbed by the stirring noise in the next bedroom.

She shoved Dougie with both hands.

"Quick, me Dad's getting up," she panicked.

Dougie jumped up and put his jeans on. Mr McFaye walked into the bathroom and ran the hot water for a shave. Dougie tiptoed past him as he lathered the shaving foam on his chin. Downstairs Maca was making tea and toast.

"Nearly got you," he laughed.

"I know," admitted Dougie, "why didn't you give us a shout?"

Maca shrugged, handing him a cup of tea and a plate of thick buttered toast. "You could have been on the nest".

Dougie smiled and shook his head, chomping away at the lump of toast in his mouth and slurping his tea. He had been courting Vicky for four years. He had come to look on Maca as his little brother. Just then Mr McFaye walked into the room.

"Alright lads," he breezed. "Alright Mr McFaye," replied Dougie.

"Big day today son," he said to Maca, referring to the morning's football match.

Maca shrugged. He stuffed his shin pads into his boots and dropped them into his sports bag.

"I'm not interested in signing schoolboy forms for no-one. I play the game because I enjoy it. I don't want some no-mark giving me all this wank. Do this, do that. I've probably got more skill in the crack of me arse than they've ever had in their life."

Maca was fifteen with the body of a twenty one year old. He was dwarfed only by Dougie's exceptional muscular frame. He was already playing football for the local pub team, one of the best football teams in the city. His father was hounded by scouts for top teams from up and down the country, in fact there was little doubt that one day he would make the grade and turn professional. But he was a free spirit. He hated being regimented by coaches and being told what to do all the time. He was still young and immature and didn't know yet what he wanted from life.

"That's the wrong attitude son," said Mr McFaye. "Do you want to end up on the dole with the rest of your mates?" The father looked at his son, wanting an answer. None came. "There aren't many jobs around now, what makes you think you're going to get one when you leave school?"

"I suppose you're right," admitted Maca. You decide what the best offer is. I'll sign the paper and play the football."

Smigger arrived at the front gate, his football boots and shin pads dangling from his finger tips behind his back.

"Alright boys," he greeted the four kids in the path.

"Alright Smigger," chirped little Maca. "How many are you going to let in today?"

"Don't be cheeky," replied Smigger, the team goalie. "Where are you going?" he asked.

"Southport," came the reply.

"I wonder what for," laughed Smigger, looking at the old home made bikes in the path.

Time seemed to go slowly that day. The man driving the van which took the football team turned up late. The lads spent the time kicking the ball around outside the local pub, some sat on the steps reading the Sunday papers.

The four kids were cycling along the bypass. A big sign on the left said 'Southport 18 miles".

It was about that time that the match kicked off. It was the start of a hard uncompromising tussle with another of the city's leading sides. Maca had been warned to keep an eye out for the right back and the midfield player marking him because they were both well known for their dirty play.

The ball swung out to the left. Maca recovered it with his marker tight at his back. Maca killed the ball dead with his first touch, dummied one way and then went the other way with the ball leaving his marker flat footed. Just as he was about to sweep upfield with the ball, he was dumped unceremoniously into a muddy puddle. It was the veteran full back covering his midfield man.

"Sorry ref," he called, making out it was an accident and helping the kid up out of the puddle.

"Playing with the big boys now son," said the old campaigner, patting the youth on the head.

Maca nodded but said nothing. He knew the man was trying to get him into a slanging match to put him off his game.

The four kids cycled along a leafy country lane in Aughton, (a neighbouring area to Southport), populated mainly by rich and well-off people. Up the road on the left was the local church hall where the local scout pack was holding one of its weekly meetings. It was little Maca who spotted them first. Three unattended racing bikes leaning against the church hall. The four kids slipped off their bikes and crept up the path to the church hall. Little Maca peeped in.

The scout master was standing on the stage addressing the assembly, all spotless in their tidy uniforms.

"What are the spoilt bastards doing?" asked Sykesy.

"They're all dib dib dobbing themselves to fuck," replied little Maca.

The four kids clambered onto the stolen bikes and pedalled off down the lane. Little Maca stayed on his own bike. There was still plenty of time for him to pinch one later.

Maca landed on his backside for the umpteenth time. The referee blew for the foul and came running up.-Maca sat there shaking his head.

"Get hold of the game. The cunts kicked the kid more often than he's kicked the ball" called the line.

The full back gestured as though he was masturbating himself, insinuating that the line was a crowd of wankers. Maca got up and carried on with the game.

In the following ten minutes he was kicked, tipped, barged, elbowed, and fouled off the ball. His father watched anxiously from the line and shook his head at the treatment that the opposing side meted out to his son and got away with. The score was nil nil. The opposing side were attacking and forced a corner on the far side of the pitch. Everybody was back in defence except Maca who stood on the half way line marked by the midfield player and the full back.

The corner was taken and the ball cleared upfield. Maca held off the challenge and controlled the ball. The full back bundled him to the ground. The referee gave a foul. The full back stood there arguing at the decision. Maca kicked the ball against his legs and then played it into their half of the field. There was nobody else back. It was a straightforward race for the ball between Maca and the two players. Maca was yards and yards faster leaving the men struggling in his wake. He had time to drop his shorts and show his white buttocks to his pursuers before he hammered the ball past the unprotected goalkeeper. He turned in triumph, his arm raised, a broad grin on his face. He was engulfed by a horde of team mates,

"Playing with the big boys now son?" he called to the full back as he ran past. The man shook his head. There was nothing he could say. The kid had made a show of him. He also had to suffer the howls of laughter and torrents of abuse from the line. There was nothing else he could do except laugh.

The four youngsters were waiting for the traffic lights to change at a small crossroad. A youth on a racing bike cycled past them toward Freshfield. Sykesy saw him first and nudged little Maca. His eyes lit up at the sight of the ten geared well maintained bicycle the youth rode.

"That'll do me," he said.

The lights changed and the lads turned right and set off in careful pursuit of their quarry.

The football match had ended in a one nil win. The players from both teams trudged in unison across the park towards the dressing rooms, the rivalries and personal battles ending with the final whistle. Some discussed the game as old foes who had played against each other many times, others carried crossbars and goalposts towards the safe-keeping behind the dressing rooms. Smigger gave Maca a shout and motioned to his father. Maca watched the talent scout introduce himself to his father from a distance.

"Is he bringing the forms up the alehouse for you to sign?" asked Dougie.

"Fuck off," replied Maca.

The youth rode his bike calmly along the road oblivious to his four young pursuers following him at a distance, biding their time. He bumped onto the pavement and skipped off his bike outside a small newsagents. He leant his bike against the bubble-gum machine and went inside the shop. Little Maca came riding along the pavement, hopped off his own wreck, dropping it onto the floor. He grabbed the youth's bike, scurried along with it for a few strides and then skipped onto it and pedalled furiously up the street.

The youth came running out of the shop.

"Come back you little bastard!" he roared.

Little Maca pedalled as fast as he could along the street undeterred.

"Why do they always shout come back?" he asked Sykesy philosophically.

"They must think we're fuckin' soft!"

It was Sunday lunch time. The pub was crowded. It didn't seem to matter how depressed the area was, it was surprising how many people could scrape together enough money for a couple of pints at last orders on a Sunday afternoon. The football team was huddled together in a corner, the tables before them full of ale. The conversation was mainly about the game. Maca took a swig of his pint and declined a go of the raffle for a bottle of whisky. Maca's father walked in and took a sip of the pint of bitter that had been reserved for him on the table. The raucous din quietened as the lads listened to what he had to say.

"He's bringing the forms around to the house tomorrow night, for you to sign," he annnounced proudly.

There was a loud cheer around the pub. Dougie patted Maca on the back of the head and Maca ducked away blushing but trying to remain modest.

Smigger jumped up with a pint in his hand, swinging his arm and stamping his foot. He started the team off in their victory song. Everyone joined in and the pub seemed to bounce as the noise rebounded off the walls.

"Oh it's a grand old team we play for
It's a grand old team to know
And if you know their history
It's enough to make your heart go
Oh! Oh! Oh! Oh!
We don't care if we win lose or draw
What the hell do we care

Cos we only know that there's gonna be a show
And that St. Philomena's will be there."
The song ended. The lads burst in a loud cheer and boisterous laughter. Maca caught his old fella's eye. He saw the pride and delight on his father's face. Maca smiled and took a swig of his ale. It was a good thing for a son to know that his father was proud of him.

The four kids came speeding along the dual carriage way on the way home. They were faced with the dilemma of either keeping on going, where the police might be lying in wait for them or travelling through one of two estates roamed by rival gangs.

"What d'you reckon?" asked Sykesy.

"Fuck it," decided little Maca. "We'll swing right and cut up the Melling Road and then past the cemetery and the park."

A group of lads were playing football in the park as the four lads cut up the Melling Road which ran across the racecourse. One team launched an attack down the wing. Gatesy, the local yob, came running across the pitch dressed in his Airwair boots and Wrangler jacket. He hammered the ball high and mighty into the air over the fence. The ball bounced off the cemetery railings and back into the road. There were howls of laughter from his own team and shouts of derision from the opposition.

"Go away you fuckin' big yard dog," accused one lad.

"Who are you calling a yard dog?" retorted Gatesy, walking menacingly towards the lad.

"You," came the reply as the lad rose to the challenge. The rest of the lads stepped in and restrained the two youths. Gatesy struggled like a wild man growling threats and insults.

"Let him go," snarled the other youth unimpressed.

One of the younger lads was sent for the ball while the fuss was going on. He clambered over the fence and ran down the road after the ball. It was when he picked the ball up that he saw the four youths on racing bikes turn into the lane. He stared at them for a moment until he realised who it was. He picked up the ball and went scurrying over the fence calling to the rest of the gang.

"Here's four Sparrowhall kids on bikes."

The four youths came tearing down the road. They knew this was the stretch of road where they were most vulnerable, once past it they were safe.

The gang forgot its argument and ran for the fence trying to cut them off. Little Maca changed gear and the chain slipped. The other three kids hurtled past to safety as the leaders of the mob came over the fence. One lad caught the back of little Maca's seat. Gatesy grabbed the handle bars and stood blocking his path.

"Get off it," he ordered.

"I won't," said little Maca defiantly.

Gatesy tried to wrest his hands free but couldn't do it.

One kid punched little Maca in the face and pushed the bike over. Gatesy volleyed him in the nose as he fell. Little Maca's nose burst open pouring blood. His friends watched from a distance, unable to help. Gatesy leapt on the bike and cycled down the lane on it crowing like the lout he was. The rest of the gang started kicking little Maca. He struggled to his feet and ran away up the lane.

"You've had it, I'll get our kid on you," he called back down the lane, once he was safe.

"Get who you fuckin' like," yelled Gatesy, riding the bike in a circle and laughing like a yob.

Maca was asleep in bed when his little brother arrived home. Vicky answered the door.

"What happened to you?" she asked on seeing the bloody nose and tear stained face on her younger brother.

"Got jumped by the "George"," he said, giving the gang their name. "They robbed me bike off me."

"Never mind. Our Maca will get it back for you," she said.

She led him away upstairs to the bathroom to clean him up. She opened Maca's bedroom door. Maca was still asleep. She shoved him - still there was no reaction. She slapped him across the face.

"What the fuck " growled Maca jumping up.

"I thought you might like to see the state of your little brother before I clean him up," she said.

Macca jumped out of bed, oblivious to his nudity and the effect the afternoon's drink had had on his loins.

"What happened?" he asked earnestly.

"Put it away" said his elder sister sarcastically, referring to his piss proud.

"Shut up you". You'd think you'd never seen one before," said Maca, covering himself with the eiderdown. "What happened?" he asked.

"I got jumped by the George," said little Maca, wiping his nose on his sleeve. "And they robbed me bike."

"Who hit you?" asked Maca.

"One of them booted me in the nose to make me let go of the bike," whimpered little Maca. "Will you get it back for me?"

"Tell me when I've ever let anyone get away with hitting you?" asked Maca, annoyed at the question.

There was no reply.

"I'll get you the bike back tonight and put the shithouse in hospital. O.K.?"

"O.K." agreed little Maca.

"Come on," said Vicky, taking little Maca to the bathroom. "Aren't you glad that your Dad let Maca stay up to see all the John Wayne films when he was a lad?"

"Piss off'" called Maca from the bedroom.

Maca and Smigger's younger brother Joey sat on the alehouse steps among a gang of teenage lads. It was the local meeting place for the kids who had nowhere to go and nothing better to do. Joey took a last drag on his cigarette and flicked it away into the night sky. He blew the smoke out of his nose and watched the dog end tumble gracefully through the air like a small firework.

"Right, are we ready?" he said.

Maca nodded. The two lads got up and walked down the road into the top end of the estate followed by an ever growing number of youths arming themselves with sticks, stones, bottles and any other object that could be turned into a useful missile or weapon. By the time the small cortege of around a dozen lads had made their way through the estate to the school at the top of the lane leading to the desolate unlit no-man's land between the two gangs' territories, their number had swelled to forty six. Two lads stood necking with two schoolgirls by the school fence as the mob approached. It was Cummo and Stevie. The gang crossed to the island in the middle of the road. Stevie jumped over the school fence and handed Cummo the two crates of empty milk bottles they had hidden there. They kissed their girlfriends again and stepped into the mob.

"Chuck come back," called Joey in an American accent, much to the amusement of the company.

The gang made its way down the dark spooky unlit lane that wound its way past the old golf course, the playing fields and the rubbish dump, around past the cemetery and hospital annexe, past the plots and finally to the old hump-backed railway bridge that marked the beginning of enemy turf.

Old Jack doddered up to the bar in the pub.

"Pint of Guinness please love," he stammered counting the loose change in his hand. "And a packet of crisps for the dog." He opened the packet of crisps and put them on the floor for his little Jack Russell. He doddered back to his seat near the window and sat down. He took a sip from his drink and smiled. It was the only real pleasure left to the old pensioner now. His quiet pint on a Sunday night. He looked round at the dozen or so regulars in the bar and thought at eighty-six, how good it was to be alive.

The gang arrived at the humpbacked bridge. Joey and Maca crept up to it to check it was all clear. They signalled to the rest of the gang to follow. Crouching in the shadows they half ran half trotted through the dark side streets of the estate up to the pub where the rival gang hung round.

They stopped at the end of the street just before the dual carriage way that separated one side of the estate from the other. Maca peeped round the corner at the group of sixteen or so lads hanging round the pub. One lad was dressed in denims and Airwair boots sitting on a racing bike that leant against the pub wall.

"That's him," piped up little Maca.

Maca nodded. The problem was to get to him before he could get away on the bike.

Cummo and Stevie placed the crates of empty milk bottles on the floor. Those who didn't already have artillery snatched up the fresh ammunition. Maca took two bottles from the crates the same as Joey, Cummo and Stevie.

"Aim to both sides of them to try and stop them running," ordered Maca, "Then take no prisoners. Us four will be after the guy on the bike. The rest of you get stuck into the rest."

The lads nodded as Maca peeped round the corner waiting for a break in the traffic.

"As soon as you get the bike - fuck off on it. I'll meet you back home," he told little Maca.

Little Maca nodded.

The break in the traffic came. Maca led the charge across the street. They were spotted just as they got into throwing distance. The milk bottles shattered down on both sides of the gang as they looked for an escape in panic.

Old Jack showed a speed that belied his years as a milk bottle came sailing through the pub window. He hurled himself under the seat, clutching his dog to his chest and the pub was bombarded with debris and flying splintered glass.

Gatesy knew he wouldn't have sufficient time to get enough speed up on the bike to get away. He dropped it and ran. About four of the gang managed to run into the estate with Maca, Cummo, Joey and Stevie hard on Gatesy' heels. The rest of the gang ran into the pub doorway and just managed to get it shut under a barrage of stones, sticks and bottles. The gang laid seige to the pub and tried to force the door open. The pub regulars jumped up and helped the kids keep it shut. Little Maca picked up his bike in the confusion and made off on it. Gatesy ran round the corner and into his house. His four pursuers chased him into the parlour where they caught him. His father was at work, only his mother was home. The stricken youth had no chance as the four angry young men plunged into him with sticks, hands and feet. His mother jumped into the melee, trying to pull the lads off him, screaming at the top of her voice. Maca turned and butted her in the face, dropping her on the floor. He pinned her down on the floor while his three friends continued with the beating. Battered and unconscious Gatesy lay limply on the floor when the lads had finished with him. His mother was in hysterics.

"You bastards, you bastards," she cried in tears.

"The sun doesn't shine out of his arse darling. He started it," growled Maca, letting her go.

"Here's the bizzies," shouted a youth seeing the police car in the distance. The gang scattered and ran across the road down back entries and into the hospital annexe. Maca, Cummo, Joey and Stevie climbed the railing into the cemetery and from the darkness wondered how many of the lads would get caught. It was every man for himself.

It was seven o'clock on Monday evening. Maca sat at the table in the parlour. The football team scout slid a form across in front of him.

60

"Where do I sign?" asked Maca.

The scout pointed to the dotted line designated for his signature. Maca nodded and signed. His father also signed and the form was witnessed by the two men from the football club. The scout checked the form was valid. It was. He got up and shook Maca's hand.

"Good luck son," he said.

The company exchanged handshakes and good wishes and then the two men left.

Maca looked at his admiring little brother. "So now I'm a footballer!" he shrugged.

"I know," said little Maca," I bet we make a few bob fiddle on them F.A. Cup tickets!"

Mrs Smith turned the cooker off and moved the empty chip-pan onto a cold ring. She picked up the plate of sausages, egg and chips and carried her meal into the kitchen. As usual she was the last one to have her tea, having already cooked meals for her three sons. It was Monday tea-time. Billy, the eldest lad, sat in the armchair near the fire reading the Echo. Smigger, the middle son, was curled up on the other armchair watching the local news. Joey, the youngest lad, was just finishing his tea.

"That was lovely that, Mum," he chirped, picking up his empty plate and carrying it into the kitchen.

Mrs Smith sat down to enjoy her meal. Joey walked into the lobby and picked his coat off the bannister.

"I'm going out Mum," he called as he slung his jacket on.

"Where are you going?" she called.

"Just out," came the reply.

"Where are you going?" his mother asked again.

"Out," scowled young Joey slamming the door behind him.

It was six thirty in the evening and it was already dark. Joey's mates would all be playing football under the lamp at the top end of the estate. He had a short five minute walk up the lane past the school and down the avenue to the top end of the estate, where his friends were playing football. As Joey reached the top end of the school and turned into the avenue he heard a noise behind him. He looked round and saw a huge mob of teenagers coming down the lane next to the school, four of whom were trying to sneak up behind him.

It was the "George". They had joined forces with another gang and had come to settle the previous night's score. Joey ran for his life as bricks and stones landed all around him. One hit him on the back but Joey kept running. A padlock and chain flew past his head. One of his pursuers threw a stick at his feet to try and bring him down. The stick hit him across the back of the legs but Joey kept running.

"Look out, it's the George," he yelled to his mates at the bottom end of the street. The football match stopped. The kids began ripping up garden fences to use as weapons, some ran up garden paths and stole the empty milk bottles. Maca picked a stick up from the gutter and stood his ground. He was almost immediately joined by Cummo and Stevie who had just armed themselves with part of Mrs Shaw's garden fence. Mrs Shaw came to the door shouting abuse but was silenced when she saw the approaching horde of thugs.

"Oh my God." she cried.

She dashed back into the house and dialled nine nine nine .

"Hello," she said, "get me the police."

Although outnumbered, the kids from the estate stood their ground in a line across the street led by Maca, Joey, Cummo and Stevie. Everyone was nervous but no-one wanted to be tarred with the name of being the first one to run. Little Maca arrived back from his package tour of the gardens with a dozen or so milk bottles. He placed them on the floor and stood his ground next to his big brother, undaunted by the huge mob and bathed in the unshakeable belief that his big brother was unbeatable.

The estate had been built thirty years previously and had always had a gang, father and son in their turn had been gang members. In those thirty years even in the face of formidable enemies the kids were proud of the fact that their ground had never been taken. Their attackers grouped up in the middle of the street and advanced slowly on the gang. They finally broke into a charge under the cover of a huge bombardment of bricks, bottles, stones and other assorted missiles. The air was agog with debris. However most of it fell short. The kids dodged the bouncing debris and flailing masonry. The gang stood its ground. The charge began to falter. A lot of the attackers were unarmed now. They stopped. Maca led the charge firing two milk bottles into the crowd and chasing them in with his stick. The gang turned and fled. The slow runners at the back kicked and punched at each other, trying to trip one another up in the hope that their pursuers would stop and attack the fallen quarry, thus giving the others time to escape. One lad was tripped by his friend in the frenzied scramble. The kids piled into him like bees around a honey-pot. Joey smashed a bottle and gouged it into his stomach. Another stabbed him in the back.

The stricken youth shouted "Is this the way to Croxteth?" like a drowning man clutching for a straw, trying to make out he was only passing through, as the boots, fists, sticks and kicks rained in on him.

A little further up the street, Maca caught the traitor who had tripped his friend - his treachery had done him no good. Maca whacked him repeatedly across his head with a stick. The lad crumpled under the onslaught. Little Maca arrived just in time to volley the youth in the face as he fell, breaking a bottle over his head in the same movement. Another group of youths gathered round and began kicking him across the street. The youth bravely tried to struggle to his feet and run under the onslaught but was beaten down every time.

Mrs Turner came dashing out of her house and up the street, her extremely large bosom swinging wildly as she ran to the rescue.

"Look out, it's Mrs Turner," called one youth. The lads scattered and tried to run but they were too late. She lambasted four of them, including Maca, across the street. The two youths were saved.

"Go 'way you little bastards," she shrieked in temper.

"They would have done it to us," moaned Maca indignantly, clutching his swelling ear.

"Go on, sod off," said Mrs Turner, having none of it. "You wait till I see your mother."

"Here's the bizzies:!" shouted a voice warning the others that the police were coming. The unmistakeable sound of a police car engine being screwed could be heard from the other end of the estate. The lads quickly dispersed.

It was just after eleven o'clock. The police had been, done their business and gone again. The gang had drifted back to the grass verge behind the traffic barrier. Skint and bored with nothing to do and nowhere to go, they waited for the highlight of the evening - the robbed car - to come round. Stevie puffed at a battered old cigarette.

"I'm next on it," claimed Joey, waiting for a turn at the cigarette.

"No you're not," argued Cummo. "I'm after him and Maca's after me."

Joey scowled and reluctantly accepted the fact that he'd have to settle for the last drag on the battered old dog end.

Dougie came walking past with his girlfriend, Vicky, Maca's elder sister.

"Alright Dougie lad. Have you got any smokes on you?" chirped Joey jumping to his feet, seeing his chance.

Dougie was half cut. He took his arm from around Vicky's shoulder, fumbled in his pocket for his cigarettes. Vicky smiled and hung on to her drunk around the waist.

Dougie lit a cigarette.

"When's Jerry out?" asked Cummo.

"Tomorrow," replied Dougie out of the corner of his mouth. He placed a cigarette behind his ear. "That's for in the morning," he said, knowing how desperate he was for a cigarette every time he woke up.

He tossed the packet to Joey. Joey accepted it gleefully and tossed the other three lads a ciggie each.

"One left," he said quietly to the rest of the gang, looking deep into the cigarette packet. He closed the lid and tossed the cigarette packet into the air for the kids to fight over. Six of them jumped for it and fell to the floor in a heap. Joey watched the scuffle in silence.

"Where's your kid tonight?" asked Dougie.

"Who - Smigger?"

Dougie nodded.

"He's out with Julie Hopkins."

Dougie winced. "She's a fuckin' monster. She'd frighten the life out of you," said Dougie exasperated.

"You know what our Smigger's like, doesn't care who he gets it off with as long as he gets it."

A youth emerged from the scramble with the bent cigarette in the corner of his mouth and a happy smile on his face.

"Give Smigger his due," Dougie told Vicky on the way up the street, "he's got some bottle."

His girlfriend laughed and they disappeared round the corner out of sight.

The lads pulled happily at the cigarettes while the other lads argued whose turn it was next on them. Suddenly life seemed a lot better.

There was a loud squeal of brakes. A red car swerved to avoid the brown Mark IV Cortina that sped through the lights, its occupants hooded with balaclavas. The traffic with the right of way stopped or accelerated out of the way.

"Little bastards," cursed the driver of the red car, as the Cortina sped round in a circle with smoke roaring from its exhaust. The car shot back the way it had come and swung to a halt at the grass verge in front of the gang.

The gang gathered to inspect the car. The lads removed their hoods. It was Ritchie and little George, two lads from a rival area.

"Where's all your car robbers?" taunted Ritchie, revving the engine.

"It's a shed," said Stevie. "When we rob a car, we rob a car."

"What d'you know about cars, soft arse. You couldn't handle a lawn mower," scowled little George.

"Good job I haven't got one. It would go quicker than this," replied Stevie. "Watch no pandas chase you or you'll have to hit the back gardens. You'll never get away in this."

"Fuck off!" replied Ritchie and sped away, smoke pouring from the exhaust. The car shot across the junction and down the East Lancs Road out of sight. A minute later it reappeared speeding back up the other side of the road. Ritchie took the sharp bend too fast and lost it. The car smashed into a street lamp across the street from the gang. Little George saw the windscreen hurtling towards him and tried to shoo it away. Thankfully it didn't break. George's nose bled profusely. He tried to get out of the door but it wouldn't open. He started climbing out of the door window.

The engine was still running, although the front end was off the floor and wrapped round the lamp. The wheels screeched as Ritchie managed to reverse back into the road. He gave George time to scramble clear and then shot away up the street. He turned off and parked the car. He calmly got out and walked away as though nothing had happened.

Little George ran across to the gang. Stevie gave him his coat so the police wouldn't recognise him. The rivalry shown earlier was forgotten as the lads joined forces against their most hated enemy - the police. The lads walked half way into enemy territory to see little George got home alright before they themselves eventually dispersed to their beds.

It was tea time the next day. Mrs Smith had finished her meal and was just lighting a cigarette. She shook the match and dropped it into the ashtray before her. She took a long pull on the cigarette and exhaled the smoke. She sat at the table laden with empty plates and cups and saucers, watching the local news on the television. It was just the couple of minutes relaxation she afforded herself every night after tea before she did the dishes. Her three sons lazed in front of her watching the television. Joey got up off the couch.

"I'm going out Mum," he said.

"Where are you going?" she asked.

"Out," he replied indignantly.

"I said where are you going?" insisted his mother.

"Just out," replied Joey.

"So you're not going anywhere in particular?"

"No," replied Joey.

"I hope you weren't involved in that trouble last night," she nagged.

"I was at me bird's," lied Joey, as though butter wouldn't melt in his mouth.

"Well you stay away from that Maca. He was one of the ones fighting last night."

"I'm only going for a game of football under the lamp," replied Joey.

"Well that's alright then. Why didn't you say that in the first place?"

Joey didn't answer. He walked out into the lobby and slung his coat on. He opened the door.

"If you want me I'll be at the bingo down the pensioners' club," called his mother.

"O.K." he said and shut the door behind him.

Maca, Cummo and Stevie were waiting for him under the lamp.

"What kept you?" called Stevie as the lads set off up the street."

"Me Ma," replied Joey. "I've got to go through a steward's enquiry everytime I go out."

Little Maca watched his brother walk away up the street. The rest of the kids were playing football under the lamp.

"Where's your kid going?" asked Sykesy.

"Childwall for a car," replied little Maca.

The 61 bus arrived at the bus stop. The four lads climbed on the near empty bus. Cummo paid the fares while the rest of the lads trooped upstairs.

"How much have we got left?" asked Stevie.

"Just enough for smokes. No bus fare home," replied Cummo.

"So it's either a car or a six mile hike in this shit weather," laughed Maca, knowing that they never took enough money to return home when they went car robbing. It gave them them added incentive to get one.

Joey took a bunch of car keys from his jacket pocket and looked at them.

"Don't worry," he said, "it will be a car".

Childwall was a very respectable area, populated by a mixture of middle class, rich and well off people. It often provided rich pickings for the likes of the four gang rogues alighting from the 61 bus at Childwall roundabout. The lads walked into the dark estate away from the bright lights and the prying eyes from the main road. They spotted a claret coloured Capri parked outside a house. The four lads walked past it in silence.

"Is it bugged?" asked Cummo?

"Dunno," replied Maca. "I can't see."

The lads stopped about forty yards up the street. Joey fumbled through his bunch of keys until he found a suitable one.

"You's wait here," he said to Cummo and Stevie.

He nodded to Maca and the two lads approached the car. Cummo and Stevie looked furtively about for any sign of danger. There was none.

Joey crept up to the car door. Maca looked at the house. The light was on but the curtains were drawn. Joey worked the key into the lock. A deafening siren blared out obscenely into the cold night. The alarm had gone off. Joey and Maca ran like hell. The hall light went on. A man with a large beer gut, dressed in trousers vest and slippers came running out. He saw the two youths disappear round the corner.

"Come back you little bastards. I'll tan the arse off you," he shouted, chasing them down the street. Cummo and Stevie walked the other way up the street as lights came on and doors opened, neighbours wanting to know what the commotion was. The man reached the corner knackered and out of breath. There was no-one in sight.

"Little bastards," he muttered and leant against the garden wall, gasping for breath. The two youths sat in the bushes behind the privet hedge, no more than a yard or two from the fat man.

Joey held his nose and covered his eyes, trying to stop himself from laughing, the tears beginning to stream down his face. He looked at the ground so he couldn't see the comical sight in front of him. Maca stuffed a handkerchief into his mouth, his body shaking, bursting to laugh out loud.

The fat man coughed and wheezed. The two lads saw each other. It was the final straw. They both roared with laughter. They jumped up in front of the startled man and ran for the back gardens rolling with laughter.

The man ran up the garden path as the lads cleared the garden wall. He stood panting, out of breath. He knew he couldn't catch them. The house owner came out.

"What's going on?" he asked.

"Two little bastards trying to rob me car," spluttered the fat man. "No chance of catching them now."

The house owner looked into the night air. The noise of bodies blundering through bushes and privet stopped and the laughter faded away in the distance.

Cummo and Stevie stood patiently in the bus shelter waiting for Maca and Joey.

"I wonder if they got away," worried Cummo.

66

"Here they are now," said Stevie, spotting the two lads walking up the street towards them.

"What happened to you's?" asked Joey as he breezed into the bus shelter.

"Nothing," said Cummo. "We just walked away, didn't get a tug or nothing."

"What now?" asked Stevie.

"We'll hang around for a few minutes then we'll go back," said Maca.

Stevie spotted a brand new white Rover parked in the driveway of one of the houses behind the bus shelter.

"What do you reckon?" he said, drawing the lads' attention by nodding towards it.

"Bit near the main road isn't it?" said Cummo.

"Is it fuck," said Joey defiantly pulling his car keys from his pocket with a confident smile.

Maca and Joey slipped over the fence into the front garden. Joey scampered towards the car door while Maca crept up to the front window of the house and peered in.

A man sat in an armchair in front of the fire watching television. His young son lay at his feet in front of the fire, with his head resting on a cushion like his father. He was deeply engrossed in the television. Maca ducked as the lady of the house walked in carrying a tray with three mugs of tea and a plate full of thickly buttered toast. He peeped in again. The woman held the tray as her husband picked off it a cup of tea in one hand and a thick piece of buttered toast in the other. Joey stared fixedly at Maca and waited for the go ahead. The man had a sip of tea and then placed the mug on the floor by his feet as his wife placed a mug of tea and the plate of toast on the floor next to her son but within easy reach of her husband.

She walked out of the lounge and into the kitchen. Maca gave Joey the nod. He jiggled the key into the lock and the car door clicked open. he sat half in and half out of the car trying to get one of his keys into the ignition. The woman took three slices of toast from the grill and turned it off. She began buttering the toast. Joey signalled to the rest of the lads. Maca climbed into the seat next to him. Stevie and Cummo opened the gates and climbed into the back of the car. The woman stopped as she came into the living room with the toast.

"Wasn't that the gate squeaking?" she said to her husband.

"Probably the wind. You must have left it open when you came in," he replied not wanting to be disturbed.

Suddenly the engine started. The man jumped up and knocked his hot tea over his son as he ran to the door.

Joey had reversed the car onto the road and was waiting for the man to arrive at the door so they could wave to him before they drove off. The door flew open. The man stopped for a moment, horrified at the two youths wearing balaclavas sitting in his car. He dashed down the path towards them.

"Ta ta fat shites," called Joey out the window. "You don't deserve a good car if you don't look after it properly."

The car drove slowly away. The lads roared with laughter as Joey drove slowly on purpose so the irate car owner would chase them. Just as the unfortunate man drew close, Joey accelerated away much to the approval of the rest of the gang. Maca slipped a tape into the cassette deck - loud music blared out the speakers. The car owner watched as the car shot round the roundabout and back down the other side of the dual carriage way.

"Bastards," he muttered. "Call the police," he yelled to his wife.

Joey screwed the car down Queen's Drive towards home where the rest of the gang would be waiting for them.

The gang sat on the grass verge watching the officer on the beat move the kids playing football under the lamp on.

"What's up with that cunt? Didn't he ever play football when he was a kid?" scowled one youth.

"Yeah, the kids aren't doing any harm," agreed another of the lads.

"It's probably the old cunt on the corner complaining. He must be on earlies this week. Mind you - you can't blame him. It's a bit late for playing football now."

"Look out'" called one of the gang. There was a loud squeal of burning rubber as a white Rover hurtled towards them across the pavement and onto the grass verge. The gang scattered in panic. The car stopped.

"Hello lads," chirped Maca in a posh accent. "Did we give you a bit of a fright, what?"

The officer over on the estate was on his radio immediately. He watched the gang gather round the stolen car.

"This is PC 249 reporting a stolen white Rover parked on the grass verge at the junction of the East Lancs Road and Townsend Avenue. Request a Tango Charlie pursuit vehicle to intercept."

"Where did you get it from" asked one of the lads.

"Childwall," replied Cummo.

"It's a fuckin' cracker," said one of the lads, listening to the loud music.

"It's brand new," said Maca. "It's only got sixty miles on the clock!"

Joey sat in silence watching the policeman on the beat. He turned the music off and called to him mockingly "Yoohoo' Officer'"

The policeman stood there helpless, but with the knowledge that help was on the way. The Tango Charlie unit with its blue light flashing was tearing up the road about two miles away.

''Yoohoo! Officer," called Joey. "Come and get me."

The policeman did nothing at the jibe.

The gang guffawed with laughter at the policeman's indignity. It wasn't often they had the chance to put one over on their most hated enemy.

"Come and get me tithead," mocked Joey, waving to the officer out of the car window.

The pursuit unit sped through the junction and swung left at the lights. The lads watched the car come hurtling down the other side of the dual carriage way and do a 'U' turn at the junction, its blue light flashing.

Joey threw the car into gear and wheelied away into the road. The gang roared their approval as their new champion stepped into the gladiators' arena to do battle.

"Show him your fuckin' arse," called one youth.

"Go on, Joey lad," called another as the car shot away with the police car in pursuit. Little Maca stood with his ball under his arm. The look of pride had changed to one of worry as the two cars shot away out of sight.

The Rover flew up the road in fourth gear towards the red traffic lights. The music banging loudly in Joey's head and the blue flashing light in the rear view mirror. Joey decided against taking the chance of finding a break in the flow of traffic and threw the car down a gear. The car veered left and shot through the red lights and tried to slip into the flow of traffic rather than go through it. He blasted hard on the horn to make the driver of a Capri slow down so he could get out unscathed. He braked and changed gear. The car lurched and swung left into a winding side street with the police car struggling to keep in touch.

"You're starting to lose him, Joey," laughed Cummo in the back.

Stevie looked behind at the trailing police car but said nothing. It wasn't over yet.

Joey turned left at the first cross road, travelling too fast. The back end scrambled away from him and hit the kerb. Joey put his foot down trying not to lose any momentum as he tried to haul the car level. He shot past a parked transit van but over corrected his earlier mistake. He clipped the parked van and lost control. The Rover veered into a tree with a sickening crunch. The left wing crumpled. The lads bounced back in their seats after the initial impact.

"Twat," groaned Cummo clutching his knee. Maca and Joey snatched their seat belts off and scrambled out of the car. Stevie was already out.

"Get out," he screamed at Cummo as the police car turned the corner. Cummo was still clutching his injured knee. He jumped out of the car. He half limped and hopped into the back gardens. Stevie hurled a housebrick through the police car windscreen trying to draw the policemen off in the opposite direction from Cummo. The police car skidded to a halt and bumped gently into the transit van. The first policeman leapt out after Stevie who was already clearing the back garden fence. An old dog barked and leapt at him. Stevie booted it and kept running. The dog yowled in pain and only made a token bark of disapproval as the policeman landed in the back yard. The policeman stopped and then chased the noise in front of him, too dark and too far behind to see his quarry. He blundered through the darkness of the adjoining garden until he came out on the main road. Stevie watched him from a front garden on the other side.

The officer watched the traffic go past. There was no sign of anyone. The lad could be anywhere by now. He returned back to the car through the back gardens.

He was greeted by the other officers returning out of breath and empty-handed.

"Two of them are away but there is another one who has hurt his leg. He's probably hiding nearby until it all blows over," said the officer.

Jerry stood at the front gate and listened. He had only got out that day. He walked back up the path past Teresa, his girlfriend, into the house.

"What are you doing?" she asked..

"Giving the kid a chance," replied Jerry.

Outside more police officers arrived and began searching the back garden. Jerry opened the back kitchen door with the light on. He whistled twice and stood in the doorway so he could be seen. He turned the light off and shut the door.

Cummo was sitting in the corner of the garden behind a tree and some hedging. He rocked gently back and forward, sucking the blood from his cut knee. He saw Jerry and understood but did nothing. He heard the two policemen come in to the back garden. From the light of the house he watched the two officers in silence still sucking his knee.

"I'll take this one, you take the other," said one policeman.

One officer went next door. The other began sweeping the back garden with his torch. Slowly and carefully he checked every nook and cranny systematically, determined not to miss anything. Cummo winced and shut his eyes as the beam eventually reached and fell right on him and then passed. Amazingly the officer had not seen him. The officer retreated from the garden to search elsewhere. Cummo scurried silently to the back door and slipped in. Jerry smiled in triumph at Teresa.

"Alright Cummo lad. How's it going?" asked Jerry.

"Sound. I'll need about five stitches in me knee, though," replied Cummo.

"When did you get out?"

Today," replied Teresa. "Take him in the front room while I clean that cut up," she said, running some hot water into a bowl.

"Great stuff," said Cummo. "I thought I was collared there."

"Well you weren't, were you. We'll take you to the hozzie after, and get you stitched up," said Jerry. "Will you make us a cup of tea please, Teresa?" he continued.

Teresa carried the bowl of hot water into the kitchen and examined Cummo's cut knee. She dabbed it clean with a warm flannel. Cummo winced in pain.

"You'll never learn, will you?" she said.

70

Outside the police locked the stolen car and drove away - their search had proved fruitless and was abandoned.

The following day Vicky and Teresa took the day off work to take Jerry and Dougie out for the day as a special treat for Jerry. They were going to the bowling alley across the water in New Brighton. Just as they were leaving Jerry's house, the car-owner and her husband arrived to pick up the stolen car. She burst into tears when she saw the damage. Her husband consoled her, resting her head on his shoulder.

"Poor cow," said Dougie in shame. "There's only sixty miles on the clock. The engine is probably fucked because it's been screwed before it's been run in."

"She probably hasn't even started the HP payments yet," sympathised Vicky.

"Yeah," agreed Teresa quietly.

"A tart shouldn't have a car like that anyway," said Jerry unsympathetically.

"Why shouldn't they?" growled Vicky in contempt.

"They can't even drive," said Jerry.

"They don't go smashing into trees though, do they?" interrupted Teresa, ganging up on him.

"Yeah - putting your mate's head through the windscreen," bitched Vicky.

"You've got a lot to say considering," snarled Jerry.

"Considering what?" asked Vicky.

"Put it this way. Where was your little brother last night?"

"Don't know," shrugged Vicky.

Jerry looked up the street at the stolen car and the weeping woman being led away by her husband.

The two girls followed his gaze. Vicky turned and looked at Jerry in surprise. For once in her life she was stuck for words.

"Exactly," said Jerry, confirming her worst fears. "So keep your trap shut you big mouth cow."

"That's not a very nice way to speak," said Teresa.

"She asked for it," replied Jerry. "It wasn't my fault I crashed into the tree. It was that old bastard who pulled out in front of me."

"Let's give the arguments a miss and just enjoy the day out," said Dougie.

The two couples walked quietly down the street to the bus stop.

Smigger was hard at work. He worked on shifts, on low pay with no prospects, loading and unloading wagons at one of the local factories. Smigger's workmate, another young lad, tossed him the boxes from the loading bay and Smigger stacked them in the back of the wagon muttering angrily to himself, dripping in sweat.

"What's the matter Smigger?" his friend asked.

"That job I was after in the computer room fell through," replied Smigger.

"How come? There was only you and Jimmy Caine after it, and he's only a "divvy". Anyway, you've been here longer than him."

"I know," snarled Smigger, plonking himself down on one of the boxes.

"Did you fuck the interview up?" queried the lad.

"No. I thought the interview went well," said Smigger. "I'm gutted. Pig sick. That was me chance to get out of throwing boxes on a wagon for the rest of me life. There's good prospects in that computer room if you work hard."

"Well how did Cainey get the job?" asked his mate.

"The bosses have got their own canteen upstairs, and Cainey's ma does the waitressing," answered Smigger.

"Oh"' realised the lad. "I'll give you extra pieces of toast if you give our Jimmy the job?" he said in a funny voice.

"Something like that," replied Smigger.

"Don't you know this wagon has got to be in Manchester this afternoon. Smigger, get up off your lazy arse and get some work done."

Smigger sat on the boxes drenched in sweat and glared at the slightly built mustachioed man in his early thirties. That was the final straw.

"Who are you talking to? You fuckin' maggot. I've been running this bay for the past three years for buttons. If it wasn't for me the wagons would never get out on time, but you never get off me back, you crying little bastard."

Smigger tore his boiler suit off and hurled the overalls at him.

"I had enough. Stick the job up your arse."

Smigger stormed off the wagon and onto the loading bay.

"Don't go, I need you," pleaded the manager, grabbing Smigger's arm.

Smigger's head simultaneously lashed out at lightning speed and landed with an awful bump on the bridge of the manager's nose.

Smigger stood over the bloodied and dazed man.

"You need me?" he growled. "Yeah, we all need somewhere to stick our dick. Well I'm sick of being shagged," he roared his training shoe crashed into the man's face.

Smigger stepped over him and disappeared into the factory.

The next morning Smigger sat in Jerry's front room relating the story to Dougie and Jerry.

"So what are you gonna do? You won't get any dole for six weeks," said Dougie.

"I know. Me Ma went mad. She called me all the soft bastards under the sun. ' What are you going to live on - fresh air?' she said," moaned Smigger.

"Well what are you going to do? Eat shit on the dole all your life?" asked Jerry.

Smigger shook his head.

"Why don't all them old bastards drop dead. They've had their lives. Why won't they let us live ours?"

"It's no good sitting round with your head up arse wingeing like a fanny. If you want something out of life you've got to go out and take it. It's the survival of the fittest," said Dougie. "The cavemen had the right idea. They took the best things in life and let the others live on the scraps. Could you imagine them letting some decrepit old civil servant getting ready to snuff it palm them off with a poxy giro every week? Being on the bones of their arses while the old bastards are out playing golf and swigging gin and tonics in the golf club bar?"

"No," laughed Smigger. "What have you got in mind?"

"Me, you and Jerry against the world," said Dougie.

"We know all the good robbers," said Smigger, shaking his head. "They're all only waiting to do bird. They get a few grand now and again and blow it. Sooner or later they go to the well one time too many and get nicked."

"Not us though," said Jerry. "We'll use the money from the first touch to buy a decent car to go on the mooch in. We'll put a share away from each touch and save up for the tenancy in an alehouse, maybe a nightclub or two. Then we can get some other soft cunt to run them for us while we sit back getting fat."

"Have you got a touch in mind?" asked Smigger.

"Yeah. A sneak on a pub in Walton," said Jerry. "the manager sells his own ale and keeps his fiddle in a shoebox on top of the wardrobe."

"How do you know?" asked Smigger.

Jerry tapped the side of his nose.

Smigger laughed.

"Should be enough for a decent car and some ale money for the boys left over," laughed Dougie. "Are you in?"

"Bollock deep," replied Smigger.

Chapter Four:

Mrs Smith twisted the mop in her hands, draining the excess water back into the bucket. She slapped the mop onto the corridor floor and carried on mopping like the expert she was. She worked part time as a cleaner in the local school. It was almost half past five. She was nearly finished. The only people left in the school were the handful of teachers who supervised the extra curricular activities, such as five-a-side in the gym, chess, table-tennis and drawing for the younger kids. Mrs Smith picked up her bucket and hurried down the corridor, the mop leaning against her shoulder. She placed her tools in the cupboard and put her overcoat on over her overalls. If she hurried she'd just have time to get some pork chops from the shop for the lads' tea.

"Hello Mrs Smith," greeted the P.E. teacher dressed in a tracksuit. He'd just finished supervising the five-a-side in the gym. "How's your Joey doing? Has he got a job yet?" he asked.

"Oh hello Mr Blake," said Mrs Smith, turning to see who was addressing her. "Yes, he's got a job on the Youth Opportunities as a trainee car mechanic in that college up Muirhead Avenue. He likes it. He's mad about cars. But he finds some of the instructors very snotty and difficult to get on with."

"Well," said Mr Blake, "It's difficult to maintain discipline, especially with kids that age. Some of them resent having to settle for a job on a scheme. They can't be bothered working because they don't see them as proper jobs. They distract the kids who do want to get on and lead them astray. They suspend the trouble makers for three days without pay and dock late comers half a day's pay...so I'm told," said Mr Blake.

"Well our Joey's got no excuse for being late. I get him up in time for work every morning," said Mrs Smith, strolling along the corridor.

"It's a shame really. There's nothing for the kids. A lot of people on these schemes are right cowboys any way. Most of them have been on the dole or made redundant and managed to bluff their way in. You can't blame them really. They've probably all got families and mouths to feed."

"Yes," said Mrs Smith listening.

"So most of the kids are just wasting their time. We need to attract new industry. This city has been going down the nick ever since we joined the Common Market."

"Yes, but we've paid too much in to pull out now," argued Mrs Smith.

"True. But we've got to do something soon. We're breeding a generation of no-hopers. Some of them won't accept that. They'll go robbing - getting into trouble with the police. There'll be riots before long."

"None of my kids have ever been in trouble with the police. I'll tan their bleedin' arses," said Mrs Smith.

Mr Blake laughed. He taught all her sons at one time or other.

"How's Smigger?" he asked.

74

"Oh, He's just packed his job in," said Mrs Smith in a worried voice. "He said they were exploiting him. I believe he punched one of the managers on the way out."

"Who? Smigger did?" said Mr Blake. "The fella must have done something to deserve it. Your Smigger's very easy going, very difficult to upset."

"I know," said Mrs Smith, lying but considering the new light thrown on the subject.

"There's a lot of disillusioned young people about. Somebody better do something about it soon before someone lights the bonfire. Goodnight Mrs Smith."

"Goodnight Mr Blake," said Mrs Smith, reaching the door. She rushed off through the yard and up the road towards the shops.

Billy Smith turned the corner into the road and walked up towards the house. He'd just finished work in the local biscuit factory. He opened the door and hung his coat up in the hall. He trudged up the stairs to get changed.

Young Joey was in the bathroom trying to scrub the oil off the cuff of Smigger's best sweat shirt.

"Come off you bastard," he muttered as he scrubbed desperately at it.

"What's the matter Joe?" asked his eldest brother on hearing the remark as he walked past. Joey turned to look at him for a split second. He'd thought it was Smigger.

"I've had our Smigger's best shirt on for work and I got oil on the cuff and it won't come off."

Billy started laughing. "He'll kill you," he said. "What did you wear it for in the first place?"

"You've got to look smart. There's loads of tasty women at that college," replied Joey.

The door opened downstairs.

"Anyone in?" called Smigger.

"Yes," called Billy.

Joey flapped and dashed past him into the bedroom and hid the sweatshirt under a pile of clothes in Smigger's drawer. Smigger walked into the parlour and put the telly on. Joey walked past Billy on the landing.

"Don't leave me on me own with him," he whispered.

Joey breezed into the parlour. "Alright Smig?" he said.

"Alright Joe," replied Smigger. "Good day at work?"

"Sound," said Joey, settling down to watch telly.

The front door opened. It was Mrs Smith.

"Is everyone in?" she called.

"Yes," came the reply.

"Right, your tea will be ready in half an hour," she said, taking her coat off.

She carried her shopping into the kitchen and put the kettle on and began peeling spuds.

75

Smigger tossed the evening paper to Billy. "Right. I better get ready. I've got to be out early tonight," he said.

Smigger placed a pair of leather gloves and a balaclava helmet respectively into the deep pockets of his bomber jacket. He got a swill in the bathroom and dried his face.

Mrs Smith peeled the spuds and dropped them into the pan of cold water to clean.

"Mum, have you seen my light blue sweatshirt?" called Smigger.

"It's in your drawer. I washed it yesterday," came the reply. Billy and Joey looked at each other. Smigger found it in the corner of the drawer under a pile of clothes. He spotted the dark patch of oil on the sleeve and instinctively sniffed the armpit.

"Bastard'" he cursed. He knew Joey had been wearing it.

He stormed down the stairs, dropping his coat over the bannister and marched into the parlour to confront Joey with the evidence.

"You been wearing my clothes? You little bastard," growled Smigger, holding the sweat shirt aloft.

"Yes," admitted Joey, cowering on the end of the couch.

Smigger kicked and punched him before Billy could drag him off. The punch cut Joey's lip and put one of his teeth out.

"You little twat. Two days' pay that cost me, pulling me bollocks off in that shit-hole," roared Smigger.

"Don't you use language like that in this house," shouted Mrs Smith, entering the commotion and slapping Smigger twice across the side of the head.

"What's going on here?" she said, then slipped her sandal off and set about Smigger with it as she saw Joey's cut mouth. She forced him back into an armchair and vigorously whacked him all over the body with the sandal as Smigger vainly tried to fend the painful blows off - eventually he lost his temper with her. He flung her back onto the couch.

"This is a bleeding mad house," he roared, "and you're a nutter," he said to his mother. "No wonder me dad fucked off on you."

Mrs Smith's sandal crashed into the door as Smigger slammed it behind him. Billy, his anger roused by the last remark, tried to run after him but was stopped by Mrs Smith.

"Leave him alone," said Mrs Smith. "He's having a difficult time over work. And you stop wearing his clothes," she shouted at Joey.

Joey rubbed his face. "Don't worry. I'll get the bastard when he's asleep," he said ruefully.

That night, Smigger sat alone in a stolen car with his balaclava on, watching the pellets of rain splash open on the windscreen. Down the entry, two shadowy figures tossed a blanket over the broken glass cemented into the top of the pub yard wall. Jerry gave Dougie a bunk up and was then in turn helped over the wall by Dougie. They landed silently and simultaneously in the back-yard. Dougie crept up to the pub and shinned up the drainpipe towards the lit bedroom window. Jerry pulled a made-to-measure, sawn-off pick axe handle out of the front of his bomber jacket and stood guard in the shadows, ignoring the rain.

The pub manager's wife sat at her dressing table putting her make-up on. She was in her early forties and dressed in a black underskirt. She continued putting on her mascara, oblivious to the masked man at her window. From his vantage point Dougie could see the shoebox on top of the wardrobe.

Some time passed. The rain poured down. Jerry concentrated on the bedroom window. Dougie watched the woman put on her dress. She stepped into her shoes and put her coat on. One last check of her hair and she was ready to go out. She picked up her handbag from the dressing table, turned the light off and walked out.

Dougie stepped onto the window sill and tried to open the window. It wouldn't budge. He couldn't risk smashing the window with his hand because of the lack of room and for fear of overbalancing. He motioned to Jerry in the yard below. Jerry tossed him the pick axe handle. Dougie caught it and in the same movement smashed the window by the catch and dropped the club to Jerry below. Dougie reached in, opened the window and climbed in. He snatched the shoebox off the wardrobe, pausing only to check the money was inside. It was. He climbed straight back out of the window. The pub manager was at the bottom of the stairs and his wife coming down them when they heard the window smash. They looked at each other for a split second, realising they were being robbed The manager charged past his wife up the stairs and crashed into the bedroom. He saw the shoebox was missing and ran to the broken window.

"Come back you pair of bastards," he roared as the two lads disappeared over the wall, followed by the blanket. Jerry and Dougie ran down the entry and jumped into the car. Smigger pulled away.

"D'you get it?" he asked excitedly.

"Yeah. No problem," laughed Dougie, triumphantly opening the box and showing off the wad of money.

The three lads knelt on the floor of Jerry's parlour counting the money. Dougie counted the money into wads of one hundred pounds. Jerry checked each bundle, while Smigger wrapped an elastic band around each wad and placed the money into a small waste paper bin. Dougie counted the last wad. It came to sixty-five pounds.

"How much altogether?" he asked Smigger.

"Eighteen hundred and sixty-five pounds," announced Smigger, tipping the bundles of money onto the floor.

"Let's go and get pissed on the odd sixty-five quid."

The local pub was fairly busy that night because the manager had hired a group for the evening. Jerry walked up the steps to the pub, followed by Smigger and Dougie. The local tramp nicknamed "the Wooden Indian" stood forlornly in the doorway, out of the elements and trying to bum enough money for a pint.

"Have you got two bob on yer?" he said to Jerry in a gruff voice, trying to intimidate the young man into giving him money by his rough manner and haggard appearance.

Jerry stopped and stared at him, waiting for the snarl. The Wooden Indian quickly realised that he'd used wrong way of extricating money from the young man and his hard stare changed to the sorrowful eyes of a dog that hadn't eaten for two days. Jerry walked past the frightened man but said nothing. Dougie stuffed a pound note into his hand on the way in.

"You're mad," said Smigger. "He's barred anyway, He won't get served."

"He's harmless," replied Dougie. "He'll get one of the lads to get his drink for him."

Jerry ordered the drinks. "You wouldn't say he was harmless if you were a bit skint and it was your ale he was minesweeping," he said.

"I feel sorry for him," said Dougie. "Years ago in the sixties when everyone had money he was the best dressed fella in the ale house. He had a big row with his mother and then she snuffed it. He blamed himself and went off his head. Been living out the bin ever since."

"Unlucky," shrugged Jerry.

The football team had been training and were sitting by the wall. The local girls were gathered down the end of the bar, right by the group. The three lads squeezed into the company of the football team.

"Alright boys," said Docker, the local window cleaner and football team manager. "Why haven't you been training?"

"Had to go and see about a job," said Jerry. "Still not working?" said Docker.

"No," replied Jerry.

Smigger sat and met his brother Billy's hostile gaze.

The Wooden Indian tapped Billy on the shoulder, interrupting the situation. "Will you get us a pint please Billy," he said, handing Billy the pound note.

Billy paused for a moment. "O.K. Chris," he said, calling the Wooden Indian by his real name.

Billy got up and squeezed through to the bar. Smigger took a sip of his ale and watched him go. He noticed a group of girls down by the group.

"Oh 'ere y'are. Me Sunday shag's in," he said, referring to the rather plump buck-toothed girl in the green dress sitting near the group. Smigger made a habit of taking her home every Sunday night.

"D'you fancy getting a grip of her sister?" he asked Dougie.

"Bit rough isn't she?" said Dougie, not too keen.

"Oh aye yeah. Look at the teeth on her, if you butted her in the mouth you'd have a head on you like a jig-saw puzzle," quipped Jerry.

"She's the one I'm with," said Smigger unashamedly. "You get a grip of her sister. The one in the red top."

Dougie looked at her dubiously. She was fairly attractive.

"I thought she was courting," he said.

78

"She was," said Smigger. "But she finished with him about two months ago. Come on, she'll be dying for it."

"What happens if we get knocked back?" asked Dougie unconvinced.

"We won't," said Smigger. "I'll go and talk to the one I'm taking and you come up and offer them a drink. The girls round here think it's Christmas when some one offers them a drink. Everyone's that hard up."

"O.K." said Dougie, finally convinced.

Billy handed the Wooden Indian his pint of Guinness and sat back. He watched Smigger chatting up the girl down the end of the bar.

"I believe you're getting engaged," Billy said to Jerry.

"Yeah. You're all invited to the do," came the reply.

"Wait till you start getting all the lecky and gas bills and start having to pay for the food and rent," chastised Docker. "I've got a couple of spare ladders in the back garden if you want to start your own round to pay for your ale money.

The company all laughed.

The Wooden Indian took a drink of his pint and had a brain storm.

"Oh 'ere y'are," said Docker, knocking Jerry's arm. The Wooden Indian walked down the bar with his hands in his pockets. Suddenly he drew his hands from his pockets and began excitedly shooting his imaginary attackers like a child with his fingertips.

The pub manager shook his head and then buried it in his hands. "I'm tired of throwing the cunt out," he told the regulars standing near him.

The Wooden Indian stopped shooting and blew the gunsmoke away from his fingertips. He put his hands back in their pockets. A look of calm serenity returned to his face. He turned and walked calmly back to his drink, while the pub howled laughing at him.

Dougie joined Smigger and the girls.

"What do you want, Smigger? Pint of lager?"

"Yes," replied Smigger.

"D'you want a bevy, girls?" asked Dougie.

"Vodka and Orange," replied the girl with Smigger.

Her sister paused for a moment. She looked at Dougie and then at her sister and finally back at Dougie.

"Bacardi and Coke please," she said.

Dougie went to the bar. "Who's paying for the do?" Docker asked Jerry. "You're only just out of the clink."

"She's got a few bob saved," replied Jerry, "and I've still got some money left in the trust fund me mum set aside for me out of the insurance money when me dad died."

"Oh," said Docker.

"I've only got to find the money for a ring. I'll have to get her a good one, because she works in an office full of girls. And you know how bitchy they get over things like that."

79

The conversation was drowned out by the loud noise of the group starting up. Jerry looked down the bar. Smigger and Dougie were heavily engrossed in chatting up the two girls.

A short stocky woman with long black tied-back hair got up from her chair and ignored the television. She walked into the kitchen to check on the meal of roast beef, potatoes, peas and gravy she was trying to keep warm for her husband. The meat had dried up and the gravy had partly evaporated and partly formed a brown skin over the food. She burned her fingers on the plate and withdrew them quickly.

"Where is he?" she said aloud, looking at the clock.

Her husband was the bearded full-back who had given Maca a hard time in the football match. He sat in a quiet country pub with an attractive young blonde from work. She was beginning to feel a bit tipsy.

"Another drink?" he asked and went to the bar without waiting for a reply.

An hour or so later, Jerry, Smigger and Dougie were the last ones out of the pub. The manager locked the door behind them.

Smigger and Dougie walked the two girls home. Dougie deliberately took his time and lagged behind in an effort to split the two girls up.

Smigger sat on the couch as Ann put the kettle on. Her parents were in bed. She walked back into the parlour and sat on the couch, kissing and cuddling, waiting for the kettle to boil.

Dougie strolled along with Linda towards the row of shops.

"I thought you were going with Vicky anyway," said Linda.

"No, I finished with her last night," lied Dougie. "I'm fed up with her always nagging. She won't let me go out with me mates."

"I'd let you go out with your mates," she said.

Dougie looked away and smiled slyly. He knew he had her.

"But I'll probably end up back with her," he said solemnly, as though he didn't want to.

"Why?" asked Linda. "Well where am I going to find someone as sexually adventurous as her?"

The girl looked at him. Dougie stopped walking by the shops.

"Well, most girls only want to have sex on the couch in front of the fire when their mum and dad are out. And even then they think they've only got to drop their draws and open their legs and that's it."

Linda laughed. She'd fancied Dougie for a long time. This was her chance.

"I'm not like that," she said, taking him by the hand and leading him to the cake shop doorway. She turned and embraced him. She began kissing the face off him.

Smigger's naked buttocks pummelled up and down on the couch. He was naked except for his socks. The girl moaned underneath him.

"Don't leave it in....Please."

80

Smigger managed to arch his back and dismount her as he ejaculated over her body rather than in it. The girl lay still and Smigger bent over her motionless, getting his breath. Smigger lifted his head and wiped a bead of sweat from her brow.

"Well me old tater. It's been really great, really terrif," he said, mimicking David Bellamy. He rolled off and began to get dressed. Ann lay naked but still on the couch and wondered whether she was a fool to herself in continuing their relationship the way it was. Smigger was dressed. He kissed her goodnight and left.

Dougie's trousers were round by his ankles. He clutched Linda's buttocks tightly and gamely battered away at her.

"Dougie' Dougie" she moaned, more high pitched the harder Dougie pressed. She tore at the hair on the back of his head. Dougie went faster and faster reaching a climax. Suddenly it was all over. His body stiffened and then relaxed. His knees trembled. The girl clung onto him. Dougie broke away from her and pulled his underpants and trousers up. Linda fixed her dishevelled clothes and covered her naked left breast that was hanging out of her blouse.

"I've got to shoot off" said Dougie.

"What?" said Linda. "Aren't you walking me home?"

"No," said Dougie. "I can't. If I don't get in by a certain time me ma will lock me out. See you later," he said, running off up the road, laughing his head off.

The girl watched him go for a moment.

"Bastard," she cursed, and continued fixing her dress.

The television screen disintegrated to a white blip in the middle. The day's programmes were over. The dark haired woman turned the television off and looked at the clock.

"Where is he the bastard?" she said.

The man was making love in his car parked down a dark country lane. His foot hung out the window as he tried to make room for himself in the cramped space. The car bounded rythmically back and forward and the man's shoe eventually fell off as he tried to change his angle of thrust because of cramp.

Half an hour later he pulled up outside his own house. His wife heard the car door slam. She turned the landing light on as he opened the door.

"Where've you been?" she asked aggressively.

The man looked at her and took his coat off, slinging it over the banister. It was time to come clean.

"Where do you think?" he asked. She paused for a moment, expecting what was coming but still shocked by the truth.

"You've been seeing another woman, you dirty bastard," she exclaimed.

"Other women," he corrected her and walked into the parlour.

She charged down the stairs.

"You can pack your bags," she roared. "You're not staying here."

81

"Fuck off," replied the husband. "You pack your bags. This is my house as much as your's. Anyway it's as much your fault as it is mine."

"What d'you mean?" asked his wife, flabbergasted, following her husband upstairs. He sat on the bed and started taking his shoes off.

"We've been drifting apart now for a long time. Even when we make love there's no passion. You just lie there like it's something you've got to go through. And when it's over you turn over, like I've done something bad to you"

The wife sat down on the bed in shock. The truth hurt.

"I never thought," she said.

"Maybe we've been together too long," said the husband getting into bed. "We've let things go stale."

"What do you want to do?" asked the wife. "D'you want a divorce?"

"I don't know," replied the husband. "But I do know I don't want things to go on like they are."

He reached out and turned the light off. His wife climbed into bed next to him and lay awake thinking.

The following morning Jerry, Dougie and Smigger walked up the street to Yardsy's house, commonly known in the area as 'the pits' because all the young robbers went to Yardsy to have their cars fixed. Yardsy was lying underneath a car welding a gap together in the back of an old wreck. Three lads sat in their car further up the street waiting for the timing to be fixed in their car.

Yardsy slid from under the car and removed his mask, still checking his handy work.

"Alright Yardsy lad. Where d'you learn to do that?" asked Smigger.

"Alright Smigger. Borstal," replied Yardsy.

"You must make a few bob here," said Smigger. "All the good robbers that come here to get their cars fixed. Why don't you charge them a percentage of their earnings?"

"What d'you think I am," replied Yardsy, "A fucking Tory."

The lads all laughed.

"I do get a dropsy now and again," admitted Yardsy. "What can I do for you?"

"We're buying a car," said Jerry. "We want you to see we don't get ripped off."

"I'm a bit busy just now," said Yardsy. "The boys have been waiting two days to have their timing fixed," he said, nodding to the car up the steet.

"There might be a 'oner' in it for you if you do a good job," said Dougie.

"O.K;" laughed Yardsy. "I'll just see if I can get away," he said, strolling up the street to the parked car.

"Listen boys, I've got to shoot off to sign on. I'll be back in half an hour then I'll make a start on this," he said through the window to the lads in the car.

"O.K." agreed the lads. Yardsy got into his own car accompanied by Jerry, Dougie and Smigger and drove off.

The three lads stood next to the salesman in the showroom and watched Yardsy do his stuff. The car was a dark blue mark IV Cortina with £1850 emblazoned in large orange letters across the windscreen. Yardsy slipped underneath the vehicle and studied the bodywork. He said nothing as he got up and checked the tyres. Then he opened the bonnet and peered inside. He climbed into the car and started the engine. He listened very carefully for any rumblings or any noise that may tell him there was something wrong with the car. The lads watched him work in silence. He turned the ignition off and got out of the car.

"I wouldn't pay more than fifteen hundred for it," he said, putting the hood down.

"Oh I don't know about that," said the salesman pensively as the lads turned to look at him.

"Cash," said Jerry firmly.

The man relented.

"Done," he said, shaking hands. "Your friend certainly knows his business."

Dougie counted fifteen wads of one hundred pounds onto the bonnet whilst Smigger started the engine up. Dougie tossed the sixteenth wad to Yardsy who promptly caught it.

"Pleasure doing business with you," he said.

The young woman walked along the corridor and opened the door to the careers office. It was the woman who had caught her husband being unfaithful the night before. Her face was pale and her eyes heavy with the loss of sleep. She walked past the kids waiting to see her and into her office. She draped her coat over the chair and placed her handbag on the desk. There was a furtive knock at the door.

"Come in," she said firmly.

Joey walked gingerly into the office, his face slightly swollen from the night before.

"Sit down," she ordered, pulling a folder from her drawer and placing it on the desk before her. "Now then, what can I do for you?" she asked.

"Please miss, I want to go to the dentist this afternoon," said Joey. "I got a tooth knocked out last night and me mouth's dead sore."

The careers officer looked at him. "It doesn't look that sore to me," she said unsympathetically.

"It is," replied Joey.

"Well you can't go. You've got exams this afternoon," replied the careers officer.

"I've already made the appointment," said Joey.

"Well you shall just have to cancel it then, won't you?" said the careers officer, used to dealing with lead-swingers and malingerers.

"I won't," replied Joey indignantly. "I'm entitled to go for half an hour. It says so in me contract. You can't stop me."

"And I'm entitled to suspend you for three days for being cheeky," snapped the teacher. "It says that in your contract as well."

"You're suspending me just because I want to go to the dentist for half an hour," ranted Joey. "What am I going to tell me ma when she wants her money on Friday?"

"I'm sure you'll think of something," said the careers officer, filling a form in on the desk and not even looking at him.

"What's the matter with you. Did your old man turn his arse on you last night?"

The woman looked at the angry youth in alarm, perhaps there was some truth in what he was saying.

"You fucking old bitch," roared Joey, slamming the door behind him.

Smigger had dropped the lads off and was driving home when he saw Joey getting off the bus.

"What's the matter" said Smigger

"Got suspended for three days," said Joey.

"What for?" asked Smigger.

"Arguing," said Joey. "The cow wouldn't let me go to the dentist. Where d'you get the car?"

"Tell you in a minute," said Smigger, spotting his mother struggling with the shopping. He stopped the car and got out, breezed along behind her and picked the shopping up effortlessly.

"Sorry about last night, mum. I'll carry them," he said.

"Alright lad," she replied.

He walked towards the car with a smile on his face. Mrs Smith spotted Joey sitting in the back.

"Where d'you get that?" she asked.

"It's a company car," smiled Smigger, passing the shopping to Joey. "I've got a new job."

"Doing what?" asked Mrs Smith.

"Salesman with a double glazing firm."

Mrs Smith looked at him flabbergasted.

"What happens is I drive a team of salesman anywhere up and down the country. They pick out a rich housing estate and go selling double glazing. I get paid on a commission basis. There's loads of money in it."

"That's good isn't it?" said Mrs Smith, completely taken in.

"Yeah. Be able to buy the house for you soon."

"Hey mum, is it alright if I buy a pair of jeans this week instead of giving you any money? I need trousers for work," asked Joey.

"O.K. lad," agreed Mrs Smith in a good mood. At last one of her lads was making something of himself.

That evening Jerry, Dougie and Smigger were sat huddled round a table in the local pub when Marty walked in. Smigger nudged the others. It was the first time they'd seen him since the crash. One eye was half closed and lower than the other. His face was held together by a mass of scar tissue still clearly visible despite the surgeon's brilliant efforts. He smiled when he saw his friends and greeted them in a slurred but still audible voice.

"D'you want a bevy?" asked Smigger getting up.

"Pint of lager," stammered Marty, sitting down.

Jerry looked at him without saying anything.

"How are you doing?" asked Dougie.

"Sound," replied Marty.

"Are you coming for a bevy with the boys?" asked Dougie.

"No," replied Marty, "I've got to go somewhere. See you later," he said, picking his pint up and walking to the bar.

The lads watched their friend's unsteady gait up the bar in silence. Jerry looked deep into the bottom of his pint, remembering his friend the way he had been.

"It wasn't your fault," said Dougie.

"It was his arse slapped next to mine in the window. We all knew what we were getting into," said Smigger.

"It's a cruel, cruel world," said Jerry, thinking deeply.

"Do we care," shrugged Smigger.

"No," replied Dougie. "I'd sooner be in me box than on the dole all me life." Just then Collo, Ged and Whitey walked into the bar.

"Hello boys. What are you's drinking?" asked Collo.

"Lager," replied Dougie, happy to see his friends he'd met in the nick.

"Six pints of lager please, luv," Collo called to the barmaid.

"What can we do for you?" asked Smigger as the lads drew seats up to the table.

"Gotta bit of business lined up. We're looking for a top jockey?"

"What's the touch?" asked Jerry.

"A nitty" (night safe) interrupted Ged.

"Supermarket?" assumed Jerry.

"Yeah," replied Collo.

"How much?" asked Jerry.

"Between three and five grand we reckon," said Ged.

"What's the score over the driver?" asked Smigger.

"There's a cop-shop round the corner. We need a good jockey in case something goes wrong - no virgins," said Whitey.

The three lads looked at each other. Ged and Collo were good lads but they wouldn't trust Whitey as far as they could throw him.

Just then the Wooden Indian caught Ged's eye. He stopped speaking.

The old bum stalked shiftily up the bar with his hands in his coat pockets, his eyes wild and insane.

"On guard"' he cried at the top of his voice and began a frenzied swordfence up the bar with an imaginary attacker. The whole pub stopped to watch and roared with laughter. The Wooden Indian eventually cornered his attacker and killed him with a desperate lunge. He kissed his blade and returned it to its scabbard. A look of calm serenity returned to his face. He put his hands back in his pockets and walked back down the bar and sat down in his place.

The pub manager buried his head in his hands. He took a deep breath and surfaced, shaking his head.

"Who's he?" asked Ged."He's great him."

"The Wooden Indian," replied Dougie."He used to be one of the lads but his ma died and he went off his cake."

"He's harmless but he causes hassle because he's a terrible minesweeper. He'll drink anything," said Smigger."Watch this," he said, getting a brainwave.

He picked up a half empty pint glass and walked into the toilet followed by Collo and Whitey. He unzipped his flies and began urinating into the glass.

"Why isn't Cagsy driving?" asked Jerry.

"He's locked up over his fines," replied Ged. "He set the touch up, the getaway route, the lot."

"What's Whitey got to do with it?" asked Dougie.

"Nothing really," replied Ged. "We just needed someone with a legitimate car for getting to and from the touch."

"He's definitely one bad shady character," said Dougie. "There's no way Smigger will drive. He won't have anything to do with a dickhead like that."

"I'll drive," said Jerry.

Dougie looked at him in surprise.

"The money will do as an engagement ring for me tart," Jerry enlightened him. "We'll clock the job tomorrow and if it's on I'll drive."

Just then Smigger returned from the toilet. He placed the pint on an empty table in full view of the Wooden Indian, and then continued walking back to his place.

The lads ignored the pint as they watched the Wooden Indian sight his prey. He looked furtively about him. No-one was watching. He walked past the table and turned. No-one was paying him any attention. He swooped on the pint as he walked past and returned to his seat. He gulped heavily at the drink as the Croxteth lads groaned in disgust. The Wooden Indian was unperturbed. He placed the drink on the table before him and didn't turn a hair.

The lads laughed half in disgust. Jerry kept a straight face. He'd seen the trick done before.

"Another few years and it'll be Marty sitting there," he said, wiping the smile off Smigger's face.

The following evening, Jerry sat eating his tea with his mother and his younger sister, Karen. Jerry buttered a piece of bread and made a sandwich from the plate of scouse he was eating.

"Can I have some money to go the disco?" Karen asked her mother.

"I've got no money," said Mrs Kinsella. "What I've got I need for shopping tomorrow."

"Oh go on, Mum," implored Karen. "All me mates are going."

"I can't even afford to go the bingo meself, never mind pay for you to go to the disco," said Mrs Kinsella.

Her daughter began to sulk. Outside a car horn beeped. It was Collo, Ged and Whitey come to pick Jerry up. Jerry polished off the remnants of the bowl of scouse with a slice of bread.

"If I give you some money, will you iron me shirts and jeans when I ask you?" he asked, sticking the last piece of bread into his mouth.

"Yes," said Karen gleefully.

Jerry stood up and pulled a small roll of fivers from his back pocket. He tossed a fiver on the table in front of his sister.

"Oh thanks Jerry," she said gratefully as Jerry peeled off a tenner and dropped it on the table for his mother.

"Where do you get that?" asked his mother inquisitively.

"Won it on the horses," laughed Jerry. "You get down the bingo tonight and win a few bob. That's lucky money there, you can't go wrong."

Mrs Kinsella smiled. Jerry was a good lad.

"Thanks son," she said.

Jerry smiled. "I'll see you later. I'm going out."

The front door opened and Jerry strolled down the path, putting his jacket on, he climbed into the car and Whitey drove off.

The stolen car to be used on the job was parked on a quiet road that ran along the edge of an estate in between a block of flats and a small cemetery. Mrs O'Brien stood in the back kitchen washing the dishes. She looked at the powerful car outside and wondered who owned it. Just then Whitey pulled up next to it in his car. Mrs O'Brien watched the four lads get out of one car and into the other.

"The car O.K?" Jerry asked Collo as they got in.

"Sound," replied Collo.

Mrs O'Brien's suspicions were aroused as she watched Jerry drive the car away. She picked up the pad she used for her shopping lists and wrote down the licence number of Whitey's car.

Jerry parked the car in the village street, a little down the road from the bank, where they could see the night safe clearly without raising too much suspicion. They waited. Nobody spoke. Jerry cleaned his teeth with a match. Across the street, two women were waiting for a bus. A man in a mac walked slowly up to the bus stop and joined the two women already standing there. He sighed and looked at his watch. It had been a long day at work and the bus was overdue. He watched the four lads sitting in the powerful car across the street. The driver sat with his elbow out of the window chewing a match. The man wondered what they were waiting for. Jerry felt the man's eyes on him and rested his head against his hand so as to obscure the man's view of him. A car passed them and pulled up outside the bank.

"That's him," said Collo.

Jerry nodded, chewing patiently on the match. The man at the bus-stop stamped his feet and blew on his hands. It was getting cold. The supermarket manager opened the glove compartment and pulled out the thick bank wallet. He tucked it discreetly into the front of his jacket and got out of car. The supermarket manager stepped onto the pavement and walked towards the night safe. The people at the bus stop looked on in surprise as the powerful car screeched away up the street. The supermarket manager turned to see what was going on as the car skidded to a halt at the bank. The startled man froze in shock - caught in the no-man's land between the car and the bank. The car door flew open and Ged and Collo flew towards him. He recovered quickly but it was too late. They were on him. He turned away as Ged grabbed the bank wallet and tried to wrench it away from him. Collo grabbed him by the-hair and volleyed him in the face as he fell. The man released the money as his head bounced on the floor. Ged kicked him in the groin as he snatched the wallet.

The man from the bus stop came running up but it was too late. The raiders were back in the car and Jerry sped round the corner past the police station and magistrates' court.

The man reached the stricken supermarket manager and looked helplessly in the direction the raiders had gone. It was all over that quickly he'had no time to help.

"Bastards," he cursed.

The car swung left down a dual carriage way, overtaking traffic as it went. Jerry chewed impassively on the matchstick, swinging the car right, through the dual carriage way before speeding away down a suburban street.

Ged stared out the back. There was no sign of any pursuit.

"We're O.K." he said.

Whitey heaved a sigh of relief as he trembled nervously in the corner.

Jerry motored coolly down the drive and stopped at the lights. They waited. The lights changed. Jerry pulled calmly away and watched the lads' excited rabitting about the snatch.

"That was brilliant that," declared Ged.

"I didn't think he was ever going to let go of the money," babbled Collo.

"See the gob on him when Ged kicked him in the bollocks," enthused Whitey.

Jerry looked at him disdainfully in the rear view mirror. He didn't like that lad one bit. He turned the car into the estate and parked behind Whitey's car. Mrs O'Brien watched the four lads get out of the car and get back into Whitey's car. The car pulled away. Mrs O'Brien thought to herself. The kettle clicked as the water boiled and the kettle turned itself off. She poured herself a cup of coffee, her suspicious line of thought disturbed. No. them young lads couldn't be up to no good.

The four young men arrived at Collo's flat where he lived with his common law wife and their young daughter.

"Did you get it?" his woman asked excitedly.

"Yes luv," said Collo, giving her a kiss and cuddle. "Go and put the kettle on," he said, slapping her backside.

"What are we going to open it with?" asked Whitey.

"'Ere y'are. Give us it," said Jerry. Ged tossed him the money. Jerry produced a stanley knife from his pocket and cut an L shape in the back of the wallet. He ripped the leather back. He tossed the money to Whitey who was sitting in front of the fire with a bag of elastic bands, waiting to count and bundle the money. Collo sat quietly in the armchair. His young lady sat on the arm of the chair as Ged and Whitey bundled and counted the money. Jerry sipped quietly at his coffee, watching the joy on Collo and his wife's faces as the money was counted.

"How much is there?" asked Collo when the count had ended. Whitey had already begun stacking the money in four separate piles.

"Four thousand five hundred, seven pound and eighteen pence," answered Whitey.

"Hurray," cheered Collo's girl, embracing her husband.

"That's one thousand, one hundred, twenty six pound, seventy nine and half pence each." He began putting one pile inside his jacket.

"Get your fuckin hands off," snarled Jerry.

Everyone froze. Whitey put the money back.

"What about Cagsy?" asked Jerry

"Yeah, that's a point," said Ged. "A nice few bob won't do him any harm when he gets out of the nick."

"Why? What did Cagsy do?" snarled Whitey.

"What did you do?" answered Jerry picking up and passing the odd seven pounds eighteen pence to Collo's wife.

"Cagsy clocked the job and set up the get-away route," said Collo.

"He won't expect nothing," said Ged philosophically.

"Well it will be a nice surprise for him then won't it?" said Collo.

"What do you reckon?" asked Jerry. "A grand each and five hundred for Cagsy?"

"Seems fair enough," said Collo.

"Yeah," agreed Ged.

"No way, I'm not having it," moaned Whitey and went to reach for the money.

Jerry stood on his fingers. Whitey withdrew his hand in pain.

"What did Whitey do today?" Jerry asked.

"Nothing," replied Ged and Collo.

Jerry turned and looked Whitey in the eye.

"What's a full share of nothing?" he asked.

Whitey didn't reply.

"Get the picture?" insisted Jerry.

"Yeah," replied Whitey reluctantly.

Jerry picked up his money.

"It was a pleasure working with you's," he said, shaking hands with Ged and Collo.

"If you ever want a lift again don't bring the dickhead with you because you'll only be wasting your time."

Jerry walked out and shut the door behind him.

It was dark when the police found the stolen car. Mrs O'Brien was on her way home from the bingo with one of her neighbours. A policeman was locking the car up so it could be examined the next morning.

"What's going on here, officer," asked the neighbour.

"Stolen car luv," replied the officer. "Been used in a robbery."

"I saw the four lads get out of it about tea-time. I thought there was something funny going on," said Mrs O'Brien.

"Would you know them again?" asked the officer.

"I think so," said Mrs O'Brien. "I even wrote down the number of the car they drove off in. Come on, I'll get it for you."

It was just after three o'clock in the morning. Whitey was driving home from a night on the town with Collo and Ged who were singing in the back. The car stopped outside Ged's house.

"Goodnight boys," said Ged and staggered out of the car drunk. He slammed the car door behind him and waved as it pulled away. Whitey beeped the horn twice regardless of the neighbours.

They stopped outside the flats.

"See you tomorrow Whitey lad," said Collo, getting out

"See you tomorrow Collo," replied Whitey and then pulled away. Collo walked into the flats.

Four detectives sat in an unmanned police car across the street from Whitey's house.

"This is him," said Detective Constable Holmes as the headlights turned into the street. The officers watched him lock the car and walk up the path to his house. It was obvious he was drunk. Two of the officers snatched him from behind.

"Police officers," said one, splashing an identity in front of his face.

"I haven't done nothing," whined Whitey as he was pinned against the wall.

"Well you've got nothing to worry about then, have you?" replied Holmes as he frisked him. He found a roll of money in his pocket. Sergeant Hughes watched from behind.

"Fifty quid sir," said Holmes.

"Where did you get the money?" asked Hughes.

"I won it on the horses," replied Whitey.

"Which betting shop?" asked Hughes. There was no reply. "Take him away. Search the house," ordered the sergeant.

Whitey's mother let the police in as her son was led away. She had no option. The police had a search warrant.

"What's going on?" she asked in surprise, dressed only in a nightdress.

"We have reason to believe your son was involved in a robbery yesterday evening," the sergeant informed her. Whitey's family were dragged from their beds. The whole house was searched. Drawers were opened, clothes scattered about the rooms, cushions were ripped open, furniture taken apart. The house was in a state of complete disarray. Chalky, Whitey's elder brother stood there helplessly and watched the police.

"Bastards," he cursed as his mother sobbed on his father's shoulder.

Outside in the back yard the family pet alsation was going berserk trying to break away from the chain that tethered it next to the kennel. One officer was searching the guttering and the windowsill in the back bedroom. He looked down at the ferocious animal hungry for his blood.

"Search the backyard," ordered Officer Holmes.

"Sod off," replied the detective. "You friggin' search it."

"You wait till I see the Council in the morning," roared Mrs White as the police walked down the path back to their cars - the raid had been fruitless. The cars pulled away. Chalky calmed the dog down in the backyard. It licked his face.

"There's a good boy," he said.

He reached inside the kennel and pulled out the evidence the police were looking for. He kissed it and returned the money to its hiding place.

Whitey sat suddenly sober at the table in the interview room at the police station.

"What was your car doing in the Huyton area today?" asked Sergeant Hughes.

"I'm not saying nothing," replied Whitey.

"You don't have to son," replied Hughes. "We've got you bang to rights."

Whitey looked at the officer beginning to get scared. "You were seen getting in and out of a stolen car used in serious crime before and after the robbery," continued Hughes.

"Bollocks," replied Whitey, unsure of himself.

The sergeant laughed. "You were positively identified by an old school mate, apparently the guy went to school with you years ago," bluffed the sergeant.

Whitey began to think - just maybe it was true.

"How do you think we picked you up so soon?" asked the sergeant.

"The guy's on the critical list," lied the sergeant, stirring things up.

Whitey looked at him and began to panic.

"Banged his head on the floor when you hit him. Turns out he's got a thin skull."

"I never hit no-one," panicked Whitey. "I didn't do nothing."

"Tell that to the judge," sneered Hughes. "If the guy dies he'll work you a ten or maybe even a fifteen year stretch."

"It wasn't me," pleaded Whitey.

"Who was it then?" demanded the officer.

Whitey went silent, strongly tempted to tell.

"It was your mates," said the sergeant, walking around the table. "But I don't know who they are. They're in the clear. You're the dickhead whose gonna do the bird." Whitey started to cry. "It wasn't me," he snivelled.

The sergeant looked at the uniformed officer in the room taking notes and then back at Whitey in disgust.

"Who was it?" asked the sergeant in a quieter tone.

"D'you think I'm going to do fifteen years in a cell with three nutters I'd grassed up?" moaned Whitey, the tears flowing freely. "I wouldn't last five minutes."

"You can turn Queen's evidence and give evidence against them," said the officer.

Whitey continued snivelling but said nothing.

"Look," said Sergeant Hughes, "I know you're only a stink. You've only just got the bottle to get out of bed. It's not you I want - it's your friends. They're the danger to society."

Whitey kept snivelling with his head hung low but said nothing.

There was a knock on the door. It was Detective Constable Holmes. Sergeant Hughes went outside to speak with him.

"Turned the place upside down. Nothing there sir," said Constable Holmes.

"O.K." replied Hughes and walked back into the interview room.

"That was a message from the hospital," lied the sergeant. "The priest's been in and given the man the last rites. If you've got anything to say, you better say it now because once he dies I can't do nothing for you."

The sergeant look at Whitey waiting for an answer. Finally he relented.

"It was Jerry Kinsella, Ged Cotton and Jimmy Collins. They needed a legitimate car so they could get up to Huyton without getting a tug. I didn't know what was going on. They made me get in the robbed car. They done the job and gave me sixty quid and said I'd better keep me mouth shut. We went out on the ale. That fifty quid you found on me is the change out of it," snivelled the grass.

"O.K." said the sergeant. "I'll buy that. Where do they live?"

It was seven o'clock in the morning when they knocked on Ged's door. There was no answer. Sergeant Hughes nodded to Detective Constable Brennan who then went around the back of the house. Sergeant Hughes knocked again louder. There was still no reply. Hughes knocked again and waited. Ged woke from his drunken sleep and looked at the alarm clock. It was only seven o'clock. He groaned and turned over. He heard the loud knock on the door and his father's heavy foot steps on the stairs. Suddenly it dawned on him what was happening.

"Alright, alright," called his father, coming down the stairs as the caller knocked again.

Ged jumped out of bed, dressed only in his underpants. He saw the unmarked police car outside and ran for the back bedroom as his father slipped the bolt off the door.

"Police officers," snapped the sergeant. "We've a warrant for your son's arrest," waving the identification and handing Mr Cotton the warrant.

Holmes burst past them and ran up the stairs. Ged ran into his mother's bedroom, the back bedroom, opened the window and clambered out just as Holmes burst into the room.

"Ha ha! You'll have to be quicker than that," called Ged, climbing down the drainpipe.

"What's going on?" screamed his startled mother, sitting up in bed.

D.C. Holmes watched D.C. Brennan pounce on Ged as he reached the ground. The burly officer snatched him from behind and pinned the nearly naked man face down on the ground. The officer quickly handcuffed Ged's hands behind him. He picked the man up and led him to the police car.

"Ha ha!" called D.C. Holmes out of the window. "You'll have to be quicker than that."

"What's going on?" asked Ged's bewildered father as his son was led down the garden path and placed in the back of the police car.

"We have reason to believe your son was involved in a robbery yesterday evening," answered Sergeant Hughes.

"Who? Our Gerald?" asked Mr Cotton in disbelief.

D.C. Holmes came down the stairs. "Found this in a drawer next to his bed, sarge," he said, holding up a thick wad of money - Ged's entire share from the job.

The sergeant looked at Mr Cotton. "Yes, your Gerald," he replied.

Collo was lying tucked up in the arms of his girlfriend when the police called. His reaction to the first knock was to snuggle a bit closer to his girl.

Sergeant Hughes knocked again, louder. Collo's eyes flashed open.

"Shit - it's the bizzies," he gasped, jumping out of of bed.

His girlfriend looked at him In alarm. Collo dragged his jeans on. The banging continued.

"Delay them'" he panicked.

"I'm coming," called his girl, not making a move.

"I'll leave the money down the drainpipe," said Collo, putting on his training shoes.

Collo ran through the living room and onto the verandah. He climbed over the railing and wedged the money into the drainpipe before beginning the long climb down. His girlfriend opened the door.

"What do you's want?" she asked.

D.C. Brennan slipped into the back yard and watched Collo climb down. He hid out of sight and waited for his quarry to hit the ground. Collo dropped the last ten-foot into the yard below. Brennan pounced on him as soon as he landed. The big man pinned the struggling youth to the ground.

"Get off me, you big bastard," cursed the angry young man, struggling like a wildcat.

His girlfriend cradled their baby in her arms and watched her boyfriend's vain struggle next to the sergeant on the balcony.

D.C. Holmes joined the fray and handcuffed Collo's ankles together. The two officers picked him up by the chains and carted him off to the police car.

"Let me go, you bastards," screamed Collo, struggling violently.

"Where's the money?" Sergeant Hughes asked the girl.

She didn't reply. She just cuddled her crying baby.

"We can do this the hard way or the easy way," insisted the sergeant. "Where's the money?"

"I don't know what you're talking about," replied the girl.

It was Saturday morning. Jerry got up early. He came down the steps dressed only in a pair of jeans, opened the front door and picked up the two pints of milk. He sleepily watched little Maca, Sykesy and two friends down the street. They were going to play football for the school team.

"Can you fight Billy Atkinson out of our class?" one youth asked.

"Dunno," shrugged Sykesy.

"He said he could fight you. Why don't you have him out?" continued the youth.

Jerry smiled and shook his head. He'd seen it all before. He closed the front door behind him with his heel. He walked into the back kitchen and poured himself a bowl of Rice Krispies. He turned the television on and settled down to watch "Tizwas" as he ate his breakfast.

There was a knock on the door. Jerry answered it. It was the police.

"Police officers," snapped Hughes, flashing his identity card.

"What do you want?" asked Jerry innocently.

"You," replied D.C. Holmes, handing him the search warrant.

"Who is it Jerry?" called Mrs Kinsella from upstairs.

"The police," answered Jerry.

"What do they want?" called Mrs Kinsella, getting out of bed.

"Get dressed," the sergeant ordered.

Holmes accompanied Jerry upstairs, passing Mrs Kinsella on the way.

"What's going on?" she asked bewildered.

"We have reason to believe your son was involved in a robbery yesterday evening," answered Sergeant Hughes.

"You're a cool one," said Holmes. "You're going down for four years and you don't even turn a hair."

"I don't know what you're talking about," said Jerry, refusing to rise to the bait.

Karen came out of the bedroom dressed in a short negligee and briefs.

"What's happening Jerry?" she asked.

"Get back in the bedroom," snapped Jerry, "and get dressed," annoyed at the way Holmes goggled at his scantily clad young sister.

The officer followed Jerry into the back bedroom and watched him dress. "Touchy aren't we?" said the officer, trying to upset Jerry into making a mistake. "Never mind, I'll look after her for you for the next four years." "Get home lad, your ma's got cake," growled Jerry, informing the officer he was out of his league. Jerry was handcuffed by the angry officer and led downstairs.

"Don't worry mum, I never had nothing to do with it. I don't know what they're on about."

The sergeant watched in silence. He had seen it all before.

"Don't forget to cash me giro and give me brief a ring," called Jerry as he was led down the path.

Mrs Kinsella watched the car pull away, frantic with worry.

The sergeant looked at Jerry in the rear-view mirror.

"Your giro won't do you any good where you're going, son," he said.

Jerry glared back at him. "Stick your smart remarks up your well shagged arse," snarled Jerry.

D.C. Holmes smacked Jerry a backhander across the face. The blow cut his lip. Jerry felt the wound begin to bleed.

"We've got a long way to go. I'd keep me mouth shut if I was you."

Jerry scowled but said nothing.

It was some time later when Sergeant Hughes emerged from the interview room. He was tired and he wanted to go to bed.

"Well?" asked the duty inspector, wanting to know how he'd got on.

"Nothing," said the sergeant shaking his head. "I've tried everything. He won't even tell us how many sugars he takes in his tea."

"Well," replied the inspector, "maybe the identity parade will throw some new light on the matter."

Jerry took his place at the front of the line-up, shortly after the supermarket manager was led into the yard escorted by a uniformed officer. The manager looked carefully at Jerry and passed him by. Jerry winked at D.C. Holmes who was standing next to Sergeant Hughes, who was directing the procedure. The constable scowled and said nothing. He was angry that a young tearaway could commit a violent crime and then cock a snook at the law. Jerry was growing with confidence. He was sure the police had nothing on him, having to resort to an identity parade was the last straw. The manager walked up to the sergeant and shook his head. He was led out of the yard.

The first woman from the bus stop was led in. She looked long and hard at Jerry, trying to remember. Jerry stared fixedly at the wall in front of him. He breathed a sigh of relief and stuck his tongue out unceremoniously at D.C. Holmes. The woman moved along the line of young men examining the faces. She returned to the sergeant.

"I think the first one might be one of them but I'm not sure," said the woman thoughtfully.

"O.K. Thanks very much," said the sergeant, knowing that her evidence wouldn't stand up in court.

The man who had come to the aid of the shop manager was led in. He didn't spare Jerry a second look. He moved down the line to the sixth man and pointed at him.

"That's one of the bastards'" he declared, turning to the sergeant.

"Are you sure?" asked Sergeant Holmes.

"Positive," replied the man.

Jerry stood looking at D.C. Holmes and near burst out laughing, much to the officer's discomfort.

The second woman was led in. She walked up to Jerry and looked closely at him.

"That's him. He was the driver," she declared. A smile appeared on D.C. Holmes' face.

"Are you sure?" asked the sergeant.

"Positive," declared the woman.

"Thanks a lot luv," said Jerry sarcastically. "I hope the milkman is getting plenty."

The woman slapped him across the face.

Jerry was led away to the cells by D.C. Holmes and the uniformed officer.

"You're not laughing now, are you golden boy?" said the detective, pushing him into the cell.

"That's alright," replied Jerry. "You bring the woman to court as a witness. I'm going to bring the other two and the other fella who got positively identified as witnesses for the defence."

The smile on the detective's face disappeared. Jerry had a point.

"Bring who you like. You're going down," said the officer, slamming the cell door shut.

It was almost one o'clock. Smigger and Dougie arrived outside Jerry's house to go and play football. Smigger beeped the horn. Karen came down the path dressed in tight grey corduroy trousers and a tight white T shirt. She was a well built and very attractive girl.

"Cor, what wouldn't you do to her?" asked Smigger.

"True," admitted Dougie as she approached. "But what wouldn't Jerry do to you."

Karen put her hand on the roof of the car and leant in.

"Where's Jerry? We've come to pick him up to play football?" said Smigger.

"He got lifted this morning over a snatch last night," said Karen.

"Bastards" cursed Smigger. "I told him not to go with those dickheads."

"He was trying to get some money to buy Teresa a good engagement ring," said Dougie, shutting Smigger up.

"Me mam's going mad. They've turned the house upside down. I don't know who she wants to batter the most Jerry or the police."

"Did they find anything?" asked Dougie.

"No," replied Karen.

"Who was the arresting officer?"

"Don't know," shrugged Karen.

"Was one an old fella and the other one young, about twenty-five, with blonde hair?"

"Yes," replied Karen.

"Jerry wasn't giving them any cheek was he?" asked Dougie.

"He was a bit. The young one was trying to wind him up."

"Shit," cursed Dougie.

The two lads looked at each other in dismay.

"What's the matter?" asked Karen, even more worried.

"The young one's a bastard, He's always trying to impress the old sergeant. If Jerry gives them any shit he'll get his head kicked in," said Smigger.

"We'll call back later and see how he got on," said Dougie.

"O.K." said Karen. "See you later."

The car pulled away.

Jerry stood disconsolately against the cell wall, propped up by one leg. He looked at the ceiling and gently tapped his head against the wall. His solicitor sat on the cell bench.

"How long if I get found guilty?" asked Jerry.

"Three to five years," answered the brief.

"I can't understand how they got us so quick. Everything went sweet," said Jerry.

"The other two lads said the same thing," replied the brief.

"There was four of us," replied Jerry.

"Well the police seem to think they've got everyone," replied the lawyer.

"Everyone except Whitey, I'll bet," said Jerry.

"The other two lads both got caught with their share of the money so their cases are cut and dried. You've still got a chance. We'll have to see what evidence they have against you at the commital. You may even get bail yet. If you do I'd go missing if I was you because if they charge you they must be pretty certain they can make it stick."

Detective Sergeant Hughes sat in the Detective Inspector's office discussing the case.

"Do you think you've got enough evidence to prove the case against Kinsella?" asked the inspector.

"Not yet," replied the sergeant. "We're waiting for the forensic's saliva test on a half-chewed matchstick in the car even though we know the kid was in on the job."

"What do you suggest?" asked the inspector.

"I think we should charge him and then give him bail. The chances are he'll pick up his share of the money and hightail it. Then we pick him up and the case is proved."

"What if he doesn't run?" asked the inspector.

"Then we're still in the same position as we are now.",

"O.K." replied the inspector. "Charge him and release him on police bail of £100 to appear in court on Monday."

It was almost five thirty. Smigger and Dougie drove slowly past a small supermarket in Walton. Dougie stared long and hard. He watched the cashier sitting idly waiting for a customer. He noticed how close the till was to the door.

"Sound," said Dougie. -"We'll have this."

Smigger parked the car in a side street down the road.

"Have you got any money?" asked Dougie.

"What for?" asked Smigger, reluctant to part with his pennies.

"I'll have to buy something to make sure she opens the till," answered Dougie.

Smigger arched his back and struggled to get his hand into his tight trouser pockets.

"'Ere y'are. Get us a yoghurt," he said, handing Dougie twenty pence.

Dougie laughed. He slammed the car door behind him and set off up a series of back entries, taking great care to avoid the sporadic dog turds.

Smigger's meanness amused Dougie. He knew it didn't matter how much money he brought back, but Smigger would be annoyed if he didn't get a yoghurt or his twenty pence back, he was that tight.

Dougie entered the shop and browsed slowly along the shelves. A young schoolboy was sticking the price tags on tins of peas further up the passage way.

"He must be the Saturday lad," Dougie thought to himself. He watched the cashier ringing up the grocery prices for a young mother.

"Four pounds thirty six pence, please," she chirped as the till pinged open.

Dougie moved on to the freezer. He picked up a yoghurt and peeled the price tag off, taking great care to replace it on the bottom of the yoghurt. Hopefully it would give him an extra bit of time as the cashier looked for the price tag. The manager was nowhere to be seen. He was in the stock room filling in an order form. Dougie glanced to the back of the shop where the meat counter was. The girl threw half a pound of boiled ham into a plastic bag and scribbled the price on the bag with a pencil.

"Oh that bacon looks nice. I'll have half a pound of that," said the customer as Dougie walked past. The girl picked up the bacon and weighed it on the scales.

Dougie placed the yoghurt on the counter in front of the bored cashier girl. She picked up the yoghurt, looking for the price. She found it immediately and rang it up on the till. The till flew open.

"Eighteen pence please," asked the girl.

Dougie fumbled in his pockets, looking for his money. The girl looked at Dougie, waiting for the money. Dougie smiled ineptly back at her. The girl raised her eyebrows and looked away, momentarily, at the clock on the wall.

Dougie's hand flashed out and grabbed the wad of five and ten pound notes. The girl screamed. Dougie was out the door and sprinting towards the entry, clutching the money in one hand and the yoghurt in the other. The manager came running out. The girl was out in the street. She pointed to the entry Dougie had run down. The manager set off in pursuit. Dougie came tearing out of the entry. Smigger started the car. Dougie jumped in, slamming the door behind him. Smigger scorched away. The manager came dashing out of the entry, puffing and panting. He was out of breath. He'd heard the car pull away. To make matters worse he stepped in a large dog turd in the entry.

"Bastard," he cursed as he leant against the lamp post, gasping for breath.

Smigger took his eye off the road and watched Dougie counting the money. "How much did you get?" he asked.

"About fifty," said Dougie winding Smigger up.

"There's more than that there," said Smigger alarmed.

"One hundred and seventy five quid to be exact," laughed Dougie. Eighty five quid each and a fiver for petrol."

"Gis that yoghurt," asked Smigger.

"No," said Dougie, "Here's your four bob back."

Dougie peeled the lid back and took a swig. He smiled smugly at Smigger.

"Bastard," cursed Smigger. "Save us some."

It was eight o'clock that evening when Smigger and Dougie called for Jerry. His mother was ironing a shirt for him.

"Alright Jerry," said Smigger, "What happened?"

"Hundred pound bail. I'm in court Monday morning," replied Jerry putting his shirt on.

"How's that?" asked Dougie.

"Got grassed on," replied Jerry.

"Whitey," replied Dougie.

Jerry nodded.

"It was a nap," replied Dougie.

"What do you mean, you got grassed on?" asked his mother flabbergasted. "I thought you didn't do it."

"Well I did," said Jerry coldly, admitting his slip of the tongue.

"Your father would turn in his grave if he knew he had a thief for a son," declared his mother.

Jerry calmly brushed his hair in the mirror.

"Is it alright if I stay in yours next week?" he asked Dougie.

"Yeah, sound," replied Dougie.

"What do you want to stay in Dougie's for?" asked his mother. "You're in court on Monday."

"I'm not going," replied Jerry. "Me solicitor told me not to."

"Solicitors don't say things like that," replied his shocked mother.

"Mine did mum," replied Jerry, putting his coat on. "Don't worry, I'll give you your hundred back."

Mrs Kinsella sat down in shock.

"Listen mum," said Jerry, trying to explain. "There's never going to be any work in this city anymore. I can't live on the dole, never mind eat shit on the dole the rest of my life. What happens if I have a wife and kids and live on handouts all my life? What kind of a man will I be in the eyes of my kids?"

"What kind of a man will you be if you're in jail?" argued his mother.

"That's a chance you take, mum," replied Jerry. "You said me dad would turn in his grave if he knew I was a thief. He wouldn't. Not if he knew the reason. He'd turn in his grave if he knew a Tory was screwing me. Mrs Thatcher has sold two million people down the river. People of all ages, people who've worked all their lives and people who've never worked plus their kids. People never count them as their victims, do they? Well I'll tell you straight, mum, she's not selling my arse down the river. She's not pimping for me!"

Jerry stalked out of the house followed by his mates. Mrs Kinsella sat down in shock. The lads climbed into the car.

"Bit heavy wasn't it, Jerry," said Smigger.

"Yeah," admitted Jerry, cooling off. "I'm out of order taking it out on me ma. I'm more annoyed with meself than anything."

"Looks like your Joey's in trouble," said Dougie.

Joey was walking along the street. He looked back to the police officer on the beat and muttered some profanity to himself. The officer strolled arrogantly after him. Smigger swung the car over.

"What's up Joe?" he asked.

"I was just walking out the offie eating a Mars bar and the bastard brought me back in to make sure I'd paid for it. He made a right cunt out of me," grumbled Joey.

"Jump in Joey," said Jerry, noticing the policeman taking an interest in the scene. The car pulled away.

"Where are you going?" asked Dougie.

"Nowhere," he replied. "I'm skint."

"I thought you were working?" said Jerry.

"I am," replied Joey. "I'm on one of them poxy twenty three nicker a week schemes. The supervisor suspended me for arguing. They dock your money. I had to tell me Ma I'd brought a pair of jeans for work because I had no money to give her."

"Terrible, isn't it?" said Dougie. "Isn't Maca working with you?"

"Yeah," replied Joey. "He's suspended as well."

"What do you do?" asked Smigger.

"We do painting - Well Maca does the painting. I'm no good at it. I just get the tins of paint for him and sit there reading the papers all day."

"What's Maca suspended for?" asked Dougie.

"Well, you know what Maca's like. If I'm in the shit and he isn't, he's not happy."

The lads laughed.

"What did he do?" asked Dougie.

"He said he couldn't work without his labourer," replied Joey.

The lads laughed.

"You's are cases," said Jerry. "Well Smigger, you've got eighty five quid there, are you gonna give your kid some money?"

Joey's face lit up as Smigger's dropped. The car stopped outside Maca's. Smigger indignantly slipped him two pounds.

"How much? A deuce out of eighty five quid. You fuckin' mingebag," laughed Jerry.

Dougie tossed Joey a fiver. "Give that to Maca," he said.

Smigger was forced to do likewise, much to the merriment of his friends.

"Cor thanks, Smig," said Joey, pocketing the money and getting out of the car.

"I'll tell you what, Smigger," said Dougie. "You're a tight bastard. There's no need for it".

The car pulled away.

Half an hour later the three lads stopped off at a pub on the way to town. Smigger ordered the drinks.

"Three pints of lager please mate."

"What are you going to do then, Jerry, work away for the summer?" asked Dougie.

"You're joking aren't you? Get ripped off working for buttons? No chance!" replied Jerry.

"What are you gonna do then?" asked Smigger, gripping his ale.

"As many snatches as are possible and put it all in the building society. Then I'll console myself with the thought of my nice little nest egg building up while I'm doing my bird," replied Jerry.

"Hey Smigger, there's your Dad," said Dougie, noticing a man sitting with a woman in the far corner of the pub.

Smigger looked round in surprise. His worst suspicions were confirmed.

"Bastard," he cursed. "I haven't seen him since the day he walked out on me ma."

"How long ago was that?" asked Jerry.

"About two years ago," replied Smigger.

"Why don't you go over and say hello?" asked Dougie.

"I hate him," replied Smigger.

"I don't know," said Jerry. "Why don't you go over and say hello. Tell your ma how he is. You might even get them back together again."

"Do you think so?" said Smigger.

"Why not?" said Dougie.

Smigger picked up his pint and walked over to the couple.

"Hello dad. Can I buy you a drink?" he said, taking the couple by surprise.

Mr Smith's face dropped in surprise but it soon turned to one of joy.

"Hello son," he said, shaking Smigger's hand. "This is one of me lads, luv."
The woman smiled. Smigger nodded.

"This is your new mum," declared Mr Smith tactlessly.

"What?" snarled Smigger angrily. "That old stink's not my mother. Look at the fuckin' state of her. She's only an old rip."

Mr Smith made a grab at Smigger in temper.

Smigger stepped back and threw his pint in his father's face, blinding him. Mr Smith stumbled forward over the fallen table, landing at Smigger's feet.

Smigger volleyed his father in the face. His fringe bounced, his nose bled and his glasses flew off from the force of the blow. Smigger attempted to throw the empty pint glass at his father's head. Dougie snatched his arm and put him off his aim. The glass smashed harmlesly on the floor. Dougie dragged Smigger away.

"You fuckin' old bastard" roared Smigger. "I hope you die screaming of cancer."

Mr Smith jumped up to continue the fight but Jerry held him, trying to calm him down.

"Little bastard," growled Mr Smith, blood pouring from his nose.

"Take it easy," said Jerry. "Calm down."

"What kind of son would try to hit his own father in the face with a beer glass," said the woman.

"He only came over because he thought he might be able to get you back with his ma," said Jerry.

The remark knocked the wind out of Mr Smith's sails. He felt ashamed. He hadn't meant to say what he had.

The car drove out of the car park as Mr Smith and his lady friend left the pub. Smigger wound the window down to shout abuse.

"You fuckin' old bastard!"

Jerry put his foot down.

"Shurrup will you Smigger. You should be grateful you've got an old fella," said Jerry.

"My old fella died the day he walked out on me ma two years ago," snarled Smigger.

Mr Smith watched the car disappear into the distance.

Three bouncers stood at the door of a club in town. It was after one o'clock in the morning. A taxi pulled up outside. Three girls alighted, one stopping to pay the fare.

"Hello Joe," breezed the first girl. "Are we alright?" she said, referring to the admission fee.

"Yes, go 'ead," replied the doorman.

The girl walked upstairs into the club, followed by her two companions.

"Who's that?" asked one of the bouncers.

"Mr Russell's daughter," came the reply.

102

Upstairs in the club, the blare of amplifiers was almost deafening. The dance floor was packed. The lights flashed rythmically in time with music, cascading colour and atmosphere around the room. Dougie and Jerry were sitting with two nice girls from Gateacre in a quiet corner of the club. Smigger was at the bar, getting the drinks in.

Two girls from Kirkby watched the drunken youth reach into his pocket and pull out his wad of money. He pushed his way into the bar to get served. Jean looked at her friend. They had obviously found a victim here.

"A large brandy and three halves of lager, please," called Smigger, catching the barmaid's attention.

Jean tapped Smigger on the back.

"Hey mate, will you get ours for us? We're never gonna get served here."

Smigger turned and looked at the girl. He saw the handful of change she'd carefully selected to pay for their drinks, so that Smigger would think that they were skint. His drunken gaze fell on her pretty face, her large bosom and the large nipples prodding through her T shirt and Smigger was in love.

"What d'you want luv?" asked Smigger.

"Two vodka and oranges," she replied, trying to hand him the money, knowing he wouldn't take it.

"No, yer alright," said Smigger, refusing the money.

"And two large vodka and oranges, please luv," Smigger ordered.

Smigger knocked back the large brandy.

"What's your name?" asked Smigger.

"Jean," she replied.

"Where are you from?"

"Kirkby," she replied, as Smigger handed her the drink.

"Where are you from?" she asked, sipping her booze.

"Norris Green," Smigger replied, picking up the three lagers.

"What's your name?" she asked.

"Smigger," he replied. "Even me mum calls me Smigger. Why don't you come and have a drink with us?"

"O.K." she replied with a smile.

Smigger led the way.

Jean gave her friend the nod and laughed. It looked as though they had a right mug here. Dougie saw the nod and clicked what the girls were up to right away.

He watched the party approach.

"D'you clock that Jerry?" he asked.

"No, what?" he asked, turning his attention from his girl.

"Two rip off merchants with Smigger," answered Dougie.

Jerry watched them approach.

"He's a case, isn't he. Screams like fuck if he's got to give their kid a couple of quid, then he gets pissed and lets two skunks put the knife into him."

"Come on, let's get the girls up to dance then we'll get off. They won't rip him for much in the next two minutes - their glasses are full."

103

Smigger reached the table as his mates were departing for the dance floor. "We're just getting up for a drunken shuffle. We'll be back in a minute."

"O.K." said Smigger, sitting down at the table with the two girls from Kirkby.

The slow records were on. The dance floor was full of couples smooching to the romantic music. Russell's daughter was dancing with a very good looking black youth. Her coloured friend was dancing with his friend. Her other friend, a fat white girl, sat disconsolate and alone at a nearby table.

Dougie's girl was called Julie. She had short brown hair and was dressed in a multi-coloured boob-tube and tight pink trousers.

"Who are those two girls?" she asked as they smooched on the dance floor.

"Two scrubbers trying to rip Smigger off," Dougie replied. "If they get their way Smigger will buy their ale all night, pay for the taxi home and he'll be lucky to get a goodnight kiss for his trouble."

"That's terrible, isn't it?" Julie replied.

"We've all got to live. It's hard to have a good time on the dole," shrugged Dougie.

He looked across over her shoulder at Jerry. Jerry clutched hungrily at his partner's buttocks and pulled her closer towards him. He winked at Dougie, signalling that he would be alright with this girl. Dougie laughed.

The girl's name was Elaine. She had auburn hair and was dressed in a short leopard skin coloured dress.

"You must have a few bob living in Gateacre," said Jerry. "What does Daddy do for a living?"

"He's a policeman," replied Elaine.

"Oh, that's nice," lied Jerry, pretending to be impressed.

The record finished.

"Listen, girls," said Dougie. "You's go and get your coats and we'll meet you outside. We'll just go and drag Smigger away from the two skunks. That way there won't be any hassle."

"O.K." replied the girls and set off in the direction of the cloakroom.

Smigger was holding court in the corner.

"So you're not working then, girls?" he said.

"No," replied Jean. "Me dad reckons it's the common market, especially the French."

"Yeah, that's right," agreed Smigger. "We won the war for them. Now they're telling us what we can and can't do. I think we better go over there and smack a few chins."

The girls laughed. Jean placed her hand on the top of his thigh and rubbed it.

"Are you going to buy us another drink, Smigger?" she asked.

"No he's not, you fuckin' old stink," answered Dougie returning.

"Who d'you think you're talking to?" she snarled, as Dougie helped Smigger to his feet.

"You," growled Dougie defiantly.

Jean threw a drink in his face. Dougie's head immediately lashed out and caught her on the bridge of the nose. She fell like a stone. A young man, enraged by the incident, tried to jump on Dougie's back but Jerry knocked him out with one dig. The lad's friends stood back, frightened to do anything.

"Can we have some doormen up here?" called the D.J. over the tannoy.

The three lads pushed their way through the crowd and out of the club. The doormen arrived on the scene. The injured girl lay doubled up on the floor. Her face cut and contorted in agony. She was still unable to get up, despite the attentions of her friend. The young man still lay unconscious.

"Shit!" cursed the bouncer.

The car stopped outside Smigger's house. Smigger got out and staggered up the path.

"See you tomorrow," he drawled.

"We'll pick you up tomorrow morning for the football," called Dougie.

Twenty minutes later the car arrived at Gateacre Drive. Dougie and Julie got out.

"See you tomorrow," said Dougie.

"Give us a ring tomorrow," Julie said to Elaine.

"O.K." she replied.

The car pulled away.

"Friggin' hell, it's not half posh round here," remarked Dougie, looking at the area.

"Shush, you'll wake me dad up," whispered Julie, opening the door.

Dougie followed her into the house and sat down on the couch. Julie went straight into the kitchen and filled the kettle.

Jerry and Elaine arrived outside her father's house. The couple embraced each other and kissed long and hard for a moment. Jerry was the first one to come up for air.

"Are you inviting me in for a cup of coffee?" he asked.

"I'm not that kind of girl," she said, smiling wickedly. "Anyway, I'm not on the pill."

Jerry kissed her again.

"Neither am I," he said. "Mind you, I'm too young to start a family. Good job there's ways and means round that."

Elaine smiled and kissed him again.

"Come on," she purred, "you'll have to be gentle with me."

Jerry followed her into the house. She went into the kitchen and put the kettle on. Jerry stood alone in the parlour. He picked up a photograph of a policeman from off the sideboard. He recognised him immediately. It was P.C. Ash. Jerry's mind flashed back to the beating he received in the back of the police van. His dark mood was disturbed by Elaine floating into the room and tossing her coat on to the armchair.

105

"Is this your dad?" he asked.

"Yes," she smiled, embracing him.

The water boiled in Julie's kitchen. The kettle turned itself off unnoticed. The couple had other things on their minds. They embraced each other passionately on the couch.

Dougie's tongue darted from her mouth to her neck, diverting Julie's attention as he pulled slyly at her boob tube with his free hand. Julie's hands were running riot. One was tangled in Dougie's hair pulling his head towards her as she almost ate him. The other was at the back of his shirt, stroking his back with her long fingernails. Dougie switched his attention to her chest, devouring her left nipple as soon as the boob tube was pulled down far enough. Julie feebly tried to resist, wanting Dougie to force her. Dougie would not be denied. He brushed aside her half hearted efforts to save herself. She began to breathe heavily as she got more excited. Dougie reached down to open her trouser button. Julie snatched his hand and sat up on the couch.

"No"! she said firmly.

"What's up?" asked Dougie in anger.

"What d'you think?" snapped Julie.

"Dunno," said Dougie innocently.

"Time of the month," she explained.

"Shit," cursed Dougie, deflating back on the couch. He said nothing. He toyed aimlessly with one of her nipples.

"Anyway, I had a hard day at work," she sulked.

"Why? What d'you do?"

"I work in a betting office. Today's our busy day."

"What's hard about a betting office?" scoffed Dougie, unimpressed.

"There's this fella who always does £500 and £1000 wins when I'm always busy. I wouldn't mind, he usually loses. He lost £3000 today, said Julie, not realising the information she was giving away.

"Terrible, isn't it," said Dougie. "Some people have got money to throw away. I feel sorry for the manager having to go to the night safe with all that money."

"Oh it's in a nice area," replied Julie. "We don't have any trouble like that."

"Whereabouts do you work then?" asked Dougie innocently.

Jerry was busy making love in front of the fire. He was naked except for his socks. The floor was littered with various articles of discarded clothing. The room was silent except for the gas fire humming low and Elaine beginning to moan in excitement.

"Jerry...Oh Jerry," she whimpered in a half muted squeal, clutching the back of his head as though for dear life. Her legs were spread across his hips and her feet folded over his backside.

"Faster' Faster'" she implored over and over again.

Jerry pumped furiously at her. His brow became beaded with sweat. Elaine moaned louder and louder, became more and more excited.

Jerry pressed on and on, faster and faster. Elaine let out a series of highly excited squeals as her body convulsed in ecstasy. She threw her swirling hips towards him even harder. She whimpered slowly as if she was about to die. Jerry tore on even more vigorously and exploded into a climax with no intention of dismounting her. Elaine's eyes near popped out when she realised he'd ejaculated into her.

"You bastard," she cried. "I told you I wasn't on the pill. "

She struggled and hit out at him but Jerry was too strong. He held her in position until he had finished. Jerry dismounted and quickly began to get dressed. Elaine was almost hysterical.

"You knew I wasn't on the pill. You said you were going to jump off."

Jerry pulled his trousers up and sat on the couch as he put his shoes and socks on.

"Why didn't you jump off'" shrieked Elaine.

"Your dad's a copper. I hate coppers," growled Jerry.

Elaine's chin dropped in shock. She couldn't believe what she was hearing. She sat back on her heels. Jerry continued to dress.

"If you have a little lad in nine months time you can call it Old Bill if you want," growled Jerry. "You bastard!" she shrieked, her large breasts swinging as she hurled a shoe at him.

P.C. Ash woke up in bed.

"Is that you Elaine, making all that noise?" he called inquisitively.

Elaine froze in horror and clutched at her nakedness. Jerry laughed and walked to the front door.

"Does your Dad know you're a slut?" he asked in triumph as he left.

Elaine hurled another shoe at him and missed. P.C. Ash heard the crash and jumped out of bed. Elaine clutched at her naked body when she heard her father's footsteps overhead. Jerry jumped in the car and sped away.

"He does now," he said to himself.

P.C. Ash watched the car speed away and marched into the parlour.

"What's going on?" he asked.

Elaine was panicking, trying to get dressed. She hand't even got her panties past her knees when her father walked in. P.C. Ash froze in horror. His daughter burst into tears and tried to cover herself with a coat.

Teresa's father sat in his armchair reading the newspaper. He turned a page and noticed the light shining in the hall from the landing.

"She still in the bathroom?" he asked his wife.

"Yes," replied his wife, looking up from her book.

"Where's she going?" asked her husband.

"Out with Jerry," she replied.

It was almost eight o'clock in the evening. The traffic was sporadic but gradually growing in numbers as the first of the night's revellers began to come out. The noise of a hackney cab braking to turn a corner, pierced the evening's tranquility. Jerry sat comfortably in the back. He watched a courting couple enter a pub in the Old Swan area as the cab sped past. The taxi driver glanced at him in the rear view mirror and caught Jerry's eye.

"Take your next right," directed Jerry. "This is it here."

The taxi stopped. Jerry stuffed two pounds through the wire grill to the driver.

"Keep the change," he said, getting out of the cab.

Jerry knocked at the door.

"Hello Mrs Sims" he said as Teresa's mother answered.

"Hello Jerry. Come in. She's not ready yet," she replied.

"I won't be a minute," called Teresa, fixing her earrings.

"Hello Mr Sims," said Jerry, walking into the lounge.

"Hello lad," said Mr Sims, looking up from his paper.

"Aren't you going out tonight?" asked Jerry.

"No," replied Mr Sims. "There's a film I want to watch on the telly."

Teresa breezed into the room wearing a green mini-skirt. She picked up her handbag from the table and the couple left.

"Where d'you want to go tonight?" asked Jerry. "The wine bar?"

"No," replied Teresa, "it's too crowded. It's more like a football match than a pub."

Jerry flagged a taxi. "Yeah, you're gonna need a bit of quiet - give you room to faint," muttered Jerry.

Teresa's face dropped. "Why? What's wrong?"

"Lots," replied Jerry. "Tell me," persisted Teresa.

"I'll tell you later," replied Jerry, opening the taxi door for her. The couple climbed in.

It was after midnight.

"We've missed the last bus," declared Jerry, unsuccessfully trying to flag a passing taxi that was already occupied. They began to walk arm in arm along a dark country lane away from the quiet village and its two small pubs that they'd spent the evening in. Teresa had a fit of the giggles as her drunken boyfriend almost tripped them both up. Jerry stopped to get a stone out of his shoe. Teresa hailed a passing taxi. The shrill braking noise preceded the steady thrub of the engine.

"Hurry up Jerry," called Teresa, climbing in.

Jerry was leaning against the wall with his shoe in his hand. He stamped his foot into the shoe and climbed into the taxi. The driver pulled away. Jerry belched. Teresa laughed and rested her head on his shoulder.

"Pig," she said.

Jerry looked at her out of the corner of his eye and farted loudly.

"That you, driver?" asked Jerry with a straight face and a serious voice.

The driver looked at him in the rear view mirror and laughed.

"You behave yourself," said Teresa, punching Jerry in the arm. Jerry pulled a face like a naughty school boy.

The taxi arrived outside Teresa's house. Teresa waltzed up the path, rummaging in her handbag for the key. Jerry paid the taxi and staggered after her.

"Shush," said Teresa, opening the door. "Mum and dad are in bed."

Teresa turned the light on in the lounge and went into the back kitchen. Jerry tossed his coat onto the armchair and lay down on the couch.

Presently Teresa came in with two cups of coffee and a plate of cheese sandwiches.

"Are you gonna tell me now?" asked Teresa, climbing on the couch next to him.

"In a minute," said Jerry, wolfing a sandwich.

They finished their snack. Jerry lay back on the couch staring at the ceiling. Teresa cuddled up close to him and slipped her hand up his shirt, playing with the hairs on his chest as he related the story of the robbery. The story finished. Teresa cleared her throat and asked "Why?"

"You're only young once, girl," said Jerry "I've got to make the grade now before I'm old and decrepit and can't afford my heating bills or any bills in the winter. This government is going to give us nothing, so I've got to take what I want out of life while I'm young and capable. I can't live the rest of my life sweating on a giro."

"It's still wrong," said Teresa.

"I don't want to get into the whys and wherefores of it. I've given it a lot of thought and I know I'm right. If there was a job anywhere doing anything I'd take it - but there isn't. I've got no option."

"What are you going to do about the engagement?" asked Teresa.

"That's up to you," said Jerry. "I still love you and I want to marry you. But this is going to be my life while I get enough money to start my own business. Then I'll give myself up, hopefully get a reduced sentence, come out, get married and have kids and live a normal life. I could have done all that anyway if it hadn't been for that grassing bastard. I still want to go ahead with the engagement, but I can't get married until my troubles are behind me." Teresa's eyes began to well up. Jerry kept staring at the ceiling.

"You're a very attractive girl. Lots of fellas would give their right arm to go with you. All with better prospects than me. All able to give you a better life than I can. You don't need the worry and the hassle you'll get over the next couple of years with me. If you want to stay together we can still get engaged and see how things go. After all, I'm not asking you to jump out of a robbed car with me with your balaclava on".

Teresa laughed.

"Anyway I've got to go now because me head's done in. Let me know what you want to do when you're ready." Jerry kissed her and walked out.

Dougie sat at the back of the court. He watched as Collo and Ged were lead away to the cells. He felt sorry for Collo's girl as she sat there cradling her baby in court. Dougie got up and walked out.

Teresa sat in the works canteen having her lunch. The idle chatter of her friends went straight over her head. Jerry was on her mind. The rest of her life was on her mind. She made a token effort to eat a few chips but couldn't. She pushed the plate away from her.

Jerry was playing the invader machine in a pub down Westminster Road. The pool table was set up behind him. Smigger was at the bar.

"Two bottles of lager mate" he ordered.

Jerry was blasting away on the machine as Smigger walked in with the beer. Jerry was hit by one of the spaceship bombs. Smigger heard the explosion.

"Everyone's blowing you up lately," he quipped.

"I've got one life left," said Jerry. "Go on your break."

The room was silent except for the steady drone of the descending spacemen and Jerry's incessant firing to keep them at bay. There was a loud crack as Smigger broke the balls - a stripe went down. Jerry got blown up and Smigger missed.

"GAME OVER" flashed up on the screen.

"My shot," said Jerry, picking up a pool-cue.

He potted a ball and followed in after it.

"Two shots," guffawed Smigger in triumph.

Just then Dougie walked in.

"It's definitely Whitey who grassed," said Dougie.

"What happened?" asked Jerry.

Smigger was cheating as his friends spoke, he moved his balls over pockets so they were easy to pot.

"They got remanded to the Crown Court for sentence," said Dougie. "They've issued a warrant for your arrest".

Smigger was sneakily potting the balls as they spoke.

"Have you told Teresa yet?" asked Dougie.

"Yes," replied Jerry.

"What's the S.P. - have you finished?"

"Don't know yet," said Jerry. "I give her a bit of time to make her mind up."

"That one," interrupted Smigger naming his pocket for the black.

"What d'you mean, I've only had one shot," declared Jerry.

"Yeah, but you give me two shots," insisted Smigger.

Jerry had to accept it.

"You're a cheat," he said.

"I'm not," said Smigger smirking. "I'm just a great player," he said, lining up the shot.

He potted the black and the white bounced off the cushion and rolled ominously towards the corner pocket.

"Go on you beaut," encouraged Jerry. The white duly obliged much to Smigger's dismay.

Jerry and Dougie roared laughing.

"Bastard," cursed Smigger, hurling his cue down. "I'm going for a burst," he said.

110

"I'm just a great player," Jerry called after him. "You couldn't win a farting contest with a bellyful of beans."

Detective Sergeant Hughes and Detective Constable Holmes arrived outside Jerry's house. Hughes knocked on the door. Mrs Kinsella let them in. It was obvious that Jerry wasn't there. Karen felt uncomfortable under the lecherous gaze of Constable Holmes.

"He's only making it worse for himself," said the experienced Sergeant Hughes.

"I've told him," said Mrs Kinsella.

"He hasn't done nothing," said Karen.

"Where is he?" said Constable Holmes, moving closer.

"I don't know," said Karen, "but I wouldn't tell you anyway."

"It doesn't matter. We'll get him in the end anyway,' said the sergeant. "Thanks very much for your help, Mrs Kinsella," said the sergeant as they walked towards the door.

Mrs Kinsella shut the door behind them.

It was after closing time that night. Jerry and Dougie arrived at Dougie's house and knocked on the door. Mrs Lacey answered.

"Hello lads," she said.

"Alright mum," said Dougie. "Is it alright if Jerry stays at ours for a few days. He's had a row with his mum."

"Yes," said Mrs Lacey, "of course it is. Come in".

"I'll walk you home again Kathleen," sang Mr Lacey, sitting blind drunk in his armchair in the living room. He paused to pour himself another whisky.

Mrs Lacey smiled. "Your dad's having a little drink again. You best go upstairs," she said.

Jerry began taking his clothes off and climbed into bed. He could still hear Mr Lacey in full voice downstairs.

"Your dad's on form tonight," laughed Jerry.

"He's just been made redundant," said Dougie.

"He's been on the ale since he got his ninety days notice. He's forty seven, he's got no trade. He knows there's hardly any chance of him getting a job. He's worked all his life since he left school at fourteen. He can't handle the thought of being on the scrap heap at the age of forty seven."

"I know how he feels," said Jerry. "I can't handle being on the scrap heap at nineteen."

"I can't remember the last time I seen him sober. God knows what he's going to do when the redundancy money runs out," said Dougie.

It was just after twelve o'clock the next day. The two lads strolled round to Jerry's house, ignoring the steady downpour of light drizzle.

111

The lollipop woman was dressed in a white oilskin. Three school girls dressed in duffle coats stood obediently at the kerb. The lollipop woman kept an eye on the traffic and one eye on the three school boys playing off ground tick on the pavement behind her. The lights changed. The lollipop woman planted her stick in the middle of the road. The three girls walked across, three in a line, one of them offered her a sweet as the passed.

"Thank you," said the woman, smiling as she took one. "Come on, you boys," she called to the mischievous boys who ran across the road.

The lights changed. The lollipop woman scurried to the pavement after safely guiding her children across.

Jerry and Dougie had crossed the road and plodded on into the rain.

"Everton are playing West Brom away tonight," said Dougie. "D'you fancy going down there, watch the game and see what we can rob while we're at it."

"Sounds good to me," said Jerry, turning the corner into his street.

A sandy coloured dog crouched disconsolately in the rain outside its master's house. Its tail stood up in defiance as it saw Jerry and Dougie approach. Jerry spotted it first. He shoved Dougie towards it and the dog went for him as Jerry dashed across the street. Dougie swung a kick at it and then dashed across the street after his laughing friend. The dog attacked Dougie from behind, snapping at his heels. Dougie cried out in fear, thinking the dog was going to bite him. It didn't. It turned and headed back to the front gate. Dougie fired a stone after it. The dog darted through a gap in the privet to safety.

"You bastard," cursed Dougie at his friend, laughing and seeing the joke.

Mrs Kinsella was hoovering in the parlour when Jerry and Dougie arrived. She turned the hoover off with her foot.

"The police have been," she said.

"They'll probably call a couple of times and then stop bothering," said Jerry.

"What's that young one's name?" asked Mrs Kinsella. "He gives me the creeps."

"Detective Constable Holmes. They call him Sherlock," replied Jerry.

Mrs Kinsella laughed.

"I'll shoot up and get changed mum," said Jerry. "The less time I spend here at the moment the better."

Smigger was stretched out in bed when Jerry and Dougie called. Young Joey turned his beefburgers over in the frying pan and answered the door.

"Come in lads," he said. "Smigger - Jerry and Dougie's here."

Smigger mumbled something upstairs and turned over.

"Not working today, Joey?" asked Dougie.

"Nah. Me and Maca got the sack yesterday. D'you wanna cup of tea?"

"Yes please," said Dougie.

"What d'you get the sack for?" asked Jerry.

"Messing about," said Joey. "There's nothing else to do. When you're on them schemes you're either getting used as scab labour or there's nothing for you to do at all which means you're only on the scheme to fiddle the unemployment figures. It's just a pisstake."

Joey handed the lads their cups of tea as Smigger breezed into the room, wearing only a pair of jeans.

"State of that," said Dougie.

"Well, what d'you expect knocking for me at six o'clock in the morning?"

"It's eleven o'clock," said Jerry.

"It's six o'clock to me," said Smigger.

Joey returned with a cup of tea and a beefburger sandwich.

"Give us a bite of your butty," said Jerry.

"I'll save you some," said Joey, taking a bite.

"Your Joey's got no luck," said Dougie. "He got the bullet off that poxy scheme yesterday."

"Yeah, me ma's going mad. No dole for six weeks," said Smigger.

"No dole for six weeks that's terrible," said Jerry.

"I was comparing myself with Prince Edward the other day because he is the same age as me. He was complaining about the photographers taking pictures of him while he was shooting grouse. Wish that was all I had to complain about. What does he want to shoot grouse for anyway?"

"Probably been shitting on his ma's washing," replied Jerry.

"Where are you going?" asked Smigger as Joey handed Jerry the last bit of beefburger butty.

"The match," said Dougie.

"Can I come?" asked Joey, his eyes lighting up.

"No'" said Smigger. "You've got no money."

"I'll pay for him," said Jerry, chewing the burger. "He might earn a few quid. He'll need it if he's gonna be short for the next six weeks."

The car sped down the motorway. The countryside flashed by as the car dodged in and out between the sluggish heavy goods vehicles.

Dougie gazed out the window in boredom.

"Have you ever wondered what would happen if we ever went to war?"

"I wouldn't fight for Thatcher," growled Smigger and Dougie agreed with him.

"Maybe things wouldn't be so bad under the Russians," said Joey.

"Shut up, Joey, you're only a stupid kid," said his brother. "Anyway, it won't be the Russians what start it. It'll be 'Ronnie Ray Guns'."

"Yeah," said Jerry. "A typical yank. A nomark with a big mouth. The Ayatollah has already shown him his arse over the hostages."

"See what I see," said Dougie, spotting a wagon advertising Hitachi signalling to turn into the service station.

"That'll do us," said Smigger switching lanes and following the lorry.

The lorry stopped. There was a hard rush of compressed air as the driver braked. Smigger pulled into a parking space and watched from a distance. The

113

driver grabbed his newspaper and leapt from the wagon. He walked towards the the cafeteria area of the service station. Jerry opened the glove compartment and put on a black pair of leather gloves. Dougie was donning his. Jerry pulled a set of bolt cutters from under the front seat.

"What's going on?" asked Joey.

"Just shut up and open the boot when I tell you," said Smigger.

The car rolled up behind the wagon. Jerry and Dougie jumped out. Jerry wrenched the container door open. Dougie leapt up and started unloading boxes of radio cassette recorders out of the back.

"Open the boot and fill it," Smigger ordered his brother.

The lorry driver placed a cup of tea on his tray to wash down the large meal he had selected. He paid his money and turned to find a seat to eat his food. He glanced out of the window and noticed the back door of his wagon swinging in the wind.

"Bastard'" he cursed and charged out of the restaurant. He was too late - the lads were already speeding towards Birmingham.

"How many did you get?" asked Smigger, tearing along the outside.

"Dunno," said Dougie, opening a box.

"Eighteen," answered Joey.

"What are they?" asked Jerry.

"Radio Cassette recorders," replied Dougie.

"They're worth about £300 in the shops," blurted Joey.

"Yeah but there's no plugs on them," said Dougie disappointedly.

"That's alright," replied Jerry. "We'll buy some and put them on in the morning."

"Yeah, but where are you gonna get rid of all them for a good price?" asked Joey.

There was a moment's silence as the three older lads looked at each other.

"Radio City on 194" - the lads burst into song singing the signature tune of the local independent radio station. Every dinner hour the station ran an hour long show called 'Trading Post' when listeners rang in offering goods for sale.

The next day the four lads were sitting in Smigger's house, attaching the plugs to the cassettes.

"It's nearly a quarter to twelve. Hurry up or we'll miss it," said Dougie.

The lads loaded their swag into the car and raced round to a public telephone box. The lads stood in silence as Jerry dialled the radio station. Joey watched in amazement.

The station's receptionist answered.

"Radio City, can I help you?" she chirped.

"Yes luv," said Jerry. "I've got a radio cassette recorder to sell for £100 or nearest offer."

"What's your address and phone number?"

Jerry gave a false address and the phone number of the public phone.

"O.K. You'll be on the air in five minutes. Hold the line."

Jerry put his hand over the phone's mouth piece and gave the lads the thumbs up. The lads were packed into the phone box. Smigger gyrated his hips against Jerry's backside as though they were having sex. Jerry panted and moaned. Dougie burst out laughing.

"You's are mad," said Joey in astonishment.

The receptionist warned Jerry that he would be on the air in a moment.

The D.J. introduced himself and asked what Jerry had for his listeners today. Jerry cupped his hands around his testicles and the lads burst out laughing.

"Who have you got with you?" asked the D.J., trying to get in on the joke.

"Just a few of the lads out of work," said Jerry. "We'll have to be quick before the boss catches us."

"Go on then," said the D.J. with a phoney laugh.

"I've got a radio cassette recorder worth £300. It's almost brand new. I want £100 or nearest offer." "How come you're selling it so cheap?" asked the D.J.

"I'm emigrating to Australia so I'm selling everything except me toothbrush," said Jerry.

The D.J.'s phoney laugh echoed over the phone. And then he read out Jerry's phone number twice over the air.

"Thanks very much and good luck in Australia," concluded the D.J.

Jerry hadn't put the phone down two seconds when it started ringing again.

"Hello," said the caller, "I'm calling about the radio cassette recorder."

"Well just give me your name and address and the best time to drop it round," answered Jerry.

"You've got to be hard faced if you want to get on in life," Smigger informed his younger brother.

It was almost tea time. The lads sat in a leafy suburb waiting for Dougie to return. The lady handed him the money and he turned towards the car.

"That's the last one," said Jerry. Little Joey sat in the back.

"How much are we giving our kid?" said Smigger, not wanting to give him a full share.

"A full chop," said Jerry. "He was with us, wasn't he? Since when have we been Tories ripping people off?"

Smigger started the car. Dougie and Jerry divided the money. Jerry handed Smigger his cash. Joey watched wide-eyed as Dougie handed him his share.

"How much is there there?" said Joey, looking at the thick wad of twenties.

"Four hundred and fifty," said Dougie.

"Bleeding hell. Can I come with you next time?"

"No you can't" said Smigger glaring in the rear-view mirror. "It'll be bad enough if I get collared but if you get caught too I'll really be in trouble."

"We'll give you a shout if we need a lift with anything," said Jerry. "Meanwhile you give your ma a hundred out of that. Tell her you won it on the horses because she'll be a bit stuck for her pennies if you don't get any dole for six weeks."

The car stopped outside Smigger's. The two Smiths got out. Jerry jumped in the driver's seat.

"We'll see you up the pub for last orders," said Jerry, "we're on the arm tonight."

It was almost ten o'clock. Smigger stood alone at the bar in the crowded pub. The band belted out loud music down the other end of the bar. Smigger laughed in his ale. Joey was sitting near the front of the stage, drunk as a lord, with a table full of ale, surrounded by his good friends Maca, Cummo and Stevie.

Paula pushed her way into the bar by Smigger.

"Two halfs of lager please," she called.

The barmaid began to serve her.

"Hello Ann," said Smigger. "I'll get them," and passed the barmaid a pound.

"Hello Smigger," she replied. "How's it going?"

"Alright," replied Smigger.

"Where's Dougie tonight?" she asked.

"Oh he'll be in later on," he replied. "Why?"

"Well between you and me," she said, nodding to her sister Linda, "he's going to be a dad. She's hoping to tell him tonight."

"Well that's good news," said Smigger after being dumbstruck and trying not to laugh.

"I'll see you later, he said.

Just then Dougie, Vicky, Jerry and Teresa walked into the bar. The girls sat down at an empty table while the lads went to the bar. Smigger was almost in tears laughing.

"What are you laughing at?" asked his two friends, tickled by his good humour.

"Oh this is gonna be some crack this," blurted Smigger. "I don't know whether to tell you or sit back and watch the pantomime."

"Tell me what?" asked Dougie laughing.

"Do you remember cakeshop doorway Lil?" said Smigger in between guffaws of laughter.

"Yeah," replied Dougie.

"Well, she's humped and she's waiting to sting you with the good news tonight."

Linda watched the scene from across the room and realised the joke was on her.

"Abandon ship," said Jerry. "Let's get out of here quick."

"Too late," said Dougie, spotting Linda making a bee-line for him.

The band finished playing just as she delivered the first of her broadsides. The whole pub was about to witness the scene.

"I thought you and her were finished," she snarled.

Vicky and Teresa looked up from their conversation.

"Well we're not," rapped Dougie, confronted by the angry girl.

"You bastard. I'm carrying your child," she cried.

"Bollocks," replied Dougie. "It could be anyone's."

The girl went mad. She tried to hit him in the face with her glass. Dougie blocked it and punched her in the eye. The girl went down. People jumped in trying to stop the row. Linda hurled her glass in Dougie's direction.

"Don't think you can shag me and fuck me off," she roared. She was ushered away into the ladies' toilet.

Dougie sat down at the table under Vicky's murderous gaze.

"Well?" she said.

Dougie couldn't look her in the eye.

"Red fuckin' handed," he replied.

"Where did this monumental achievement happen then? Somewhere exotic?"

"Cakeshop doorway," mumbled Dougie.

Vicky nodded to Teresa.

"I'm gonna see this cow. She knew he was my fella."

The two girls headed for the toilet. Linda was holding an ice-cube over her eye.

"What's the idea of going with my fella?" asked Vicky.

"He said you were finished. He said you weren't sexually adventurous enough," Linda replied.

"No, not really," said Vicky. "I've just got more respect for myself to let some one shag me in a cakeshop doorway. Anyway you can have him if you want him. The question is, does he want you. I'll just console myself with the laugh I'll have everytime I walk past the cakeshop."

"Bitch," said Linda as Vicky stormed out.

She picked up one of the drinks Jerry had bought and poured it slowly over Dougie's head. Dougie sat there meekly and accepted it.

"We're finished," said Vicky and stormed out of the pub.

Dougie ran out after her. Teresa went to storm off in a huff after them. Jerry caught her by the arm.

"What's the matter with you?" he asked.

"What about her friend?" she asked, upset.

"You mean Smigger's friend. He takes her home every Sunday."

Outside, Vicky hailed a taxi.

"I was drunk," Dougie pleaded with her. "She doesn't mean anything to me."

Vicky climbed into the cab, slamming the door behind her. Dougie watched it fade away into the distance. Jerry and Teresa watched from the pub step.

"Come on, I'll have to take a chance and stay in our house tonight," he said.

"Have the police been yet?" Teresa asked.

117

"Yes," replied Jerry. "The young one always leers after our Karen. Me mum can't stand him. She said she'd love to throw a bucket of piss over him." Teresa laughed.

"Have you decided what to do over the engagement?" asked Jerry.

"Fraid so," said Teresa. "I'm addicted to you, I can't help it."

"Good girl," said Jerry, squeezing her. "Strange isn't it. I thought it was me that was getting the elbow tonight, not Dougie."

It was almost one o'clock in the morning. Jerry and Teresa lay necking on the couch. Jerry slipped his hand up Teresa's T shirt.

"What do you think I am?" she snapped, angrily tearing his hand away.

An unmarked police car pulled up outside.

"Back door," whispered Sergeant Hughes to his burly detective constable.

"What do you think I am?" growled Jerry. "A bleeding altar boy. I've been going with you for two years and you still haven't come across."

"You cheeky bastard," snapped Teresa.

Jerry clapped his hand over her mouth. He heard the gate squeak outside. He jumped up and saw the car parked outside.

"Shit!" he cursed and ran into the lobby. He could hear the policemen outside. He raced upstairs. The officer heard him.

D.C. Holmes crashed the door in and chased him up the stairs. It was too late - Jerry was out of the back bedroom window and onto the sill. He didn't see the policeman waiting below. Jerry leapt with all his might and landed on next-door's garden shed. The old wooden shed collapsed on impact. Jerry landed heavily on the floor.

"Are you alright son?" asked the burly officer, concerned for the lad's safety after the heavy fall. Jerry pretended to be groggy as the officer helped him to his feet.

Jerry's head lashed out. There was an almighty crack. The headbutt landed full in the officer's face who in turn landed on his backside in the garden. Jerry was away over the garden fence. He blundered through a series of back gardens and then landed running in the street. He was spotted by the detective sergeant. They chased him across two back gardens and watched him sprint across the dual carriageway and disappear into a block of flats whose gardens led onto a huge playing field. The police chased him into the garden flats and gave up.

"It's no use," panted Sergeant Hughes. "He's young and fit and running for his life," he said, looking at the burly officer's cut mouth. "Come on, we'll catch him another night."

Jerry sat quietly in the bushes. He noticed the light on in one of the flats. A fat woman in her early thirties lay awake reading a book. Bored and restless she couldn't get interested. She tossed the book to one side.

"Books'" she said. "What I need is a man."

There was a tap on the door.

"Annie, are you up?" whispered the voice.

118

"Smigger - is that you?" called Annie, jumping out of bed in delight.

"It's me, Jerry," he called through the letter box.

"What d'you want?" she said, half opening the door.

"I'm on the run. The police are after me. Can I stay the night?" he asked.

Annie smiled wickedly. "On one condition," she said.

"Anything," panted Jerry, worried and out of breath.

Annie pulled her negligee over her head and stood fully naked in the doorway all glorious sixteen stone of her.

"Fucks sake," exclaimed Jerry.

Annie grabbed him and pulled him in.

"Come on, you can shut your eyes and imagine it's someone else," she said, closing the door behind him.

Jerry was just out of the shower. He phoned Teresa at work.

"Hello Teresa."

"Hello Jerry. Are you alright?"

"Yeah," replied Jerry. "Sorry about last night. Did the police give you a hard time?"

"No, I just walked out. They were too busy chasing you. I phoned your mum. She's going mad over the front door and the neighbours aren't too happy over their garden shed."

"Don't worry about that. I'll pick you up at one o'clock and we'll choose a ring."

"O.K." said Teresa.

"See you later," replied Jerry.

"Bye," she replied and hung up.

"Everything alright?" asked Vicky.

"Yeah, he got away," replied Teresa happily.

"Well at least one of us is in a good mood this morning. I'm glad Jerry got away. For all his faults at least he looks after you. At least he's faithful."

"I know," said Teresa. "That was a terrible night last night."

"You're telling me," said Vicky grimly. "Four years I was going out with the bastard. I'd have trusted him with anything. Then he shits on me in front of the whole alehouse."

"How many times has he phoned this morning?" asked Teresa.

"Three," replied Vicky. "He can't get it through his thick skull that he's all washed up."

The phone rang. Vicky answered it. "Hello."

"Hello Vicky, it's Dougie," he said.

"How many times have I got to tell you?" she said.

"I just want to talk to you," he pleaded.

"We're finished," she snapped and hung up.

Jerry met Teresa in the town centre.

"Just pick up whichever one you like the look of," said Jerry. "I haven't a clue about rings."

"Come on," said Teresa linking him. "I know the best place to go. There's hundreds of girls in our place always showing off their rings when they get engaged."

"And all the other girls talk about them behind their backs about either how cheap the ring is or how expensive it is," replied Jerry.

"Yes," replied Teresa laughing.

"Cases you's are," said Jerry. "What's the average price that everyone pays for an engagement ring?" asked Jerry.

"About three hundred to four hundred," replied Teresa. "I think the most expensive one I've seen was just over five hundred. Julie McGregor's, out of the accounts department. She's always flashing it and showing it off, because she knows she's got the best. Vicky said it would take a five million pound ring to make her get engaged to the gobshite she's going with."

Jerry started laughing as they approached the jeweller's shop.

"I bet she's not flashing it as much after that. Right, just pick one."

"How much have I got to spend?" asked Teresa.

"Well, I've got about two hundred on me but if you fancy one a bit more expensive we can come back again when I've got some more money," said Jerry solemnly.

Teresa smiled and kissed him. "Two hundred is fine," she said. "It's not the price of the ring it's the man who's asking me to wear it."

Jerry looked deep into her eyes and winked. "I'm only joking," he said. "Will five hundred do you? But we'll have to walk home after that."

Teresa laughed and hugged him. "Oh look at that one," she said, unable to contain herself. "Isn't it lovely?" referring to a £1200 ring.

Jerry looked at the big diamond ring set in gold - even he could see it was a smasher.

"God bless us, it's like going out with the Queen of Sheba. Get looking down there at the four and half hundred tray."

Teresa started laughing. "There's some lovely ones there, let's go in and have a closer look."

"Good morning," the jeweller said, greeting them. "What can I do for you?"

"I'd like a look at your engagement rings around the four hundred and fifty to five hundred range, please," answered Teresa.

"Certainly," replied the jeweller reaching into the cabinet and placing a tray on the counter in front of them.

"Oh aren't they lovely?" said Teresa.

Jerry shook his head. "Women and jewellery," he said.

"I like that one there, can I try it on please," she said, referring to a four hundred and eighty pound ring.

"Certainly miss," replied the jeweller.

Teresa placed the ring on her finger.

"It fits perfectly, she said, admiring it. "Can I have this one?" she said, turning to Jerry.

Jerry ignored her. "I'd like to look at the twelve hundred pound diamond ring in the window, please," said Jerry firmly.

"Yes sir," said the jeweller in surprise and scurried away to get it. Teresa looked at Jerry in bewilderment. The jeweller returned.

"Try it on," ordered Jerry.

Teresa placed it on her finger in silent delight.

"Does it fit?" asked Jerry.

Teresa turned and nodded with a big smile on her face.

"I'd like to make you an offer for this one," he said.

"Certainly sir," said the jeweller.

"A grand cash," replied Jerry.

"I'll just have a word with my partner," replied the jeweller. He whispered to the baldy middle-aged man's ear who was standing next to him behind the counter, serving other customers.

"Yes sir," replied the jeweller. "That will be fine."

Jerry slapped his wad on the table as Teresa jumped on him and kissed him.

Jerry and Teresa sat in a plush restaurant enjoying a romantic meal. The waiter opened a bottle of wine and poured it for Jerry to taste.

"That's fine," said Jerry.

The waiter placed the bottle on the table and left. Jerry poured the wine.

"Don't you think that's a bit expensive," said Teresa dubiously.

"You only get engaged once, girl," said Jerry.

"Yes, but I don't want to end up doing the dishes," joked Teresa.

"Don't worry, I've still got a hundred and seventy left," said Jerry. "I feel great," he said. "It's a pity I've got that bit of porridge hanging over me."

"I wish life was only as complicated as those daft women's in the washing powder adverts," said Teresa, refusing to have a damper put on the night.

"What do you mean?" asked Jerry.

"All they've got to worry about is whether the washing comes out white," she replied. "Me mam and dad are in Manchester this weekend for me cousin's wedding," said Teresa. "They should be gone by the time you take me home."

Jerry kissed her hand and smiled. "Two years courting and a thousand pound engagement ring. It's about time."

Teresa pulled tongues at him. "Don't get smart or I might change me mind."

A taxi arrived outside Teresa's house. She fumbled in her bag for the front door key. She was still a little tipsy and couldn't find the keyhole in the dark.

"Hurry up," laughed Jerry. "If you've waited two years, you can wait another two minutes," she replied. She finally succeeded in opening the door and went in. Jerry went into the front room while Teresa took her coat off in the hall.

"D'you want a cup of tea?" she called.

"No thanks," called Jerry as he fumbled through the assorted collection of records and tapes, looking for some suitable music to play. He slid a cassette into the tape deck. Upstairs the toilet flushed. Jerry sat down on the couch and listened to Teresa's footsteps on the stairs. Presently she sat down on the couch next to him.

"I'm tired," she said.

Jerry caressed her lips with a long slow kiss. "As long as you haven't got a headache," said Jerry, coming up for air.

She punched him playfully in the chest. The couple embraced passionately. Teresa felt Jerry's hand slide slowly up her body to her breast. She leaned back and looked him in the eye. She knew what he wanted. He pressed forward kissing her lips and fondling one of her breasts. She wrapped her arms around the back of his head, enjoying the taste of his mouth. Jerry picked her up off the couch and carried her upstairs to her mother's room. She did not resist. She hung her head meekly against his chest.

Jerry gently bounced her on her mother's bed. He stopped and looked at her, savouring the moment. She lay back and waited for him. His body engulfed her. She felt his hot tongue run from her ear to her neck and back to her mouth while she was vaguely conscious of various articles of clothing being undone and removed. She was soon down to her bra. She stopped him and climbed into bed.

"I'll take that off myself," she said shyly, covering herself with the bed-clothes.

Jerry climbed in next to her dressed only in a pair of boxer shorts. He pulled them off quickly and lashed them blindly across the room. He helped her off with her bra. She rolled the blankets up to cover her naked breasts. Jerry kissed her passionately rolling his tongue around her mouth. She could feel his warm strong hands running tenderly over her body and slowly pulling her panties down. She felt them slide slowly down her thighs. She meekly tried to stop him but Jerry brushed her aside. The panties slid down her legs and over her feet. She was completely naked. Jerry returned his attention to her chest, kissing and caressing her breasts - first one then the other, then back again. She could feel his powerful erection hot against her stomach. Jerry's tongue moved towards the lower part of her body, licking and probing and tantalising her erogenous zones. She moaned shrilly in anticipation. His body pulled the blankets away, revealing her naked breasts. His tongue was tickling the inside of her thighs. She could stand it no longer. She pulled his head up by the hair. He stopped at her breasts for a while before moving on to her lips, his fingers caressing up and down her thighs, probing and tickling. He straddled her hips and guided himself into the right position. He nudged gently against her. She pulled him towards her by his buttocks. She was breathing faster with excitement and opened her legs, gyrating her hips towards him. Jerry watched her face as he felt himself penetrate her. Her eyes rolled open wide as if in pain and shock. He felt her body go taut then relax. She gasped at the top of her voice and her head fell back on the pillow. She nibbled lecherously at Jerry's ear as he slowly made love to her. He buried his head in the pillow as he became more and more excited. His slow careful thrust was over-taken by pure lust as his powerful hips battered back and forth at break neck speed. They were both sweating slightly. Teresa began to feel the same strange sensation building up in her body as Jerry went faster and faster. It seemed strange that it hurt her but she didn't want him to stop. She squealed in excitement. Jerry pulled her towards him by the buttocks. She let out a long cry, twisted in ecstasy. She collapsed back on the pillow - life seemed to have gone out of her. Jerry felt himself coming and pushed even harder. She groaned. He was hurting her now but he didn't care. He tried to time it to the last moment before jumping off. He climaxed up and down her body. He lay beside her, a spent force gasping for breath, his heart almost beating out of his chest.

Teresa lay looking up at the ceiling for a moment, collecting her thoughts. Beads of sweat were gathered on her brow. She turned and rested her head on his chest. He ran his fingers through her hair and noticed the tears welling up in her eyes.

"What's the matter?" he asked gently.

"Shush," she replied.

Jerry cuddled close to her and buried his head in her shoulder.

"Aren't men's things horrible?" she declared.

Jerry didn't reply.

Their heaving bodies began to breathe as one as the young couple fell into a deep sleep.

The bacon and egg chattered back and forth and Teresa lifted them from the pan onto Jerry's plate the next morning. Jerry was on the phone.

The phone rang in Smigger's house. Smigger took his face out of a bowl of Rice Krispies and answered it.

"Hello," he said speaking with his mouth full.

"Hello Smigger, it's Jerry."

"Alright Jerry, where are you?"

"In me birds. Pick up Dougie and I'll see you in an hour."

"Are we doing that one Dougie sussed?"

"Yeah," replied Jerry, "if we can get some suitable transport in town."

"O.K." said Smigger, "see you later.

There was an air of tension in the car as Dougie and Smigger drove up to Teresa's. Dougie didn't speak. Vicky was still very much on his mind. Smigger swung the car over and beeped the horn.

Jerry stuffed a twenty pound note into Teresa's hand as she kissed him goodbye.

"Get some grub, a good video and a few bottles of plonk. We'll have a night in if you want."

O.K." replied Teresa. "See you later."

Ten minutes later the car arrived in a city centre car park. Dougie was still silent. Jerry and Smigger knew his head was done in but they didn't know what to do or say.

"There's one there'" said Smigger, spotting a suitable car."

"No good, it's bugged," said Dougie, spotting the alarm system on it. "Try that Cortina further up."

Smigger pulled in next to it. Jerry approached the car as though he owned it. He pulled a bunch of keys out of his leather jacket and opened the door. He sat half in-half out of the car fumbling through his key ring until he found a key that fitted the ignition. Dougie and Smigger kept a watchful eye for any sign of danger.

Suddenly the car started.

"He's got it," said Dougie.

Jerry closed the door behind him. He reversed out and drove around to the car park exit, followed by Dougie and Smigger. They drove out onto the main road unchallenged.

"Sweet as a nut," said Jerry, sliding a tape into the tape deck and turning the volume up.

Ten minutes later Jerry parked the car in a quiet council estate. He walked through the estate to where Smigger and Dougie were waiting.

"Should be safe until we need it," he said getting into the car.

"Let's go and have a look at the victim," replied Smigger.

The car arrived outside the betting shop.

"I'd better stay here in case she recognises me," said Dougie.

"I hope the info is right,said Smigger. "Maybe she was just trying to impress you.

"Oh she impressed me alright," said Dougie. "Anyway, nothing ventured, nothing gained."

The betting shop was quite busy with a lot of punters putting their bets on before they went to the pub or the football match for the afternoon.

Julie took a bite out of one of her cheese sandwiches. She wiped some crumbs away from the corner of her mouth with her long fingernails as she accepted a bet and rang it up in the till.

"Is that her?" whispered Smigger, impressed. "She's tasty."

"That's her," confirmed Jerry.

"Did Dougie shag her?"

"Said he did," replied Jerry.

"The jammy bastard," replied Smigger.

Just then the manager stood up and started making some price changes on the board behind the bandit screen.

The two lads left the betting shop. Dougie sat in the car deep in thought, almost in a trance. Smigger looked at Jerry. Jerry shrugged. The two lads got back in the car.

"What d'you reckon?" asked Dougie.

"The man from Del Monte - he say yes," replied Smigger.

"What time is the last race?" asked Dougie.

"Quarter to five," replied Jerry. "should give us plenty of time to play footy and get back here."

It was nearly half past five. The betting shop manager was checking his takings with his two clerks. The board marker was sweeping all the discarded betting slips up from the floor.

Outside the three lads sat patiently up the street in their stolen car. Presently one of the clerks and the board marker left. The lads watched them cross the road. Dougie's mind wasn't right.

"Talk to me. I can't concentrate. I've let that cow do me head in," he panicked.

Jerry leant forward and growled down his ear.

"Banged up in a cell twenty three hours a day. Some old homme pulling the head off himself every time you use the piss bucket. Screws spitting in your dinner. An old pensioner getting ready to snuff it wearing a stupid wig and cloak made out of his old girl's front curtains giving you four years. Are you gonna get us all nicked, you cunt."

"I'm alright," said Dougie.

"Here they are now," said Smigger watching Julie and the manager step out of the betting shop. They turned to lock the door. The boys donned their balaclavas.

"Are you sure you don't want a lift?" asked the manager.

"No thanks," said Julie, "I've got some messages to get on the way home."

"O.K." said the manager, turning away and noticing the robbed car pulling up. The two bandits flew at them.

"Don't hit me'" screamed the manager, and handed Jerry the bank wallet as he was cornered against the wall. Jerry snatched the money and the two stick wielding thugs fled back to the car which sped away. It was all over in seconds. The manager slid down the wall clutching his chest.

"Oh my God," he said, bursting into tears.

Julie ran into the road stopping a car.

"Get the police. There's been a robbery," she shrieked at the top of her voice.

The stolen car swung left and sped along the main road towards a roundabout. Jerry ripped his balaclava off and checked to see if they were being chased. Smigger threw the car down a gear and shot into the flow of traffic around the roundabout. The car darted inside a lorry and flew away up the street across another junction and into a suburban street. There was no sign of pursuit.

"Slow down, act normal, we're away," stated Jerry.

They turned left into a side street and parked the car. They stashed the weapons and balaclavas into their sports bags.

"Leave nothing in the car," said Dougie.

"Let's take it easy. The police won't even be at the scene yet," said Smigger.

The lads got out and walked back into the suburban street. They crossed a main road and went down a flight of steps to where their own car was waiting.

The three lads walked into the pub where the rest of the team were already drinking.

"Where've you been?" asked Docker, the team manager.

"Had to pick up a few bob I won on the horses, Dock," replied Jerry.

Smigger and Dougie looked at each other and smiled knowingly.

"We'll count the money in Dougie's later," said Smigger. "Then we'll go into town on the sniff."

"Yeah, that'll do me," said Dougie.

"Drop me off at me birds on the way," said Jerry.

His two friends looked at him in amazement.

"Her mum and dad are away for the weekend, we're having a nice meal and a night in," he explained.

"Staying in on Saturday night with your bird. You're getting serious aren't you?"

"We're getting engaged soon. I spent a grand on an engagement ring yesterday."

Smigger looked at Dougie. "They never learn, do they?" he said, shaking his head. "

I'm saying nothing," said Dougie, "after the state the other one's got me into."

"Oh you'll get her back or another one, after a bit of time goes by," said Smigger. "I bet you she's not too happy about the situation either."

"I don't know what you're taking the piss for anyway," said Jerry. "At least I'll be marrying a virgin. I'm not getting stuck with a second hand fanny like you'll end up with."

"Second, third, a million and first - they're all lovely to me lad," replied Smigger.

"Why don't you get yourself a steady bird Smigger?" asked Dougie.

"Steady bird. I've got about twenty of them already. There's no such thing as an ugly woman to me, big, fat, small, thin, whatever - I love them all. There's just something about each individual that drives me wild. But I think I'm nuts. I go mad to bonk them but once I have I hate them."

"Fucks sake," said Dougie. "I believe the Yorkshire Ripper started off like that."

"No, he's right" said Jerry. "I can understand why"

"What d'you mean?" said Dougie.

"Well keep this dark. This is between us and it's not to go any further." Jerry took a sip of his pint. "I wasn't going to tell anyone about this. D'you remember the other night when I butted the copper and got away through the back gardens? You'll never guess where I spent the night."

"Where?" asked his friends.

"Big Annie's," admitted Jerry, laughing to himself. "You dirty bastard' She's one of mine," said Smigger.

"You never," said Dougie. "She's about twenty stone."

Jerry nodded his head. "I did," he said, "But wait till I tell you. I seen the light on and knocked on the door, two o'clock in the morning. D'you know what she said?"

The two young men shook their heads.

"Smigger - is that you?" called Jerry, impersonating her.

The three of them burst out laughing.

"Anyway, if she's anything to go by it's no wonder you hate them after you've bonked them."

"Why?" asked Dougie.

"Well you can imagine what the price of bed and breakfast was for the night?"

"Yes," said Dougie," go on."

"Well," said Jerry," I'm riding her and she starts moaning and groaning and then she comes out with "Empty those bags!".

The lads started laughing.

"I'm looking round while I'm riding her, looking for some rubbish bags I thought she wanted me to put out. Next thing she's got me by the back of me head, pulling me hair, swearing and effing and blinding at me."

"I taught that girl everything she knows," laughed Smigger.

"Then she started scratching me back, digging them big nails of hers in. It wasn't the fact that me bird might see the scratch marks, it was just the fact that she was hurting me."

"What did you do?" asked Dougie, enthralled.

"I butted her right in the fuckin nose and give her the hammer all night."

"What did she do when you butted her?'' asked Smigger.

"She called me a kinky bastard" replied Jerry, roaring with laughter. "I said that'll give you something to fuckin shout about. There was no way a woman can get the better of me, no matter how big and strong they think they are. It's amazing the more of a bastard you are the more they love you. She was like a kitten in the morning, purring with pleasure. I was growling like fuck. I thought the police had me bird down the station and I'm lying in bed with this animal. I kicked her in the shitter said make me breakfast you fat bitch. D'you know what she said?"

The lads shook their heads and giggled in anticipation.

"You're the best shag I've ever had, you can come here anytime they're after you."

Smigger's face dropped. His pride was hurt.

"She never said that," he protested.

"She did," declared Jerry.

"Anyway," answered Smigger, "I never shagged her. I made love to her."

It was almost eight thirty p.m. The lads had counted the money, showered, shaved and were dressed to kill. Dougie was driving the car to Teresa's to drop Jerry off. He and Smigger were going on to town for a night on the tiles.

"Four grand. Not bad for a day's work," laughed Smigger, watching the scenery fly by.

The music blared out of the speakers of the car. The boys were jubilant, in fine fettle after the day's success. Suddenly Dougie slammed the brakes on.

"What the fuck" said Smigger, bouncing back in his seat.

Dougie was out of the car and running across the street towards a young man and woman.

"Shit," cursed his friends, diving out the car.

It was Vicky with her new boyfriend, a lad from work. She heard the car screech to a halt and saw Dougie dive out the car with a look of murder on his face.

"Run'" she shouted to her boyfriend.

The lad tried but Dougie was on him. Dougie piled in with his hands and feet. The lad went down under the onslaught.

"You bastard!" screamed Vicky, diving at Dougie and clawing at his face.

Dougie lashed her to one side. She landed on the floor in a heap. There was a hole in the knee of her tights. Dougie landed another frenzied kick before Jerry and Smigger grabbed him and dragged him away. Dougie struggled like a wild man.

"I'll kill you! You bastard! She's mine!" he roared.

Vicky picked herself up off the floor. She grabbed one of her stilletto heels and attacked Dougie in a wild temper with it.

"You bastard! she cried in fury and hit Jerry over the head with it.

Smigger dragged Dougie away. Jerrry put his hand on his head and saw the blood on his fingertips while he was restraining Vicky.

"I'm sorry about this girl, try and get the right swede next time," he said, rubbing his head.

Tears of rage poured down Vicky's face.

"I'll kill the bastard," she screamed.

"Looks like you're going to have to," said Jerry, running to give Smigger a hand. "It doesn't look as though he's going to be reasonable about this."

It was Sunday morning. A man was walking his dog in the park. He could hear the sound of laughter coming from three young girls playing under a tree. It was a lovely autumn day, a perfect break from the week's slog at work.

One little girl held a buttercup under her sister's throat.

"Let's see if you like butter," she said. It was a game children played. If the sun reflected off the flowers onto the girl's throat it was said she liked butter. If not, vice versa.

Hostile eyes watched dangerously from the bushes. His hair was unwashed and he was unshaven. He watched the man with the dog disappear out of sight, his burning gaze returned to the young girls.

"It's my turn now," said the youngest girl, holding the buttercup to her sister's throat.

"Ahh'" she screamed, sensing the evil presence next to her.

She turned and saw Marty standing about a yard away from them, indecently exposing himself.

The little girls screamed and ran. Marty stood there chortling to himself. The man with the dog came running. Marty turned with a smile right in to a big crashing right hand blow from the man. Marty cowered and screamed like a young boy as the kicks and blows rained in on him. A police car arrived. Battered, bleeding and crying like a child, Marty was bundled into the back of the police car.

It was Monday morning. Cummo was upstairs in the shower. His mum was downstairs in the dining room, polishing his best shoes. His father poked his head from behind a newspaper at the breakfast table.

"Shouldn't he be at school?" he asked his wife.

"No. He's got the day off because he's got an interview with the D.H.S.S." replied Mrs Cummins.

"Well if he gets that he should have a job for life. It looks as if there's going to be enough people around here on the dole for life."

Cummo bounced down the stairs.

"Thanks mum," he said, slipping his shoes on. "I better go or I'll be late."

"Good luck son," called his mother.

Cummo arrived outside the Social Security building in Stanley Road dressed in his best trousers, jacket and tie and sparkling shoes. He looked at the tall building and fixed his tie.

"Me bottle's gone," he said to himself. He took a deep breath and walked into the building.

"I've come for a job interview - Cummins," he told the smiling receptionist.

"Upstairs on the third floor," replied the receptionist, smiling pleasantly.

Cummo got into the lift with an attractive office girl. He nervously watched the lift ascend through the fluorescent floor numbers. It stopped suddenly. They were there. The girl could sense his nervousness.

"Just give your name in to the girl down the corridor. Relax, you'll be alright," she reassured him.

"Thanks," replied Cummo nervously.

Cummo walked up to the office girl.

"Er, hello. I've got an interview for a quarter to ten," he said, handing her his appointment card.

"That's fine," replied the girl. "Just take a seat in the waiting room."

"Thanks," replied Cummo and turned to sit down in the small room.

There were three school leavers already in the room. Two girls and a boy. Cummo sat down and looked at the attractive girl opposite. She was smartly dressed and sat quietly. The boy next to her had a smart suit on and spoke confidently to the equally confident heavy girl sat next to him.

"How d'you think you'll do in your exams?" asked the fat girl.

"I got 'A' grades in my mock exams before Christmas, so I'm quite confident," he said.

Thought so - fuckin' knowall, pondered Cummo. Looks like daddy's got a few shilling as well going by the suit the bastard's got on.

"What about you?" asked the youth.

"Yes, I'm expecting to do well in my exams. We even got taught how to answer properly and how to put ourselves over properly in interviews," replied the heavy girl.

Cummo winced. He closed his eyes and looked at the fluorescent light on the ceiling.

I'd put you over the table and kick you in the shitter, you fat cow, Cummo thought to himself. I wonder how many jobs are going and how many people are applying for them. Are all the other applicants going to be as well educated as these two.

The other girl looked at him and smiled. She was obviously as nervous as him.

"Mr Backhouse," called the receptionist. "They're ready for you now."

The youth got up. "This is it," he said.

"Good luck," proffered the heavy girl.

Drop dead, thought Cummo.

The time on the clock ticked slowly by. The sweat began to gather on the palms of his hands. Cummo waited patiently as it turned ten o'clock.

"Mr Cummins, they're ready for you now," chirped the receptionist.

Cummo was shown into a room where a man and woman were sat at a table waiting to interview him.

"Good morning," said the man, "I'm Mr Goodfellow. This is Mrs Brown".

Cummo shook hands with them both.

"Pleased to meet you. This is my reference from school," he replied, handing it to the man.

"Please take a seat," said Mr Goodfellow, referring to the seat in front of their table.

"Thank you," said Cummo and sat down.

Cummo regarded the man as he sat down and watched him read his reference. He didn't like the look of him. He was in his mid to late thirties with thick grey shoulder length hair and plenty of dandruff on his jacket to go with it. Cummo looked at the flared trousers and the raised heel and out of date shoes the man was wearing. His worst fears seemed about to be realised.

Oh no! Cummo thought to himself.

"That's a good reference," breezed the man, handing it to his colleague.

Cummo watched her as she read it. She picked her glasses up from her chest. They were strung round her neck on a silver coloured chain. She was in her early fifties with grey hair tinted slightly purple. She handed Cummo his reference back.

"Very good," she said with a phoney smile.

"Thank you," replied Cummo, taking it back. Shit, I've got no chance, he thought, seeing right through the woman.

"How many exams are you taking?" asked the man.

"Seven G.C.S.E's," replied Cummo.

"How many are you expecting to pass?" asked the woman.

"All of them. Grade One, I hope," replied Cummo.

"What d'you think of violence at football matches?" asked the woman.

Cummo paused. What's that got to do with anything? he thought. The cow must think I'm a football hooligan.

"It's a disgrace," replied Cummo, "but what can I do about it? I don't go to the game."

"Have you ever seen any trouble?" asked the woman.

"No," replied Cummo. "Only on the telly."

"What hobbies do you have?" asked the man.

"Reading, chess, swimming -" for fuck's sake don't say horse-riding, he thought "and, er, tennis."

"What kind of books d'you read?" asked the man.

Cummo shrugged his shoulders. "Anything interesting", he replied.

The man wrote something down. Cummo watched him.

"D'you think Coronation Street is an old woman's programme?" asked Mrs Brown, waving her pen and looking at the clock on the wall behind Cummo.

"In what way?" asked Cummo.

"D'you think it's suitable viewing for a wide range of people or just old women?"

Cummo paused for a moment. He knew he hadn't got the job. Why should I sit here and subject myself to this crap from these two clowns just because I want a job, he thought.

"Coronation Street is suitable for a wide range of people with the mentality of old women," answered Cummo, finally losing his temper. "I came here looking for a job and you two ask me dickhead questions about football hooligans and Coronation Street. My career, if I'm going to get a career, the rest of my working life is on the line here in the hands of two clowns like you. You need some dandruff shampoo and a haircut, you scruffy get," he said to the startled man. "And you haven't even got the manners to look at me when you speak to me," he said to the woman. "Then you ask me dickhead questions about Coronation Bastard Street. What makes you think I want to work for a pair of cunts like you. Stick your job up your arse," he roared, slamming the door behind him.

The man sat looking at the gawping woman next to him.

"I don't think he likes Coronation Street," said the man, drily.

The lift arrived and Cummo stepped in.

131

Joey and Maca staggered out of the pub drunk, laughing like two lunatics. It was just after ten o'clock. The young lads had been in the pub since opening time that evening. Joey stopped laughing.

"D'you see what I see?" he said, pointing to a moped parked in an alley across the road.

Maca looked at him and burst out laughing again.

"Are you going to give me a lift home?" he asked playfully.

Joey was halfway across the street. He fired a key in and pedalled like mad down the alley, being pushed by Maca until the bike started. The engine spluttered into life. Joey turned the moped around. Maca climbed on the back. Joey drove up the entry while Maca swung wild kicks at the bins that had been left out for collection the next day.

The bike shot across the road and round the car park behind the pub and out past the off licence against the flow of traffic. The noise of the engine and plumes of smoke filled the air. The young lads hanging around outside the off licence roared with laughter.

"Hey Maca, your kid's got a robbed bike?" called Sykesy to his friend.

The youngsters were laughing at the antics of the two drunks on the stolen moped. Then it got serious.

Maca spotted the police car first.

"Shit, it's the old Bill," he cried.

Joey shot away down the lane with the police in pursuit. The police closed in on the moped. It was far too fast for them.

"This is Charlie Victor One in pursuit of two youths on a stolen moped down Stopgate Lane. Over."

"They're too fast for us," yelled Maca, looking back. "Bump on the side and hit the back gardens."

Joey sped across the road against the oncoming traffic and onto the pavement. He charged across the grass verge but lost the back wheel on the wet grass. The two lads and the machine slid across the wet grass. Joey was up and running. Maca was up and running but lost his footing and fell. He regained his feet and started running again but the first officer felled him with a rugby tackle. Joey was into the front gardens and pursued down the entry between two houses by the second officer. He vaulted over the door and shot up the back garden and flew over the back yard wall, cutting his hand on the broken glass set in cement along the back wall. He landed in the safety of the darkness of the girls' school playing field and ran for his life. The policeman vaulted the door and landed on the bin, sending himself sprawling. He clambered to his feet and ran to the back garden wall. He thought better of trying to clear it, preferring to stay in one piece instead.

"Bastard" he cursed.

He returned to the car. His colleague had Maca in the back of the police car.

"What's your friend's name?" the officer asked.

"I don't know him. He just offered me a lift home!", lied Maca.

"Where's your crash helmets then?" asked the officer.

Maca shrugged.

"I'll ask you one more time. What's your friend's name?"

Maca looked at him in the eye and then stared out of the window.

The blow landed across his mouth, cutting his lip.

"You can't do that," said Maca.

"Can't I son?' said Constable Ash. "Cut lip - you got that when you fell off the stolen bike son. Wait till I get you to the station. You'll tell me your family tree, never mind your friend's name."

"I'll tell you fuck all,'' growled Maca defiantly.

Maca sat alone in the cell in his bare feet. The two policemen walked in and handcuffed him behind his back and stood him in the corner of the cell.

"What's your friend's name?" asked Constable Ash.

There was no answer. The officer stamped on his toes. Maca roared at the top of his voice and stood in the corner on one leg.

"What's your friend's name?" asked the officer again, showing no mercy.

There was no answer. The officer stamped on his other foot. Maca screamed in pain and went down. The officer watched him writhe around the floor on his back.

If I stay on the floor and keep me feet in the air they can't stamp on me toes, thought Maca.

"Brave little bastard, isn't he?" said Ash coldly to his colleague.

"O.K. Smartarse, one last chance. You either tell us the name of the driver or we'll charge you with driving it with no insurance etc. etc."

"I wasn't driving it," said Maca.

"We'll say you were," replied Ash. "What difference is one dickhead to another to us?"

Maca stared at him in disbelief. He knew the man was serious.

"Fuck you," Maca defied him.

Ash blasted him in the stomach with his size ten boots. Maca gasped in pain.

"Foul mouthed little cunt, aren't you?" said the constable sarcastically. "Who's the judge going to believe - you or us?"

It was morning break in school next day. The fourth year girls had finished their gym lesson and were pouring into the changing rooms and the showers. Stevie and Cummo stood against the wall in the school playground.

"I believe Maca got captured on a robbed bike last night. They reckon he broke a couple of his toes when he wrapped up," said Stevie.

"Poor bastard," said Cummo. "Liverpool will fuck him off now for getting in trouble with the police. His dad will kill him."

"What happened at the interview yesterday?" asked Stevie.

"No good," replied Cummo. "You should have seen the two pricks who interviewed me."

"Something will turn up. Never give in to the bastards, no matter what," replied Stevie.

There was a loud bang and a scream and a football thudded against the ventillator shaft for the girls' changing room and smashed it. The ball bounced down and the young lads continued with their football match.

Steve put two and two together with the scream.

"What do you mean?" asked Cummo.

"The fourth years are in the shower. Quick, give us a bunk up."

Stevie climbed onto Cummo's shoulder and peeped through the hole. "Fuckin hell," stammered Stevie.

"What can you see?" gasped Cummo excitedly.

There were four naked girls in the shower and a lot more were coming and going.

"Tits and fannies' everywhere," blurted Stevie.

"It's my turn," pleaded Cummo.

"In a minute. I've only just got here," argued Stevie.

"Who can you see?" persisted Cummo.

"Burnsey's bird," answered Stevie.

"Who? Vera Howard?" said Cummo.

"Yes," said Stevie. "They're not tits. They're melons. Nipples like cups and saucers.'

"What's her fanny like?" pleaded Cummo.

"Oh, you want to see the growler on her. Fuckin big mat of hair," enthused Stevie.

"Let me have a look," cried Cummo.

Vera wiped the soap out of her eyes and spotted the peeping tom.

"Ahh!"she screamed. "You wait, Stevie, you wait"'

She made a dash out of the shower for the changing room. There was panic and pandemonium everywhere. Girls screaming and running, others trying to cover their modesty, then running. Stevie fell off Cummo's shoulders with laughter and landed heavily on the ground.

"What are you two boys doing?" asked the teacher on playground duty. The lads didn't answer. The teacher heard the pandemonium and the angry girls' screams.

"You dirty bastards," called one girl hysterically.

The teacher looked coldly at the two boys. "Quite," he said. "Headmaster's office."

The two lads trudged along the corridor to the headmaster's office.

"You bastard," cursed Cummo, laughing. "I'm gonna get the stick now and I didn't even get a blimp".

Stevie burst out laughing.

The bell rang for the end of playtime and the kids lined up in their different classes. Vera Howard was speaking to her boy friend, Tony Burns, a stocky dark haired lad.

"O.K., O.K." he could be seen saying from a distance, trying to placate her. Cummo stood outside the headmaster's office.

"Looks like we better have a new cock of the school tonight," said Cummo.

"What d'you mean?" said Stevie.

"Burnsey's bound to do something and I can't fight him. If you don't do him in he'll kill me."

Stevie burst out laughing with a fit of the giggles.

"You fight him - you got all the blimps," moaned Cummo.

"Don't panic," said Stevie. "It's been on the cards for ages. He's a bullying bastard, it's about time someone gave him a hiding."

The various classes were filing past the office, some along the corridor, some up the stairs to their various classrooms. The fourth year girls filed past upstairs.

"You dirty bastards."

"You perverts," harangued the angry girls.

"You wait," said Vera Howard.

"I think she loves you," said Cummo out of the corner of his mouth.

Stevie doubled over laughing.

Burnsey's class filed past upstairs.

"Behind the shops four o'clock," he growled at Cummo, pointing his finger.

"He never seen nothing," growled Stevie. "If you want to see someone see me."

Burnsey glared at him. "Four o'clock behind the shops," he agreed.

"She was standing there for ages rubbing her tits for me. She knew I was watching. She only started panicking when the other girls spotted me!" said Stevie, going through the motions.

The fight near started there and then. Burnsey tried to go for him but was stopped by his mates because of the approach of the teachers.

"Was she?" asked Cummo astonished, when they had left.

"No'" said Stevie. "I was only saying that cos I hate the bastard. Remember he battered me when I was in the first year. I'll get him back tonight."

"You two boys - into my office," said the headmaster sternly.

The headmaster pulled a cane out of his cabinet. The two boys stood there on parade, heads bowed, hands behind their backs. Upstairs the classroom door was open in the fourth year girls' class. They could hear the terrible scolding and thrashing strokes of the cane landing. Even the girls winced as they counted the number of strokes of the cane. They looked at each other in silence, feeling sorry for the boys. The beating ended. Presently the two boys arrived in the room. Cummo had his hands under his armpits, his eyes were near popping out trying to hold back the tears. Stevie shook his hands vigorously and blew on them. He pulled the seat of his pants away from his backside as he walked into the classroom followed by Cummo.

I'd just like to apologise to the girls, sir," Stevie told the class. "I'm sorry if I upset any of them."

The girls sat in silence. Cummo was obviously in great pain, he couldn't talk, he was trying to keep it all in.

"Well Cummo, what about you? Did you think it was worth it?" asked the teacher.

"No sir," gasped Cummo, blowing on his hands.

"Why's that?" asked the teacher.

"I never saw nothing," answered Cummo.

There was a giggle of laughter around the class and then silence as the teacher turned sternly on them.

"And what about you boy?" said the teacher, turning to Stevie who was much tougher than Cummo.

"I think I'm in love sir," he replied, trying not to laugh.

The teacher looked at them for a moment. "Go on, get back to your class," he said.

There was a buzz of excitement around the school for the rest of that day as news of the big fight spread. Come four o'clock the pupils, boys and girls alike, of all ages, flocked to the wasteland behind the shops where for generations the pupils had settled their differences.

Cummo walked up to the shops with Stevie, surrounded by a posse of excited schoolkids.

"Watch his head. It's fast and rock hard," warned Cummo.

Stevie nodded, saying nothing.

"Kick him in the balls, you've got him then," advised Cummo.

"D'you want to fight him for me?" asked Stevie drily.

"No," replied Cummo bemused.

"Well shut up then," answered Stevie.

A huge crowd of schoolboys had gathered on the wasteland behind the shops. Burnsey was already there with some of his mates. He passed his girlfriend his coat. Stevie took his coat off and fastened his laces tight. Burnsey rolled up his sleeves.

The two lads began squaring up. The crowd was silent in anticipation. Burnsey smiled at Stevie, trying to throw him off guard. He leapt forward kicking and punching. The crowd burst into voice in a crescendo of noise, shouting encouragement for their own particular favourite. Stevie met the charge head on and traded blows with his hands and feet. The partisan crowd bayed, pushing and shoving at each other to get a better view. Burnsey landed a butt that cut Stevie's nose. Stevie fought him inside, kneeing him in the groin and following it up with a heavy right hand. Burnsey managed to trip him as he came forward catching Stevie by the hair and volleying him in the face as he landed. Stevie swept Burnsey's feet away.

"Go on Tony," roared Vera hysterically.

"Kill the bastard'" screamed Cummo.

Burnsey landed on top of his adversary. Stevie kicked him off. The two youths struggled to their feet. Burnsey snatched up a piece of garden fence and came at Stevie with it. He broke it across Stevie's shoulder and followed it up with a head butt. Stevie flew back against the shop wall. Burnsey came forward onto a powerful kick in the groin. His body doubled up under the blow. Stevie brought his head smashing against the brick wall. Burnsey yielded under a heavy attack from Stevie's hands and feet.

"I've had enough" he cried.

"I'll tell you when you've had enough ," growled Stevie, smashing half a house brick onto his head. Cummo dragged Stevie away still snarling.

Vera ran over to Burnsey, crying her eyes out. "D'you think she's worth it?" roared Stevie.

"D'you think she's worth it? I've seen everything and she's worth fuck all."

"You bastard," bleated Vera.

Cummo dragged Stevie away up the street, waiting for him to calm down.

"D'you know what?" said Cummo.

"What?" said Stevie.

"She's a right cow if she doesn't give him his hole after that".

It was almost midnight. Teresa got out of bed dressed in a short seethrough negligee. She checked her bedroom door. The local radio station's midnight show, the peaceful hour which played smoochy music for all young lovers, was on the air. She walked to the window and watched the cool spring wind blowing fallen leaves down the street. The window was open. She wondered to herself whether he would come tonight.

Jerry parked the car. He looked furtively around to check no-one was looking. He flitted quickly and quietly over a fence into the back gardens. A house dog barked momentarily in the distance. Jerry crouched in the bushes. Teresa sat up in bed. Jerry shinned up the drainpipe to the gutter and stepped in the window. Teresa smiled lovingly at him and watched him undress without saying a word.

He hopped into bed next to her, and kissed and hugged her. Teresa snuggled up to his chest. Jerry tried to lift her negligee off.

"Stop it," said Teresa angrily.

"What's the matter?" asked Jerry, knowing something was wrong.

"Nothing," sulked Teresa.

"Listen, whatever it is I'm on your side," he said.

"I could be wrong," said Teresa. "I think I'm pregnant."

Jerry smiled at her. "So what's bad about that?"

"Me dad will kill me," she said.

"No he won't. I won't let him. I can easy get us a flat, we can do it up nice and move in together," he said.

"How can you do that?" she asked, liking the idea.

Jerry winked. "Trust me," he said.

137

Saturday night arrived. The young couple had hired the local community hall to announce their engagement. A large buffet was spread out in front of the stage. A couple of tables had been set aside as a display of the presents the couple had been given by their guests. Dougie, Maca and Karen were working behind the bar, giving out the free drinks. Little Maca and his mates were collecting the empty glasses. Teresa and Jerry were at the door greeting their guests.

Joey came to the bar and ordered three pints of lager and three whiskies.

"You'll have three pints of lager and that's it," said Dougie. "Slow down or you'll be pissed before the night's even got going."

Vicky walked in with her new boyfriend from work. She handed Teresa a gift and kissed the happy couple.

"Thanks for coming," said Jerry.

"This is Tony, he works with us," replied Vicky, introducing the new boyfriend. He was a thin good looking lad with a moustache.

"Pleased to meet you," said Jerry, shaking his hand. "What would you like to drink?"

"Pint of lager," said Tony.

"And" said Jerry, waiting for Vicky.

"A bacardi and coke please."

"Pint of lager and a bacardi and coke please," ordered Jerry at the bar. His sister Karen served him.

"Dougie," said Jerry.

"I know," replied Dougie. "I seen her."

"This is me and Teresa's night - don't spoil it for us".

"I won't let you down," said Dougie.

"She's only doing it to get you jealous," piped up Vicky's brother, Maca.

"It's working," replied Dougie.

Karen handed Jerry the drinks, listening to the conversation.

"Kick her head in and get back with her," advised Maca.

"Tch'" butted in Karen. "The men round here are all cavemen," she laughed.

The buffet was finished. The lights dimmed and the disco started with a slow, smoochy record. Jerry got up to dance with Teresa. Her father asked Jerry's mum to dance.

"Me dad's having a good time," said Teresa.

"I know," said Jerry. "He's just been lecturing me for ten minutes about paying phone bills, lecky bills and rude awakening bills."

Teresa laughed. "He's pissed," she said. Her father had been hammering the whisky all night. Vicky was up dancing with Tony. Karen could see the hurt in Dougie's eyes though he was trying to disguise it.

"D'you wanna dance?" she asked. "Love to," he smiled.

Vicky's expression changed to a glower as she watched them walk on to the dance floor and begin to dance. Karen was a very attractive girl.

138

Vicky felt someone pulling at the back of her dress. It was her baby brother, little Maca. He stood there with a pile of pint glasses stashed under his arm.

"Vicky, our Maca said where did you get the cardboard cut-out from?"

"Tch," replied Vicky and glared at Maca who leant over the bar with a big smile on his face.

Just then a big hand crudely grabbed a big chunk of female backside on the dance floor. The girl leaned back in fury and belted her assailant across the face.

"What was that for?" asked Smigger innocently as the girl stormed away and the boys at the bar fell about laughing.

"She's married, you daft cunt," explained Jerry, dancing next to him.

Smigger returned to the rest of the laughing men at the bar. It was the lads from the football team.

"She wants me!" he declared unperturbed by even more hoots of laughter.

It was the end of the evening. Jerry got up on the stage.

"I'd like to thank everyone for coming. The caretaker has got to close the hall now but there's plenty of drinks back at our house. Everyone's welcome. And if anyone's still hungry there's a pan of scouse and loads of bacon ribs and peewack soup on the go. If anyone's got any transport we need a lift getting all the leftover ale back the house. Thank you."

The drink was stashed in the back kitchen at Jerry's house and the party was in full swing.

"Me mum's took me dad home," said Teresa to Jerry.

Suddenly there was chaos in the parlour. Docker was up in the middle of the floor dancing with a pint on his head.

"How's your Albie doing Jerry?" asked Billy Smith, Smigger's big brother.

"Sound," said Jerry. "He couldn't get leave to come home for the engagement but he said he'll be home for the wedding."

"Me and him used to be best mates before he joined the army. D'you remember the time he used to work on the buses as a bus conductor. He was a mad gambler in those days. He stopped the bus outside the betting shop one day to see how his horses had got on. He'd done his wages in the lot. D'you know what he done?" said Billy in fits of laughter.

"No, " said Jerry laughing.

"He put all his bus money on the favourite on the next race and it fell at the first fence. He just walked out of the shop and gave the driver his empty money bag and his ticket machine. Tell them I've packed in," he said. The two men rolled laughing.

The lights were dimmed and the music played softly. Joey's legs started going as he leant against the wall. He slowly slipped down it onto his haunches in a deep drunken sleep, still clutching his empty glass. Tony was kissing the face off Vicky on the couch. Dougie swallowed a large whisky and poured another one. Karen watched him. His jealousy was beginning to show. She noticed one of the local girls wearing red shoes taking a purse from a blue handbag that was left alone at the end of the couch.

"Strange," thought Karen, but dismissed the idea, her attention taken by Dougie walking out of the room with the half bottle of whisky.

Smigger was sitting chatting to one of Teresa's friends from work. She was a poser, a real stunner. The only problem was that she knew it.

"What d'you do for a living?" she asked him snottily.

"I'm at university studying computer electronic engineering. I'm only home for the weekend for Jerry's engagement party."

"Oh are you?" said Cherry, all of a sudden interested.

The one thing that always impresses a poser is an intelligent man who earns plenty of money - so that they can spend it all for them and be even more of a pain in the arse, thought Smigger.

"I'm a computer programmer," said Cherry, beaming. "Isn't that a coincidence?"

"Are you?" said Smigger, as if in surprise. I know, you daft cow. I asked Teresa before, so I could lay the right patter on you thought Smigger to himself. "Listen, I've got to go back to Oxford tomorrow, but I might be back up next weekend. How would you like to go for a drive in my new car. Say out for a meal in a rather exclusive restaurant I know out in the country."

"Well," said Cherry, delighted.

"Don't be misguided by my intentions," said Smigger. "It's just that I very rarely meet a woman as beautiful as you, with intelligence and the same interests as me. I'm sure we could have lots of stimulating conversations together."

"That'll be great," said Cherry, her poser's act beginning to fall. "What college d'you go to at Oxford?"

"Er, Jesus Christ," replied Smigger.

"Really," replied Cherry.

"Yes," replied Smigger. "That's what the dean said when I arrived. Would you like another drink?"

"Cherry, your taxi's here," called Teresa.

"O.K." she called.

She picked up her blue handbag from next to the couch that matched her blue shoes.

"I'll give you my phone number and you phone me next time you're in town."

Her face dropped as she rummaged through her bag.

"Me purse - it's gone'" she panicked.

Karen recognised the blue bag and her gaze fell instinctively on the local girl with the red shoes who now had a red bag over her shoulder.

"You cow'" she screamed at the top of her voice. "Robbing fuckin purses in our house."

She punched the girl in the face and they grabbed each others' hair and fell to the floor, screaming and fighting. Mrs Kinsella separated them.

"Right, what's going on?" she demanded.

"She's been robbing purses'" shrieked Karen.

"No I haven't," argued the other girl. "There's my bag, I haven't got any money." She handed Mrs Kinsella the bag. Mrs Kinsella rummaged through the bag.

"There's no money here," she said, looking at her daughter.

"I seen her," insisted Karen. "Red shoes blue bag, that's why I noticed her. The purse was black."

"That's right," said Cherry.

"O.K. upstairs," ordered Mrs Kinsella.

Teresa, Vicky, Cherry, Karen and Mrs Kinsella frogmarched the girl upstairs.

Jerry looked at Dougie and Smigger.

"Just leave it"' Docker told everyone. "The women will sort it out."

"Take your clothes off," said Mrs Kinsella.

"No'" said the girl.

The other girls held her while Mrs Kinsella stripped her. The clothes came off one at a time, dress, blouse, bra. The girl struggled to get away. There was nothing.

Mrs Kinsella noticed the bulge in the front of her panties. She pulled the girl's drawers down and pulled the money out from them. The girl stopped struggling.

"What's this?" Mrs Kinsella growled triumphantly.

There was no answer. just a look of guilt.

Mrs Kinsella handed Cherry her money and punched the thief in the eye. She dragged the screaming, almost naked girl downstairs by the hair and flung her out into the front garden. The girls tossed her clothes after her.

"Go on now, fuck off," Mrs Kinsella told the sobbing girl. "And don't come back."

The party resumed again and everyone settled back to enjoy the drink and music.

Dougie watched Vicky canoodling on the couch again and disappeared invisibly out of the room. He couldn't stand it any more.

"Docker, have you got a minute?" asked Jerry.

"Yes Jerry, what can I do for you?" replied Docker.

"You know I'm on me toes?" said Jerry.

Docker nodded.

"There's a chance me missus might be pregnant. You know all them councillors down the labour club - d'you think you can get her a flat as an unmarried mum or something.'

"Might be able to," said Docker. "But they're grabbing bastards. It'll cost money

"Here's fifty," said Jerry, handing him a fifty pound note. "Tell him there's another fifty when he gets the flat. But keep it dark, I want to be able to hide there safely with all these bastards that are after me."

141

"Don't worry, I'll sort it out for you," promised Docker.

Dougie sat down under the window in Jerry's room. He hadn't bothered to put the light on. He took a swig of his whisky and peered into the darkness before him. The drink was eating his defences away. He didn't have to hide his hurt and jealousy here - no-one could see him.

He began to build a joint of canabis. He finished it and lit the reefer, taking a long drag on it. He sipped his whisky deep in thought and said nothing.

Karen walked into the room.

"Are you alright?" she said, sitting next to him in the darkness.

"I'm fine," said Dougie. "And what about you, hardcase. Any lumps or bruises?"

"No," laughed Karen.

"D'you wanna drink - pass us that glass," said Dougie. He poured her a drink.

"Euk - that's horrible," she said, tasting it and pulling faces.

Dougie laughed. "Go on, have a pull on that," he said, offering the joint. "It won't do you any harm."

She puffed nervously on the end of it as Dougie held it for her, and started coughing.

Dougie laughed and put his arm around her, hugging her against his chest.

"How come you're not courting yet?" asked Dougie, "a lovely girl like you."

Karen smiled and looked him in the eye. Then looked away, saying "you haven't asked me yet."

Dougie smiled and looked back at her. "Well, I'm asking you now," said Dougie gently.

"Ask me when you're sober and I'll think about it," she answered cheekily.

Dougie kissed her softly on the cheek. "Looks like it's going to be pistols at dawn," said Dougie.

"What d'you mean?" said Karen.

"Me and your Jerry fighting over you," laughed Dougie.

The party was drawing to a close. Most of the guests had left or had crashed out.

"Everybody's welcome to stay," announced Jerry. "Make yourselves comfortable. I'll see you in the morning."

He and Teresa strolled off arm in arm to bed.

Jerry put the light on in his room and found his sister asleep cuddled up to his best friend. He didn't know whether to be angry or what to do. Teresa pulled him by the arm.

"She's a big girl now. She can look after herself. Let it run its course," she advised. "Come on, we'll sleep in her bed."

"O.K." agreed Jerry. "It's been a strange old night."

It was Monday morning. Maca and Joey knocked at a door on the old council estate. Docker answered it in a vest and pair of trousers.

"Hello boys," he said, taking the piece of toast out of his mouth.

"Have you got them ladders you said you'd lend us?" said Joey.

"Come on lads, round the back," said Docker, leading the way. He dragged two ladders out that were laying next to his garden fence. "I've got buckets and chamois leathers for you, anything you want.

"How do we start?" asked Maca.

"I've got a list of streets for you where they haven't got a window cleaner. Just knock on the door, ask if they want their windows washing. If they do just write the address down in the book and come back to clean them the next week."

"How much do we charge?" asked Joey.

"I'd start off at forty pence for now. That's cheaper than anyone else. You charge more for doing shops and offices, even schools."

The two lads looked at each other and smiled.

"If you want to make money - you've got to work for yourself."

"You sound like a Tory," said Joey. "I thought you were a socialist."

"I'm sociable," replied Docker, "with a few pints in me. Just keep thinking every five houses - that's two pound for us, if you work hard you can't go wrong."

Half an hour later there was a knock on a door. A woman answered it.

"Hello missus," chirped Joey. "D'you want your windows washing?"

"How much," asked the housewife, weighing up the plucky youngsters.

"Forty pence," replied Joey.

"Go on then," she said. "Make sure you do a good job."

Cummo sat lolling back in his chair watching the flies buzz round the fluorescent light in the classroom.

The class was discussing pre-marital sex during its biology lesson. Cummo looked at the clock - the time was dragging.

Another two weeks in this dump and I can sign on then. No sign of work after doing five years in this hole.

"Right then, " asked the teacher. "What d'you think of sex before marriage?"

Jill Armstrong, the class bike, put her hand up and said "I think it's wrong sir. I think you should save yourself for the man you marry because if you don't you get a bad name."

Cummo blew his fringe out of his eyes and turned his attention to Mary Hills' large breasts. He watched them protrude massively out of her chest, filling her clean white blouse.

I wonder exactly where her nipples are, he asked himself. If you draw a line across each of them, say corner to corner, the nipple should be about an inch below where the lines cross.

Timmy Garvey put his hand up. He was the only lad in the class still to reach puberty.

"Sir, I think sex before marriage is right," he said. "You only get a bad name if you're a girl. You get a good name if you're a lad!"

143

I wonder how big her nipples are, thought Cummo. Are they bright pink or dark crimson red. Are they small and pert or like football studs with crowns like fried eggs.

Mary felt his eyes burning into her. She pulled her cardigan over her breasts and scowled at him. Cummo smirked to himself.

"And what are you laughing at, Cummins?" growled the teacher.

I'm sick of this bastard, he's always trying to make a show of me, thought Cummo.

"You must have a very childish mind laddie if you can't indulge in a meaningful adult debate without sniggering like a little schoolboy every time a rude word is mentioned," shouted the teacher.

The class replied with muffled laughter. Cummo stood up. He'd had enough.

"Is this a meaningful debate?" he growled. "Miss Bang at it making herself out to be a virgin and soft arse who's frightened to take his undies off in the shower because he hasn't got any hair on his dick yet making himself out to be a stud."

"No I'm not you -" roared Jill amid the chaos and laughter.

"Yes sir, she is, I was with her last night," said Stevie.

The teacher fired the chalk duster at Cummo and missed. He rushed down the class in temper. Stevie leapt up and turned their desks over. The teacher stopped in his tracks. Stevie was no Cummo. He knew a young lion when he saw one. Stevie pulled his false teeth out of the front of his mouth and tucked them in his top jacket pocket.

"Want a fight cunt? Fight me!"

The teacher knew not to provoke him. He stood in shock staring at him.

"I'll stick that cane so far up your arse you'll be wearing it as a lump on your head to keep your cap on," he warned him.

"I'm finished with school. I can sign me name on a bastard giro. Looks like that's all I need to know for the rest of my life. I'm not putting up with this crap no more," said Cummo.

"And me," said Stevie.

The two lads strolled out past the teacher to the front of the class. Stevie turned at the door and flicked his tongue in and out of the gap between his teeth.

"See you later baby," he called to Jill, who fired a text book at him as he dodged out the door.

It was three o'clock on Sunday morning. A blue Cortina with its headlights dipped cruised slowly along the gravel path towards the big house. The car stopped at the front door. It was Russell's daughter Angie returning home after a date with her boyfriend, the good looking black man she'd been dating since Jerry and Dougie had the fight in the night club over the two girls trying to rip Smigger off. She leaned across the car and kissed his lips.

"Good night Larry," she said, "thanks for a lovely evening."

She got out of the car and watched it pull away. She turned to the house and noticed the light on in her mother's room.

"Shit - me mum's still up," she cursed, flitting into the house.

Mrs Russell stood looking out of the window. The noise of the approaching car had woken her from her uneasy slumber.

"She's been going with this new boyfriend for a while now. She seems quite attached to him. Going by what I've just seen in the driveway he seems to be a gentleman. But three o'clock in the morning is no time for a seventeen year old girl to be coming in. I think it's time we met this new boyfriend. What d'you think?" she asked her husband.

Russell grunted and turned over, pretending to be asleep.

"What d'you think?" she persisted, wanting an answer.

"We'll sort it out in the morning, now turn the light out and let's get some sleep," he growled. "I've got to be up in a few hours."

Angie came down for breakfast the next day. Her mother was waiting for her.

"Where's me dad?" she asked.

"He's gone to play golf," answered her mother. "I'm not happy about the hours you're keeping, young lady. We haven't even met this new boyfriend of yours. We don't know anything about him."

"His name's Larry, he's from the South End near Toxteth and he's coming to pick me up to take me out today. You can meet him then if you want," said Angie.

"O.K." replied her mother.

Larry arrived outside the house later that day. He stubbed a cigarette out in the ash tray and fixed his hair in the rear view mirror. Angie opened the front door of the house.

"Come on in, me mum wants to meet you," she called.

Mrs Russell was pushing her hair into place in the mirror when she heard them approach.

"Mum, this is Larry," said Angie.

Mrs Russell's happy face dropped when she saw the good looking black man.

"Pleased to meet you," said Larry.

"Oh my God. He'll be home any minute now," blabbered Mrs Russell. "Go on, you go and have a good time," she said, sinking back on the sofa.

Russell entered the driveway in the back of his Rolls Royce as Angie and Larry were leaving. Russell's eyes near popped out.

"Am I fuckin seeing things?" he growled, seething with rage.

"No boss," answered his driver quietly.

Russell stormed into the house, slamming the door shut behind him. His wife ran to hide.

"My daughter's going with a fuckin monkey," he roared at the top of his voice! "What's she gonna give me for a grandchild, a bastard chimp?" He snatched up the nearest phone and began dialling, slobbering with rage.

A frail old lady was busy cooking Sunday dinner in a small back kitchen. She was a widow who lived with her only son. She walked to the bottom of the stairs and called him in a shrill voice.

"Anthony! Your dinner's ready."

There was no reply. She opened the oven door and took out a roasting dish full of roast potatoes. She could hear the heavy footsteps of her son overhead. She fussed her way into the dining room to make sure she'd laid the table properly. A lavatory flushed upstairs. The old woman satisfied herself that everything was all right and returned to the kitchen. The running water in the bathroom stopped. She came back carrying a roast shoulder of lamb on a stainless steel salver.

"Hurry up Anthony!" she called.

Animal made his way downstairs. His mother was in the back kitchen when he arrived in the dining room. He turned the television on to watch the football. He was a huge monster of a man dressed only in a vest and a pair of trousers. He stood well over six feet tall and weighed twenty stone. He wore thick glasses and had a thick unkempt beard. At forty six years of age it was no wonder he'd never married.

His mother smiled lovingly at him and placed a huge meal in front of him.

"Thanks mum," he said. He dispensed with the conventional use of the knife and fork, and began to tear at the joint with his bare hands. Wolfing lumps of meat off it and stuffing roast potatoes in his mouth. He stared intently at the

television. The phone rang. Animal stood up and wiped the meat juices and bits of potatoes from his mouth. He burped and answered the phone.

"Hello Mr Russell," he said. "Yes boss....yes boss..." and hung up.

"Mr Russell got some work for you son?" asked his mum.

"Yes mum," he replied, sitting back down.

"Tonight?" she asked.

"No mum. Tomorrow night," he answered, continuing his meal.

It was Monday night. The barmaid in a pub in the south end of Liverpool tilted the pint glass at an angle to stop the pint she was pouring from becoming too frothy.

"One pound thirty," she piped, placing the pint on the bar next to another pint she'd just poured. She rang the money up in the till and gave him his change.

"Looks like we're in for another boring night, Albert," she said.

In the corner an arm appeared from behind a Liverpool Echo its owner was reading and disappeared again with the pint. After taking a drink the man returned the pint to the table. Further along from the man sat two workmen in overalls.

"In for a crafty one boys?" she called, "some job you've got."

Several men stood at the bar drinking, some of them had lunchboxes with them.

"Nightshift again lads?" she asked.

"Yes Mary, just steeling ourselves before we go in," answered one of the men.

"You've got to be anaesthetised before you go to that place on the night shift, never mind steeling yourself." The man laughed.

One of the four youths in the corner put money in the juke box. His friends were playing pool.

"Missed'" laughed one youth, holding his cue.

Larry hung his head over the table. "It was the sudden noise of the juke box putting me off."

His friend lined up his shot. A red Jaguar pulled up outside.

"That's the car," said Mad-dog to Bombhead, referring to Larry's motor.

Animal and Mad-dog walked towards the pub. Sydney stayed in the car. Bombhead began smashing Larry's car up with a sledgehammer. Animal and Mad-dog watched his efforts for a few minutes then entered the pub.

The people inside the pub were getting curious to know what the smashing noise was outside when Animal and Mad-dog walked ln. Everybody in the pub except the barmaid was black. The regulars looked up in surprise. They knew trouble when they saw it. The man in the corner peeped nervously from behind his newspaper.

What do these two giants want, he thought to himself.

The men at the bar eyed each other nervously. Mad-dog and Animal stared ferociously around the pub. Larry and his friends stood in silence and shrugged at each other. No-one knew what was going on.

Mad-dog and Animal said nothing. The four youths were the only young men in the pub. Animal knew it was a young man they wanted. The two monsters looked at each other in agreement, both thinking the same thing.

Toby continued chalking his cue in silence. If these men want trouble they can have it, he thought to himself as Mad-dog and Animal approached.

Mad-dog produced a photograph from his top pocket and examined the young men's faces. He nodded towards Larry, passing Animal the photograph. Animal nodded in agreement.

Larry almost had twins. Mad-dog grabbed him by the throat. Larry squealed in fright as he saw the powerful set of yellow teeth coming towards his face. He grabbed desperately at Mad-dog's bearded chin, vainly trying to keep the powerful jaws away. Some of Larry's fingers inadvertently slipped into Mad-dog's mouth. Larry screamed in pain as Mad-dog gnawed hungrily at them.

Larry's friends expected trouble and were quick to react. Toby smashed his cue across the back of Mad-dog's head. Animal lunged at him but had to stop and duck as Chukta hurled a pool ball past his head. He jumped on the pool table and dived at him. Animal stopped him in mid air with a fist like a ham shank. Chukta hit the deck, already unconscious as Elvis swung a cue at Animal's head. Animal warded the blow off with his forearm. The cue smashed on

147

impact. Animal caught him by the back of the head and smashed his face against the pool table. Then he sent his dazed adversary flying head first into the wall with a sickening thud. Elvis hit the deck, lights out.

Seeing his pool-cue smash ineffectively against Mad-dog's head did not deter Toby. He snatched up a pool ball and jumped on Mad-dog's back, beating him around the head with it. Mad-dog let Larry go, grabbing Toby by the scruff of the neck in the same instant. He pulled Toby up onto his shoulder and fired him up into the air. Toby grabbed vainly at the light bulb flex and landed heavily like a broken doll across the now out of order juke box. Mad-dog spun round - where was Larry? Animal had him face down across the pool table.

The fight was over in seconds. They held him down one arm each.

"What have I done man?" pleaded Larry, almost in tears.

Both men began smashing his knuckles in a frenzied attack with pool balls. The barmaid winced and burst into tears. Larry screamed in agony.

Animal jerked Larry's head back by the hair. Mad-dog pressed his horrible screwed-up face in front of Larry.

"You won't be putting your horrible black hands on white girls no more will you lad? Stay away from the white girl, nigger, understand?" he emphasised.

"Yeah man, I understand. I won't see her no more," he whimpered.

Mad-dog nodded to Animal. He'd got the message. Animal dragged Larry to his feet and smashed a vicious right hand into his face. Larry landed unconscious on his back, his legs splayed invitingly. Animal blasted him in the privates.

Mad-dog looked round the room.

"Is that it?" he asked the customers.

The men at the bar turned meekly away. The two workmen hurriedly began a conversation. Mad-dog's gaze fell on the man in the corner. The startled man disappeared again behind his evening paper.

"That's it," answered Animal. They started towards the door.

"You pair of bastards," blurted the barmaid in tears.

Mad-dog stopped and stared at her. She froze in fear. What had she done?

Mad-dog laughed like a crazy man and walked out.

Bombhead was still smashing away on the roof of the car with the sledgehammer in a lather of sweat. Animal sneered, pleased at the state the car was in. Bombhead stopped, panting for breath. Mad-dog signalled to him. He jumped down from the car and the three men got in the Jaguar and drove away.

"Drop me off at the Chinky's, Sydney, I'm starving," said Mad-dog.

"You must spend a few bob in that place. You're never out of there and you eat like a horse," replied Sydney.

"Fuck that," said Mad-dog in alarm. "I never pay."

Mad-dog sat alone at a table in the Chinese restaurant, an array of Chinese dishes before him. He dispensed with the chopsticks and unceremoniously battered into the food with a soup spoon.

The owner peeped at him from the kitchen door.

"He always come here never pay," he said, "soon we go bust if he carries on like this."

His son looked at him. "He come here no more I fix," said the young man, pleased with himself.

"What have you done?" asked the father sternly.

"Plenty toilet I fix not now later."

"You put laxatives in meal? You stupid boy, he find out he come back and wreck the place."

"He no find out father," said the young man.

The owner looked at Mad-dog and watched him gorging himself.

"I hope so," he said.

Two hours later the night was quiet and dark. The only light on in Mad-dog's street was his toilet light. "Oh! Ow! me arse is on fire," moaned Mad-dog as the water splashed beneath him. "I'll kill them flat faced bastards for this!"

It was late the following night. The audience from the theatre flocked out into the street. Henry Fraser, a bespectacled man in his mid thirties, strolled arm in arm with his wife.

"It's been a wonderful evening darling," said his wife, kissing him.

"How would you like to round it off with a nice Chinese meal and a good bottle of wine?" he asked.

"I'd love to," she said.

Twenty minutes later Henry sat quietly in the corner of the restaurant. The waiter poured the wine and left them alone.

The couple smiled lovingly at each other.

"Happy anniversary," they chorused, clinking their glasses as Mad-dog burst through the door wielding a pick axe handle. A startled waiter dropped his tray of meals in fright. Mad-dog crashed his pick axe handle down on a table that smashed in bits. The four young men sitting there panicked in fright as their meals flew everywhere.

Mad-dog was attacked by two young Chinese men. He whacked the first one across the head with the pick axe handle. The second aimed a revolving karate kick at his jaw. Mad-dog snatched the man by the ankle and lobbed him out of the window. Sydney sat outside in the Jag. He shook his head and laughed as the waiter came flying out the window into the street. Mad-dog tore up a table that was bolted to the floor and fired it over the bar at the optics.

Mad-dog stormed into the kitchen. A meat cleaver flew past his head and embedded in the door. The owner's son picked up another missile but Mad-dog whacked him across the skull before he could throw it. The owner picked up a wok full of cooking food and threw it in Mad-dog's face. Mad-dog roared

149

in pain at his scalded face. He caught the old man by the back of the neck and dipped his face into the open flame that the wok had been cooking on. The old man screamed and rushed blindly about holding his burning face. Mad-dog surveyed the carnage. The damage was done. He strode towards the door. The waiter who had dropped the tray of food attacked him with a kitchen knife. Mad-dog caught him by the arm and squeezed it. He leered at the stricken man. He bent forward and bit the tip of his nose off and spat it out

"I say'" said Mr Fraser, horrified,-rushing over to remonstrate with Mad-dog. Mad-dog flung him to one side. He landed in a heap on the table in front of his wife.

Mad-dog got into the car and drove off. Fraser burst into the street and scribbled down the registration number.

Inspector Benson watched Mad-dog being bundled into the cell.

"Well sergeant," asked the inspector.

"The Chinese people won't talk, sir," said Johnson. "But an accountant who was eating at the restaurant has positively identified him and given a full statement as to the attack."

"So we've got him?"

"Yes sir," replied Johnson.

Mitchell was at a topless photo session with his schoolgirl model when the phone rang.

"Damn'" he cursed, coming away from his camera.

"Hello," he said, answering the phone. "Tomorrow morning. Same deal as the last time. What's the name and address?" he said, writing it down.

The next morning Mr Fraser left the house to go to work. He climbed into his car. Mitchell sat across the street, taking photographs.

Russell sat in his office surrounded by Sydney, Animal, Bombhead and Mitchell.

"He's not the type who can be frightened easy," said Mitchell. "He's one of these fellas who's too clever for his own good."

"What does he do?" asked Russell.

"He's an accountant," replied Mitchell.

"No form," asked Russell.

"Nothing really. He's got an indecent exposure against him, he got caught having a pee in the car park coming home drunk from a student rag when he was at college. It goes on his record as a sex offence, but it's nothing we can use against him."

The gravedigger kicked off his wellington boots and walked into the house. He sat reading the evening paper waiting for his tea. There was a photograph of Mr Fraser in the paper.

"Accountant witnesses gangland protection battle," was the headline. Michael-Edward's wife walked in and put his tea on the table.

"C'mon love, it's ready," she said.

Michael-Edward flicked his paper as he got up and saw the advert in the back. "Specialists work required."

Two days later Michael-Edward sat in his hut eating a cheese sandwich. He pulled his new dossier out from the drawer. The name printed on it was Henry Fraser. The strange atmosphere settled round him again and he could hear the choir of angels begin singing to a crescendo agaln.

Russell sat having a business lunch with Mr Bletchley, his lawyer, in one of Liverpool's finest restaurants.

"Excuse me one minute, Cyril," said Russell. "Must go to the little boys' room."

He walked to the toilet, unzipped himself and began using the urinal before him.

Suddenly there was a gun fitted with a silencer under his throat.

"On your toes," advised the man in a Belfast accent.

"It's you," said Russell nervously. "Keep looking straight ahead at the wall. If you see me I'll have to kill you. Now we wouldn't want that, would we?"

"What's wrong?" asked Russell.

"I do God's work," said Michael-Edward fanatically,

"You get me evil men and I send them to hell where they belong".

"Yes," said Russell terrified, trying to humour the psychopath.

"Well then. You tell me in one second why you want me to kill this man because he's a good man or I'll put your brains all over that wall in front of you."

"You mustn't have read his record," blurted Russell quickly. "He's a child molester. Little boys. Look at his record."

Michael-Edward's face changed. That answered everything.

Russell was in a cold sweat and gasping for breath.

The door opened and Bletchley walked in to use the toilet. There was nobody else in the room. Russell near collapsed.

"Oh my God!" he cried.

"What's the matter?" asked Bletchley.

"Let's get out of here," spluttered Russell. "I'm gonna have to find out who this bastard is."

Mr Fraser sat reading the paper at the breakfast table the next morning with his wife and two young sons.

"Are you taking us the baths today after school dad?" asked young Peter excitedly.

"Yes son," replied his father.

"Don't speak with your mouth full Peter," scolded his mother.

Mr Fraser looked at his watch and realised he was late.

151

"You two be good boys for your mother, and I'll see you tonught. He kissed his wife and left the house.

Michael-Edward watched him coldly from down the street in his Escort van. Fraser got into his car and drove away. Michael-Edward started the van and followed him, unaware of the predatory eyes that were following him.

Mitchell walked out of the alley into the street with his zoom lens camera draped round his neck and down his fat belly. He watched the van drive away out of sight.

Fraser hooked his pen into his jacket pocket.

"That's enough for today'" he said to his secretary, closing the folder in front of him.

"Taking the boys swimming tonight?" asked his secretary.

"Yes," replied Fraser. "Every Thursday regular as clockwork."

Mr Fraser arrived outside his sons' school. The youngest, Peter, was leaning against the wall waiting for him. His tie was slung untidily around his neck. He looked up at his father through a pair of thick National Health glasses.

"Hiya dad," he called, climbing into the back of the car.

"Hello son, where's Roger?" asked his father.

"Don't know," said Peter as Roger came running up the road, carrying a heavy sports bag.

"Sorry I'm late dad," shouted Roger, climbing into the car.

Michael-Edward watched the scene from down the street in horror, as he saw the two young boys get into the car. He was taking a bite from an apple as he watched. He stopped in mid bite, Russell's words ringing in his ears.

"He's a child molester. Little boys".

The Frasers arrived outside the baths.

"Can you dive off the high board dad?" asked little Peter.

"Easy," replied his father, paying their entrance fees.

They walked down the path next to the bathing area. Roger ran off and returned with three coloured baskets to put their clothes in for safe keeping. Michael-Edward watched them enter three adjoining changing cubicles.

Michael-Edward could hear the squeals of delight from the young children in the baths as the voices in his head got louder and louder. His brain was almost bursting as he entered the empty changing cubicle next to Mr Fraser's.

Fraser took his trousers off and folded them neatly into the clothes basket when he heard the words of Michael-Edward.

"Sinner repent ye your sins for the day of judgement is at hand," said the crazed killer with his silencer and gun in his hand.

"Tut tut. It takes all kinds," said Fraser to himself just as three holes splintered through the side of the wooden cubicles in quick succession. His body jolting in shock as the bullets landed in his stomach and chest.

Roger banged on the cubicle door. "Hurry up dad," he called and ran down to the room where he handed his basket of clothes in for safe keeping. The clothing attendant handed him a pin with a number on it. The boy pinned it into his costume and dived into the water.

Little Peter placed his basket of clothes on the floor outside his dad's cubicle, dressed only in his glasses and costume.

"Hurry up dad," he called, his little lip puckering when there was no answer.

"What's wrong son?" asked a passing bathing attendant.

"Me dad won't answer me," whined little Peter.

The attendant noticed the thick trickle of blood beginning to ooze out of the locker.

"Well you go and put your basket in and get your pin and I'll give your dad a shout, eh? Go on, there's a big boy. Your dad will be ready in a minute."

Peter scurried down the pathway with his basket.

The attendant peered over the locker. "Shit!" he cursed.

Blood was trickling from the corner of Fraser's mouth. His glasses lay lopsided round his face and the three bullet wounds leaked heavily down his body, mixing with the soil that adorned his face and body.

"Come on," breezed the attendant. "Your dad told me to give you some chocolate and crisps while you're waiting for him. He's gone to see someone."

The attendant led him back to the entry kiosk where they paid to come in.

"Come on, let's put some two bobs in the machine and get some sweets." He handed Peter a handful of change. "Get the police quick - someone's shot the kids' dad," he whispered. The lady picked up the phone.

Peter sat in the office with his sweets.

"My dad can dive in off the high board, you know'" he bragged, with sweets in his mouth. "And he can do the backstroke and the butterfly."

"Can he lad?" replied the lady, trying to keep a straight face but the tears were welling up in her eyes.

Roger dived in and came out the other side of the bath, just as the police came in. He watched the uniformed officers walk round the pathway to where his father had been. He saw the blood pouring from the cubicle and it dawned on him.

"Dad, Dad" he bleated at the top of his voice.

Inspector Benson turned in horror and looked at the frightened boy. A burly sergeant dragged the screaming child away under his arm.

Michael-Edward pulled into the cemetery and parked his van. Mitchell watched him get out of the van and go into the sexton's house. His wife greeted him at the door. She kissed him on the lips.

"Your tea's ready love," she said.

Teresa got off the bus in the city centre. She looked nervously at the pregnancy testing centre across the street, deep in thought.

"Just walk in. You're nearly married, it's not a crime." She looked away reluctantly, still not convinced. "Just walk straight in like you work there, no-one will take any notice. Come on, it's got to be done," she said to herself. She was halfway across the road and in the building before she knew it.

Jerry, Smigger and Dougie watched the manager of a supermarket come out of his shop accompanied by two security guards, on his way to the bank.

"D'you think that case is handcuffed to his wrist?" asked Dougie.

"If it is we'll have to chop his hand off," said Smigger, following the car.

"Behave yourself", said Jerry.

The lads watched the men pull up in a small village and walk across the fifty yard pavement to the bank in the shopping centre. They delivered the money into the night safe.

"This fella's been done a few times," said Smigger, watching the security measures.

"The pretend hardcases won't bother us much," said Jerry, referring to the security men. "The only problem is whether the money is chained to his wrist."

"Why not have a pair of bolt cutters in the car. If the money is handcuffed to him, we'll give him an headache and take him with us. Snap it in the car," said Dougie.

Smigger and Jerry looked at each other. That was the answer.

"The man from Del Monte - he say yes," they chorused.

"I meant to tell you," said Smigger, "I forgot."

"What?" asked Jerry as they drove away.

"Ged and Collo got sentenced yesterday," replied Smigger.

"How long?" asked Dougie.

"Four years," replied Smigger.

Dougie waited for Jerry's reaction.

"Unlucky," he said, staring out of the window, hiding behind his thick skin again.

Teresa sat at the table picking at her evening meal with her parents. Her mother noticed her uneasy manner and caught her husband's eye. Mr Simms followed his wife's worried look to his daughter. He sensed something was wrong.

"What's the matter girl?" he asked.

Teresa looked at him and looked away. Her worried parents looked at each other. Teresa plucked up her courage.

"I've got some good news dad, and bad news. I may as well tell you it all."

Her parents waited.

"You're gonna be grandparents."

"That's alright girl, we'll just bring the wedding forward," said her father reasssuringly.

"We can't," said Teresa.

Mr Sims looked at his wife. Her happy face had changed to one of worry.

154

"Why Teresa?" asked her mother suspiciously.

"He's on the run. The police are going to give him four years when they get him."

Mrs Sims tried to forestall the coming storm, knowing her husband only too well.

"Any one can make a mistake," she said.

"A mistake!" bellowed Mr Sims in rage. "What a stupid slut I've got for a daughter."

Teresa ran out of the room in tears and started packing suitcase in her room.

"You shouldn't have said that," snarled Mrs Sims.

"If she's got to sleep around why can't she use some kind of protection? There's enough of it about. But no, not her", he ranted, pacing the room.

"Arthur," scolded his wife, trying to silence him.

"She's giving me a bastard for me first grandchild and a thief for a son in law and I'm supposed to be happy," he roared at the top of his voice.

Teresa sobbed, throwing some clothes into a suitcase.

"We'll have the police calling here next," he roared, sitting back down in the front room. He heard his daughter's footsteps on the stairs.

"There's only one thing worse than having a slut for a daughter - that's having a stupid slut."

The front door slammed shut. Teresa hurried down the path as the television came crashing out of the window.

"Don't come fuckin back," roared her father.

Mr Sims plonked himself in his armchair. There was silence. His wife was in tears.

"Bastard," he said. "I never meant to say that - I never meant none of it," and kicked the cat.

Teresa sat having a cry at Jerry's house.

"Your dad just needs a bit of time to get over it," said Mrs Kinsella. Jerry sat on the settee with his arm around her.

"You can stay in my room until we get the flat. I'll get it in a couple of weeks. I'll stay in Dougie's".

Jerry, Dougie and Smigger sat in a stolen car outside the bank.

The supermarket manager arrived with the two security men. They walked the fifty yards to the safety of the bank. Smigger started the car and put his foot down. The car bounced onto the pavement. The security men were in no man's land - no cover.

"Throw the money down and run before they run us over," shouted one. The three men dropped the money and ran as Smigger swung the car round in a hand brake turn. Dougie and Jerry leapt out. Dougie snatched the money and the two men leapt back into the car, which sped away.

"See the way the shithouses ran," blurted Smigger as the car flew away.

The three lads counted the money into hundreds in Dougie's room. They wrapped each bundle of a hundred with elastic bands and shoved them into three piles.

"Another easy four grand," said Smigger. "On the town tonight with the boys, Jerry?" asked Dougie.

"Yes, I'll drop some money off on the way," he replied.

Smigger sat in the car outside Jerry's house. The three lads were dressed to kill.

Mrs. Kinsella was sitting at the table with Teresa. Karen was making cups of coffee in the kitchen. Jerry walked straight into the kitchen to see her.

"Alright Karen, he said. "Here's a tenner for the bingo tonight. Everything all right?"

"Thanks Jerry," she said. "D'you want a cup of coffee?"

"No thanks," he replied, "you know I can't stay long."

Jerry breezed into the front room. Dougie was sitting on the settee.

"Where's Karen?" he asked.

"In the kitchen making coffee," replied Jerry.

"I'll just go and get a drink of water while I'm waiting for you," he said.

Jerry fired a wad of one hundred pounds on the table for his mum. Mrs Kinsella eyed it suspiciously. She wanted the money but didn't want it.

"What's this?" she asked.

Jerry looked her in the eye. "I can't live on fresh air mum, and I'll never give you anything I didn't earn," said Jerry.

"Are you working now then?" she asked.

"If I risk my life to get money as far as I'm concerned I've earned it."

Mrs Kinsella looked deep into him.

"I never hurt no-one mum."

"O.K. lad," she said, accepting it.

He sat down next to Teresa and started nibbling her ear. She elbowed him off playfully.

"Get off me. You're still in the bad books."

"I've got a present for you," he said.

"What is it?" she asked. "I still haven't got over the last present you gave me."

Jerry tossed a wad of a thousand pounds into her lap. Teresa gasped. Jerry smiled.

"Put it in the bank towards the flat."

"Thanks Jerry," she said, kissing him on the lips.

"You take me back thirty years," said Mrs Kinsella. "You always come up smelling of roses just like your father."

"Hello Karen," said Dougie.

"Hello Dougie," replied Karen. "I'm sober now," he smiled.

"Are you now?" she smiled. "Well?"

"I'm asking," laughed Dougie. "Saturday night do for starters?"

"O.K." replied Karen pouring the coffee.

Dougie fired two wads of one hundred pounds onto the work top.

"What's this?" she asked.

"You might want to buy yourself a new jumper or something," he laughed, walking out the door.

The two young men left. Karen came into the parlour with the coffee.

"Dougie just give me two hundred quid to buy some clothes. He's taking me out on Saturday night," she said excitedly.

"Terrible, isn't it?" said Mrs Kinsella, "surrounded by generous men who keep giving us some other poor bastard's money".

The three young lads were drinking in one of the pubs in the city centre. It was packed with young men and women. It was one of the pubs they used to have a few drinks before they went on to the various night clubs in town.

The three lads sat in a corner drinking. Two attractive girls came over looking for somewhere to sit.

"Is there anyone sitting there?" asked the dark haired girl in the short dress.

Smigger ran his eyes up her long shapely legs, over her firm breasts with her nipples protruding through her dress and finally onto her pretty face.

"You are love," replied Smigger.

"Thanks," replied the girl, smiling and turning her back. She sat down with her friend at the table.

"Listen girls - " said Smigger, his eyes were distracted by the four lads who'd just walked into the pub.

'Shit, not now," cursed Smigger.

His friends followed his gaze to the four young men at the bar. It was Whitey, his elder brother Chalky and two friends.

Jerry was on his feet in a split second, followed by Dougie. Smigger swigged the remainder of his pint and followed his two friends.

"Hey you. You grassing bastard," growled Jerry.

Whitey turned straight onto a head butt. His nose burst open with blood as he landed on the seat of his pants. Whitey's friend Jimmy tried to jump on Jerry from the blindside but Dougie butted him three times in the face and followed up the attacks with his feet as the man hit the floor.

Smigger had the lad who was ordering the round by the throat at the bar.

"Nothing to do with me'" he cried with his arms out in surrender. "I'm not sticking up for any grassers.

Chalky stepped in between Jerry and his fallen brother with a Stanley knife in his hand.

"Come on cunt," he goaded.

Jerry attacked him. Chalky flashed the blade at Jerry's face. Jerry flicked his head to one side to avoid the blow and unloaded a crashing right hand at the same time. The blade sliced open a small thin gash over Jerry's eye. The blood poured out. Jerry was immediately blinded in one eye by the blood. The right crashed against Chalky's jaw. He crashed to the floor unconscious.

The blade fell from his hand. Whitey got up and ran for the toilets. It was his only way out. Jerry picked up a table and smashed it three times into Chalky's stricken body, breaking his ribs and his arm.

"Where is he" growled Jerry.

"Toilet," said Smigger, still holding the other lad at the bar.

Whitey was standing on top of the urinals, trying to pull the locked window open.

"Please God open," he panicked with the blood pouring from his nose.

The toilet door crashed open. Whitey jumped to the floor and cowered in the corner in tears.

"It wasn't me. They made me do it," he implored.

Jerry tore into him, hands, head and finally feet.

Whitey screamed for mercy and his calls were finally answered as he fell into unconsciousness and could no longer feel the speed or viciousness of the frenzied attack.

Jerry stopped for breath and looked down with contempt at his stricken opponent lying with his head in the urinal. Jerry unzipped his flies. His urine bounced off Whitey's face, cleaning some of the blood away.

The door opened behind him. It was Dougie.

"Hurry up, the bizzies are coming," he said.

Jerry shook his penis dry over Whitey's face and tucked it back into his trousers. He booted Whitey again in the face and walked out of the pub.

The bingo had finished and a band was now playing on the stage in the pensioners' club. Mrs Kinsella was up dancing with a man called Eddie. Karen and Teresa looked at each other and laughed.

"She's having a good time. Who's the fella?"

"Eddie," replied Karen. "They used to go to school together. His wife died about six months ago. He always comes over talking when we go to the bingo. Me mum loves it but says nothing. I feel like a gooseberry."

"Get Dougie to take you out on bingo nights and see what happens. Your mum's dead nice, she deserves to have someone in her life," said Teresa.

"Yeah," replied Karen. "I like Eddie, he's dead funny. I hope he can fight?"

"What makes you say that?" asked Teresa.

"Our Jerry," said Karen. "He was very close to me dad. Wanted to go everywhere with him. The thought of me mum and another man - he'd think it was high treason, even though me dad's been dead ten years."

It was Monday afternoon. Maca, Joey, Cummo and Stevie were on their way to the job centre. It had been raining heavily all day and had thus stopped the window cleaning round for the day. Maca had been in court over the moped.

"How d'you get on?" asked Cummo.

"Seventy-five pound fine and 120 community hours," replied Maca.

"Sod them. You don't pay fines," growled Joey, entering the job centre.

Stevie had no seat in the left side of his pants - and no underpants. His left buttock was quite clearly visible as they moved around the job displays, laughing at the ridiculous jobs on offer.

"Look at this," said Joey, "vacancy for an office worker - thirty-five pound a week."

"They'd expect you to piss out of your earhole for forty quid a week," remarked Stevie drily.

"Look at this one for a computer programmer - £250 a week," said Cummo.

"Yeah, we've got no chance of getting that. They're just taking the piss," said Joey.

"Well, if they're taking the piss out of me - I'm taking the piss out of them. Watch this."

Stevie strode boldly up to the receptionist, a young man dressed in a jacket and tie and of smart appearance.

"I'd like to enquire about job number one six one," said Stevie, sitting down with a serious face.

"O.K." said the receptionist, fumbling through his file looking for the reference number.

"The vacancy is for a computer analyst with two 'A' levels and five 'O' levels." The receptionist looked at the untidy youth in astonishment. "You need two years previous experience.

Stevie nodded his head repeatedly, trying to look intelligent and trying not to laugh. He could hear his mates sniggering in the background.

"The salary is a thousand pounds a month," said the receptionist. "D'you have the necessary qualifications?"

"No, but I'll just give them a bit of bluff," said Stevie seriously.

"What! you can't do that," said the receptionist, gaping.

"Well stick the job up your arse then," said Stevie eventually, bursting out laughing with the rest of the lads.

Stevie flashed his backside on the way to the door.

"Go on, fuck off you useless cunt. You're a waste of bloody time," he called.

"Shall we do a few windows this afternoon?" said Maca. "It's starting to dry up. We can take Cummo and Stevie with us."

"Yes," said Joey. "We'll get some ale money for tonight."

Cummo and Stevie were in a front garden. Cummo footed the ladder and Stevie was up top, cleaning a window.

Vera Howard walked past on the other side of the road spotting Maca and Joey at work as well. I'll get me own back on you bastards, she thought to herself. She opened the front door to her home and picked up the telephone directory in the hall. She dialled a number on the phone.

"Hello. Is that the Social Security? I'd like to make a complaint about somebody who's claiming dole and working at the same time."

The day's work was done. The hundreds of bank staff poured out of the building and into the street. Teresa was walking to the driveway entrance with Vicky.

"Hello girls," said Jerry. "I've got a surprise for you."

The two girls got into the car.

"What is it?" asked Teresa.

"A two bedroomed flat," beamed Jerry.

"Have you!" exclaimed Teresa, kissing him. "What's it like?"

"Well it needs a bit of work on it. Billy Smith said he'd install central heating for us for next to nothing. He's a plumber and he can get all the gear trade price. He said he'd install it for free. I'll give him a few bob like."

Vicky found it hard to conceal her jealousy but she was happy for her friend Teresa.

"I've got just over a grand to give you as well to furnish the place" said Jerry, "but that will leave me more or less skint."

"We'll just get the bare necessities at first," said Teresa. "We can get all the luxuries later when we've settled in. I'm sure it's not going to take you long to get some money.

Jerry winked. "I've got something in mind already. There's only one thing. You'll have to keep this quiet."

"Why?" said Vicky.

"I just don't want the police turning the place over looking for me. If they don't know where you live - they don't know where I live," replied Jerry.

Jerry and the two girls walked round the flat.

"It needs a lot of cleaning up," said Teresa.

"Nothing that a bit of elbow grease can't handle," said Jerry.

"When d'you plan on moving in?" asked Vicky.

"Soon as we've tidied it up, redecorated it and furnished it," answered Jerry. "We start work on it tomorrow - if Teresa likes it - and the place should be almost perfect in a couple of weeks."

"It doesn't look up to much," said Teresa dubiously, looking round the place.

"Trust me," said Jerry, kissing her. "Rome wasn't built in a day."

The work started on the flat the next day. The three lads scraped the old wallpaper off and set about redecorating the place. Billy Smith came round in the evening and ripped the floorboards up and started installing the central heating. They ripped the old bath out and replaced it with a new deluxe shower and bath and completely retiled the bathroom. Karen and Teresa took the week off from school and work respectively to help out. They scrubbed round where the old sink, the cooker and the fridge had been before replacing them with a brand new hi-tech cooker, fridge freezer, washing machine, dryer and microwave oven set in a flash kitchen suite fitted by the multi-talented Smigger. The romance between Karen and Dougie blossomed through the work as everyone pitched in. Soon the job was almost finished. The painting and decorating was done, now all they had to do was select the furniture they wanted.

Karen bought tea and sandwiches into the room. Everybody tucked in.

"Bastard," cursed Smigger, taking a bite out of his sandwich and hurling the newspaper on the floor.

"What's up?" said Karen, fearing it was her sandwiches.

"Fuckin England team," growled Smigger. "Talking about doing well to qualify for the World Cup Finals. Should be going to Spain to win it."

"Yeah," said Dougie. "It's all this nonsense about continental styles of play. Why don't we just attack them and play them off the park."

"What's continental style of play?" asked Smigger. "Rolling round the floor like a fanny when someone's hardly touched you? You play for England you can beat everyone in the world. Just play the English way."

"Yeah," agreed Jerry. "Never mind letting them kick you and not retaliating - they'll just keep on kicking you. If they want to mix it our lads will give as good as they get and more."

"Excuse me," said a blonde woman in her mid thirties, poking her head round the door. "My name's Sarah Gray. I live in the flat above. I just called in to see if you wanted anything. A cup of tea or a hand with something."

"I'm Teresa Sims," Teresa said, getting up and shaking hands. "This is me boyfriend, Jerry. Why don't you come in and have a cup of coffee."

"Mum I'm hungry'" called the little boy from the doorway.

"Can we have fish fingers for tea?" asked his big sister.

The two women looked at each other and smiled.

"You never get two minutes d'you," said Teresa laughing.

"No," replied Sara, "just call up if you need anything, O.K?"

"O.K. Thanks," said Teresa as her neighbour walked out the door.

Jerry and Teresa spent the following day bargain hunting for furniture for their flat. Teresa did all the talking and selecting of furniture and Jerry just seemed happy to agree with whatever Teresa wanted.

They bought a three piece suite, a television and video recorder and a bedroom unit, along with notably a big double bed that Jerry insisted on bouncing on in the shop window "to test it".

Joey, Maca, Stevie and Cummo sat in the waiting room of the local social security department.

"I wonder why they've got us all here?" asked Cummo.

"It's obvious isn't it?" replied Joey. "Someone's grassed us up. It's the only thing it can be."

"Deny everything," said Maca, "admit fuck all."

The four lads were called in separately for an interview over a space of fifteen minutes. Stevie was the last one called. As his name came over the tannoy he was instructed which box number he was to attend in the interview room.

Stevie sat down in cubicle number five. A clerk in her mid thirties was waiting to interview him.

"I'm from the fraud department," she announced. "It's my job to investigate fraudulent claims."

"What's that got to do with me?" shrugged Stevie unimpressed.

"D'you realise that it's an offence to work and claim dole at the same time?"

"Yes," replied Stevie.

"It's been brought to our attention that you have a window cleaning round," accused the investigating officer.

"Not me, love, I'm scared of heights" replied Stevie.

"Well we've received anonymous information to the contrary," continued the officer.

"It's not my fault love if some headcase wants to waste your time," he replied.

"You do realise that you have to keep yourself available for work at all times when you're claiming unemployment benefit?"

"Yes," replied Stevie.

"O.K." replied the officer. "We'll let the matter drop for the time being but if we get any concrete evidence I can assure you that you'll find yourself in court facing fraud charges."

"O.K." replied Stevie.

The four lads strolled away from the social security offices.

"What d'you reckon now?" asked Stevie. "Do we go legit?"

"No," replied Maca. "There's not enough money in it".

"I think we should do what our Smigger and the lads are doing," said Joey. "Let's go and buy a wreck with the window cleaning money and go on the mooch in it."

"No," said Stevie. "I don't want to get into robbing."

"I went to the match with them once. We robbed a load of gear out of this waggon and they gave me four hundred and fifty quid - my share."

"Did they?" gasped Stevie.

"I was looking through our Smigger's drawer the other week. I was looking for one of his good shirts for going out in. You'll never guess what I found?"

"What?" said Cummo.

"Nearly three grand in cash," Joey replied.

"I've changed me mind," said Stevie. "I want to get into robbing".

The small post office was set in a row of five shops facing a playing field. Smigger, Jerry and Dougie sat watching the post office men delivering money to the shop. A guard got out and looked furtively around. He went into the post office and informed the Postmaster of the delivery. The guard returned and checked everything was all clear. He signalled to another guard in the van. The guard got out of the van carrying the money. He walked quickly into the post office.

"We'll need three motors for the snatch," said Dougie. "A wagon to ram the van with and a car behind to stop it reversing, plus the getaway car."

"Yeah," replied Jerry. "Let's check out the 'Hoffmans', meaning the getaway route."

Smigger started the car.

It was Saturday night. Dougie called round to Karen's house to take her out for the evening. Mrs Kinsella let him in.

"She won't be a minute, Dougie. Come in and sit down."

"Thanks Mrs Kinsella," replied Dougie.

Dougie was surprised to find a man in the living room waiting to take Mrs Kinsella out for the evening.

"This is Dougie, our Karen's boyfriend," said Mrs Kinsella, introducing the two men. "This is Eddie, an old friend of mine."

"Pleased to meet you," echoed the two men.

Karen came down the stairs.

"See you later mum," she said and left the house with Dougie.

"Have a good time," called her mother.

"What's this?" asked Dougie. "Your mum doing a spot of courting?"

"Looks that way," replied Karen.

"Does Jerry know?" asked Dougie.

"No'" said Karen. "And make sure you don't tell him. Me mum will tell him when the time is right in her own way. I don't want him learning it second hand from you."

"O.K." replied Dougie.

"I don't want that homicidal bastard of a brother of mine spoiling things for me mum. Eddie's a nice guy. Me mum deserves to have some one nice in her life. She's been lonely too long."

"I won't say nothing," repeated Dougie, seeing it was a touchy subject.

Teresa lay on top of Jerry in bed. She rested her head against his chest. Jerry ran his fingers through her hair and lay back staring impassively at the ceiling. The couple had just finished making love.

"You're up to no good tomorrow, aren't you? What is it?" asked Teresa, breaking the silence.

"Post Office snatch," replied Jerry curtly.

"What happens if someone gets hurt?"

Jerry shrugged. "Unlikely," he said.

"There'll be old people and pensioners waiting for their money. They'll be put out if they have to wait extra days for their money."

Jerry didn't answer.

"Say one of them gets hurt?" continued Teresa.

"They've had their lives and blew it," growled Jerry in anger. "That's why they've got to hang around waiting for their pension money every week!"

"You'll grow old one day," replied Teresa.

"No, I'll die young," replied Jerry, his voice calmer and more sombre now. "I won't suffer the indignities of growing old and decrepit. Pissing the bed and having to have somebody wipe me arse for me. I'd sooner be dead."

"Don't talk like that," sulked Teresa. "You can't afford to die. You've got responsibilities."

Jerry laughed.

"Your alright giving me pressure over how I get me money but you're alright spending it, aren't you?"

Teresa laughed.

"Would we have all this if I just waited round for me giro to come? And how would we live on it if we did? It wouldn't go far. Am I supposed to stay in every night and watch all the pathetic repeats on the telly?"

Teresa rolled off him.

"I can't argue with you when you're like this," she said.

Jeff Baird entered the block of flats. He was in his mid thirties, wearing jeans and a donkey jacket. He stopped to take a swig from the bottle of whisky in his pocket and gasped. He screwed the top back on and replaced it in his pocket and made his way up the stairs past Jerry's flat to Sarah's place. Sarah was a divorcee. She was Jeff's ex-girlfriend but Jeff couldn't take no for an answer.

Jeff banged on the door. Sarah crept up to the door, holding a poker for protection.

"Who is it?" she asked nervously.

"It's me - Jeff," replied the man.

"What d'you want?" she asked, half opening the door on the lock and chain.

"I only want to talk to you. Can I come in?" he asked.

"No," replied Sarah. "I finished with you two weeks ago. You're bad news. I don't want to see you anymore."

She tried to close the door but Jeff jammed his foot in it. Sarah panicked, trying to force the door shut, hurting Jeff's foot in the process.

Jeff banged the door to free himself. The lock and chain snapped. Sarah was forced back into the hall by the impact. She belted Jeff over the head wlth the poker as he forced his way in. Jeff blocked the second blow and knocked Sarah to the floor with a back hander.

"I only wanted to talk to you!'' growled Jeff.

"I've got no money for you'" yelled Sarah running into the living room and hurling ornaments at him.

Teresa looked at Jerry, disturbed by the heavy thuds and breakages and screaming overhead.

"Sounds like her boyfriend's beating her up," said Teresa.

"Maybe she's been playing around. Anyway it's none of our business," replied Jerry.

Jeff stormed through the barrage of ornaments and knocked Sarah to the ground. He kicked her in the stomach in a rage of temper encouraged by the whisky. He ripped the negligee off her, leaving her only in her panties. He dragged her into the bedroom by the hair. Sarah screamed for her life. Jeff kept punching her across the face, trying to shut her up.

"Shut fuckin up!" roared Jerry downstairs, sitting up in bed and staring at the ceiling.

Jeff closed a hand over Sarah's mouth and produced a flick knife from his pocket with the other hand. He jabbed the tip into Sarah's eye socket, just below the eye at the top of her cheek bone.

"One more word and I'll put your fuckin eye out," snarled Jeff.

Sarah looked up at him in pain. He was bigger and stronger than she was and he was vicious. She knew he meant what he said.

Jeff looked down in anger at her swollen and disfigured face. He stared evily at her magnificent breasts. He pulled at her skimpy knickers. First they slid down her thighs. Then the elastic snapped as he ripped them off.

"Oh no," whimpered Sarah, the blade still against her eye.

"Oh yes," growled Jeff, dropping his trousers.

She closed her eyes and turned her head as she felt Jeff's hand touch her. She looked down the bed in disgust. Jeff had his massive weapon in his hand. He looked down at the beautiful body before him. The angry bush of mousey hair in a sea of pure white skin really excited him.

Sarah felt his brutal thrust strike home.

"You bastard," she cried, tears streaming down her face.

Jeff pulled her ankles up onto his shoulders. The more he hurt her the more it excited him, the more vigorous he became. He watched her breasts shake back and forwards in rhythm with his powerful frenzied and hurried thrust. Sarah felt like dirt. She could feel his horrible eyes enjoying the hurt he was doing her. She grabbed a pillow and sobbed heavily into it, burying her face so she didn't have to look at him any more.

It was early the following morning. Jeff pulled his trousers up.

"You got your giro yesterday. Have you got any money for me?"

"I've got no money. I haven't paid the rent for five weeks," replied Sarah.

Jeff picked her handbag up, unimpressed.

"I got the final demand for the lecky, that's got to be paid this week'" she begged.

Jeff rummaged through the handbag and produced a small wad of notes. He placed it in his back pocket.

"What am I going to feed the kids on?" roared Sarah, jumping off the bed and attacking him.

Jeff butted her in the nose. She crashed to the floor unconscious.

Jeff put his coat on. He stepped over her stricken body and walked out of the flat. He passed Jerry on the stairs as Jerry left his flat.

"Alright mate?" said Jeff smiling.

Alright mate," replied Jerry, acknowledging the greeting and suspiciously watching the man descending the stairs.

Jerry bounced down the stairs. Smigger and Dougie were waiting outside to pick him up. He got in the car and drove away.

Teresa was getting up for work some hours later. There was a loud banging on the front door. Teresa opened it.

"Come quick," shouted five year old Peter, Sarah's son. "Me mum's sick."

Teresa followed him up the steps to the top flat. She found Sarah lying battered and naked in the bedroom.

"You take your sister and go down to my flat and have some breakfast while I make your mum better," she said, shepherding them away from the bedroom.

Teresa got some ice cubes from the fridge and revived Sarah.

"What happened?" asked Teresa. "The bastard's raped me," said Sarah. She lifted her handbag upside down. There was no money in it. "And he's took me last penny."

"Who is he?" asked Teresa, bathing her wounds.

"He's an old boyfriend. He always comes when he's skint because he's bigger and stronger than me and he know's I've got no one to turn to."

"Why don't you call the police?"

"No, don't do that'" panicked Sarah. "The social will take me kids off me. I just want a good bath to wash all this dirt off me."

The post office van arrived on time outside the post office set in a row of five shops facing the playing fields. The guard got out to inform the postmaster of the delivery. He returned from the shop and gave his mate the all clear. A second guard jumped from the van. Suddenly a large Bedford wagon crashed head on into the post office van. A car screeched to a halt at the back of the van, blocking it in. Dougie and Smigger leapt out. Dougie jumped at the guards and snatched the money covered by Jerry. Smigger jumped into the getaway car and switched on the ignition. Jerry tried the back of the van but there was no more money in it. The two raiders leapt into the getaway car. The car sped away up the street. They zig-zagged through a couple of side streets and out across a dual carriage way. They stopped in another side street and switched back to their own car.

"Another easy one," guffawed Smigger in triumph.

The three lads returned to Jerry's flat to count the money.

Jerry was stunned to see Sarah's swollen and bruised face. The cup of tea trembled in her hands. Her two children stood silently by. Jerry knew instinctively what had happened.

"The cheeky bastard even let on to me this morning coming down the stairs," he said in dismay.

"You're partly to blame," snarled Teresa. "I told you to go up there but you wouldn't have it."

"Have you called the police?" asked Dougie.

"Don't want any police," snapped Sarah.

"Well how are you going to get your own back?" he asked.

"I'll stab the bastard next time he comes," answered Sarah.

"Surely he won't come back," said Smigger. "He can't be that stupid."

"He'll be back," said Sarah morosely, "just as soon as his money runs out and he needs an easy touch."

"And I'll be waiting for him," growled Jerry. The bastard won't bother you no more.

It was a wet windy evening. The incessant drizzle was being buffeted in squalls by the gusts of wind as the old banger drove into the hospital car park. It was visiting time, the car park was full.

"Twenty quid for this. It's a cracker'" said Joey driving.

"We'll have to earn some money quick," said Maca. "We're potless after buying it."

"That one will do", said Cummo, spotting a Ford Escort.

Joey parked the car.

"Stevie, you keep dixie in the bus stop," he said.

The three lads sat in the car as Stevie made his way to the bus stop. Maca and Cummo stepped out of the car as Stevie reached the bus stop. Cummo opened the boot and picked up two oil cans. Maca picked up a rubber tube. They crept over to the Escort. Maca slid the petrol cap off and fed one end of the rubber tube into the petrol tank. He sucked hard on the other end of the tube and placed it in the can.

"It tastes fuckin horrible'" he spat as the petrol was siphoned into the two oil cans.

Cummo took the first can as it was filled. He ran over to their own car and began tipping the petrol into the tank. Maca came running over with the other can and poured the petrol into the tank.

"That's us," he said, "first day at work tomorrow - on the mooch."

Joey drove out of the car park and picked up Stevie at the bus stop. The car sped out into the night.

It was ten o'clock the following day. A wagon stopped outside a supermarket in the high street. The driver jumped from his cab, clutching a despatch sheet. He opened the back of the wagon and began gathering the deliveries together before taking them into the shops. He placed four stacks of ten trays of tinned salmon at the back of the wagon. He jumped down into the street and carried one stack into the supermarket with his despatch note in his teeth. As soon as he entered the shop Maca, Stevie and Cummo appeared from nowhere. They each lifted a stack of salmon and piled back into the car with it.

Joey said nothing and drove calmly away as though nothing had happened.

"What did we get?" he asked presently.

"Salmon," replied Cummo excitedly. "We'll sell them easy in the pub tonight. Three tins of salmon for a nicker."

167

"Yeah, that's two hundred and forty quid between us," said Maca. "Sixty quid each for a day's work. Not bad for starters."

It was almost five to six. The pub had been open for nearly an hour. It was packed full of working men who'd mainly stopped in for a pint on the way home. The four young lads entered carrying the stolen salmon in plastic carrier bags.

"Anybody want to buy tins of salmon? Three for a pound," shouted Stevie at the top of his voice.

"I'll have some lad," called one man, as the lads moved round the bar doing a brisk trade.

A group of scaffolders were sitting in the corner playing cards. They had been rained off earlier that day and had been on the drink for the rest of it.

"Hey son. What are you selling?" asked one of the men calling him over.

"Tins of salmon," replied Maca. "Three for a pound."

"Can I have a look?" asked the man.

"Yes," replied Maca opening the bag.

The man dipped his hand in and pulled out three tins. "That'll do us," he said, placing them in his pocket.

"That's a nicker mate," said Maca.

The man smirked a fake grin and waved Maca away. "Go away son, I'm not paying."

Maca looked at the ceiling and then focused his vision on the tip of his finger. The man was with a group of friends - big strong working men - and they outnumbered the young lads.

"Go on, give the lad his money," goaded one of his workmates.

The four lads confronted the scaffolders.

"Are you gonna pay or what?" asked Cummo.

"Go on, fuck off," growled the scaffolder. "It's not your salmon in the first place. You only robbed it off someone, now I'm robbing it off you."

"What's all this hassle over a nicker for," asked Joey. "You're a mate of our Billy's aren't you?" he said to another of the men. "Are you gonna let this fella rip us off?"

"Look son I'll give you the nicker," proffered Billy's friend.

"Don't want you to pay," said Maca, who had so far remained silent. "I want the hardcase to pay."

"Go on, fuck off before I break your fuckin back , you cheeky young cunt."

"Come then," growled Maca.

The man lunged at him but was stopped by his friends.

"He's only a kid," shouted one of them, trying to calm things down.

"I'd go home son if I was you, before you get your arse smacked," growled the man sitting down.

"You're not going to get home in one piece tonight, shitbag," answered Maca calmly. "So enjoy your pint. You're going to need the anaesthetic." The four lads turned and left the pub.

It was after eleven o'clock when the drunk finally left the pub. The four lads watched him stagger down the steps in the pouring rain. They sat in silence in their car across the street, as the hardcase got into Billy's friend's car.

Three of the lads stuffed a tin of salmon into a sock each. The car pulled away. Joey followed at a discreet distance.

"Just drop me off here," said the hardcase arriving at the corner of his street.

"Are you sure you're alright?" asked his friend.

"Yes, I'll see you in the morning. Thanks for the lift home. Goodnight," he replied. The car pulled away.

Stevie got out of the car and followed the man. The car drove past him. Maca and Cummo got out and walked up the street towards him. The hardcase paid them no attention at first. He didn't recognise them. Cummo crossed the street. He shinned up the lamp and took the bulb out. Everything went dark. It was then that the hardcase realised he was in trouble.

"Shit," he gasped.

Suddenly Stevie cracked him over the head from behind with a tin of salmon. The hardcase hit the deck. He grunted and groaned as the three lads piled into him with the tins of salmon and their feet. A vigilant house dog barked like mad but no one came to the man's aid.

"Alright, Alright," he shouted at the top of his voice, trying to block and fend of the barrage of blows. he passed into unconsciousness, battered and bruised and bleeding heavily. The three lads stopped - out of breath. Maca, the main assailant, gave him an extra kick in the face for good measure.

Cummo reached into his pockets for the salmon.

"Leave them," said Maca. "He's paid for them."

A few days later Dougie and Karen were invited round to Jerry's and Teresa's for a meal. Jerry poured the wine as they sat around the table enjoying the meal.

"How much did you get from the post office snatch?" asked Karen.

Jerry and Dougie looked at each other and said nothing.

"Twenty four thousand," replied Teresa, "and it's still not enough.

Karen's chin dropped.

"Yeah! but sooner or later you'll get caught. You'll go to the well one time too many," she said, recovering herself. She didn't want Dougie or Jerry to be a robber.

"We know that," said Dougie. "That's why we put twenty thousand into a special account between the three of us. As soon as we think we've got enough we'll stop. Start our own business."

"What does Smigger think of all this?" asked Karen.

"It was his idea," replied Jerry.

"Where is he?" she asked.

"He's out with Cherry from our place," said Teresa. "She still thinks he's a university student."

The log fire burst into glowing crimson red embers. The waiter poured the wine. Smigger sat at the table in the plush restaurant, dressed in a suit. Cherry was dressed in a stunning black low-cut dress.

Smigger tasted the wine and nodded his approval to the waiter. The waiter immediately filled their glasses and left the young couple alone.

"Rather a fruity little number," remarked Smigger. "A good bouquet."

"Yes," replied Cherry, enthralled, slurping her red wine.

"What d'you think of the Toxteth riots?" she asked, trying to be intelligent. "The politicians put it down to bad housing, unemployment and police harassment."

"No," disagreed Smigger. "They're just a gang of clowns trying to get their names in the paper. Half of them have never been there. A policeman was killed in town the night before the riots. The police came down hard on everyone and that's what sparked it off."

The four lads pulled up in a dark suburban street. Maca and Stevie got out of the car. They opened the driveway gates and approached the Ford Granada parked near the house. Maca jiggled a key in the lock. A loud piercing alarm went off. The two startled youths sprinted back to their car and drove off as the car owner opened the door of his house.

The wine was beginning to take effect as Smigger gave Cherry his comic version of the Toxteth riots.

"The police had to draft in police from surrounding areas for support," said Smigger. "The scouse police sent them all to the front line while they sat around in braces and longjohns, smoking pot and drinking knock-off whisky looted from some of the shops. The poor old woollyback police were all getting carried away on stretchers with ZZZ's coming out of their heads. There was a load of big black mommas dropping television sets from the flats onto the

policemen's heads. The coppers were all walking round with TV sets wrapped round their heads, reading the nine o'clock news."

Cherry was highly amused with Smigger's comic analysis of a serious situation.

"Even when they arrested the lad who drove the JCB at them he said it was just because he was black," said Smigger.

Joey, Maca, Cummo and Stevie drove slowly into a pub car park looking for a car to steal. Joey parked the car next to a white Cortina Mark Three. Maca opened the door and tried the ignition. The car started. Cummo jumped in next to him. He drove out of the car park, followed by Joey and Stevie.

Karen and Dougie arrived home. Mrs Kinsella was still up .

"Is it O.K. if Dougie stays in Jerry's room tonight, mum?" asked Karen.

Mrs Kinsella looked at the young couple suspiciously.

"Me mum and dad are fighting again. Me dad's rotten drunk and she can't do nothing with him. I just want to stay out of the way if I can."

"O.K." said Mrs Kinsella, "but if there's any hanky panky tonight you'll get the back of my hand."

"O.K." laughed Dougie. "I'll just get me head down now, I'm knackered."

Karen followed him into the hall and kissed him goodnight.

"I'll be in to see you later," she whispered.

Dougie stripped to his underpants and got into bed. He turned the radio on and began to doze off.

The local kids were hanging round the edge of the estate hoping a robbed car would come round. Maca burst across the dual carriage way driving in circles round the busy junction, wheels screeching and smoke pouring from the exhaust. He pulled in at a bus stop so all the youngsters could examine the car.

"Gis a go," said Stevie.

"Are you sure," said Maca. "You're not that good a driver."

"I'm sure," said Stevie. "I've got to learn somewhere."

"Let me out," said Cummo. "I'm not getting in with him."

Stevie got into the car and screeched away on his own just as a police motorbike came down the road. The sergeant sped past the crowd of youths in pursuit. Stevie spotted him and did a U turn through the dual carriage way. The powerful police motorbike closed up on him in a matter of yards. Stevie swung the car left then right through another dual carriageway and sped up a side street. Still the motorbike stayed with him only ten yards behind his quarry.

Dougie leapt off the bed as soon as he heard the car engine being screwed. He looked out of the bedroom window and saw the white Cortina picking up speed as it accelerated up the road.

"Slam on," he urged as he saw how close the motorbike was to the car.

The car hurtled through a chicane of parked cars just clipping the last car with its back end. Stevie struggled like a jockey trying impossibly to hold his horse together after a bad mistake at a fence. The car seemed to straighten for a moment but the back wheel hit the kerb. The car rose diagonally, Stevie closed his eyes as the world came at him - the car rolled three times and eventually landed upright some sixty yards away from the original impact. The experienced police officer hung back expecting the car to explode. Stevie snapped off the seat belt and ran through a garden and down the entry and vaulted into a back garden.

Dougie dragged his jeans on and sprinted up the street, People in various states of undress began to arrive on the scene. A transit van arrived and a police officer with an alsatian disappeared down the entry after Stevie.

The crowd waited. Maca, Joey and Cummo came running up the street.

"Did he get away?" asked Maca.

"Don't know," said Dougie. "They're after him with dogs."

The dog handler returned empty handed.

"Thank fuck for that," said Dougie. "Now I can go back to bed."

The car was parked on a deserted stretch of beach near Formby. The pure white foam danced along the edge of the waves as they crashed remorselessly onto the beach. The soft smoochy music gave the car the warm romantic atmosphere Smigger wanted as a light rain began to fall on the windscreen.

Smigger was in the mood for love. He kissed Cherry passionately and groped her breast.

"No!" said Cherry knocking his hand away for the umpteenth time and continued kissing him.

"What's the matter with you?" asked Smigger, angrily breaking away from her embrace.

"Just because you've bought me a few drinks doesn't mean I have to have sex with you," she answered.

"What did you come to the beach with me for then?" asked Smigger.

Cherry avoided his gaze. There was no answer.

"You're not one of those dopey cows who like to be forced. Try valiantly to resist before you're hopelessly overpowered by the big strong man are you?" asked Smigger.

"Don't be a dickhead," replied Cherry.

"Yeah, you're just a prick teaser," decided Smigger. "Well, I don't think you'll be bragging to your friends about me taking you out for an expensive meal and buying your ale all night without getting me leg over. Get out of the car."

"It's twenty miles back to Liverpool," said Cherry in alarm.

"Get out of the car," growled Smigger.

"No," said Cherry defiantly.

Smigger got out of the car and dragged Cherry from the passenger seat and lashed her onto the beach.

"You bastard!" cursed Cherry.

"Little miss posing arse, you don't look so clever now, do you?" muttered Smigger, getting into the car.

Smigger wheelied the car round and threw her handbag at her.

"Been a few girls raped on this beach, even murdered over the years," he said calmly.

Cherry stared at him in horror. She knew what he was saying was true and the rain was getting heavier.

"They reckon a lot of devil worship goes on here at certain times of the year as well. Goodbye".

"Wait," called Cherry as he went to drive away.

Smigger waited. Cherry hung her head in submission. She was terrified of being left out in the middle of nowhere in such a spooky place. Smigger was the lesser of two evils.

"I'm not on the pill," she mumbled. "Is it alright if I give you a wank?"

Smigger looked her up and down out of the car window.

"No," he said. "I can't stand that type of nail varnish," and wheelied away.

"You bastard." shrieked Cherry.

She was all alone as the car shot out of sight - just the sound of the crashing sea. Suddenly something moved behind her in the shadows. Then she heard a noise.

"Oh shit," she cursed, realising someone or something was there.

"Smigger," she shrieked. "Smigger," and she ran away up the beach in the direction Smigger had driven off in.

Smigger and Dougie sat in the back of the almost empty courtroom. Marty stood in the dock for sentencing. The judge stared at his battered and terribly scarred face and read details on the charge sheet before him. Marty's mother clutched her husband's hand.

"I find it very worrying that young girls aren't safe to play in a public park in broad daylight without being bothered by the likes of you. It must have been a terrifying experience for them. One little girl still has nightmares about it,"'said the judge.

Marty haplessly returned the judge's gaze, not really understanding what was going on.

"I sentence you to two years imprisonment," glowered the judge. "Take him down."

Marty's mother collapsed in tears. His father put his arm round her to comfort her. Marty was led down the steps.

"It would have been better if he was killed in the car crash," muttered Dougie in dismay.

"Bollocks," replied Smigger. "He did die in the car crash. I don't know what the fuckin hell that is," referring to the new Marty.

"Look at his ma," said Dougie as she was led away in tears. "I hope to God I never hurt me ma like that. If you ever crash the car make sure you kill me outright."

Jerry potted the final pool ball in the pub and went to the bar to refill his glass. Just then a distinguished looking man in his early fifties walked in.

"Hello Mr Davis," said Jerry. "Long time no see"

"Hello Jerry son. Are you still playing football?" the man asked.

"Yes," replied Jerry. "Can I buy you a drink?"

"I'll have a scotch and lemonade, please," replied Mr Davis. "What brings you to this neck of the woods?"

"One of the lads is in court today. A few of the boys have gone to see how he gets on. They're picking me up later. I don't like courts," answered Jerry.

The barman placed the drinks on the bar and Jerry paid for them.

"Come and sit down and tell me how you're doing."

"I'm doing fine," said Jerry. "How about yourself? Are you still driving the wagon?"

Mr Davis laughed. "No son, I've got a small wholesale business now and two pubs."

"Must have been some fiddle on them wagons," laughed Jerry.

"Don't be spreading malicious gossip now," laughed Davis, almost admitting it. "It's funny you know. I've got an old sparring partner of your dads working the door for me on one of me pubs," said Davis. "I remember one day your old fella near killed him."

"Tell me about it," said Jerry. "I love hearing stories about me dad."

"Well, your old fella was a bomber. He couldn't half punch, but he was quiet and never looked for trouble, and the other fella made the mistake of underestimating him. I remember your dad winking at him just before he banged him - caught him completely off guard. The big dope thought he was going to let it go."

"What happened?" asked Jerry.

"Well the fella's name was Lennie Casey, and he used to work the welt on the dock with your dad," recollected Davis.

"What's that?" asked Jerry.

"Well in those days," said Davis, the job would be overmanned. So one fella would go the pub for a couple of hours while his mate did the work. Then the other fella would come back and it was his mate's turn to go the pub."

"And they'd get paid for it?" asked Jerry.

"Yes," replied Davis, "but there were some right bullies down there. If you couldn't handle yourself you'd find yourself working all day while your partner was in the pub all day. Anyway, Casey went to the pub first and didn't come back. Your dad finished the shift and went looking for him. Found him in the pub with two of his cronies. Casey seen him coming but didn't expect anything because of the quiet way your dad acted like nothing was wrong. I'll always remember the wink then the big right. There was teeth everywhere. He battered the three of them - hands, head, feet, speed, power - he had everything. It took two big dockers to drag him off. Casey was on the sick for two weeks."

Jerry laughed. "Listen, Mr Davis, are you interested in buying some knock off vodka?" he asked.

"A couple of lousy bottles?" scoffed Davis.

"No, a wagon load," replied Jerry.

"When can you get them?" asked Davis.

"They're subject to availability," replied Jerry. "Give us your phone number and we'll sort something out when they're ready."

Just then Smigger and Dougie walked in.

"I've got to go," said Jerry, accepting Davis's business card. "I'll be in touch."

The following morning the three young men were parked opposite a vodka making factory in Warrington. They watched the lorries drive out with their deliveries.

"How many on a wagon d'you reckon?" asked Smigger.

"Thousands on some of them," guessed Dougie.

"We'll cop the biggest one," said Jerry. "We'll just pick out the slowest and most cumbersome - that means it's carrying a heavy load. As soon as the driver stops for his dinner we'll throw him in the boot of a car and fuck off with him and the wagon in different directions."

"Sounds good to me," said Smigger.

"And me," replied Dougie. "Let's go and discuss how much we're going to get paid for it."

The three lads arrived at the wholesalers yard an hour later. A ferocious alsatian tethered with an old rope barked angrily at them.

Lennie Casey stood idly against the wall with one of his cronies.

"Mr Davis about?" asked Dougie.

"In the office," scowled Casey.

Jerry glared at him. There seemed to be bad blood between them almost immediately.

"Smart arse young kids with money," muttered Casey, following them into the hut.

"Hello boys," said Davis, looking up from his desk. "Would you like a drink?"

"No thanks," said Dougie, sitting down.

"What can I do for you?" asked Davis.

"It's about that wagon load of vodka," said Jerry. "Dougie usually does our negotiating for us," nodding to the young man in the chair.

Casey sneered at his friend.

"How many bottles of Vodka will there be and what type?" asked Davis.

"Only the best," said Dougie, "and about five thousand of them."

"When can you make the delivery?" asked Davis.

"Whenever you like," replied Dougie.

"How much a bottle?" asked Davis.

"Three pound," replied Dougie.

"No, it doesn't leave enough room for the sort of profit I'm looking for," replied Davis.

"Don't give me any crap," growled Dougie

Casey started towards him, but Davis waved him away. Jerry raised an eyebrow and stared coldly at Casey.

"Vodka retails over six pounds a bottle," continued Dougie, unaware of the situation behind him. "You'll still make a good profit."

"O.K." replied Davis. "On one condition. You don't get paid until I've sold the gear."

175

"What!" said Dougie. "I don't like the smell of that."

Casey flew at Dougie, unable to contain his temper any longer. Jerry leapt across and butted him in the face, almost simultaneously punching his crony in the mouth. Casey was unconscious. His pal didn't want to know. A cut lip and a sore face was enough. He lay on his back looking up.

"You'll have to accept the deal the way it was offered. I can't spare the capital up front right now," said Davis, ignoring the incident.

Dougie looked at Jerry. Jerry nodded. Smigger shrugged.

"O.K." said Dougie, shaking hands.

Jerry was the last of the three of them to leave. He stepped over Casey's carcass in the doorway. He turned and winked at Davis.

"Definitely a chip of the old block," said Davis.

The car was jacked up outside the block of flats. Jerry lay on his back changing the brake shoes. Peter and his sister Helen were playing in the front garden. Sarah their mother was frying sausages for their dinner. She turned them over for the last time and went to the window. She spotted her children playing below.

"Helen, Peter. Your dinner's ready," she called.

Helen ran into the flats and up the stairs. Peter tried to kick the ball up the first flight of steps. The ball bounced down towards him. Peter booted the ball back upstairs as it rebounded to him.

Jeff Baird came strolling down the road dressed in a long black leather trench coat. He saw the legs sticking out from under the car and disappeared into the flats.

Helen sat at the table. She cut the tip off a sausage and put it in her mouth."
"Where is he?" fussed Peter's mother, knowing his dinner was going cold.

Jeff passed him on the stairs. Peter froze as he watched the large man striding up the stairs. His football bounced past him, down the stairs. Peter turned and ran after it.

"Jerry! Jerry! That man's back," he shouted at the top of his voice, running down to the car.

"What man?" asked Jerry, coming from underneath the car.

The anxious look on the little boy's face told him what man. Jerry flew into the flats and sprinted up the stairs.

Sarah walked along the hall towards the partly open door.

"Where is he?" she said talking to herself. The door opened and in walked Jeff.

"Oh my God!" she cried in anguish, having expected to see Peter. "What d'you want this time?" she gasped, backing off into the kitchen.

Jeff didn't answer. He just stared impassively at her. Sarah snatched the bread knife up from the work top behind her.

"Keep back you bastard," she panicked, holding the knife up in front of her.

Jeff heard the door bang and spun round. Jerry stopped momentarily. Their eyes met briefly. Jeff instinctively went for the flick knife in his back pocket as Jerry charged at him. The blade sprung open in Jeff's hand just as Jerry charged in on him. The blade flew from his hand as both men flew over the settee. Jerry was first to his feet tearing vicious blows into the man's body and face. Jeff tried to contain him at close quarters but Jerry butted him in the nose. Jeff's head ricocheted off the wall behind him. Jerry kneed him in the crotch. Jeff crumpled forward. Jerry dragged him down the hall by the hair. He stamped on the man's foot and shoved him down the stairs. Jerry chased after him, aiming kicks at the tumbling body. Jeff half ran, half staggered into the street. His legs were gone. He couldn't get away.

Jerry battered him up the street tearing into his opponent with his hands and feet. He deliberately tore the long trenchcoat in half up the back seam. Jerry banged a big right into Jeff's jaw. Jeff collapsed in a heap, battered and out of breath. His face was cut and bleeding. He nursed his rib cage unable to get his breath. He knew a few of them were broken.

"You ever come back here again and I'll kill you, you cunt! Understand?" gasped Jerry.

Jeff nodded, unable to speak.

"Well go on then. Fuck off!" Jeff staggered to his feet and his dodgy legs carried him away up the street to safety.

Teresa lay on her back staring at the ceiling. Jerry's head was barely visible above the quilt as he cuddled into her. They had not long finished making love but Teresa had something on her mind.

"You're grafting again tomorrow, aren't you? What if an innocent bystander gets hurt?" she asked.

Jerry was silent for a moment before he answered her question with a question.

"How do you always know when I've got something on?" asked Jerry.

"Because you always make love to me as though it's for the last time," answered Teresa.

"I'll be able to stop soon," he said reassuringly.

He kissed her on the cheek and disappeared under the blankets again.

"What if someone gets hurt?" persisted Teresa.

Jerry turned over and lay with his back to her.

"Don't start," he said.

"Haven't you go any conscience?" asked Teresa.

"Conscience!" laughed Jerry. "What's that. It's just a word the nobles invented years ago after they'd ripped everyone off. It's just bullshit they used to keep the dopey peasants in order."

"You don't really believe that," said Teresa. Jerry didn't answer. "Conscience is the little voice in your head telling you right from wrong," she said.

Jerry ignored her much to her annoyance.

177

"You always get paid back in the end," she snapped. "Just wait till something happens to you in a few years time. You'll think - why me? What have I done? You'll know then won't you?"

There was no immediate answer.

"Would you like to see me in jail for ten years?" said Jerry deeply. "Would you like to see me on a slab down the morgue with me legs and arms or even me head missing if we crash? Would you like to see me getting two years for flashing to little girls in the park like Marty?"

"Course I wouldn't," said Teresa, waiting to see what the outburst was leading to.

"Well why d'you always try and fuck me head up before I go on a touch. I need a clear head. I can't afford a mistake or I'll get me arse bit. D'you think I like taking me life in me hands every time I try to get some money. When I jump out of that robbed car with me balaclava and me headache stick I'm terrified. I'm scared shitless and so are the others. It's just that we're all too macho to admit it. When you see us buzzing after a touch it's not the money, it's the fact we're safe and we can all laugh and brag how brave and tough we are."

Teresa cuddled into him. Her nagging question had at long last touched a nerve.

"It won't be long before I can pack in, but just remember next time you twig I'm up to no good - you can make all the difference between getting caught and not getting caught - between getting hurt and not getting hurt."

"O.K." said Teresa guiltily and cuddled into his chest.

The three lads sat in the car watching the lorries pull out of the depot and go off in different directions. One lorry pulled away slowly, obviously struggling for speed with the weight of its load.

"That'll do us," said Smigger.

Jerry and Dougie got out of the car and climbed into the stolen car parked behind them. The two cars set off on the trail of the vodka laden lorry.

The driver plodded steadily along the motorway. He looked at his watch as he passed a sign advertising the service station one mile further up the road.

Jerry and Dougie watched him indicate and turn in the service area. Jerry placed his balaclava on his head as though it was a hat. It only needed pulling down over his face.

There was a sudden rush of escaping air as the lorry driver parked next to another lorry. He jumped down from his cab hidden from view by the adjoining lorry. Jerry whacked him over the head with a club. They bundled the dazed man into the boot of the car, Dougie snatching the keys off him as Jerry tucked him into the boot.

Jerry climbed into the cab and started the lorry. He drove out of the service station followed by Dougie in the stolen car. Smigger sat in his car making sure there was no sign of pursuit. There was none. Smigger caught them up on the motorway and gave them the all clear. Jerry came off the motorway at the next turn and headed back to Liverpool. Dougie kept going in the opposite direction followed by Smigger.

An hour later Dougie stopped their car in a deserted country lane. He ignored the irate driver's muffled cries for help coming from the boot.

"Let me out you bastards," he called as Dougie climbed in next to Smigger. The two lads headed back to Liverpool.

Jerry stood watching Casey unload the lorry with a fork lift truck.

"Five hundred cases I make it," said Jerry.

"That's right," said Davis. "That's thirty six grand I owe you."

Jerry laughed and jumped into the lorry. "I'll go and park this in Manchester out of the way. The police can sniff around there for the vodka."

Teresa was heavily pregnant. It was Saturday morning. The young couple came out of a boutique laden with shopping. They had spent the morning buying clothes for the forthcoming baby.

"D'you fancy a cup of tea?" asked Jerry.

"Love one," replied Teresa.

Whitey was across the street - window shopping. He was in town to buy a shirt. He glanced up and saw the happy couple enter the cafe. There was only one thing on his mind - revenge. Out of the corner of his eye he spotted a row of phone boxes.

Whitey dialled the number. He listened to the phone ring.

"Hello, can I speak to Sergeant Hughes of the serious crime squad please," he blurted, not giving the officer a chance to answer.

The telephonist switched him through. Hughes sat at his desk in his shirt sleeves drinking coffee from a plastic cup. The phone rang.

"Hello, Sergeant Hughes," he answered.

"Hello Mr Hughes, this is Whitey. I've just seen Jerry Kinsella go into George's cafe in town with his bird. You'll have to be quick if you're going to catch him."

Whitey hung up.

"Holmes! Brennan!" shouted the sergeant, calling his men. The three officers walked out of the police station and got into an unmarked police car and headed for the town centre.

"A lot of people are present at the birth these days," said Teresa.

"Not me," said Jerry. "I'd probably knock the doctor out. I don't like the idea of anyone looking at you with no clothes on except me."

Teresa laughed. "You're daft," she said, finishing her coffee.

Whitey watched from the safe vantage point in the shopping precinct, waiting for the police to arrive.

"Shit!" he cursed as Jerry and Teresa came walking out of the cafe. He watched them cross the road towards a waiting row of taxis. An evil smile came over his face as he saw the police car pull up outside. Holmes went to get out of the car but Hughes stopped him.

"There he is," said the sergeant. "Let's take him in."

Holmes got out of the car and followed Jerry. The sergeant drove the car up the street and Detective Constable Brennan got out. Jerry was trapped.

He spotted Brennan walking innocently towards him but didn't recognise him at first.

"You want to watch yourself in town," said Teresa, "there's police all over the place."

"I know," said Jerry looking at him. "He's got 'jack' written all over him," referring to Brennan coming towards him.

A picture of Jerry butting him in the face in the back garden flashed in his mind. He dropped the shopping and ran. It was too late. Brennan was on him. Jerry handed him off and sprinted away with Holmes in pursuit. Brennan picked himself up and charged after him.

Jerry's head tipped back in the wind as he ran for his life, his heart bursting. His mind began to work overtime as he tried to think where to run. Holmes was only ten yards behind him as the two powerful men sprinted through the crowd of startled shoppers. Sergeant Hughes drove off up the street to try and cut Jerry off. Teresa jumped into the nearest taxi with the fallen shopping. Whitey cursed as the cab pulled away.

Jerry watched the traffic coming towards him but didn't stop. He went for the gap between two cars in the flow of traffic and just made it as the angry driver slammed the brakes on. Jerry gained precious yards as Detective Constable Holmes had to stop momentarily to get across the road. Jerry raced down an alley with Holmes in hot pursuit. Jerry knew he had to shake him off now or he'd be caught. He darted down the alley and out of sight. Holmes raced round the corner and hurtled face first into a head butt. There was a terrific crack. The top half of Holmes' body stopped dead while the bottom half kept travelling. Holmes landed unconscious on the floor with his leg bent up behind his back. Jerry looked down at his battered and bleeding face and was felled by a rugby tackle from Brennan who shot round the corner from nowhere. The impetus of the diving tackle sent the two men sprawling up the alley. A lorry driver delivering goods to the department store was joined by the two young warehouse boys as he watched the struggle.

Jerry lay on his back trying to get up. He struggled vainly. He kicked and punched and attempted to butt the officer, but he couldn't shake the brave policeman off.

Sergeant Hughes arrived at the top of the alley and came running down to aid his fellow officer. Brennan laughed in triumph as Jerry struggled like a wild man to get free. The burly constable contained him.

"You're going nowhere, cunt! You're nicked," he laughed.

Jerry poked him in the eye with one finger. Brennan squealed and released his grip, clutching his face. Jerry kneed him in the groin and broke free from the stricken officer. He watched the old sergeant running towards him. He knew the old man was too slow to catch him.

He gestured to the sergeant as though Jerry was masturbating himself. He kicked Brennan in the face and ran off down the entry. The sergeant didn't chase him. He stopped to help the fallen men.

"Get an ambulance," he called to the warehousemen.

It was Sunday night. The local pub was packed. Sykesy and little Maca were round the back in the pub car park trying to steal an old Morris Oxford. Little Maca got the car door open and turned the ignition. There was no response.

"It's no good," said Sykesy. "We'll have to bump start it."

The rest of the young teenagers were playing cards for pennies at the front of the pub.

"Come on," said Sykesy. "We need a push."

The card school scattered as the gang of young kids raced round the back of the pub.

Little Maca and Sykesy got into the car. The rest of the gang began to push.

"We'll meet you over the playing fields," called Sykesy as the gang of twelve year olds pushed the car.

Little Maca released the clutch. The car darted forward in hops, smoke poured from the engine as little Maca struggled to drive it.

The lights changed and the corporation bus started up on the way to Kirkby.

The driver slammed the brakes on as the Morris Oxford shot out from nowhere in front of him.

"Stupid little bastards," called the driver. "You're going to get yourselves killed."

Smoke poured from the exhaust and the engine screamed as little Maca couldn't change gear as the car chugged down the East Lancashire Road.

Maca, Joey, Cummo and Stevie stood at the bar watching the man playing the one armed bandit.

"There must be some money in that," said Joey. "Someone's been on it all night."

"When does it get emptied?" asked Cummo.

"Tomorrow," replied Maca.

"I reckon the barmaids wouldn't notice if we carried it out at last orders."

"We'll make a joke of it if we get captured. The manager's too scared to say anything."

Smigger was sitting talking to Ann, his so-called Sunday girl. He walked her home every Sunday without fail, even though Dougie had put her sister in the family way.

"There was this queer in the merchant navy," said Smigger, "when the ship put into port, the crew would go ashore and get mad with it. The queer would wait for them to come back rotten drunk and pretend to help them back to the ship. Then he'd stick it up their arse when they crashed out. If they woke up before he'd finished he'd tell them to go back to sleep, it was only a dream!"

"You're terrible," said Pauline.

"It's true," said Smigger. "One fella needed eight stitches in the arse."

"Did they ever catch him?" asked Pauline.

"Oh aye. They got him in the end. Gave him a terrible hiding," replied Smigger. "I think I'm seeing things."

He watched the four lads unplug the one armed bandit and carry it out of the pub. A man coming into the pub held the door open for them and carried on into the pub as though nothing had happened.

They smashed the back of the machine open around the back of the pub. They piled all the ten and fifty pences into a plastic bag.

"Hey Maca," said a young lad, "your kid's got a robbed car over the field."

Maca looked at his friends. "I'd better go and see he's alright."

The four lads took a short cut over wasteland to the field, dropping the bag of money into their car on the way.

Little Maca had stopped near the garages in the corner of the field, surrounded by the rest of the young lads when his big brother arrived.

"Get out you little bastard! I'll get the blame if you get collared in this."

Maca kicked his younger brother up the backside as he got out of the car. Stevie climbed into the car.

"I think my driving could do with a little practice. Climb on the back. The last one I shake off is the winner."

Cummo jumped into the car beside him as half a dozen lads climbed onto the back of the car, using the bumper as support and using any hand grip for safety.

Cummo rooted through the car looking for valuables.

"Don't waste your time," said Stevie. "Sykesy will have had anything worth taking."

Joey banged his hands on the roof of the car. "Go ahead Stevie, we're ready" he roared.

The rest of the young teenagers ran and climbed onto the garage roof where they could watch the show in safety.

Stevie started the car, building up speed, zig-zagging this way and that. The lads on the back held on for dear life. The car slowed as Stevie threw it into a tight turn. Two lads in the most precarious positions sensibly jumped off as the car slowed. They picked themselves up and sprinted for the safety of the garages. Stevie swung the car round and watched the two youths running for their lives. It was part of the game to try and run the runners down. Stevie smiled as he jammed his foot down on the accelerator. He knew they wouldn't get away as the car picked up speed. The first youth reached the wall and leapt straight at it, clinging to the top. He was helped up by two other lads.

The second was too slow. He shrieked in terror as Stevie swung the speeding car away from him at the last minute. The crowd on the roof jumped up and down and cheered as though a goal had been scored. Stevie turned the car round near the garages. Two lads sneakily jumped off the back of the car as they wouldn't have far to run.

The gang on the garage roof booed and jeered them loudly.

"Fuckin bastards!" cursed Stevie speeding away as he watched them climb the wall. That left only Maca and Joey on the back.

The playing field was surrounded by back gardens. An angry householder watched the headlights driving round the field. He'd been attracted to the window by the noise of the engine being screwed.

"Little bastards!" he picked up the phone.

Stevie zig-zagged out into the middle of the field. Maca and Joey began kicking and punching each other, trying to knock one another off the speeding car. Maca was winning the fight but Joey clung desperately to his hair. Stevie threw the car into a hand brake turn. The car spun viciously. Maca and Joey flew off the back. They scrambled to their feet and sprinted to the wall.

The car began to pick up speed. Stevie laughed crazily as the car cut down the leeway between itself and its quarry on the long run to the wall. Maca pulled away from Joey. The car bore down on the slower runner. Stevie smiled wickedly to himself, Joey slipped on the wet grass and fell under the wheel. Stevie panicked and snatched at the wheel trying to turn away in time. The crowd on the roof groaned as the car flashed past. Maca reached the wall and turned to see Joey's motionless body on the floor.

"He's hit him," gasped Sykesy.

The gang sprinted across the field to their fallen friend. Joey still lay on the floor - no sign of life.

The gang stopped on reaching him. Stevie and Cummo approached the body nervously, thinking he was dead.

"Missed me! You blind bastard," he laughed, raising his head.

"Ahh!" said Stevie, kicking him in the ribs. "Don't do that again. You frightened the shit out of me!"

"Here's the bizzies," said little Maca, spotting the headlights at the top of the playing fields. The gang sprinted for the garages. Little Maca leapt at the wall three times but could not get a grip on the top.

"Maca, don't leave me here," he shrieked as the patrol car bore down on him. Maca reached down and pulled him up by the hand.

"Don't worry lad," he said. "I won't let them get you."

The gang disappeared over the wall.

The two policemen got out of the car. They surveyed the damage the car had done to the turf.

"I wouldn't fancy the groundsman's job in the morning," said P.C. Ash.

Ann was lying face down on the couch. Smigger was trying to mount her, doggy style.

183

"No!" she said. "Once is enough."

Smigger shrugged. He knew better than to argue with her when she was like this. He pulled his trousers on.

"Where are you going?" she asked.

"I'm going to go and give Big Annie a knock," he said.

"Yeah! I bet you are," said Pauline, not believing him.

"The football team are having a night out next week. Are you taking me out?" she asked.

"Take you out," said Smigger. "I'd sooner knock you out."

"You're just using me!" she said angrily. "All you want is a cheese butty and a screw!".

"Well you should appreciate that," said Smigger, closing the door behind him.

Jerry had just had a shower. He'd dried himself and wrapped the towel around his waist. He was in the process of having a shave. The phone rang. Teresa answered it.

"Jerry, it's Smigger," she called.

Jerry walked into the room and picked up the phone.

"Hello Smigger," he said.

"Alright Jerry," replied Smigger. "Mr Davis has just phoned up and said to pick the money up at two. Have you got the car?"

"No," said Jerry. "Dougie's took our Karen out for the day in it. I think they've gone to the dog racing in Manchester."

"O.K." said Smigger. "I'll pick you up in a taxi this afternoon. See you later."

Joey tucked the last wad of money into the sports bag.

"It's a pleasure doing business with you," said Davis, shaking hands with the two lads. "Where's your friend?"

"He's sitting off with a sawn off in case there's any funny business over the money," said Smigger.

Davis laughed. "I'm not that stupid," he said. "Life's too sweet to risk everything over nothing with a gang of young up and comings like you."

"Thanks Mr Davis," said Jerry, zipping the bag up. "We'll be in touch when all this blows over. You might want another delivery."

"O.K. lads! See you. Now tara," said Davis as the two young men left the hut.

Casey was stacking empty crates in the yard outside. He scowled angrily as he watched the two lads get in the waiting taxi.

"What d'you reckon?" said Smigger. "Thirty grand in the bank and two grand each spending money?"

"Yeah," replied Jerry. "Dougie will wear that."

The hare flashed past and the traps opened. The greyhounds bolted out. Trap one bust into an early lead and missed the bumping and boring at the first bend.

"Bastard!" cursed Dougie, seeing his dog's chance was gone at the first bend. "The bastards should have jockeys." "Come on One"' yelled Karen, jumping up and down.

The greyhound had pinched a four length lead at the first bend by missing the trouble. Its lead was cut to two lengths down the back stretch by the pursuing dogs.

"Come on One!" Karen yelled frantically.

Trap Five burst out of the pursuing posse on the final bend and began to cut down Trap One's lead all the way to the line.

The dogs flashed past the post together. Trap One was just the winner.

"Yes!" squealed Karen in delight.

Dougie shook his head in disappointment. He'd wagered twenty five pound on the beaten favourite.

"Alright! Alright!" he said. "You haven't won the pools. You only had fifty pence each way on it."

"You're just jealous because I won," laughed Karen.

"Thirty three to bastard one," moaned Dougie. "How did you pick that?"

"I just liked the name," replied Karen.

"The game's not straight you know," laughed Dougie putting his arm round his girl.

"What d'you mean?" asked Karen, watching the dog handlers catch their dogs and lead them away.

"Sometimes they squeeze the dogs balls as they're going in the traps to stop them running," said Dougie.

"What!" said Karen, laughing. "Behave yourself!"

"What d'you fancy in the next race?" asked Dougie handing her the race card.

Karen studied the card. "Trap Four," she finally announced.

"What!" gasped Dougie. "It's twenty to one. What made you pick that?"

"Oh I just liked the name," said Karen coyly, handing Dougie back the race card.

"Bruised Plums"! said Dougie, reading aloud and then bursting out laughing.

It was midnight when Dougie eventually brought Karen home. They'd had a nice meal in a restaurant and had stopped off in a quiet country pub for a few drinks on the way home. The two young lovers tip-toed up the stairs slightly the worst for wear.

"Shush! Don't wake me mum up," said Karen, disappearing into the toilet.

Dougie stripped off to his underpants and waited for her. Karen returned from the toilet and put her arms round his shoulders. The couple kissed passionately for a moment.

"I've just got to go to the toilet," said Dougie breaking away. "Get your kit off, I'll be right back."

Karen began undressing. Dougie flushed the toilet and tip-toed back along the landing past Mrs Kinsella's room. He stopped suddenly hearing voices coming from within. Karen was down to her panties when he rushed into her bedroom.

"Come here quick!" he said, grabbing her by the hand and dragging her along the landing, forgetting her nakedness. They stopped outside her mother's bedroom and listened at the door.

"D'you think they've gone to bed now?" asked Eddie in a worried voice.

"I think so," said Mrs Kinsella.

Karen's eyes near popped out and she grabbed her nose to stop herself laughing out loud. The young couple fled back to Karen's room in fits of muffled laughter.

"Looks like me mum's getting rid of the cobwebs," laughed Karen.

"Fairplay to her," replied Dougie, kissing her lips. He descended to her large breasts, caressing her big hard red nipples with his lips. Karen closed her eyes, enjoying the sensation and running her fingers through his hair.

"But if there's any hanky panky tonight you'll get the back of my hand," blurted Dougie, imitating Mrs Kinsella's words as he switched from one breast to the other. The couple burst out laughing and collapsed onto the bed.

Teresa turned over in bed and reached for Jerry. She woke up in alarm when she realised he wasn't there.

Jerry breezed into the room with a cup of tea for his girl.

"You're up early aren't you?" said Teresa, sitting up in bed and looking at the clock.

"Couldn't sleep," replied Jerry, handing her the cup of tea. "I've got to go to me mum's to give her a dropsy, and I've got Dougie's few quid for him as well. D'you want anything to eat before I go?"

"No thanks," replied Teresa.

Jerry kissed her on the lips and left. He bounced down the stairs out of the flat into the street. He began his mile long walk to his mum's house.

Karen straddled Dougie's loins and smiled wickedly at him as she eased herself into position. Her mouth opened momentarily as if in astonishment as she felt him pierce her. Dougie smiled and looked up at her beautiful face and body. She trailed her fingers round the hair on the back of her head as she pushed slowly down on him.

"Oohh! I'd hate to be a lad," she oozed.

"Why?" asked Dougie bemused.

"You don't know what it feels like up here," she simpered.

"It's alright down here too," said Dougie laughing.

Karen laughed. She leant forward onto his ribs and began to batter down on him building up to full speed. Dougie lay back and watched her large breasts clatter repeatedly into each other and then bounce comically away again. Suddenly she stopped as though someone had walked over her grave.

"What is it?" asked Dougie, seeing the alarm on her face.

Jerry turned the key in the lock and opened the front door.

"It's our Jerry," she blurted, sprawling under the blankets for cover.

Jerry walked up the stairs. He looked in his old bedroom where Dougie was supposed to be sleeping. He smiled to himself when he realised no-one was there. He went to Karen's room and found the two lovers in bed.

"I thought so," he laughed. "You make sure she's taking tablets, I don't want any fat bellies in this house."

Dougie laughed. Jerry tossed him a thick roll of money held together with an elastic band.

"How much is there?" asked Dougie, catching it.

"Two!" replied Jerry. "Smigger put the other thirty into the account."

"Sound!" replied Dougie.

"How come me mum's not up yet. I only came round to give her a dropsy," said Jerry, heading out of the door for his mother's room.

Karen and Dougie looked at each other in horror.

"Hang on a minute Jerry," said Dougie, trying to call him back.

Karen jumped out of bed and put her nightgown on. Dougie leapt into his jeans. Jerry knocked on his mother's door and breezed in. Jerry stopped dead in his tracks as he saw his mother in bed with the stranger. Karen and Dougie arrived behind him in the door way, too late.

Tears began to well up in his eyes. He felt betrayed. His mother was downcast. She felt ashamed. She tried to avoid his accusing eyes. Large tears began to drip down his face. Karen began to cry as she saw the anguish and heartbreak on her brother's face.

"What about me dad?" gulped Jerry, finally speaking.

Dougie stared at his friend in silence. He felt like he'd been stabbed in the stomach.

"I was only bringing a fuckin dropsy round," growled Jerry, lashing the loose two hundred pounds over the bed.

"Listen son," said Eddie, trying to speak, "I love your mother."

"I'm not your fuckin son," growled Jerry, going beserk.

He went for Eddie with his hands and head. The blows poured in. Eddie made no attempt to defend himself other than to try and fend the blows off.

"Jerry! Jerry!" shouted his mother. Dougie snatched him by the waist and dragged him away. Mrs Kinsella flung herself in front of Eddie, knowing Jerry wouldn't attack for fear of striking her.

"You're a fuckin slut!" roared Jerry. "I'm going to kill you! You old bastard," he yelled at Eddie.

"Calm down! Calm down!" said Dougie, trying to restrain him.

"And you," said Jerry, switching his attack to Dougie. "You're supposed to be me mate and you're turning a blind eye while some cunt's goosing me ma."

The powerful butt caught Dougie by surprise and on the bridge of his nose. He dropped like a stone. Jerry shoved past Karen and ran down the stairs.

187

"Fuck it! I'm giving meself up," he roared.

He leapt into the car and scorched away.

Dougie and Smigger borrowed Joey's car and searched every pub and bar they thought he might go, but nobody had seen him. Teresa was sitting near the phone when Dougie and Smigger arrived at the flat. Dougie shook his head. It was almost midnight and still there was no sign of him.

"I hope the police haven't got him," she said.

The car was parked on a piece of wasteland near the canal. There was a half overgrown towpath that ran along next to the car. Jerry sat alone in the long grass, his eyes reddened with tears. He hurled a rock into the canal. He was drunk out of his mind. He took a swig from the whisky bottle next to him and gulped the drink down with a gasp. He was beginning to hallucinate. The lonely spot on the canal was a favourite place where his father used to take him fishing when he was alive.

Jerry began to hear voices. "Quick dad! I've got a bite! Help me!" shouted a young eight year old lad.

His father sprang to his aid and snatched the straining fishing rod with one hand. Jerry tried to focus on the vision. The young boy was him. The man was his father.

"Go on, reel it in," said his father.

"What am I going to do now that me mum's bang at it?" mumbled Jerry.

"That's it," encouraged his father as the fish skipped along the water about to be landed.

"I suppose me mum's still young and she's still entitled to some fun," reasoned Jerry.

The young boy reeled the fish in. His father unhooked it and dropped it into the keep net. Jerry passed out into the long grass.

It was two o'clock the next morning. Teresa heard the screech of brakes outside. Jerry bumped onto the pavement and stopped the car. He fell out of the driver's seat rotten drunk. He kicked the car and staggered into the flats. Teresa picked up the phone. Karen answered it first ring.

"Hello," she said.

"Hello Karen, it's Teresa. Jerry's just turned up rotten drunk. He's parked the car on the pavement. You better get Dougie or Smigger to come round and move it before someone robs it or the police see it."

"How's Jerry?" asked Karen.

"I don't know. I'll just put him to bed and see what he's like when he sobers up," replied Teresa.

Jerry opened the front door.

"I've been fishing," he announced, staggering into the bedroom. He collapsed on to the bed, scruffy and unshaven. Teresa began to undress him.

"I'm giving meself up," he gibbered. "I'm giving meself up," and then passed out.

Dougie and Smigger walked into the bedroom. Teresa looked at them but said nothing.

"He's in some state," said Dougie quietly. "I don't blame him," said Smigger. "Imagine coming home and finding some cunt knocking a slice off your ma."

It was dark when Jerry started coming round. He groaned, feeling very rough.

"Come on, you get up and get a shower and a shave. You stink, you're not sleeping with me like that."

There was no movement other than a grunt.

"Come on," she said, shaking him. "I'll change the sheets."

Jerry staggered into the bathroom in obedience. He showered and shaved and walked into the living room in his track suit. Teresa was pouring coffee.

"Well, are you alright now?" she asked.

Jerry sipped his coffee. "Yeah, I'm sound," he replied.

"You've got to realise your mum's got her own life to lead," said Teresa.

"That's alright as long as she leads it away from me or I'll put her and her fancy fella in fuckin hospital," growled Jerry.

The factory guard locked the front gate as the security van drove in with the week's wages. Smigger, Dougie and Jerry strolled along the narrow public foot path that ran adjacent to the factory. They watched the guard carry the money upstairs to the wages office inside the factory.

"We'll need guns," said Smigger, gazing up at the security cameras.

"Yeah," agreed Dougie, "we'll just hacksaw a few railings off and take them by surprise. It'll be easy to get away down the path."

"Yeah," said Smigger. "The police will come to the front of the factory and have to go right round the back while we'll be gone."

"What about the guns?" asked Jerry as they strolled innocuously down the path as though nothing was happening.

"I can get the sawn-offs easy," replied Dougie, "forty five quid each."

"How d'you feel about shooting someone?" asked Jerry.

"If they're prepared to bet their life against my liberty it's got to be their life every time," replied Dougie.

"We can take bets on which way they flop," laughed Smigger.

"How much d'you think is there?" asked Dougie.

"Roughly about forty thousand going by the size of the workforce," guessed Jerry. "There's only one problem."

"What's that?" asked Smigger.

"We're going to need someone else to give us a hand," said Jerry.

"Who?" asked Dougie.

"Don't know," shrugged Jerry.

"What about our Joey?" suggested Smigger. "He can drive for us on this one."

"D'you think he's got the bottle?" asked Jerry.

Smigger shrugged. "We'll have to test him out," he said.

Two nights later the three lads and Smigger's younger brother, Joey approached the stolen white Capri that had been cleverly parked behind the local labour club - a stone's throw away from the local police station.

"That's the robbed car that was round last night," blurted Joey. "It got chased everywhere."

"Correct," said Smigger, handing him gloves and a balaclava. "So they'll be out in force looking for it tonight."

"We want to see how you perform when your shitter's twitching," said Jerry.

"D'you want to come on one with us or what?" asked Dougie. "This'll be harder than the touch."

Joey opened the car door, his three companions donned balaclavas and climbed into the car. They watched him kick the tyres to make sure they were alright. He slid into the driver's seat and started the engine. He listened to it as it turned over. Jerry turned and looked at Smigger, impressed. Smigger sat in the back with a big grin on his face.

"I've been teaching him," he announced proudly.

Joey clipped his safety belt on. He slid a cassette into the tape deck and the music boomed out the speakers as the powerful car pulled away. The car screeched out into the road past the police station and down the lane towards the countryside.

They stopped at a set of traffic lights. The lads in the back instinctively pushed the door locks down. It was a favourite ploy of the police to come up behind a stolen car at traffic lights, open the door and drag the driver out, thus capturing everyone in the car. Joey was careful to leave a gap between himself and the car in front so he could pull out and roar off if danger threatened. The lights changed and the car sped away.

Joey spent the next half hour putting the car through its paces on the country lanes to Southport. The music banged in his ears and bounced his adrenalin. It was interrupted only by the odd screech of wheels.

The car was running low on petrol. Joey slowed as he approached a petrol station. It used to be self service but now they'd employed an attendant to stop the young car thieves filling up and driving away without paying. Joey drove on.

They found a self-service station and pulled in as if to pay. They removed their balaclavas. Joey stopped at the petrol pump furthest away from the pay kiosk. Jerry got out and filled the tank up. The man in the kiosk watched them carefully but was busy with other customers in the garage. It was always suspicious when a group of teenagers pulled in in a fast car and the front passenger got out to fill up rather than the driver. Jerry shook the last drop of petrol into the tank and replaced the pump. He got back into the car and Joey drove towards the kiosk as if they were going to get out and pay. The man watched them suspiciously. Joey accelerated away and out of the forecourt as the man tried to write down the registration number, distracted by Smigger's and Dougie's bare backsides spread across the back window.

"Hello, is that the police?" asked the man as the car sped back past the garage on the other side of the dual carriage way.

The car shot away into the night. It sped along under the orange fluorescent street lamps, down country lanes and into the blue night sky. Hospital, buses and other bright lights rushed back into the distance in a blur of colour. The music reverberated around the car and through Joey's head. Nobody spoke. They were lifted by the loud beating music. Joey smiled to himself. He felt ten feet tall. He knew the police would be waiting for hlm with their best drivers and fastest cars. He couldn't wait.

The car zoomed into a bus stop on the estate. The street was packed with youngsters waiting for the robbed car to come round. The youngsters milled around the car wanting to know what was going on.

"Any cars been round?" asked Joey, referring to any stolen cars.

"Yeah!" replied Sykesy. "Ritchie and little George were round in a three thou Ghia coup."

The two lads were from a rival estate. When both gangs had a car on the same night it was customary to have a burn off. One car would lead the other in a race through the side streets or which ever course it chose to go, trying to shake off its pursuer. If it failed it would be the other car's turn to lead and try and shake off it's pursuer. There was tremendous loss of face to the loser and another glorious page in the legend of the winning driver.

"Let's go and find them," said Joey.

There was a roar from the crowd. Two fast cars, two boss drivers and police everywhere with their own top men. They were in for a show tonight.

Ritchie and little George were talking to two teenage girls in a dark suburban street. Ritchie clocked the flash of headlights behind him in the rear view mirror.

"Who's this?" he asked, breaking off his conversation with the girls.

Joey pulled alongside.

Evening chaps. Where did you get the shed?" he asked, winding the window down and Ritchie up.

"Cheeky cunt!" growled Ritchie. "This goes faster than your ma's arse on payday."

Joey laughed, ignoring the insult.

"Shall we dance?" he asked in a posh voice.

"Yeah. We'll bat first," replied Ritchie, clipping his seat belt on.

The car shot away picking up speed. Joey dogged him all the way. The speeding cars shot round the tight bends and in and out of parked cars. Neighbours came to their doors in the wake of the noisy engines knowing there was a car chase on. Ritchie burst out onto the East Lancashire Road. He was unable to shake off Joey in the dangerous side streets at high speeds. He tried his luck on the open road. Joey gunned the car after him and began to make ground. Ritchie watched him in the rear view mirror as he tried to overtake. He threw the car across to block him off as they approached the area where the young kids were gathered to watch the chase. The two cars flashed past the traffic lights flat to the boards. Joey swung the car right through the junction past the two cars at the lights and up the wrong side of the dual carriage way. Drivers pulled over in panic as they saw the headlights hurtling towards them. Inch by inch, yard by yard Joey was beginning to get ahead. The next set of traffic lights were on red. Ritchie pushed his foot down harder. The car flew through a gap in the traffic and Joey swung back at the lights onto the proper side of the road, just failing to overtake Ritchie. The cars shot away into the night. The startled drivers and passers by watched the police come tearing out of the road after them, blue lights flashing everywhere. The cars turned into more side streets and flew down the dimly lit roads. Ritchie knew he couldn't shake him off on the straight. The cars swung out at a roundabout. Ritchie drove round it twice slowing down acknowledging he couldn't shake Joey and deliberately offering him the lead. It was Joey's turn to bat. Ritchie pulled in behind him and flashed his headlights to signal he was ready. Joey shot away. Ritchie ignored the chase and shot straight off in a different direction, catching a glimpse of the speeding police car bearing down on him in the rear view mirror.

Ritchie zoomed through the shopping centre and turned right up the wrong side of the dual carriage way. The police car charged after him. Ritchie began to pull away. The police car just couldn't match the horse power of the superior car.

"He's on the radio," blurted little George looking back.

Ritchie swung the car over to the right side of the road and put his foot down. An unmarked police car came tearing out of the junction and shot down the dual carriage way after them. A blue light was stuck on the roof, Kojak style, above the driver's head. The squad car had stayed in touch long enough for the police to get one of their Tango Charlie pursuit vehicles, their top car chase units, onto the tail of the stolen car.

"Game on," said Ritchie looking back in the mirror, realising who was chasing him. He swung the car left into the side streets, trying to shake off his pursuers in the dark tight bends through the chicanes of parked cars in the lonely frightened dark streets that were brought to light by the flashing blue lights. There seemed to be police cars everywhere. They set up road blocks at different junctions and then moved on somewhere else as their quarry changed course.

The gap between hunter and hunted slowly but surely began to grow as the cars flashed through the dark streets.

"The kid's got talent," said the police driver as the quarry swung round a tight bend. A man walking his dog cowered behind a tree as he saw speeding cars hurtling towards him.

"Little bastards!" he cursed as the cars shot past.

Ritchie swung out onto the dual carriage way and headed up towards the traffic lights on the wrong side of the road. The persistent police officer refused to give in and sped after him. There was pandemonium at the traffic lights as Ritchie cut up the other startled drivers and turned left towards Croxteth at the traffic lights.

The police car zoomed after him through the chaos.

"We better break off-before someone gets killed," said the police officer in the passenger seat, looking back at the chaos at the traffic lights.

"No chance!" growled the driver, "I want this bastard!"

The cars flew left handed towards Fazackerly. Ritchie pressed his foot down hard, ignoring the red traffic lights at the junction of a busy main road that loomed up before him. Ritchie watched the cars, lorries and wagons crossing his path in front of him. He blasted his foot down and accelerated towards his fate. Little George mouthed a swear word and closed his eyes. To Ritchie the excitement of a car chase was the great experience in life. It was even better than fulfilling his wildest sexual fantasy. His heart pounded. The adrenalin flowed. Not knowing whether he was going to live or die and knowing that both the police and his father would kill him if he got caught, he hurtled towards his destiny.

The car zapped safely through the junction between traffic and down into the dark open lane beyond. He could see his pursuers beginning to lose ground. The gamble had paid off. The car raced on. Ritchie knew he had only to get past the next set of traffic lights and he was safe. He only had to turn into an estate or some side streets to lose his pursuers.

The lights changed from green to red. Ritchie smiled and put his foot down. He wasn't going to fall at the last fence with the race won. The lights facing the traffic heading towards town turned to green. The cars started. Ritchie blared his horn aloud, seeing the danger. The startled taxi driver slammed on the brakes. A young mother driving home with her two young children didn't see the speeding car that was hidden from view by the taxi. She kept going. She turned just in time to see the headlight flying towards her and death laughing at her. The car crumpled on impact in a shower of flying metal and glass.

"Shit!" cursed the taxi driver, jumping from his cab. He looked in the at the remains of the dead mother and children. He looked over in shock as little George scrambled from the wreckage of the stolen car and tried to run. His legs went completely on him. His ankle was broken and his foot looked as though it was on the wrong way round. Ritchie scrambled out and sprinted towards the wooden fence and the safety of the darkened playing fields beyond. The taxi driver didn't realise what made him do it but something just came over him. He chased after Ritchie. Ritchie vaulted onto the fence and almost made the sanctuary of the darkness. The taxi driver dragged him back from the top of the fence. He piled into him with his hands and feet as the chasing police car skidded to a halt. The police hauled the enraged driver off Ritchie and placed him in the safety of the back of the police car as police units seemed to arrive from all directions. The taxi driver, a big strong man in his early thirties, burst into tears, overcome by it all.

Joey watched the meat wagon coming towards him. He turned right, driving normally, waiting to see if they had spotted him. The police jeep turned the corner and belted after them at top speed.

"What d'you think you're going to catch with that soft arse? said Joey in the rearview mirror. The car was much too powerful to be threatened by an inferior motor as the police jeep. Joey changed gear and swept away leaving the jeep trailing in his wake. They drove down Jerry's street towards the corner of the estate where all the kids were gathered. A bobby on the beat stood at the corner of the road. He spotted the hooded men in the car and flagged it down.

"Look at this cunt," said Joey, amazed at the audacity of the man. "Just as though we are going to stop."

The car drove past the young policeman and stopped in the middle of the dual carriage way. The policeman came running over after them. As soon as he got close Joey pulled slowly away just out of the policeman's reach and stopped again on the other side of the road, waiting for and laughing at the hapless officer. The policeman could hear the young kids laugh at him from across the street. He picked up his radio and called for assistance. Joey turned the music up and shot away. The car sped through the winding side streets looking for a chase. The car closed up behind the police jeep that had chased them earlier and began to follow them.

"I wonder how long it'll take them to notice," laughed Smigger.

Joey tailed the jeep for a few minutes and got bored. He flashed the car in front and pulled up alongside. Jerry, still wearing his balaclava, wound the window down and stuck his head out. The policeman wound his window down in astonishment wondering what the man had to say.

"Er officer," said Jerry in a posh voice, "we're going that way."

The car pulled away revealing Smigger's and Dougie's backsides spread across the rear windscreen.

"Cheeky bastards" muttered the officer, setting off in pursuit and radioing in the direction the car was heading in.

The car swung left through the red lights and scorched away from its pursuers round the double roundabout under the bridge and away up the dual carriage way. A fleet of police cars braked as they saw their quarry driving in the opposite direction on the other side of the reservation.

The policeman came running up to the driver at the scene of the car crash, the radio still crackling in his ear.

"Come on," he shouted, "there's another one coming our way."

They dragged Ritchie from the back of the car and handed him to their colleagues. They scrambled into the car and sped away into the night. Joey kept driving towards Croxteth. They shot past the traffic lights and zoomed down the road past three blocks of high rise flats. The lights changed to green. Joey shot through them as the Tango Charlie pursuit vehicle burst through the lights from the left. The flashing blue light cascaded colour all around as the high performance car swung left after its quarry. "O.K.A." said Smigger

194

looking back and identifying the car. It was one of two Tango Charlie pursuit vehicles the police used in that area. The young car thieves identified them from the first three letters of their registration number. The drivers used to like to brag to each other about who they'd been chased by in their regular duels with the police.

Joey braked and swung the car right at the T junction in front of the row of shops. He watched the pursuing car scramble round the corner going too fast. Joey shot away and took the second turning on the left.

"Oh shit," cursed Smigger as they shot down the dead end. He and Dougie reached for the sun roof and began fighting who was going to get out first. Jerry shooed them back from the sun roof.

"It's not a dead end," he growled.

Joey bumped the car onto the pavement and shot across the grass lawn across more pavement and out into another street. The police car came after them but was beginning to lose ground to the superior car and driver. The car screeched round a bend and out onto the main road towards Kirkby. The police car screeched round after it and headed towards town by mistake. Smigger watched the pursuers disappear into the distance.

"Flying colours," said Dougie in the back seat.

"Pity we can't say the same about you two pricks," answered Joey, referring to the sun roof incident.

"They'll be looking for us around here before long," said Jerry. "Head towards Kirkby and then turn off to Huyton. We'll try to get back into town that way and then dump the car."

The car flew along the dark country lane towards Huyton. The road eventually led them to a large roundabout near Prescot. Joey followed the signs towards Liverpool. He stopped at the first set of traffic lights. Smigger and Dougie locked the doors. A TR7 pulled up next to them. The two young men in it looked across at the powerful car and the four hooded men on it. They laughed realising it was stolen. The driver revved the engine in challenge. Joey looked across at them and revved his engine in acceptance. The lights changed to green. The cars scorched away. Joey rattled the gear stick through the numbers first, second, third, fourth. They were much too quick for their challengers and were slowing down for the next set of red lights as the TR7 caught up. The lights changed again and the two cars shot away. The driver flashed his lights and turned off.

The car sped towards town along the empty and deserted roads. They stopped at traffic lights behind a couple of cars. The lights changed. A police car drove past them from another quarter of the junction. The lads watched anxiously to see if they'd been spotted. They could see the officer watching them and speaking into his radio. The lights changed. Joey put his foot down. He knew they were in danger again. The car shot down Rocky Lane onto Queens Drive, ignoring the red light. All the lights seemed to be on green as they tore down the road towards Bootle There was no sign of any pursuit. Joey pulled off the drive at the roundabout under Walton flyover and drove normally onto the main road to Aintree looking for somewhere to dump the car. He didn't see the unmarked police car watching them drive past. The Tango Charlie pursuit vehicle pulled out onto the road behind them. The lights changed to red just past Walton Hospital. Smigger was sitting behind Joey. He forgot to press the door lock down.

Two bikers sat on their'motorbikes opposite them at the lights. They looked at each other in surprise as they saw the two police officers get out of the car and quickly and stealthily approach the car in front. Dougie felt somebody walk on his grave. He turned just in time to see the pursuit vehicle and the policeman almost at the car.

"K.T.B." he blurted. Smigger pushed the button down a split second before the officer tried to yank the door open. Joey screeched out around the car in front. One police officer was dragged along the road and landed clutching his knee. The bikers panicked trying to get out of the way as the car just missed them. Joey sped away and turned left at the prison. They sped along past the jail. The policeman helped his injured partner back to the car. Joey swung into a side street and parked it. The lads got out. They climbed over a fence onto the disused railway line that used to serve the munitions factory during the war. They made their way home swiftly and quietly through the darkness.

The five gangsters sat downstairs on a stay-behind in one of Russell's night clubs. The phone rang. Russell, who was pouring the drinks at the bar, answered it.

"Bombhead, it's for you!" he said.

Bombhead was kissing one of the young barmaids.

"Won't be a minute," he said, breaking away. He picked up the phone.

"Hello Matthew. It's me - Harry," said a distressed voice at the other end.

Bombhead's happy go lucky attitude changed to a black mood. He knew something was wrong.

"Hello mate. What can I do for you?" he asked his boytime friend.

"I've just come from the morgue," said Harry in tears. "I had to identify the wife and kids."

"Who! Shirley? What happened?" said Bombhead in shock.

"Car crash," said Harry. "Some young tearaway in a robbed car came through a red light."

"I'll kill him for you," growled Bombhead.

"No," said Harry. "That's too quick for him. I want you to cripple him. I want him to live the rest of his life in great pain. I'll pay you anything you like."

"No I'll do it for nothing. Be my pleasure. What s the fella's name?"

"Don't know," replied Harry. "They won't tell me who it is but they've got him."

"Leave it with me. I'll sort it out and let you know when it's been done. O.K.?" said Bombhead.

"O.K." replied the distraught man and hung up.

It was dinner time the next day. Joey parked the car on the road at the top of the wasteland. The four lads got out of the car and headed for the perimeter fence in the wholesaler's yard. Maca pulled the green wire fence up from the bottom while his friends crawled underneath it. They crept over to the warehouse door and opened it. There was no-one about.

"Look at this!" said Cummo, spotting a pallet of coffee.

The boys picked up a stack each and ran to the perimeter fence with them. Joey stayed at the pallet to keep watch as his friends returned for more. They began firing the coffee under the fence. Stevie jumped after them and began ferrying them to the car.

One of the warehousemen heard a noise and came to see what was going on.

"Hey you!" he called, spotting the young thieves.

The gang fled with their coffee into the yard. Cummo and Joey fired the coffee under the fence for all they were worth while Maca held it up for them. The two lads scrambled underneath as two men from the warehouse came running up. Stevie held the fence up as Maca wriggled through just in time.

"Little bastards!" cursed the warehouseman, lifting the fence.

Maca swiped at his finger with a wooden stick. The man got his finger out of the way just in time.

"Hurry up. Get all the coffee up to the car," he ordered.

The men watched the boys carry the coffee to the car and then come back for more. Maca stood his ground.

"Come on cunt," he growled. "Stick your head through the fence and I'll knock it off."

"I'll see you again son," growled the warehouseman, knowing he was snookered.

Stevie arrived up the hill with the last of the coffee. Maca dropped the stick and fled after him. He jumped into the car and drove off.

The pub was crowded with lunchtime drinkers when the lads came in to sell the coffee. The scaffolders had finished work early, again, and were sitting in the corner.

"Anyone want to buy coffee? Two jars for a pound!" roared Joey.

The hardcase who they'd filled in over the salmon looked up and sneered on seeing his young assailants. He watched them moving from table to table selling the coffee. An idea struck him.

"I think I'll go and put a bet on," he said to his friends and left the pub.

He stopped at the public phone box on the way to the betting shop.

"Hello, is that the police? There's a gang of young lads selling knock off coffee in the Crown," he said.

He walked back over to the pub laughing to himself. He sat down with his friends and waited.

Two minutes later P.C. Ash and three other officers walked through the door. The lads were caught red handed. The four lads ran for the bar. Three of them made it. They vaulted over the bar and escaped into the lounge and out into the street. The hardcase deliberately tripped Maca as he tried to run. Ash seized him straightaway. It took three officers to drag the struggling youth away.

"I'm gonna kill you, you bastard!" Maca slobbered at the hardcase. The pub regulars began hiding and rolling the stolen coffee they'd bought away from them. W.P.C. Thatcher picked up one of the carrier bags. All of a sudden she was surrounded by rolling coffee jars that appeared as if from nowhere. The regulars avoided her accusing gaze as they looked innocently away from her.

It was late in the afternoon. Jerry, Smigger and Dougie sat in their parked car on a lonely woodland estate. Another car pulled up in front of them and a young man got out carrying a sportsbag.

"Hello Cheesy," said Dougie, shaking the man's hand. "Did you get them?"

"Yes," replied Cheesy, "shall we test them out?"

The four lads disappeared into the woods. Cheesy picked a quiet spot and produced two sawn off shotguns from the sportsbag.

"That's great," said Smigger, holding the weapon. "What kind of damage will it do?"

"See for yourself," said Cheesy, gesturing towards a tree as a target.

Smigger let rip. The shotgun blast tore into the tree amid flying bark and fresh wood.

"That's sound that," said Smigger in delight as Dougie handed the money over.

"What kind of damage will it do to humans?" asked Jerry, carrying the other gun and watching a cow feeding in the neighbouring pasture.

"Lots," replied Cheesy.

"Bang!" Jerry let rip. The cow dropped like a stone and mooed pitifully in a splatter of blood.

"What did you do that for?" asked Dougie angrily.

"Wipe its arse and fire it in a butty, I'll be back for it later," laughed Jerry.

"You're getting worse," replied Dougie.

It was two o'clock in the morning. Smigger sat alone in the car waiting. The security guard in the biscuit factory poured himself a coffee from his flask and took a bite from one of his cheese sandwiches. He gazed up at his monitors. Nothing was happening. It was another long boring night.

Dougie and Jerry were down the narrow path frenziedly sawing away at one of the railings facing the wages office. They sawed through the last remaining piece of iron and tossed the railing into the ditch behind them.

Jerry arrived home. Teresa was waiting up for him.

"What's the matter?" he asked.

"What are those two shotguns doing in the wardrobe?" she asked angrily.

"Don't start," growled Jerry.

"What happens if you kill someone?" she asked.

"The only people who might get killed are the Roy of the Rovers. Daft cunts who want to be heroes. I don't care about them. They deserve all they get," replied Jerry.

"You're going to end up dead or in prison," snapped Teresa.

"That's alright. I'm going to heaven when I die!" replied Jerry.

"You don't go to heaven if you kill people," replied Teresa.

Jerry sneered. "D'you remember that parable that God told about the master and his three servants?" he asked.

"Which one?" asked Teresa.

"The one where the master gave them all money. One went and invested his wisely. The second put his in the bank and the third went and buried his in the sand until the master got back. The master rewarded the first two and threw the other one out."

"So what?" asked Teresa.

"Well I'm not going to bury my talents in the sand," replied Jerry.

Teresa looked at him in dismay. "You're going off your head you," she retorted.

The security van arrived right on time. The factory guards closed the gates behind it as it drove in. One guard got down from the van and went to the back of it. The guard inside opened the hatch and threw the money out. The driver looked round to find a masked man holding a shotgun to his head.

"Get out!" ordered Smigger.

"Get on the floor!" yelled Jerry, bursting round the blind side of the van. The two guards were spreadeagled on the floor.

"Throw the rest of the money out," roared Dougie to the guard in the back of the van, "or we'll blow your mate's fuckin head off."

Jerry fired the shotgun into the air. The money came flying out of the hatch.

One of the security guards was beginning to get brave. Smigger jammed the gun against his head.

"Don't even think about it, soft arse. D'you think the security firm give two shits if I put a hole in your head?" he growled.

Dougie snatched the money and ran back to the railings, covered by Jerry and Smigger. Smigger hurled the van's keys into the distance as the factory guards and a posse of workmen came running after them. They sprinted down the path. A guard came charging out of the control hut at the end of the factory premises. Smigger cracked him on the jaw with the gun butt. The man collapsed unconscious. The three men ran on pursued by a posse of heroes from the factory.

Smigger and Dougie disappeared into the tunnel at the end of the path. Jerry stopped and waited at the entrance trying to buy time. He aimed his gun and his pursuers scattered off the path for cover. Jerry fired the pellets just over their heads. The guard kept running, realising the gun was empty. Jerry emptied the spend cartridges and replaced them as the man bore down on him. He snapped the gun shut and took aim as the man hurled himself at the robber. For a split second Jerry was almost going to kill him. He side stepped the flying man and slammed the gun in his face. The man collapsed unconscious. Jerry jammed the gun against his head. In his excitement he almost squeezed the trigger. The pursuing crowd stopped.

"D'you think it's worth it, eh?" Jerry yelled at the fallen man.

"Come on," called Smigger from the other end of the tunnel.

Jerry sprinted down the tunnel and baled into the waiting getaway car. Joey swung the car down the side streets and across the main road into more side streets. There was no sign of pursuit. They switched back to their own car in the car park of a nearby sports centre. Smigger safely drove away.

"No more guns," blurted Jerry. "No more."

The pub closed in the afternoon. The regulars, including Jerry, Smigger, Billy and Dougie stood outside gambling in the pitch and toss school. They had two hours to kill before opening time. A large circle of men gathered round the man holding the ten pence coins on the back of his hand - two facing up heads, one facing up tails.

"A pound he heads them" shouted Billy.

His bet was immediately accepted. The hardcase who grassed on Maca was throwing the coins. He waited until all the bets had been placed.

"Is that it?" he asked.

"Yeah, go head," came the reply.

He pitched the coins high up into the air. The crowd watched them tumble to the ground, bouncing in different directions. The first one landed on heads, the second on tails. The crowd waited with baited breath as the last coin spun. It landed on heads to roars of laughter and loud cheers. The money changed hands. The hardcase scrambled after the ten pence pieces ready to pitch them for the next bet. As he picked up the last coin somebody stepped on his hand. The hardcase looked up. It was Maca. A crashing blow landed in his face. Maca hurled a wild kick at his enemy. It flew past his head, just missing as one of the scaffolders dragged him back.

"Me and you! You grassing bastard"! snarled Maca.

"I'll have a pound on Maca," cried Billy Smith.

One of the scaffolders accepted the bet. There was a hurried rush of betting as the pitch and toss school began to bet on the fight Maca took his coat off. The hardcase wiped the trickle of blood from his mouth and removed his jacket. The two men circled each other. The two men jumped at each other throwing punches. The crowd roared their approval. The hardcase landed a heavy blow on Maca's jaw. Maca powered through not noticing the blow. The rest was one way traffic. The punches and head butts had the scaffolder reeling backwards under the barrage. He eventually went down in front of a parked car. Maca kicked him in the head. His head flew back against the registration plate.

A large gash over his temple began to bleed heavily. Maca kept kicking and punching him. Dougie dragged him off.

The money changed hands as Maca stood there out of breath. The hardcase had had enough. Two of his friends helped the battered man to his feet.

"A pound he heads them," someone shouted.

The crowd went back to its pitch and toss school as though nothing had happened.

Karen came dashing across the road.

"Jerry!" she shouted, flagging down a taxi. "Teresa's having the baby!"

Jerry, Dougie and Smigger piled into the taxi behind her and the taxi pulled away.

Jerry's and Teresa's mothers were already in the waiting room.

"How is she?" asked Jerry.

"She's fine. She's just gone into labour," replied his mother.

Jerry nodded and sat down next to them in silence. He looked up at the clock. There was nothing he could do now except wait. He paced slowly up and down, nervously chewing a match. Mrs Sims watched his anxiety and helplessness. She knew her daughter had a good man in her life.

The sister walked out into the ward. "Congratulations! You're the father of a healthy bouncing baby boy. Mother and baby are doing fine."

"Yes!" erupted Jerry, punching the air. His mother hugged and kissed him, their previous disagreement forgotten.

Smigger and Dougie queued up to shake hands.

"Well done mate," said Dougie. "Nice one," said Smigger in relief.

The clan walked into the hospital ward. Teresa lay there peaceful but drained looking.

"Oh! Isn't he lovely?" said Karen as the women gathered round the cot.

Jerry stepped nervously up to the bed.

"Are you alright?" he asked.

"I'm fine," nodded Teresa.

"How many stitches did you get?" asked Karen.

"Shut up you," snarled Jerry, affronted that Karen should bring up a topic like that in front of him.

He approached the cot and peered down at the baby. He nervously prodded it with his finger, not wanting to hurt it. The baby grabbed his fore finger.

"Ohh!" said Jerry, snatching his finger away in fright.

The women laughed at him. Jerry smiled. He didn't know what to do.

Eight hours later, the three young men were in a disco in town.

Angie Russell, her friends Cleo and Maggie, a fat girl with pimples, sat at the next table. Dougie and Smigger were arguing over which girl to pull.

"I'm not taking the pink elephant," mumbled Jerry in his drunken stupor.

"Just talk to her for a few minutes," said Smigger, "while we get them up to dance."

Jerry watched the two lads go and get the girls up to dance. The room was spinning. The lights were flashing. Jerry could see the fat girl's spotty face coming at him. He could hear her talking but couldn't hear what she was saying. He passed out.

The next morning the window cleaner placed his ladder against Jerry's window sill. Docker wrung out his chamois leather and slung it over his shoulder as he climbed the ladder. He wiped the window clean and was surprised by what he saw inside. Jerry heard the tapping on the window through his drunken stupor. He opened his eyes and looked at the window.

"Who's that?" mouthed Docker, pointing behind him. To his horror Jerry realised there was someone next to him in bed. He strained his neck, gingerly trying to see who it was without disturbing them. His worst fears were realised. It was the fat girl.

"I never, did I?" groaned Jerry, sitting up in bed.

He dragged the blankets off and jumped out of bed.

Docker nearly fell off the ladder when he saw the fat girl's naked breasts. She sat up in bed and covered herself again with the blankets and flopped back on the pillow. Docker shot down the ladder. He didn't want to miss out.

Jerry walked into the living room. Smigger was sitting on the couch, naked except for his socks. Angie walked in stark naked, carrying two cups of tea. Smigger smiled at Jerry. Jerry shook his head.

"Where's Dougie?" he asked.

"In the spare room," replied Smigger.

The door bell rang. Jerry let Docker in. He was made up to see all the naked ladies.

"Are we having a party then? he said, rubbing his hands together.

"No we're not," said Jerry, going back to bed. "Vicky's coming round to look after me while Teresa's in hospital. She better not find all you's here."

"What d'you thinks the best cream for spots?" asked the fat girl sitting up in bed.

"You'd be better off cutting your fuckin head off," said Jerry and kicked her out of the bed.

Smigger dropped the girls off in the car. Angie kissed him goodbye.

"Will I see you again?" she asked.

"Well, I'm not doing nothing on Sundays," replied Smigger.

Vicky opened the flat door with the key Teresa had given her. She could hear the falling water in the shower. She stood unnoticed watching Jerry shower. She'd fancied him for ages. Jerry felt her presence. He stepped calmly out of the shower and wrapped a towel round his waist.

"Hello girl," he said. "How are you'"

"I'm fine," smiled Vicky, watching his wet muscular body. "Is that red mark on your neck a love bite?" she asked.

"Shit!" said Jerry, scrambling to the mirror and rubbing toothpaste on the offending mark.

Vicky smiled to herself - maybe Jerry wasn't untouchable after all.

Jerry and Vicky walked into the hospital ward.

"He's lovely isn't he?" said Vicky admiring the baby.

Teresa smiled sitting up in bed. Jerry handed her a box of chocolates.

"Is there anything else you want?" he asked.

"No thanks. I'm fine," said Teresa, still drawn and tired looking. "What's that mark on your neck?" she asked suspiciously.

"What mark?" asked Jerry innocently, staring in the hand mirror to see what it was.

"Oh!" he said. "I fell over in the bushes last night coming home pissed. I had to wet the baby's head, didn't I?"

Jerry and Vicky sat in the pub after visiting time was over.

"You were lucky there," said Vicky.

"No, " said Jerry. "Teresa would never believe that I'd been carrying on. How are you getting on? I haven't seen much of you since you split with Dougie. Are you still courting?"

"No," she sighed. "That was only a way of getting back at Dougie."

"You must be dying for it then if you haven't had it for that long," laughed Jerry.

Vicky punched him in the leg. "You can talk. You can't have had much the state Teresa's been in lately," she replied.

"I'm glad," replied Jerry, "I near had twins when I woke up next to that monster this morning."

Later that evening found the couple canoodling on the couch. Vicky was tipsy. Jerry ran his hand up her shapely thigh. There was no resistance until she realised her bra was undone.

"You bastard!" she said, pushing him away and trying to refasten it.

Jerry pulled her to her feet and kissed her again. She reluctantly responded. Her mini skirt slipped to the floor and Jerry helped slide her bra off.

"No," she whispered, "it's wrong.

Jerry held her, refusing to be denied.

"Imagine getting caught doing it and we haven't done it," he replied.

She pulled his T shirt over his head. Jerry picked her up on to his shoulder and carried her into the bedroom, sliding her panties off as he went. He fired the sex starved girl backwards onto the bed. Vicky clung on to the bed sheets for dear life, moaning in delight as Jerry unceremoniously drove into her.

When it was over she lay looking up at the ceiling with a guilty conscience. Jerry caressed her nipples with his lips.

203

"Me best friend's in hospital having a baby and I'm lying in bed with her boyfriend."

Jerry prepared to mount her again, not interested in her guilt complex.

"Who's the best in bed - me or Dougie?" he asked with a wicked smile.

"Is that all this means to you?" said Vicky. "Just a grind?"

"No," replied Jerry. "I'm doing something I wanted to do for years, and I'm getting me own back on Dougie for bonking our Karen."

Vicky burst out laughing. "You're mad," she said.

"Don't worry about it," he shrugged, mounting her again.

Russell sat at his desk doing some paper work when the phone rang. It was a police officer in Russell's pay.

"The consignment en route from Amsterdam is in danger," said the voice.

"What's the score?" asked Russell.

"They're waiting to raid the ship when it docks," replied the officer. "There is a customs man and police officer on board posing as seamen. They reckon they can trace it right back to you."

Russell hung up and dialled another number.

"Hello, is that the Echo? I'd like to place an advert," he said.

The topless model stood on the set. Mitchell looked up from behind his camera.

"Now put your hands together behind your back and smile," he said in the middle of a string of shots.

The phone rang. It was Russell.

"I want you to get me information on two men," growled Russell. "Usual deal."

"Okay, Cathy get dressed. That's enough for today. What are their names?" asked Mitchell, picking up a pencil.

The ship ploughed relentlessly through the heavy seas. The radio officer took down a message and handed it to the captain.

"Get two men and dump our special cargo over the side," ordered the captain.

The two seamen watched the four deckhands throw the heavy boxes over the side into the heavy sea. They sank almost immediately as the two men stood helplessly by, unable to blow their cover.

The ship docked the following morning. The police and customs men rushed aboard and arrested the crew. Mitchell was perched high up in a warehouse with his zoom lens camera. There were two particular seamen he was interested in as he photographed the scene below.

Russell swigged back a mouthful of brandy in his office.

"Bit risky isn't it? Killing policemen and customs officials?" asked Councillor Bletchley, his lawyer.

"Fuck them," growled Russell. "They've cost me a million pounds worth of gear."

Inspector Benson sat at his desk two days later. Sergeant Johnson rushed in. "Sir, they've tried to put the customs officer's name in the obituary column." Benson jumped to his feet. "Quick, we've got to find him," snapped Benson.

The customs officer strolled out of the pub where he'd had a few lunchtime drinks. He walked to the car, taking no notice of the old van parked next to it. He climbed into the front seat.

"Police informer," said an Irish voice.

The man looked up in horror. Michael-Edward fired three shots into his head. The man fell back across the front car seats, dead. Michael-Edward got out and threw a white sheet of tarpaulin over him. He dragged the body from the car and tossed it into the back of his van. The body had to disappear without trace.

It was Friday afternoon. Michael-Edward had given his gravediggers the afternoon off. They had jumped at the chance of a long weekend. The cemetery was quiet and deserted. The wind was chasing the fallen leaves across the graveyard. In the far corner of the cemetery stood two large shovels embedded in a mound of clay and earth underneath an old sycamore tree. A coffin lay in the open grave, covered in mass cards and soil tossed in by grieving relatives. The mourners had long since gone. Only the job of burying the coffin remained.

Michael-Edward was pushing a wheelbarrow along the path towards the grave. There was a steady irritating squeak coming from the wheel. The gravedigger seemed to be struggling with the weight. His head was tipped forward into the wind, with an old chequered cap balancing precariously on it. He was dressed in an old suit that had gone shiny with age. He wore a working coat over his suit and his trousers were tucked into a muddy pair of wellington boots. His face was thin with prominent cheekbones. His nose was broken and bent. His large hands were calloused and his craggy face made him look older than he was. He reached the grave and stopped. He walked forward and stood over the grave, looking down at the coffin. The grave was about six feet deep. It had two levels of wooden braces set three feet apart to bolster it and stop it from caving in. The gravedigger returned to the wheelbarrow. He pushed it to the edge of the grave. He had one last look to make sure no-one was watching. He tipped the contents into the grave.

The blood stained tarpaulin landed with a heavy thud against the coffin. The impact loosened the rope binding and a hand fell through the gap in the tarpaulin. Michael-Edward stood at the foot of the grave, legs apart, staring up to heaven with his cold emotionless eyes. His hands were stretched out in front of him, clutching two handfuls of soil.

"Sinner! Repent ye your sins. For the day of judgement is at hand." He ritually tossed the soil over the body. He clapped his hands clean and picked up his shovel. He rammed it into the mound of earth, using his foot to work the clay loose. He tossed the first shovel full into the grave.

The two engineers were working on the ship's engine. The ship was berthed in the dock.

"O.K. Paddy, try that," called the chief engineer after finishing some adjustments with a spanner.

The propeller spun into life beneath the cold dark murky waters of the Mersey. The rope holding the body to the bottom of the dock was shaken free from the concrete block by the turbulent water. The body started to float away. A group of young kids dressed in football shorts were using the docks for a swimming poool. They dived and jumped into the murky water from the dockside.

"Hey Tommy, can you do the bullet?" called the lad on the dockside to one of the lads in the water.

"What's that?" asked Tommy.

The youngster dived in head first with his hand tight to his waist. He kicked his way to the surface. His friend laughed.

"Yes, I can do that," he said.

"What's that?" said the youngster, spotting the body that had bobbed to the surface.

Tommy swam over to it and lifted the man's face out of the water. He screamed when he saw the bullet hole in his forehead and scrambled as fast as he could to the side. It was the undercover policeman.

Bombhead sat in the corner of the room reading the Beano. He laughed crazily to himself. Mad-dog and Animal looked at him and shrugged. They knew he was like that at times. They reckoned it was all the knocks on the head during his boxing career.

Benson breezed into the room seething with anger. He walked straight over to Russell. Their faces almost touched.

"There's two officers dead with wives and young children down to you," snarled Benson. He spat in Russell's face. Russell closed his eyes as the large spittle landed.

I'm going to have you," growled the inspector.

"You're not going to have anybody," piped up Bletchley. "I suggest you and your men leave. Coming in here and making threats and unsubstantiated allegations. If you don't leave I'll report you to your senior officers. I don't know who you think you are."

Mad-dog and Animal watched in silence but ready for trouble. Benson's eyes blazed at Bletchley.

"I'll tell you who I think I am. I'm the fella whose going to nail this horrible bastard and you. You turd burgling freak. You're just as guilty as he is."

Benson stormed out followed by his men.

"Angry wasn't he?" quipped Bletchley nonchalantly.

Russell wiped the large blob of spit from his face in disgust.

206

Benson stormed to his car.

"The council elections are coming up. We take Bletchley first and discredit him. We associate him with Russell and all the organised crime in this city. He's always hanging around in the public toilets looking for new pals. Get something on him," growled the inspector.

"Yes sir," said the sergeant getting into a different car and driving off.

Joey, Maca, Cummo and Stevie drove past a shop in one of the small towns surrounding neighbouring Liverpool. It was a small shop run by a bespectacled Pakistani gentleman and his family. They specialised in selling garments known as seconds. Mr Sarheed made a comfortable living buying the goods from the manufacturer at a knock down price and selling them fairly cheaply to bargain hunters who didn't care about the minor flaws in them.

"That'll do us," said Cummo watching the shop.

Joey parked up in the next street, switching the engine off. The three lads got out and walked through the back entry and up the street to the shop.

Mr Sarheed was serving a woman customer. He put the cardigan into a bag and rang the money up in the till. He passed the lady her bag.

"Thanks very much," said the elderly gentleman.

"Thank you," replied the lady.

Maca and Stevie were browsing through some sweat shirts on a hanger.

"How much are these mate?" asked Stevie calling the man over.

"Which ones?" asked Mr Sarheed, only too eager to help.

Cummo darted behind the counter on his hands and knees as soon as Mr Sarheed turned his back. He searched around for the cashbox while his friends kept the unsuspecting man busy. He crept quietly upstairs to the living quarters. He spotted the cashbox and grabbed it.

"What are you doing?" asked Mr Sarheed's daughter in a loud voice. "Ali! Ali! We're being robbed," she shouted.

Cummo charged down the stairs chased by Mr Sarheed's two grown up sons. Cummo came tearing out from behind the counter. Mr Sarheed blocked his exit at the doorway. Cummo dived through the window. Stevie fired the tray of sweat shirts at Cummo's pursuers. The two youths tripped and fell. Maca and Stevie jumped out of the broken window and charged after Cummo. Cummo burst through the entry. Joey tried to start the car but the engine was flat.

The two Pakistani men chased the young thieves. Joey jumped out of the car and started pushing it. Cummo threw himself against the back of it and began shoving for all he was worth. Stevie and Maca came tearing up the street together. Stevie looked back at his two pursuers.

"Help them bump start it! I'll see these two off," he said.

Maca threw himself at the back of the car. The car began to pick up speed. Joey leapt into the driver's seat. The engine started. Stevie watched the two men charging towards him. The first one threw a flying drop kick at him. Stevie

207

dodged aside and smashed a big right into the man's face. Ali dived at him and the two men fell to the floor wrestling.

Get in! Get in!" roared Joey. Maca and Cummo jumped in. He roared back up the street in reverse. Stevie saw the car coming and thrust Ali into its path. The car ran over his legs. He screamed in agony and released Stevie. Stevie leapt up and jumped into the waiting car. The car sped away. Cummo looked back at the stricken man. Both his legs were broken.

"That was a bit heavy wasn't it?" he said.

"It was me or him," said Stevie.

"Don't worry about it growled Joey, soon he'll be back in the bazaar with his fucking begging bowl where he belongs".

It was the early hours. A front door opened and Ritchie came out followed by his girlfriend.

"I'm glad you got bail," she said kissing him.

"So am I," replied Ritchie. "I'll see you tomorrow."

She watched him walk down the street with a happy smile on her face. She turned and closed the door. Ritchie turned down the entry between two houses and walked halfway down it. A bear of a man appeared at the other end of the entry. Ritchie stopped in his tracks. He knew something was wrong.

"I'm glad you got bail as well," said Bombhead appearing behind him in the entry.

Ritchie saw the blade in his hand.

"D'you like wheelchairs?" asked Bombhead.

Ritchie leapt at the back garden wall. Animal dragged him down and went to punch him.

"Don't," said Bombhead, catching his prey. "I want him to feel it."

He rammed the blade into the back of Ritchie's knee. Ritchie screamed. He could feel the blade slicing through his body.

"Please God! No!" he screamed. Bombhead slashed his heels and the sinews in his elbows, driving the blade in deep. He slashed Ritchie's face as Animal held him down.

"That's you fucked! Babykiller," growled Bombhead walking away, leaving the young man screaming in agony.

It was the early hours of the morning. The baby was crying, wanting feeding. Teresa got out of bed and picked him up, gently cradling his head. She noticed a movement downstairs in the yard below.

"Jerry. There's someone in the yard. Maybe it's the police."

Jerry grabbed his jeans and jumped to his feet. He peered down into the darkness.

"It's not the police. Maybe it's that bastard from upstairs come back for more. I'll go down and see."

Jerry crept downstairs into the darkness, holding a stick. The man in the bottom flat kept a white English bull terrier with a black eye in a kennel in the back yard. Jerry approached the kennel. There was somebody there. The dog bounded forward playfully, recognising Jerry.

The young boy woke up. He was sleeping in the kennel using the dog's body heat for warmth.

"What are you doing here, Sykesy? asked Jerry, looking at the state the young lad was in.

"I'm on the run from approved school," replied Sykesy.

"Well why don't you go home? You can't live like this," said Jerry.

"I've broke out twice and me dad's sent me back," replied Sykesy.

"D'you fancy a hot bath and a hot meal?" asked Jerry.

Sykesy nodded gleefully.

"Come on then," said Jerry.

Jerry walked back into the flat with Sykesy.

"Look who I've found," said Jerry.

"Hello Sykesy," said Teresa. "What's the matter, are they after you lad?"

"Yeah," replied the young waif.

"Go on and get a hot bath and I'll cook a hot meal. Are you hungry?"

"Starvin'," replied Sykesy.

Jerry took the young lad's clothes and fired them into the washing machine. They were stinking.

Sykesy came back from the bathroom a new man, dressed in Jerry's much too large pyjamas. They watched him gulp the hot tea and wolf the bacon, egg and toast in record time.

"What are they after you for?" asked Teresa.

"Sagging school," replied Sykesy.

"What d'you sag school for?" asked Jerry.

"They used to laugh at me because I wasn't as good as the others at picking some things up. The teacher used to try but even he ended up shouting at me in the end. I don't blame him. I'm stupid," he explained. "So I just didn't bother going any more. I've run away a few times. Sometimes I break into cars for somewhere to sleep. I've been caught robbing a few times as well, but I need money to live on don't I?"

"We're looking for a lodger for our spare room. D'you know anyone looking for a place?" said Teresa, feeling sorry for him.

"No," said Sykesy, not realising she meant him. "How much is it anyway?"

"Nothing!" replied Teresa. "Just be in on time for your meals and no more trouble with the police."

"That's great that, thanks," said Sykesy.

"Just one thing," said Jerry. "Don't tell anyone you're staying here."

"Why's that?" said Sykesy.

"Because the bastards are after me as well," he laughed.

The post office guard got out of the van and informed the postmaster of the delivery. He looked round the busy shopping area crowded with shoppers and signalled the all clear to the other guard. The man got out of the van and hurried into the post office.

"What d'you think?" asked Dougie.

Smigger and Jerry looked at each other. "Yeah," they said simultaneously.

"Have you seen this?" said Dougie pulling an envelope from his pocket.

"What is it?" said Jerry.

"It's a paternity suit off cakeshop doorway Lil. She's suing him," laughed Smigger, reading the charge aloud with his Hughie Green impersonation.

"Douglas Charles Lacey, You are hereby charged with having sexual intercourse in the said city of Liverpool with one Miss Linda Maguire and are hereby charged with being the father of her bastard child."

"Shut up will you, smartarse," said Dougie.

"Does it say that?" asked Jerry.

"More or less," replied Smigger.

Little Maca sat watching his father drinking whisky in the living room.

"When's Maca up in court?" asked Vicky.

"Two weeks," replied her mother.

"That's right," said her father with drunken tears welling in his eyes. "One minute he's going to be a football player - the next minute he's a jail bird."

Little Maca watched his heartbroken father pour another drink.

Maca was upstairs in his room with Cummo, Stevie and Joey listening to some music. A John Lennon song came over the radio.

Turn that off, I can't stand him," said Cummo. "Walking round bollicko with some Japanese, what's wrong with the scouse girls?"

"They're too good for him," said Joey. "I can't stand the way all the old fellas go on about The Beatles and all the young ones think it's trendy to buy their records. They were only a gang of drughead cunts writing songs about tripping and all that crap. If they were such good fellas why didn't they build a factory and give us all jobs."

"Have you heard about that new disease in America all the queers get when they have sex?" asked Stevie. "Aids they call it. Arse injected death sentence. They're all falling off the perch with it."

"Serves them right. I can't stand them bastards either," said Cummo. "Gay? Years ago Gay was a man's name. What's gay about grown men bursting into each other."

"They can't help what they are. They're born like that," said Maca.

"They should keep themselves to themselves, never mind jumping around on Top of the Pops dressed up like women and having the cheek to sing love songs. God knows what the young kids must make of them."

"It's abortionists I hate," said Maca. "See the way they were screaming when the Yorkshire Ripper was slicing them all up. But it's alright when they're chopping little babies up into pieces just because they don't want them."

"Yeah, but they don't count them as being alive, do they?" said Joey.

"They should do as soon as they're confirmed pregnant they should be made to have it and count it as a human life," said Maca.

"Yeah," agreed Stevie.

"What about if they think it's going to be handicapped?" asked Joey.

"Well why aren't handicapped people entitled to live the same as us. They have their own little world. They're happy," replied Maca. "I hate all them lesbians who are always campaigning for it. A woman's right to control her own body they say. Can they control whether they open their legs. The fuckin sluts."

"Should hang them all," said Cummo. "The doctors, the pregnant women. Stretch a few necks, you'd soon put a stop to it."

The door flew open. Little Maca burst in.

"Me and you outside, you bastard!" he growled at his elder brother.

"What's up? What have I done?" said Maca looking at the distress on his little brother's face.

Little Maca flew at him throwing punches. Some landed. Maca didn't try to fight back. Vicky came into the room amid the commotion.

"What's the matter?" asked Maca squeezing his brother so he couldn't move.

Vicky pulled little Maca away.

"No more robbing, you bastard," he screamed, almost breaking away from his sister's grasp with tears pouring down his face.

Little Maca stormed out of the house, slamming the door behind him. Maca looked up at his sister in surprise.

"What have I done?" he asked innocently.

"You're a waster," said his sister. "He doesn't like the way you've let his dad down. You can't blame the others for robbing, but you could have been someone."

Maca's face dropped. The truth hurt. His friends sat in silence and said nothing.

Little Maca arrived outside the pub. Sykesy and two young friends were waiting for him on the doorstep.

"Where's your ball?" asked Sykesey.

"Forgot it," said little Maca gloomily.

"What are we going to do tonight then?" asked one of the lads.

"I believe there's been some queers hanging round the public toilets by the park," said the other youth. "Shall we go queerbashing?"

"Yeah. Sounds good to me," said Sykesy.

"O.K." agreed little Maca. "I could do with working out on someone tonight."

Inspector Benson and Sergeant Johnson sat across the street from the public convenience. They photographed Councillor Bletchley going in.

"That's the second bog tonight," said the inspector. "Must be desperate for it."

"Be great if we catch him with someone tonight," replied the sergeant. "That would be him all washed up."

Bletchley hung around the toilet for twenty minutes.Nobody came. The officers watched him look at his watch as he decided to try somewhere else.

The four lads stood outside the toilet near the park.

"You wait here and be the bait," said one youth. "We'll hide inside."

"What do I do?" asked little Maca.

"Just stand there and when the fella pulls up in his car - walk into the toilet."

Little Maca stood alone against the toilet wall watching the traffic go past. He almost forgot what he was there for. Suddenly a car pulled up. The young lad's bottle went. He watched the blond homosexual get out the car. The young lad walked into the toilet. The homosexual smiled.

"Here he is," panicked little Maca in a loud whisper to his friends. The four youths hid in the toilet cubicles and waited. They could hear the footsteps of the man approaching. There was no light in the toilet. The only light came from the road lights outside that shone through the opaque windows and the doorway. The road light cast a huge dark shadow as the man entered.

"Who's a pretty boy then?" he announced effeminately.

There was no answer. The man proceeded slowly into the toilet. He knew something was wrong. Suddenly two shadows darted towards him, wielding sticks. He dodged the first one and sent him crashing head first into the urinal. The boy crumpled unconscious. He blocked the second blow with his arm and smashed the youth in the face, knocking him out. Sykesy dived at him but the man tossed him aside. He landed in a heap near the doorway. Little Maca came from the end of the toilet and realised he was on his own. The man produced a sharp, evil looking knife that glinted in the darkness.

"You've been a naughty boy!" said the man menacingly.

"They made me do it," cried little Maca, beginning to blubber.

He darted into the end cubicle and tried to slam it shut but the man was too quick. He kicked the door in. The force of it threw the lad against the wall at the back of the cubicle. He was horrified as the homosexual dropped his trousers and held his weapon in his hand.

"Ah hey mister don't"! pleaded the boy.

"Suck it," ordered the man menacingly.

"No!" said the boy, cowering away from him.

"Yes," said the man, grabbing him by the hair and holding the knife to his throat.

Sykesy scrambled to his feet and ran out of the toilet. His eyes searched frantically for a weapon. He spotted the garden fence across the street. He charged across the road, ignoring the traffic at full speed. Cars slammed their brakes and drivers blared their horns. Running for his life Sykesy

212

careered feet first into the garden fence. The fence shook but Sykesy bounced off. He picked himself up and booted the fence. He wrenched a piece of wood free and went charging back across the road.

"What the..!" said the inspector seeing the whole incident as they tailed Bletchley's car.

The homosexual dragged little Maca's head down to his loins. The boy tried to turn his head away.

"This is your last chance," growled the angry man.

There was a loud crack as Sykesy crowned the man across the back of the head with part of the garden fence. Little Maca snatched up the blade and stabbed the fallen man in the back.

"Police!" shouted the sergeant arriving with the inspector. The man clutched his knife wound in agony.

"Get back!" roared little Maca in tears as he and Sykesy rounded on the officer with the knife and the club.

"It's alright son," said the inspector, trying to calm the distressed boy down.

"It's not alright!" said the boy and stabbed the man again.

The inspector came towards him to try and stop him. He just evaded the knife as the distraught boy flashed the blade inches past his face.

"Get back!" he ordered as the lads tried to make their way out of the toilet.

"Come on," shouted Sykesy, helping their two friends to their feet while little Maca kept the policemen at bay with the knife. The four youths ran out of the toilets into the night.

The inspector turned his attention to the man who was desperately clutching his wounds.

"I only came in to use the toilet," he pleaded. "They tried to roll me."

The inspector looked down at his fallen trousers in disgust, not believing the man.

"You're nicked. You piece of shit," he growled.

The man sat alone in the cell. He was stiff and in pain from his wounds that had luckily only been superficial. The cell door opened. Benson and Johnson walked in. The man sat on his bench and watched them nervously.

"The judge is going to have a field day with you. Attacking young boys in the public toilets," said the sergeant.

The man looked down in humiliation.

"It doesn't have to be like that," said the inspector.

The man looked up in silence, seeing a glimmer of hope.

"We'll drop the charge to importuning and see you get a light sentence," said the inspector.

"But I haven't been with anyone," said the man puzzled.

"Yes," replied the inspector, "but you're going to be. Tomorrow. If you want to get out of here inside the next ten years."

"O.K." replied the man. "Who is it?"

The inspector tossed him Bletchley's picture. The man nodded. The two policemen left the cell.

"The end justifies the means," said the inspector.

"Yeah, we might get two birds with one stone," said the sergeant

"What d'you mean?" asked Benson.

"With a bit of luck Russell might get the grave digger to bump off that piece of shit as well," answered the sergeant.

The two men laughed and strolled away from the cell area.

Russell was in his penthouse office surrounded by his heavies. He gazed down at the newspaper headlines.

"City Councillor Charged with Importuning. Police are holding Councillor Cyril Bletchley for questioning after attacks on young boys in public toilets."

"Stupid bastard!" cursed Russell firing his newspaper across the room. "His brains are in his Y fronts."

Bletchley sat alone in the cell feeling sorry for himself. The jailer was about to bring him his dinner.

"I'll take that constable," said Inspector Benson, picking up the plate.

The officer opened the door and the inspector walked in with a big smile on his face. He looked down at his disgraced and dishevelled prisoner - a man he'd despised for years.

"Seen tonight's paper," said the inspector, tossing him the newspaper.

The paper bounced into his lap. Bletchley didn't move. He just sat there in silence - a broken man.

"Is there anything you'd like to tell me?" asked the inspector, happily. There was no response.

"Ah well," said the inspector, "I suppose if you get a bit lonely you can stick that up your arse," tossing him a pork sausage that bounced off his bald head.

The inspector laughed handing the jailer back the plate and walked out. Bletchley looked up and scowled. The laughter ringing in his ears.

The inspector briefed his men in the briefing room.

"I want all Russell's premises raided. If they have a drunk on licensed premises- charge them. If they have a bald tyre - charge them. I want you snapping at his heels at every turn until I say different. Sooner or later something's got to give. Now go on and get out there."

Over the following weeks, the police raided Russell's night clubs, public houses, casinos and brothels. The drug squad raided his heroin houses and arrested all the pushers all the way up along the line, but no-one would talk. Inspector Benson continued the fight, refusing to give in, always believing that sooner or later a clue or bit of information would come to light that would help him nail Russell. None came.

214

Russell sat in his office.

"He's costing us plenty of money," said Animal.

"What's money?" replied Russell. "We can make money it's me he wants!"

"What do we do?" asked Mad-dog.

"We sit tight," replied Russell. "We do nothing stupid. We'll get a new young lawyer and Bletchley can pull the strings on him. Then we'll get back to normal."

It was late Sunday night. Dougie and Jerry were at a table in the pub lounge with their girlfriends. Smigger was at the bar talking to Cleo, one of Angie Russell's friends, as she ordered the drinks.

"Congratulations," she said. "You're going to be a dad."

"What!" said Smigger in surprise.

He glanced over at Angie who was sitting in the corner with her fat friend.

"Why didn't she tell me herself?" asked Smigger.

"She's going to later! I just thought I'd soften the blow. Don't tell her I told you," she said, walking away.

"O.K." replied Smigger. He rushed over to Jerry and Dougie in panic.

"Guess what - I've humped the other one," he blabbered. "She's waiting to sting me with the good news."

"What!" said Jerry.

"Smigger Smith, you are hereby charged that you did have sexual intercourse in the said city of Liverpool..." crowed Dougie as Jerry burst out laughing.

Smigger shook his head. "It's not funny," he said.

Just then a group of policemen walked in. It was after drinking up time. The customers left their drinks for fear of arrest and made their way outside. Angie was waiting for him in the doorway.

"Now let the girl down gently," laughed Dougie as they approached.

"Smigger," started Angie.

"Fuck off!" growled Smigger.

Angie burst into tears and ran off down the street. "You bastard!" she screamed.

"Call yourself a man," screamed her fat friend.

"I've just proved I'm a man," quipped Smigger walking away.

Jerry hailed a taxi and jumped in with the girls. Smigger joined the company.

"Get me out of here fast," he said.

Russell stood in the doorway of the bedroom, watching his wife comfort his inconsolable daughter. His wife came to the door and closed it.

"It's better if we leave her alone for a while," she said.

"And he told her to fuck off when she tried to tell him said Russell, half in disbelief, half in disgust.

"Yes," nodded his wife.

Russell squeezed the banister rails with his hands shaking, his head bowed in silence.

"Well he's not getting away with this," he said finally, coming up for air.

Little Maca was lying on his bed when his big brother walked in after his court appearance.

"How did you get on?" he asked, pleased to see him.

"Hundred pound fine and six months suspended sentence. Me dad got me off with it," said Maca, changing out of his best clothes.

"Good. I thought they were going to lock you up," he replied.

"No. No more robbing for me," said Maca. "We've got a big game on Saturday against one of the best teams in the league and guess what?"

"What?" said little Maca.

"They've got a young centre half everyone's after and there'll be half a dozen scouts from the third and fourth divisions to watch him," replied his big brother.

"So," said little Maca, still not understanding.

"So he's marking me and if I rip the back out of him they'll all be after me," said Maca.

"Yeah," realised the young lad. "D'you think you will," he asked in excitement.

"Bet on me," winked his big brother, much to his delight.

"I'll go and tell me dad," said little Maca, jumping up.

Saturday came. The match was a cup quarter final and the team was playing away. The pitch was rain soaked but in good condition. A massive crowd had turned out to support both teams. It was more like a cup final than a quarter final. The away team were already warming up for the game. They only had one ball. Maca was crossing it into the middle. Smigger was smoking a cigarette against the goal post. There were two defenders on the line and everyone else was going for the header. They watched the opposition run out in their smart track suit tops. Most of the players carried a football with them. They began some stretching exercises in between passing the ball round like professionals. Smigger stood with the ball in one hand and a cigarette in the other, watching one of the opposition touching his toes and doing some calf loosening exercises.

"Ooh! Isn't he lovely?" said Smigger aghast to roars of laughter from the lads.

"I hope they can play football as well as they fart around," said Dougie.

Docker, the team manager, took his teeth out and clenched his fist.

"Let's get in to them," he roared.

The game kicked off and began to live up to the expectations of the crowd straight from the start. Maca received the ball at his feet and turned away from the highly rated centre half. The centre half recovered and just managed to get a tackle in. The ball flew out of play. Maca picked himself up and winked at his brother. He knew from their first clash that he had the beating of his man. Little Maca turned and looked at his brother with a big smile. They both knew what Maca was thinking. So did the centre half.

Maca received the ball to his feet and turned slowly away from his marker. The centre half clattered into him from behind and chopped him down. The away supporters were gathered mainly down one touchline. They booed and hurled abuse at the defender.

The game began to flow. There were chances made at both ends. Smigger came rushing out and dived at the centre forward's feet, taking the ball off his toes just as everyone thought there was going to be a goal scored. The crowd roared its approval. Smigger rolled the ball out to his full back's feet and they began to attack again.

There was a throw in near the home team's area. The centre half was shadowing Maca. Dougie threw the ball in. Maca stood back on the centre half's feet, leaving his standing when he went for the ball. Jerry came steaming in on the cross and headed in just over the bar. The crowd gasped and burst into applause.

"Who's the number ten?" asked the scout on the touchline.

"That's our Maca," said his brother on the line.

The crowd roared again. Maca left the centre half for dead and beat two men. He worked a one two with Dougie and hammered a rocket shot goalward. The goalkeeper flung himself to his right and tipped the ball round the post. The crowd erupted.

"He's only sixteen," said little Maca to the scout, knowing he was interested.

The game went on. Smigger pulled off a brilliant save at the other end. The game developed into personal duels of skill and strength with chances and misses and great saves at both ends. The score was nil nil with two minutes remaining. Maca was fouled by the centre half again as he broke clear on goal outside the penalty area. The home team built its wall. Maca drove the case ball like a rocket. The crowd gasped as it bent round the wall and hit the post. Dougie smashed home the rebound. The crowd went mad. They'd knocked the favourites out of the cup. The crowd invaded the pitch at full time. The teams made their way back across the field to the dressing room.

"Excuse me son, can I have a word with you?" said the scout running up. Maca looked around.

"Listen mate, I'm soaked here. I need a shower. Why don't you have a word with me dad?" he said.

He introduced his father to the scout and walked away leaving his father in his element.

"Are you going to make it this time?" asked little Maca.

"Bet on me" winked his big brother, much to his delight.

The pub was packed with supporters when the team got back to begin the celebrations. All the talk was about the game. Stevie managed to get a space at the bar.

"Four pints of lager please," he ordered. The barmaid began to serve him. Stevie noticed the old man at the bar shaking his head. He had a mouth full of Guinness left in a half pint glass.

"Hello son," said the old man, squinting at him with his 'gosy eye'. "I need ten bob for a loaf. I've got a lump of cheese in the house and I need ten bob for a loaf for me Sunday dinner."

The barmaid handed Stevie his change. There was a fifty pence piece in it.

"'Ere y'are mate," said Stevie, feeling sorry for him and giving him it.

He sat down with the rest of the football team and told his friends what he'd done, feeling pleased with himself.

"Go away you daft cunt. He's a professional bum. He took the money on the docks two years ago," said Smigger.

Stevie looked round in dismay and saw the man buying a pint with his fifty pence.

Jerry handed him a pound note. "Shoot round the shop and get a loaf," he said.

Joey went to the bar to get served. The old bum spotted him and started shaking his head.

"What's the matter mate?" asked young Joey.

"Hello son. I need ten bob for a loaf. I've got a lump of cheese in the house and I need a loaf for me Sunday dinner."

Jerry stepped out from behind him. "'Ere y'are mate," he said, holding out the loaf as the pub fell about laughing. The old bum cracked up. He threw the loaf halfway across the room. He ran up and kicked it towards where the mocking football team were standing - slices of bread flew everywhere. Jerry clasped an arm around his shoulder and handed him a pint. The old bum began to see the joke.

Smigger came back from the bar with the round of drinks. He could see the smiles on everyone's faces. He knew something was going on. Jerry stepped out from behind the curtain onto the windowledge clutching a red sportsbag under his arm, speaking into the heel of a football boot like it was a microphone and impersonating Eamonn Andrews.

"Smigger Smith, footballer, womaniser, goalkeeper extraordinaire - this is your life," he declared in his best Irish brogue. There was a roar of laughter. Jerry waited for a lull.

"Now then here is a voice from the past. D'you recognise this voice?" he asked

"Hey! Get the fuckin ale in," shouted a voice from behind the curtain.

There was a roar of laughter as Dougie stepped out.

"Yes," said Jerry. "It's your old mate, Dougie Lacey."

The red Jaguar carrying Mad-dog, Animal, Bombhead and Sydney was followed by a cortege of three cars. They drove into the pub car park and pulled

218

up. The sixteen bouncers from town got out. Two of them were carrying plastic bags. The others picked out weapons from them, such as knuckle dusters, coshes, chains and even a sawn off shotgun, as they filed into the pub behind Mad-dog and Animal. Animal stopped and examined the photograph of Smigger and Angie. A stony silence fell on the pub as the monsters walked in. The gangsters spread out covering the door so no-one could leave. Some of the regulars got bottles and glasses ready for the ensuing fight.

Billy Smith was sitting at the table with Dougie's father.

"Someone's going to get done in," said Billy, looking at the gangsters.

"Not necessarily," said Mr Lacey. All it takes is for someone to be first in. The rest will follow."

Animal and Mad-dog approached the football team.

"We don't want any trouble," said Mad-dog pointing to Smigger who was sitting furthest away. "We just want him."

Jerry and Dougie stood up.

"Well you can't have him," said Dougie and butted Mad-dog in the nose. Mr Lacey jumped up and snatched the shotgun barrel up into the air. It blew a big hole in the ceiling as Mr Lacey whacked the man across the head with a Guinness bottle.

Jerry kicked Animal in the crotch and smashed a big right into his face. A terrible battle ensued. The outnumbered professional doormen armed with pick axe handles and chains, and the tough pub regulars armed with bottles and glasses.

The manager cowered behind the bar, phoning the police as chaos reigned. The old bum picked up an empty Guinness bottle and fired it through the mirror behind the bar. The manager looked at him in amazement.

"I've been wanting to do that since I saw John Wayne do it in a film years ago," he explained.

Jerry was struggling with Lennie Casey for possession of his pick axe handle. Animal was on the floor engulfed by Billy Smith, Smigger and Docker the team manager who was biting his leg.

Dougie was underneath Mad-dog on the floor, desperately trying to keep his dangerous teeth away from his face.

"Jerry!" he screamed for help.

Jerry wrested the pick axe handle from Casey and whacked him across the jaw with it. Smigger landed next to Jerry where Animal had thrown him. Smigger grabbed the pick axe handle and stepped back into the fray.

"Jerry!" screamed Dougie.

Jerry spun round seeing Dougie's predicament. He kicked Mad-dog in the kidneys and punched him in the face. It was no use. He unsuccessfully tried to drag Mad-dog off by the hair but he was still going for Dougie's face with his teeth.

"Hurry up!" shouted Dougie, tiring.

Jerry smashed the tip of a pint glass and rammed it into Mad-dog's face. Mad-dog screamed like a boiled crab and released Dougie. The glass was deeply embedded in his face round his eye. Animal saw the crime and roared like a bull. He tossed Billy and Docker aside like rag dolls and charged at Jerry. He caught him in a bear hug, his momentum bouncing Jerry back against the wall.

Jerry was winded. He gasped for breath. He could feel Animal crushing the life out of him. Smigger whacked him across the back with a chair. There was no effect. Bombhead butted him in the nose and Smigger went down. Dougie belted Bombhead before he could put the boot in. A terrific fist fight ensued between the evenly matched pair. Jerry was jerking his head back, unsuccessfully trying to butt Animal. He dragged his head back by the hair and sunk his teeth into Animal's nose. Animal let out a roar and released Jerry. He stepped back clutching his face. Jerry followed up the attack with his fists and feet. Animal staggered back and fell over some debris from the fight. Jerry noticed the police piling through the door and beginning to arrest everyone. Dougie got the better of Bombhead and knocked him out. Maca kicked the emergency exit open.

"Come on," he said leading the way. Most of the regulars escaped out of the door.

Lennie Casey was the only bouncer to escape. He stood in silence still carrying his wounds from the battle as Russell raged in disbelief.

"You're telling me that me best men are in hospital or jail, worked over by a crowd of young lads and drunks. Me clubs are only manned by a skeleton crew of doormen."

Sydney walked in. "Mad-dog's lost an eye," he declared.

"What!" gasped Russell. "Did you see who done it?"

"Yes," replied Casey. "A young fella by the name of Jerry Kinsella."

Inspecor Benson stood watching the men being led away to the police cells.

"Well we might get something out of this," said Sergeant Johnson. "Causing an affray is worth a couple of years."

"I doubt it," replied Benson. "Remember the last time someone tried to give evidence against these people."

"The gravedigger?" replied Johnson. The inspector nodded.

Jerry lay in front of the fire. Teresa checked the baby was asleep and came and cuddled up to him. Jerry put his arm around her.

"I've got good news for you," he said.

"What's that?" she asked.

"I've been to see my lawyer. He's advised me to give myself up. He reckons I've got a good chance of getting a not guilty."

"How come?" asked Teresa.

"He reckons the police evidence won't stand up," replied Jerry.

"That's good isn't it?" she said.

"I've got to do a bit of business with the boys tomorrow - then we should have enough money to go into something legit. We'll talk about giving meself up then if you like," said Jerry. "We'll get married if I get a not guilty."

The post office van drew up outside the post office. The guard got out to make sure everything was alright. He went inside to inform the postmaster of the delivery. He thought nothing of the cars parked on the pavement. There were always cars parked there. He signalled the 'all clear' to the guard carrying the money. Jerry put his balaclava on. The second guard stepped from the van with the money. Smigger rammed the car into the post office van as the crowd of shoppers scattered. Jerry threw his car behind the van to stop it escaping.

The guards froze in fright as Dougie leapt from Smigger's car.

"Give us the fuckin money," he roared, wielding a pick axe handle. Jerry snatched the cash from the startled guard. Smigger jumped into the getaway car and revved the engine. A middle aged woman ran out from the packed bus stop and tried to hit Dougie with her umbrella. Dougie punched her in the nose. She dropped like a stone. A passing motorist saw the commotion and careered onto the pavement. Dougie dodged out of the way. Jerry snatched the money from the guard and turned to run. The car threw him over the bonnet as it skidded to a halt. The police car raced to the scene. Dougie ran over and smashed the driver's window with the pick axe handle. The driver screamed as the flying glass flew into his face. Dougie whacked him again with the club. Jerry scrambled to his feet and hobbled into the getaway car with the money. Dougie covered him with the stick and jumped into the car.

P.C. Ash skidded the police car to a halt trying to block the pavement so they couldn't escape. Smigger screeched towards them as the police officers baled out.

W.P.C. Thatcher was too slow. She was hit and thrown up into the air as the police car was rammed. The getaway car spun right and though badly damaged escaped down the side street. W.P.C. Thatcher landed in a heap. Her legs were broken.

"Did you see that?" gasped Dougie.

"You always get paid back in the end," said Jerry gritting his teeth in pain.

"The car's going to pack up," screamed Smigger. "Can you run?"

"No," grunted Jerry.

"Jump over the privets into the front garden with the money when I tell you. We'll draw them off. Have you got your running head on, Dougie?"

"Deal me in," he nodded.

The car flew round the corner and stopped momentarily. Jerry dived into the front garden with the money as the car screeched away. Jerry lay behind the privet in agony as two police cars flew past in pursuit of the getaway car. He

221

picked himself up and made off down the street with the money trying to act normal.

The car swung out of the estate. A police car heading in the opposite direction slewed across in front of them. Smigger crashed into the school fence. The two lads leapt out the car and ran off in different directions. It was every man for himself. Smigger jumped onto the bonnet and vaulted the school fence into the playground. A police officer sprinted after him. Dougie hurtled into the estate tossing away his mask. The other policeman hurtled after him on foot.

Smigger powered across the playground and into the playing fields. His feet sloshed through the wet grass as he began to pull away from his dogged pursuer across the playing field. The determined policeman ploughed through the mud after him. A police car sped down the lane. The driver slammed the brakes on and squeezed the car through a gap in the fence that vandals had made. Smigger watched the car enter the field out of the corner of his eye. He powered on. It was all or nothing. He had to make it to the stream at the bottom of the playing field. The police car came tearing up. It was too late. Smigger jumped for his llfe and cleared the stream. The policeman jumped from the car and watched Smigger bounding into the long grass of the hospital annexe. The fresh officer charged after him as Smigger tried to make the safety of the woods in front of him. The two police men bounded through the long grass after him. Smigger disappeared into the wood and threw himself underneath some bushes. He panted for breath trying to hide in silence as he heard the footsteps of his pursuers approach. The first officer ran right past him down the small footpath into the distance. The second officer stopped right by him, panting for breath. Smigger watched him as he gasped for breath and then chased off in the same direction as his fellow officer. Smigger stood up and watched them disappear.

"You want to watch those ciggies, they're not good for you," he said disappearing into the woods in a different direction. He loped quietly through the woods. The quiet countryside was interrupted by the sound of an engine being screwed. It was coming in his direction. He scrambled down the bank into the stream and waded under the small footbridge. He crouched there in the cold water as the police car stopped on the bridge. His two pursuers appeared.

"He's around here somewhere," said the first officer.

"I'll try this way!" said the driver, driving off.

The two officers disappeared again into the woods. Smigger waded along the stream. He noticed a tall leafy tree. He scrambled up the bank and climbed the tree. He reached the top. He heard the car stop beneath him and watched the police dogs jump out, barking excitedly. Smigger closed his eyes and clung to the tree with his fingers crossed in desperation.

Dougie came tearing into the estate with the policemen twenty yards behind him. He sprinted down a road past a row of shops. The startled women shoppers turned to watch.

"Go on lad run," one mother called. The women hushed as the bobby on the beat turned the corner in front of him. Dougie didn't stop. He powered towards the officer. He knew he had to get round him. The policeman bounced into the street on his toes ready for anything. Dougie side stepped and cleverly wrong footed him. He cruised past him. The officer charged after him. He hurled his helmet at him. It struck Dougie on the back of his head. He slowed for a moment. The women groaned as though a foul had been committed. The policeman desperately threw himself at Dougie's feet in a rugby tackle. He caught Dougie by the trousers but Dougie was too strong. He shook himself free from the feeble grip and raced on. The women let out a cheer of approval. The first officer disappeared round the corner after him. Dougie's mind worked overtime. Where could he run? A police car skidded to a halt in front of him. Dougie sprinted across the main road before they could get out. He hurdled the traffic barrier on the central reservation and disappeared into the block of flats. He spotted two policemen coming from the other side as he entered it. He was trapped. He noticed the stairs door out of the corner of his eye. He had one chance. He charged through it and up the stairs. He knew if he went up into the top he'd be caught. He burst out onto the first floor landing and jumped off the balcony hoping the police were chasing him up the stairs. He stumbled as he landed. A policeman dived on his from below. He was engulfed in bodies.

"Let me go you bastards," he yelled, struggling violently.

It took six policemen to carry him to the waiting police car.

"Leave him alone you bastards," shouted a woman at the bus stop.

"Shut up or we'll have you as well," warned a policeman as Dougie was fired into the back of the van. He felt a heavy foot press down on his neck and he lay face down in the van. "I'd stay quiet if I was you son," said the burly officer. "Or I'll break your fuckin back."

Jerry limped into the flat carrying the money. He knew his collar bone was broken and he had a deep gash on his knee.

"What happened?" asked Teresa in suprise.

"Shut up," he said, picking up the phone.

"Hello," Joey answered.

"Hello Joey," replied Jerry. "Get all your Smigger's bank books and get round here."

"Has he been nicked?" asked Joey.

"Don't know," replied Jerry. "But if he has let's make sure the bastards don't get his money."

Teresa saw the wicked gash in his knee. She rushed out into the kitchen and poured a bowl of hot water. She hurried back in and began to clean it. Jerry sat on the couch on the phone to Karen.

"Hello Karen? Shoot round to Dougie's and pick up any bank books or money he's got."

"Why, what's the matter?" asked Karen in alarm. "Has he been caught?"

"I don't know yet. Don't ask dickhead questions - just do what you're told. We haven't got much time," he growled.

Jerry winced as Teresa softly rubbed the hot flannel around his cut and hung up.

Joey came round with Maca and the bank books.

"They've got Dougie," said Maca. "I saw them drag him in."

"Get out and rob a car," said Jerry. "We'll try and snatch him back at the hospital.

"How d'you know he's going to the hospital?" asked Joey.

"We ran a policewoman over when we were getting away. They're not going to get the red carpet out for him."

"Oh my God!" said Teresa.

"Don't fuckin start," growled Jerry. "It should have been me that got caught but they let them chase them so I could get away! I'm not leaving him! Drop me off at the casualty department before you go for the car. You stay here in case Smigger turns up and tell him where we are."

Dougie sat in the cell. He had been stripped naked and was shivering, wrapped in a blanket. The cell door opened and the young officer from the desk walked in.

"D'you want a ciggy?" he asked, trying to be friendly.

Dougie shook his head. The officer took a drag of his cigarette.

"You may as well tell us your name. We'll find out sooner or later," he said.

Dougie didn't answer. The officer realised he was getting nowhere and left the cell, slamming the door behind him.

"Any joy?" asked P.C. Ash outside.

"No," replied the officer.

"Fuck the niceties," growled the officer, drawing his truncheon.

He filed into the cell followed by three other men. Dougie watched them come in and close the door behind them.

"What's your name?" said a young policeman, tapping his truncheon in his hand.

There was no answer.

"How many lumps d'you want?" said the young officer, trying to impress his colleagues. And I'm not talking about in your tea!" Dougie stood up and tossed the blanket aside, knowing a good hiding was coming.

"Come on cunt! You can kill me but you're mine!" he growled, standing there naked.

P.C. Ash smashed him over the head with the truncheon. The four officers piled into him. Dougie vainly tried to fight back. He managed to wrap his teeth round the young officer's ear. He screamed in agony as the desperate man drew blood. Ash grabbed him by the testicles and squeezed. Dougie yelped and released the ear. The police continued with their battering. They pinned Dougie to the floor. The young officer held his head so he couldn't move.

Ash stood over him.

"D'you like biting people?" he asked menacingly. "You'll be lucky to gum a cheese butty after this!" He rammed the tip of his truncheon into Dougie's mouth three times, knocking his front teeth out. They left him lying on the floor. The young officer was the last one to leave, giving Dougie a last kick in the kidneys before he went.

Darkness fell. Jerry sat in the casualty department with his arm in a sling and his knee strapped up. He'd given a false name in. Smigger arrived with Joey, Maca and Stevie.

"We've got the car," said Joey. Jerry nodded

"What happened to you?" asked Jerry.

"Been sitting up a tree till it went dark," replied Smigger. "Any sign of him yet?"

"No," replied Jerry. "But he'll be here."

The friendly policeman who'd offered Dougie a cigarette peeped through the spy hole in the cell door. It was two hours after the beating and Dougie still lay prostrate in semi-consciousness on the floor.

"I'll kill all you bastards," he muttered through his broken teeth.

The policeman looked at his battered and bruised face. He returned to the desk sergeant.

"He's still out, sarge. I think he's going to die on us," he said, genuinely concerned.

"O.K." replied the sergeant. "Phone an ambulance and get his four sparring partners to take him to the hospital."

The lads watched in anger as Dougie was wheeled in surrounded by his escort.

"I'm going to kill you all," growled Dougie in his sleep.

"What have they done to him?" said Joey, seeing his battered face.

"No mercy," growled Maca. "They're not supermen. They live and die like everyone else!"

Jerry recognised P.C. Ash.

"Look who it is?" he said. "I might have known. Get ready. I'll jump him and you's sort the other three."

Jerry hobbled up behind the unsuspecting police officer. He pulled the Stanley knife from his sling and swiped it down P.C. Ash's face. Ash screamed and doubled up on the floor, kicking his feet up in agony. Blood poured through his fingers as he clutched his face. An officer went to his aid but was smashed in the mouth with a pick axe handle by Stevie. There was pandemonium. Maca stretched the third out with an iron bar. The young officer turned and ran leaving his friends to their hiding. Nurses and patients screamed as they tore into the policemen. A staff nurse tried to pull Stevie off an officer but Stevie tossed her aside. She landed on her backside. Maca chased down the corridor after the young officer. He swung the bar at his head and just missed.

225

The officer escaped round the corner. Maca raced back, not wanting to chase him too far. Smigger was trying to move Dougie.

"Don't!" shouted an Irish nurse. "You might kill him. Can't you see he's in a bad way!"

The lads realised she was right. "Dougie," shouted Smigger, shaking him, "We'll be back for you!"

The lads made their escape out of the hospital. Doctors and nurses came to the aid of the stricken policemen. The young officer came back in shock.

"Brave bastard aren't you?" muttered Dougie in his semi-consciousness. The nurse saw him squeezing his truncheon in rage.

"You dare!" said the Irish nurse, realising what he was thinking.

The lads arrived back at the flat empty handed and downcast.

"What happened?" asked Teresa.

"We done the coppers in but we couldn't move him,"said Maca.

"Why?" asked Karen.

"He was too badly hurt," replied Smigger.

Karen started crying. Jerry put his arm round his sister.

"Never mind," he said, "it could have been worse."

Russell summoned Mitchell to his office.

"How much information can you get for me on Jerry Kinsella?" he asked.

It'll be difficult," said Mitchell. "He's already on the run so he'll be hard to pin down."

"I'll double your money and give you a week to track him down before I put his name in the obituary column. It'll make anyone think twice of giving evidence against the boys."

The police were parked at the bottom of the street in an unmarked car - hoping Jerry would decide to call home.

Mitchell was encamped in the empty house across the street photographing anyone who went near it.

Smigger called at Jerry's flat. Teresa was getting ready to take the baby out in the pram.

"I'm going round to your mothers," she called, passing Smigger in the doorway.

Sykesy and Jerry were getting ready to go out.

"Where are you going?" asked Smigger.

"We're going fishing," replied Jerry. "Are you coming with us?"

"No," replied Smigger. "I'm going into town to buy a few LP's and some clobber. You take the car. I'll get the bus."

"O.K." replied Jerry.

Teresa arrived outside Mrs Kinsella's house. Mitchell peered at her behind the curtains with interest. He took pictures of her as she was greeted by Jerry's mum and entered the house.

Jerry took Sykesy to the spot where his father used to take him fishing as a boy. Sykesy looked across at his hero. He was really enjoying himself. Jerry just smiled back watching the floats waiting for a bite.

Smigger got on the bus and paid his fare. He received his ticket and strolled down to the back seat. The bus set off on its journey into town. Smigger sat in a trance watching the shops and houses go by as the bus trundled along its busy route. The bus stopped again at another bus stop. Suddenly Mad-dog was standing right next to the window, leering at him. His face was grotesque. One eye was missing. One side of his face was full of stitches. They ran almost full circle to his forehead through where his eye had been and back up into his cheek.

Smigger panicked. He saw Animal and Bombhead pushing their way through the milling crowd trying to get on the bus. He raced down the bus and tried to run upstairs. Bombhead caught him by the heel of his trousers. Smigger back heeled him in the nose and escaped upstairs. He threw himself out of the emergency exit at the back of the bus just as Bombhead and Animal closed in on him. He dropped down into the road. Bombhead dropped down after him. Smigger ran for his life with Bombhead in hot pursuit. Mad-dog and Animal leapt back into the Jaguar, Sydney scorched away trying to cut him off.

Smigger charged through the busy shopping precinct and out across a debris leaving Bombhead toiling in his wake. The Jaguar tore across the debris after him in a cloud of dust. Smigger raced into the row of derelict houses. Animal jumped out of the back of the empty house. The Jag roared round the front. Mad-dog got out.

"He's got to be round here somewhere," he said.

Smigger watched them from the empty house, realising he was trapped. He got his breath back and tried to creep away through the fallen bricks and back across the debris.

"There he is," shouted Bombhead as Smigger noisily stood on a corrugated sheet.

Smigger sprinted back into the house only to find Mad-dog coming at him down the hall. He raced up the flights of derelict stairs into the top bedroom. He picked his way across the wooden joists that were the only remainder of the floor, to the window. He looked down below at the Jag outside and the long drop beneath.

Mad-dog and Bombhead arrived in the doorway. They smiled at each other. The knew they had him trapped. Smigger jumped onto the window ledge and tried to climb onto the roof. The guttering came away in his hand. Mad-dog laughed at his plight.

"Come on you one-eyed bastard," growled Smigger wielding the guttering like a club.

Mad-dog rushed him. Smigger smashed the guttering over his forearm. Then both men tumbled across the beams. Smigger was unlucky. He landed lengthways on a beam by Mad-dog's feet. Mad-dog kicked him off. Smigger hung on to the beam, dangling desperately over the long drop below.

Mad-dog stood over the desperate man and laughed. He stood on Smigger's hand. Smigger screamed as his fingers cracked and broke. He hung on with one hand. He looked down at the long drop below and let go of the beam. He landed with a sickening thud in a cloud of dust. Mad-dog and Bombhead looked down at the lifeless body satisfied with their day's work.

"Come on, let's go," said Bombhead.

It was a little after teatime on a Friday evening. Four twelve year old schoolboys were playing football in the street using a neighbours fence as the goal. The lads hadn't been playing long when the front door flew open and the neighbour, a middle aged woman, came rushing down the path hurling abuse. It was the third time that night that the lads had been moved on.

"Go on! Sod off down your own end of the street," she cried.

"Piss off, yer old bag," shouted little Maca as they slunk away.

"You wait till I see your mother," called the woman, even more aeriated.

"Kiss me arse," muttered little Maca as they reached the corner.

"Where are we gonna play now?" asked Sykesy.

"Dunno," shrugged his friend.

The four schoolboys sat huddled together on the steps of the local pub, cold and bored with nowhere to go and nothing to do. Sykesy produced a packet of chewing gum from his back pocket and passed it round. A police car stopped nearby.

"Here we go," said one of them as the two policemen approached. One of them was the man who'd run away from the fight at the hospital.

"Empty your pockets," he ordered the schoolkids.

Little Maca produced a front door key, an old handkerchief and threepence in change. The policeman began to frisk him.

"What's your name?" he asked.

"Philip McFaye," replied the youngster uncomfortably.

"Where d'you live?" continued the officer.

"Over there," said little Maca, pointing in the direction of his home.

"Where d'you live?" snapped the policeman angrily hitting him in the stomach.

"Twenty Tenwall Road Norris Green," spluttered the lad.

"That's better," replied the officer. "Where d'you live?" he asked Sykesy.

"101 Eastham Road," he replied nervously.

The officer looked at him for a moment, recognising him.

"You're that little cunt who's on the run from approved school, aren't you?" he said, grabbing him by the scruff of the neck and marching him to the car. Sykesy looked back at his mates as he was driven away.

Teresa walked into the hospital to visit Smigger. There was a police guard on the door. Smigger lay on traction on the life support machine. There seemed to be tubes coming out of every part of his body. Joey and Billy were at his bedside - even his mother and father were back on speaking terms.

"Where's Jerry?" asked Joey.

"He can't come," said Teresa. "They're after him as well."

"What's it all about?" asked Smigger's mum.

"Smigger got some girl in trouble and didn't want anything to do with her," said Teresa. "Her dad's a gangster."

Mitchell watched Teresa leave the hospital and put two and two together.

Teresa arrived home and shut the door behind her.

Mitchell was watching from the stairs below. He took note of the number and left.

Sergeant Johnson walked into the inspector's office.

"There's another name in the obituary column," he said.

"Who is it?" asked the inspector.

"A Jerry Kinsella," replied the sergeant. "A young tearaway on the run."

"Get me the officer in charge of the case, and anyone who knows anything about him."

Half an hour later the sergeant returned with P.C. Ash and Sergeant Hughes.

"Hello Tom," said the inspector, shaking hands with first the sergeant and then the constable. "What can you tell me about this Kinsella?" asked Benson.

"Typical young and up and coming villain," replied Hughes. "We've cornered him twice and he fought his way out."

"What about you?" he asked the constable. "You've arrested him before."

"He's got no fear," replied Ash. "I think it was him that gave me this at the hospital," he said, referring to the stitched wound that ran down his face. "But I can't be sure. The lad we arrested at the post office raid is the same one we arrested with Kinsella last time. I'd bet me life it was him driving that getaway car."

"The one that put the policewoman in hospital?" asked Benson.

"Yes," replied Ash.

"Right, get his picture released to the press and give them the story. Put a thousand pound reward on his head. Someone will tell us where he is. With a bit of luck we might get the two bastards at the same time."

"D'you think the gravedigger will get him?" asked P.C. Ash.

"No," replied Hughes. "Not really. You can't kill someone that's never lived."

Russell was in his office with his heavies.

"Let me kill him please boss'" begged Mad-dog. "Give us his address'"

"No," replied Russell under pressure.

"Go on boss," said Animal, "he's cost him an eye. He's entitled."

Russell looked at Bombhead and then Sydney. They both nodded in agreement.

"O.K." said Russell. "but don't botch it."

Jeff Baird walked into the newsagent and bought the evening paper. He recognised Jerry's picture and saw the reward offered. The rapist rushed to the phone.

"Hello, is that the police? I want to claim the reward on Jerry Kinsella."

Jerry was sitting in the armchair polishing his shoes. The two children from upstairs were playing with a Scalectric set on the floor. Sarah, Teresa and Karen were getting ready to go to the bingo at the pensioners' club.

"We're going Jerry," called Teresa, rushing in to kiss him goodbye.

"Thanks for looking after the kids for me," said Sarah.

"No problem," replied Jerry, "have a good time."

The girls left. The baby was asleep and the kids were playing happily. Jerry brushed his shoes. He walked to the window and watched the girls disappear up the street. He saw the Jaguar pull up below and the three heavies get out. He rushed into the bedroom and got the shotguns from the wardrobe.

"Stay in this room kids, and don't answer the door to anyone," he said.

"O.K." replied Peter.

It was about that time that the police task force left for Jerry's flat.

Jerry put his jacket on and filled his pockets with cartridges. He closed the front door behind him and ran up the stairs to the next landing.

The three men came up the stairs and produced shotguns from inside their coats. Mad-dog and Animal positioned themselves on the stairs next to the door. Bombhead knocked on the door and threw himself flat against the wall facing the stairs that ran up to the next landing gun at the ready.

"What d'you want?" asked Jerry, taking them by surprise.

Bombhead was caught wide open. He tried to shoot Jerry. He was too slow as Jerry shot him in the stomach and dived for cover. Mad-dog and Animal emptied their guns at him, the blasts tearing away lumps of splashing concrete as Jerry ducked out of the way. Bombhead clutched his belly in disbelief. His legs buckled and he slipped down the wall leaving a red smear of blood running down it from where he'd been standing. He collapsed - dead.

Mad-dog and Animal watched his demise with empty guns. They panicked, turned and fled. Jerry dropped his empty gun and chased after them. He just missed Mad-dog. The blast tearing masonry out of the wall just behind the gangster as he fled. The two men scattered out of the door as the glass was shattered by another shotgun blast behind them. They dived into the car as Jerry came running out into the road re-loading the shotgun. The car sped away. He snapped the gun shut and fired at the Jag. The windows shattered and the men were showered with glass. Sydney sped round the corner out of sight to safety.

"Bastard'" cursed Jerry and rushed back into the flats.

He didn't see Michael-Edward sitting in his van at the top of the road. The gravedigger watched the car speed away and Jerry return to his flat. He calmly took a bite from an apple and returned his attention to his book.

Jerry raced up the stairs. He grabbed the carry cot and stuffed his bank books and wads of money from the post office snatch into it.

"Stay there till your mum gets back'" he told the children. He ran out with the carry cot and the two shotguns.

"I'll settle this once and for all," he said, putting the baby into the back of the car. He jumped into the car and sped away. The gravedigger started the ignition.

Jerry arrived at Teresa's mum's. He walked into the house with the baby. Her parents were shocked.

"Make sure Teresa gets this," he said, revealing the money. "I've got something to sort out. Look after your grandchild."

"What's going on?" asked Mr Sims in astonishment.

Jerry didn't answer. He stormed down the path, jumped into his car and drove off. The gravedigger looked up from his book and shook his head. He pulled out after him.

Jerry pulled up down the street from the night club. He loaded his two shotguns. The gravedigger fitted the silencer on the gun and got out of his van.

Casey was fronting the door at the night club. The red Jaguar was parked outside.

"You're joking aren't you?" he said. "Bombhead dead! I can't believe it."

"Neither can I," said Mad-dog.

Jerry started the car and screeched towards the club. A punter knocked on the club door. He heard the screeching of wheels and screams of the scattering passers by. He threw himself to one side as the car bounced onto the pavement. Casey opened the door a split second before the car smashed through it. He and Mad-dog had no chance. They were killed instantly. The car flew up the foyer and came to an abrupt end against the lobby wall. Jerry was dazed and coughing under the carnage. Sydney came from round the corner. He surveyed the scene and saw his dead friends. He snapped and charged at Jerry with his stilleto while he was trapped in the car. Jerry saw him coming and blasted him with both barrels as he was about to strike. His body was thrown back along the hall. Jerry got out of the car. He blasted at Animal who dodged round the corner out of sight.

The first bullet caught Jerry in the lung. He spun round in shock and saw the gravedigger aiming the gun at him from the doorway. It was in that split second he realised he was dead. He spat towards his killer as the bullets flew towards him. Two more bullets struck home. Jerry sank to the floor, dead. His large spittle landed smack in the middle of the gravedigger's face, who emptied his gun into the dead man in fury.

Animal re-appeared from round the corner, summoned by the sudden silence. The gravedigger had disappeared. He looked at the carnage and his dead friends. Something suddenly snapped. He flew at Jerry's dead body in a rage and pummelled into it. He was dragged off roaring like a bull by a posse of policemen.

231

Inspector Benson strode through the carnage into the club. Russell was downstairs in the cabaret area with Bletchley. Benson stared at him, his gaze was murderous - pure hate.

"I've been here all night," said Russell. "There's plenty of witnesses."

"You think you're so smart," growled Benson. "Well you've bit off more than you can chew this time."

Russell looked at his lawyer and back at the inspector in ignorance.

"You haven't done your homework have you? Kinsella's got an older brother in the paras. Look at the trouble the boy caused you, what trouble d'you think the man's gonna cause you?"

Russell was still bemused.

"You don't get it, do you? I've got to take you to court and prove you're responsible for all this. Albie doesn't. All he's got to do is kill you."

Albie was stationed in West Germany. He sat alone in the shower clutching the telegram containing the bad news. His head was resting on his knees in dejection. The constant stream of water bounced off his still body. His mind floated back to the first time he'd ever set eyes on Jerry.

The family were sharing a house down Scotland Road with his auntie and uncle in the early sixties. Albie was six years old. It was winter. Albie placed a chair against the window and knelt on it staring out. He watched the snow steadily drifting down on the billowing gusts of wind. He was waiting for his mother and father to return from the hospital with his new baby brother. He stared out, anxiously watching for any sign of their arrival.

"Where are they?" he said impatiently.

His auntie placed a kettle on the coal fire. "Don't worry. They'll be here soon."

The shrill noise of a taxi braking pierced the cold air. The taxi turned into the street.

"Here they are!" he shouted, rushing to the door and down the steps into the street to greet them.

His mother got out of the taxi cradling the baby against her bosom while his father paid the taxi fare. Albie pulled at his mother's skirt.

"Let me have a look," he said, jumping up and down.

"Wait till we get inside first out of the cold," replied his mum.

His uncle came down and shook his father's hand. He'd been working nights. His auntie was pouring tea.

"Would you like a cup of tea?" she asked.

"Love one," replied his mother, sitting down in front of the fire.

Albie tugged at her skirt. "Let me see," he pleaded.

His mother proudly held the baby so he could see it. He marvelled at his little brother's tiny face.

"That's your little brother. Isn't he lovely?"

Albie nodded.

"You'll never let anyone hit him, will you?"

"No," said the little lad, clearing his throat. "I'll kill them."

Albie took the next flight to London and the train to Liverpool. The train sped through the night. Albie was unaware of the rest of the passengers on the train. He stared in silence at his reflection in the window and his mind floated back down Scotland Road. It was pouring with rain. Albie and Jerry were racing matchsticks down the gutter in the fast flowing rain water.

"What are you doing out there in this weather. Get in here. You're soaked!" shouted his mother.

The two lads nervously did what they were told, knowing they were going to get a smack.

"Get in there and get dried," she scolded, clipping Albie round the ear. Jerry smiled as he escaped into the house scot free.

The train arrived in the station. Billy was waiting to meet his old friend. Albie smiled.

"Nice to see you," said Billy.

"Yeah," replied Albie. "Pity it's under these circumstances. How's Smigger?"

"He's off the danger list now," replied Billy.

The two men got into the car and drove along Lime Street. They stopped at the lights. Albie looked across at the young people waiting to meet their dates outside the Empire.

"I see nothing's changed," said Albie.

The warden shone his torch around the dormitory of the approved school. He turned and closed the door behind him.

Sykesy was only pretending to be asleep. He slipped quietly out of bed and opened the window. He climbed out onto the drainpipe and clambered down. He dropped onto the ground and crouched in the darkness, making sure no-one had seen him. An alert housedog barked momentarily in the distance. Sykesy disappeared into the night.

The funeral started at Mrs Kinsella's house. It was packed with friends and relatives. Jerry's body lay in an open coffin in the front room. A set of rosary beads were wrapped around his hands in which he held a crucifix.

The cars for the mourners arrived outside. Teresa watched in silence cradling the baby as the lid was screwed down.

"Jerry! Jerry!" cried Karen, realising she'd never see her brother again.

"Shush girl," said her mother, comforting her with a hug. "He's in heaven now."

Sykesy watched in silence. Big tears rolled down his face.

The coffin was carried out into the street to the hearse. The cortege pulled away. The church was packed with friends and relatives.

Teresa didn't remember much of the ceremony, just the noise of Karen blubbering in the church. It all went past in an unbelievable blur.

They arrived at the graveside. Jerry was being buried with his father. Albie watched as they lowered the coffin into the grave. A tear trickled down his face and his mind floated away again back to the sixties.

Albie was playing football with a burst ball in the debris with his mates. Jerry came round the corner crying on his way home.

"Who hit you?" demanded his brother. Jerry couldn't talk properly for blubbering. He couldn't get his breath.

"Some big lad," he gulped, wiping his eyes.

"Show me," said Albie.

Jerry led him round to the next street.

"That's him there," he said, pointing at the lad.

"Hey you, did you hit him?" growled Albie.

"He was calling me names," claimed the other lad.

"You're too big for him," growled Albie and punched the lad in the face. He grabbed the lad in the headlock and tipped him up. He landed on top of him and pinned his arms down with his knees. He began punching him in the face.

"Go on Albie! Kill him," roared Jerry, jumping up and down

His memories were interrupted by the gravedigger. Michael-Edward held out the shovel full of soil.

Albie looked into his eyes momentarily. He took a handful and tossed it into the grave. The gravedigger moved round the graveside as each of the mourners tossed a handful of soil onto the coffin.

The grieving mourners moved away. Albie stood alone gazing down at the coffin. The gravedigger watched him from a distance. He knew the man was trouble

Albie walked away. Billy was waiting for him at the gravel path. Albie watched as Joey, Maca, Cummo and Stevie seemed to give something to Billy as he approached. The four lads walked away.

"What's all that about?" he asked.

"Popular lad, your Jerry," said Billy, tossing a set of car keys in his hand.

"What d'you mean?" asked Albie.

"These are the keys to a fast stolen car with fake number plates. There's a pump action shotgun and cartridges in the boot. When do we start," said Billy.

"Tonight," growled Albie.

Animal was relaxing at home watching television with his mother. He was dressed in slippers, trousers and a vest. The front door bell rang.

"Who's that at this time of night," he growled, getting up to answer it.

There was a man dressed in a full length leather trenchcoat standing halfway down the path, with his back to the door."

234

"What d'you want?" growled the big bear.

Albie swung round and levelled the pump action shotgun at him.

"You," he snarled.

"Who are you?" asked Animal.

"Jerry's bróther. I believe you weren't happy with just killing him. You had to work out on him when he was dead."

Animal tried to speak. The shotgun tore into his stomach. Albie pumped it back and let the fallen man have it again. He turned and walked away. Billy was waiting for him in the car.

Animal's mother fumbled nervously into the hall. She heard the car screech away.

"Son! Son!" she cried as Animal lay dying on the doorstep. She bent down and cradled his head - but it was too late. He was gone.

It was dinner time the next day. The bin wagon was parked in a layby on a lonely country road. The binmen were inside eating their sandwiches and drinking their flasks of coffee. Two hooded men sprang from nowhere.

"Just take it easy and no-one will get hurt," said Albie.

The startled men held their hands up in surrender

Billy lifted a sandwich from the man's hand and took a bite.

"I bet you never thought your missus's sarnies were that good," he said inferring the hold-up was to rob his sandwiches. He tied the men up.

You must be Irish," claimed the binmen. "Who'd want to rob a bin wagon?"

Billy drove the wagon into the grounds of Russell's estate unchallenged by the guards on the gate. They pulled up at the back of the mansion and entered through the kitchen.

"Get on the floor," Albie ordered the kitchen staff.

Billy covered the startled people. Albie raced up into the house. Russell was still in bed after a late night's drinking session. Albie shook him.

"What the" stuttered Russell, awakening to find the masked man with a shotgun pointed at his head.

"Get dressed!" ordered Albie. "You're coming with me."

He led Russell down the stairs and through the kitchen. He ordered him into the back of the bin wagon and closed him in. Billy drove out of the estate unchallenged and disappeared. They stopped at the layby where they'd stolen the wagon. Albie opened the back up.

"What's it all about?" asked Russell.

"Tell me about the gravedigger," asked Albie.

"I don't know anything about him," said Russell terrified.

"Turn it on," ordered Albie. Billy turned the crusher on. The heavy grinding jaws began to mash the rubbish Russell was standing on.

"No - wait!" begged Russell, dodging the cumbersome jaws.

"Sooner or later you'll get tired and it'll catch your ankles. And then - you'll fall into the grinder." The crusher caught the heel of his shoe and tore it off.

"No - wait"' screamed Russell.

Albie signalled to Billy who stopped the relentless crusher.

"Who paid the gravedigger to kill our Jerry?" he asked.

"It wasn't me," panicked Russell.

"I thought he worked for you?" said Albie.

"He does," said Russell. "But I never told him to kill Jerry. It must have been Mad-dog because Jerry put his eye out."

He waited anxiously for an answer. Albie watched him in silent thought.

"That seems about right. Who's this gravedigger fella then?"

"Michael-Edward Lynch. He's the sexton at the cemetery," gasped Russell, thinking he was off the hook.

"Where does he get all his information from?" asked Albie.

"Mitchell"' replied Russell. "He's an ex-copper. He's got a photography studio in town."

"O.K." replied Albie, closing the back of the wagon. "But you'd better not be lying to us."

"I'm not. I'm not," cowered Russell as he was locked in the back of the wagon. Albie turned the crusher on. Russell screamed as the jaws caught him in the darkness. The binmen looked at each other in horror as the machine gradually silenced the bloodcurdling screams. Albie and Billy got back in the car and drove off.

Albie watched the clay fall out of the grave onto the mound of earth next to it. Michael-Edward wiped his sweating brow, pausing momentarily and then continued with his work. He felt the cold shadow of death over him. He turned and saw Albie standing over him.

"Digging your own grave?" asked Albie.

The gravedigger smiled, ignoring the remark, continuing with his work. Trying to take Albie by surprise, he threw the shovel at him and lunged for his jacket next to the grave, snatching his revolver from it. Albie dodged the flying shovel and kicked him on the jaw. The gravedigger fell into the grave on his back, his gun landed on the grass above. Albie pointed the pump action shotgun at him which he pulled from under his trenchcoat. The gravedigger looked up at him in silence, blood trickling from the corner of his mouth.

"Boom!" Albie fired the gun at point blank range into the man's legs.

The gravedigger writhed in agony, clutching his legs. He adjusted his breath, handling the pain. Albie smiled down at him. He picked a handful of soil up and tossed it carefully over his body. The gravedigger spluttered as it landed on his face.

"How does it go? Repent ye your sins for the day of judgement is at hand," smiled Albie. "Chuckie a la prick."

His smile turned to a snarl as he angrily emptied the pump action shotgun into the man. Lynch's body jumped about as though full of life. The truth was he was already dead.

236

The shots ended his macabre dance. His bullet ridden body lay still for the last time. Albie walked away, hiding the gun in his coat.

Mitchell was in his studio, photographing a topless model posing on the bed. "O.K. That's enough for today!' he smiled. "Will you lock up for me. I've got to go out on business."

"O.K." retorted the model, getting off the bed. She walked over to a chair and started to get dressed. Mitchell put his coat on and pressed the lift button. Albie walked into the apartment below and watched the lift ascend through the fluorescent numbers. The lift reached the top. Mitchell stepped into it with his camera dangling round his neck. He pushed the ground floor button. Albie watched the light descend back through the numbers. The lift stopped. The door opened. Albie spotted the camera round the fat man's neck as he went to enter it.

"Mr Mitchell?" he asked, as if taken by surprise.

"Yes," replied Mitchell inquisitively.

"Allow me to introduce myself," said Albie, tightening his grip on the Spanish bayonet in his jacket.

He rammed the blade into Mitchell's heart and twisted it. Mitchell grunted and gurgled blood. He slumped down the back of the lift onto his backside, his eyes popping out in shock.

"I'm Albie Kinsella," said his attacker, leaving the bayonet embedded in his heart.

Mitchell's startled gaze fell away from him as the last bit of life ebbed from him.

The model pressed the lift call button and the door automatically shut. Albie watched the lift ascend through the numbers and walked away. The model screamed in shock as she went to step into the lift and ran back into the studio in terror.

The betting office was packed. The pub had closed for the afternoon and the punters were trying to kill a few hours before they re-opened for the night.

Maca tossed his betting slip away. "That's me skint," he said, "what about you?"

"Brassic," replied Joey,

"I'm sweating for twenty quid on Blakesware County," said Stevie. "But if it gets beat that's me dole gone.

"I've got a nicker," said Cummo. "Hang on to it in case this one gets beat. 'Stern', me nap of the day is running in the next race."

"What price is it?" asked Cummo.

"Seven to two," replied Stevie. "Look' Blakesware County's been backed in to nine to two favourite - they must fancy it."

The lads looked up at the betting display.

"I hope it wins," said Maca. "I don't fancy sitting in on Friday night."

237

Sykesy was sitting outside with little Maca and their two friends.

"I've got to get money from somewhere," he said. "I can't live on fresh air."

"Who can we rob?" asked one youth.

"What about the milkman," said his friend.

"No," replied Sykesy, " we want someone who deserves it."

"What about the coalman? He's a robber anyway," suggested little Maca.

"How d'you work that out?" asked Sykesy.

"He's got a big yard, so he buys coal at this year's prices - then he stockpiles it and sells it to our ma's next year at next year's prices," said little Maca.

"I thought that was business?" said Sykesy.

"No, business is smartarse for robbery," replied his friend.

"O.K. The coalman it is. He'll be collecting tonight," said Sykesy.

The four schoolkids got up and walked away.

Back inside the betting shop the four lads were willing the favourite to win as the commentator relayed the race excitedly.

"Two furlongs to run and it's Blakesware County in the lead by two lengths from Premier Dancer. These two are coming away from the field. Into the final furlong and it's still Blakesware County by two lengths. And into the dip and well inside the final furlong. It's Premier Dancer coming to join the leader. It's Blakesware County and Premier Dancer! Blakesware County and Premier Dancer! And at the line it's Premier Dancer and Blakesware County in a photo."

"Bastard"' cursed Stevie. "It's got beat." "And it's a photo between number thirty six - Premier Dancer and number twenty four - Blakesware County," said the tannoy.

Maca shook his head. The horse mentioned first always seemed to win the photo finish.

"Lends that nicker," said Stevie.

Cummo handed him the pound note. Stevie scribbled out his bet. One pound win STERN in the four fifteen.

He dashed over to place his bet. The race was about to start.

"Sorry son, you're not on," said the manager.

Stevie looked at him in disbelief. "I don't think you're eighteen," explained the manager.

The commentator announced the race was off. Stevie shook his head in disbelief and tossed his betting slip away.

He stormed outside giving Cummo the pound back. "I hate that bastard! He never said that when he was taking me dole off me."

"Let's turn him over. He's got to go to the bank tonight anyway, hasn't he?" said Cummo.

The door burst open. The race was over. A squad of losing punters trailed out of the shop.

"It won seven to two," said Joey coming out.

"Bastard," cursed Stevie. "Let's get a car. The cunt's getting it."

The three lads went to walk away.

"Are you coming?" asked Joey.

"No," replied Maca. "I'm retired. It's a mugs game. You've got to get caught sooner or later. I'll see you's after."

He watch'ed the three lads disappear round the corner as he made his way home for his tea.

The betting office manager came out and locked the door. He had the days takings hidden in a bank wallet inside his jacket. The punters had gone home. He turned to walk to his car.

"Whack!" Stevie hit him over the head with a stick.

Cummo snatched the money from inside his jacket as he hit the floor. Stevie wasn't satisfied with just the money. He volleyed the man in the jaw, knocking him out.

"I learnt that in Burma fighting the Japs " he scoffed on the run to the car. A passing police car at the other side of the lights saw the incident and gave chase.

Joey powered down the road, throwing the car into top gear. The police did a U turn and chased after him. The driver was on the radio for assistance. Joey slammed on at the lights and threw the car right through the red light and across the dual carriage way and then flung the car left into a long narrow straight road.

The police car lost ground but managed to stay in touch as it careered left after them.

"This is what I joined the police for," said the young driver excitedly.

"Take it easy Clint," replied the more experienced officer.

Joey swung the car right into the side streets. He whizzed in and out of the parked cars. The kids playing in the street scattered and the police car flew after them. Joey swung the car right at a tight turn. The police flashed past and went straight on in the wrong direction.

"Lost him," said Cummo joyously. "We're not out of the woods yet! Ballbag's been on the radio," said Stevie.

Joey came out onto the main road and saw the tango charlie pursuit vehicle bearing down on him from nowhere.

"K.T.B." barked Cummo. Joey flew away from his standing start. The unmarked police car closed right up on them as the stolen car took a few seconds to reach top speed. Stevie looked out the back window at the two policemen behind them.

"Fuck off'" he snarled, putting two fingers up.

Joey flew round a roundabout and away again. The police car stayed with him. The high speed chase flew towards Huyton. Joey overtook a bus on a narrow winding lane and cut back in just in time to miss the car coming towards him the opposite way. The police car had to brake and lost ground as the car flashed by. It flew round the bus in pursuit.

"Phew," said Cummo in the passenger seat, wincing at the near miss. "Kill me outright. Don't mess me around!"

"Bet on me," snapped Joey determinedly.

The car flew past a traffic island on the wrong side of the road. A startled driver slammed the brakes on as Joey flew out in front of him. The police car zoomed past the same way a split second later.

Joey dogged it down past the hospital and adjoining police station. The junction at the top was blocked by traffic waiting for the lights to change. Joey braked and made the instant decision to swing right up the wrong side of the dual carriage way.

"Love it. Brilliant!" gasped the police driver flying after him.

Joey bumped across the central reservation in between the trees back onto the right side of the road. The police car stayed with him in dogged pursuit. Joey swung left and tore up and over the flyover into the distance beginning to pull away. Joey snatched a glance in the rear view mirror and smiled. He knew he had the beating of his old sparring partner again. The car flew into a roundabout in between traffic and out again. The police car was still there. Joey zoomed up the hill and handbraked left. The screeching car powered away, the needle racing up the speedometer as he sped downhill into the bend. He saw the police vanishing into the distance. All he needed was the right turn off and he was safe. He charged up towards the village. Two buses were stopped taking on passengers in the narrow lane through the small but busy shopping precinct. There was no room to get a car past except on the pavement crowded with shoppers. Joey flew down into the village at one hundred miles an hour. He flew around the bend and saw death look him in the eye.

"Shit," he cursed, zooming towards the roadblock. Suddenly he saw his way out onto the pavement as the terrified shoppers scattered. He saw a young mum laden with shopping pushing a pram and grabbing her frightened toddler by the arm - blocking his escape route. The price was too high to pay.

"See you in heaven!" he gasped as the car crumpled into the back of the bus. The police car skidded to a halt behind them, forewarned by the loud bang. They approached the wrecked car. It was a terrible crash. Arms and legs missing, decapitation, blood everywhere.

"Oh my God," gulped the policeman.

"I wouldn't fancy the pathologist's job," said his companion. "How's he going to find out which bit belongs to which body?"

The light was beginning to fade. Teresa sat in the darkened living room, humming softly to herself. The mourners were gone. She was left alone with her baby cradling it softly against her bosom. All she had left were her memories and a feeling of emptiness and disbelief.

There was a knock at the door in a dark quiet street. A young girl answered it.

"Mum - it's the coalman"' she called.

"O.K. love. I'm coming now," called her mother.

240

The coalman smiled and waited for his money. Across the street sat the four young schoolboys in a stolen car, watching and waiting. A petrol bomb exploded against a policeman's riot shield. The plastic began to melt. The policeman was forced to drop the shield and retreat.

The woman turned her tap on in the bath and the water crashed down on the spiders below. She came into the bathroom the next day, and the spiders were still there.

This story is dedicated to the real life spiders, living, dead and still to come.

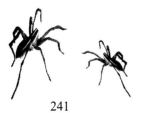

This story is a testament to a government that serves only self-interest. To a prime minister that tells us Britain is great again while four million are unemployed and serious crime is rife on the streets. This story is a testament to an opposition party infested with cranks and sexual deviants who allow this intransigent government to be re-elected again despite all its faults. How the leader of the working class can stand up with a tear in his eye and tell us how he would die for his country but he wouldn't let his country die for him, I don't know. Land doesn't make a country - it's the people that that do. The people of Great Britain never have and never will lie down and die for anybody and neither will the spiders.

R.I.P. THE BOX OF TOYS
Now you live forever.
P.S. T.J versus J. K. Tomb the Bomb would have took him.

In memory of my good friend Robbie Beardmore, the scalded cat.

Paul Breen's next book is "The Purse of Souls."